Jenny Hale

SCHOLASTIC CANADA LTD.
New York Toronto London Auckland Sydney
Mexico City New Delhi Hong Kong Buenos Aires

Scholastic Canada Ltd.
604 King Street West, Toronto, Ontario M5V 1E1, Canada

Scholastic Inc.
557 Broadway, New York, NY 10012, USA

Scholastic Australia Pty Limited
PO Box 579, Gosford, NSW 2250, Australia

Scholastic New Zealand Limited
Private Bag 94407, Botany, Manukau 2163, New Zealand

Scholastic Children's Books
Euston House, 24 Eversholt Street, London NW1 1DB, UK

Library and Archives Canada Cataloguing in Publication
Hale, Jenny
Jatta / Jenny Hale.
ISBN 978-1-4431-0277-3
I. Title.

PZ7.H136Ja 2010   j823'.92   C2009-906319-0

First published by Scholastic Australia in 2009.
This edition published by Scholastic Canada Ltd. in 2010.
Cover design by Blueboat.
Cover copyright © Scholastic Australia, 2009.
Text copyright © Jenny Hale, 2009.

6 5 4 3 2 1   Printed in Canada 116   10 11 12 13

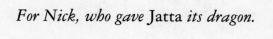

For Nick, who gave Jatta *its dragon.*

CHAPTER ONE

Princess Jatta woke on the cold marble floor, groaning weakly. Soaked in sweat. The nightmare was fading, but the horror of it lingered.

Her brother was mauled.

Instinctively she knew it, just as she knew the nightmare had been real. It had now gone, retreated deep below the throbbing in her head. 'Art, I'm sorry,' she whispered, knowing she was to blame but remembering nothing.

A face peered down at her. She strained her neck to see. Her father. Soft cloth brushed her face, mopping her forehead, the sweat from her lip. She tried to move but couldn't.

Tears pooled in his eyes. 'You've come back. My precious girl.'

You've come back? She blinked up at him, understanding nothing. He'd never cried, not that she knew. She felt one tear spatter on the marble tiles beside her face, wanting it to stop, watching his chin instead. Two ... three ... four tears for Arthmael. They fed her fear.

'Art's dead,' she moaned.

'Arthmael's alive.'

'No. It's my fault.'

He wiped his eyes, then searched her face. 'What do you remember, Jay?'

She opened her mouth. But there were no words to explain,

only confusion. A vein in her temple throbbed. She let her face roll back on the tiles and shut her eyes to recall.

Marble, cold against her cheek. Nothing. Nightgown wet with sweat. Nothing. Body shivering on the tiles. Nothing.

She opened her eyes, trying to focus. Chains clanked as she tried to move. The bedchamber tiles were smeared with bloody paw prints. They glistened in the dawn light.

'Blood.' More the repugnant smell of it than a memory.

'Blood? Yes, Arthmael's. He survived, Jay.'

'No.' But she desperately held onto his words. 'Wh—what happened?'

'Wolves.'

Wolves. Her first memory. Her mortal fear. These dark magic monsters had killed her mother.

She groaned. 'They came back for me.'

'Yes, Jay.'

'But they g-got Art instead.'

'He heard you scream.'

'Let me see him.' She tried to sit up. Iron clanked. She lifted her head to see her wrists and ankles loosely wrapped in chains. 'What—tell me, what have I done?'

Her father busied himself unravelling them. 'You had a fit. You thrashed about. I ordered the chains to stop you harming yourself.'

A fit? Nothing was making sense. She sat up, rubbing her cramped, bruised legs, focusing on the room. The wall lamps lay smashed. They'd been flung around, weaving burning oil. The scorch marks looked like ice-skating trails across the white floor. Bedding lay strewn in burgundy-spattered tatters. More bloody paw prints danced around her wardrobe, which had been dragged across the room, all ten doors of it, and

2

lay on its side through her smashed glass doors. Half of it lay in the garden beyond. How could wolves have come, and she survived? Arthmael, too? Such monsters were blood-crazed. Indestructible.

'They weren't supposed to let me live,' she whispered. 'Not if my amulet failed.'

'They shall not destroy you.' The King's voice was commanding, as she had always known it, and Jatta's pounding pulse slowed. 'Jay, we must renew your amulet's magic. This morning I'll send an ambassador to the Sorcerer.'

'Maybe this time . . . shouldn't I go, too?'

'No!' His eyes narrowed, suddenly severe. 'Never imagine you'll ever leave this palace.'

Jatta flinched.

'I'm sorry, my little Jay.' He cupped her elfin, almost child-like face in his scarred hands. 'But you know Lord Redd's magic protects you only within these palace walls. I've lost your dear mother. I won't lose you, too.'

CHAPTER TWO

The summer sun had barely risen, but most of the palace's servants were at work. As soon as her father left, Jatta slipped into a dressing gown and poked her head into the corridor. Guards had been posted outside the chambers next door. They stood to attention, shock flickering across their faces, as she hobbled painfully toward them. She knew she must look a disturbing sight, her baby-fine ash hair matted with blood, her feet bare, her ankles bruised. She limped past them and into her brother's bedchambers, anxious about what she might find.

Arthmael lay pale and still, his eyes closed. The quilts had been pulled down, exposing his heavy arms and powerful chest. Spots of blood stained their whiteness, while black thread traced across his flesh, as if some mischievous child had scribbled over him as he'd slept.

Pharmacist Yeemans bent across him, rubbing healing ointment around the surgeon's black stitches. Though his touch was light, her brother groaned.

He was alive. Jatta hadn't allowed herself to fully believe it till this moment. She tiptoed closer. Not sure what to say, she shyly stroked his hand. His eyes opened. She leaned forward, braving a smile. He registered her slowly, then his jaw hardened in aggravation.

'Go away,' he said tersely.

It felt like a slap.

'I—I was worried. I needed to see you're all right.' She bit on her lip, wincing. Of course he was *not* all right. 'How—how are you, Art?'

'Scarred for life, thanks to you.' Then he grimaced, sharply drawing in breath. Talking seemed to cause him pain. Jatta blushed with guilt.

Pharmacist Yeemans spoke gently. 'Prince, please remember none of this is your sister's fault.' But Arthmael's accusation, his rare anger too, confirmed that it was.

'I . . . Please, Art, I'm so sorry.'

He waited till the pharmacist's back was turned. 'Why, in glory's name, weren't you wearing the amulet?' he growled under his breath.

'But I never take it off.' She pulled out a pearl string from around her neck, eager to prove herself. Cupping her hands so that only he might see, she showed the disc of fiery opal set in gold.

'Then why—?' His face screwed up and he groaned through gritted teeth. After some seconds the pain seemed to ease. 'Well, it didn't work last night, did it?'

'I'm sorry.'

'Glory, Jay. What's to be done with you now?'

'Father says we'll plead for a new amulet, that everything'll be all right. Ambassador Sartora's in the treasury now, choosing a worthy gift.'

'What's to be done tonight, though?'

'Tonight?' she echoed, confused.

'Tonight, Jay.' He closed his eyes wearily. 'It'll be back tonight.'

The blood drained from her face and she stared, looking almost as ill as her brother. 'The wolves? *Tonight?*'

'*Wolves?*' His eyes opened. He stared back as if she was being deliberately stupid. Then his expression softened. 'Yes . . . the wolves. Jay, how much do you actually remember?'

'I remember sitting at my desk after supper. Drawing. Then, um—then waking up on the floor.'

'Nothing else?'

Jatta shook her head. 'Father says you heard me scream. What happened?'

He sighed and closed his eyes.

'Tell me what happened, Art.'

The pharmacist returned. 'Highness, your brother is tired.'

'All right, rest now,' she whispered. But Arthmael was already asleep.

CHAPTER THREE

The palace was prickling with rumours. As Jatta limped back from Arthmael's bedchambers, servants crowded the corridor to whisper. They fell silent and bowed while she passed, but she felt their stares on her back. She cringed inside, regretting her haste. Why hadn't she at least waited for her ladies-in-waiting to wash the blood from her hair?

Her bedchambers were full of staff. Chambermaids hurriedly finished mopping the floor, while carpenters measured the splintered oak door for repair. Two dozen guards were grunting as they righted the enormous wardrobe. Her ladies stood huddled and whispering in a corner, waiting for the others to leave.

They fed Jatta, then gasped when they undressed her. Four parallel slashes marked her calf. They were merely a scratch, Jatta argued, insisting that the blood on her nightgown was Arthmael's. She persuaded them not to wake Surgeon Tate, although no amount of begging could prevent them calling the pharmacist.

'Highness, it's only a scratch,' Pharmacist Yeemans said, bleary-eyed, as he swabbed her calf with alcohol. 'Anything else?'

Jatta shook her head. 'You won't tell Arthmael I bothered you for this?' Her brother would only laugh.

Yeemans stifled a yawn. 'We're lucky that foolish, brave

prince is still with us. Now take this potion after supper. It'll help you sleep tonight.'

She took his little blue bottle.

'Straight after your meal, Highness. No later.'

After he left, her ladies filled her bathtub and sprinkled it with rose petals. They were full of prying questions; she felt it through their thick silence. She herself was exhausted, over-whelmed by Arthmael's injuries and by a guilt she couldn't explain. She sank down into the water's warmth and slept while her ladies lathered and massaged her scalp. She awoke hungry and shivering. Hammering had begun beyond her bathroom wall.

'Highness, will you rest now?' her ladies asked as they poured hot water in with the cold. 'Shall we find you other bedchambers while the carpenters work?'

Jatta tried to rise out of the water, but her legs gave way. Her whole body ached as if she'd been stretched on a Dartithan rack. While her ladies eased her up, someone suggested re-summoning Pharmacist Yeemans.

'Please, no.' More than rest or food, more than the patently unnecessary sleeping potion, Jatta wanted her friend. 'Is Sanda back yet?' she asked. Sanda would help make sense of this whole dreadful mess. She'd know what to do.

'Highness, Baron Crewingburn's ship docked last night. His daughter should be in tapestry class.'

So she'd slept the morning away. Suffering a fit, whatever that meant, must be exhausting work.

Genteel chatter stopped as Jatta hobbled into the tapestry room. Sanda glanced up, then grinned. A dozen well-bred chins turned to watch.

'Good, um, afternoon,' murmured Jatta, blushing at the barrage of curious and compassionate stares. The noblemen's daughters and their instructors dipped their heads in deference.

Jatta slipped into the chair beside Sanda. Slowly the chatter returned as needles again wove through the great tapestry, on which were traced scenes from the twelfth Sorcerer's life.

Sanda leaned close as she worked, her gruff voice in Jatta's ear. 'So what happened? I came by your chambers. What's that hideous, siege-proof door for?'

Behind Sanda, Ambassador Sartora's daughters and several of their friends strained to listen.

'Hey, you're white as a plucked chook,' whispered Sanda.

Jatta took a deep, shaky breath. 'I'm all right,' she whispered. 'The door's to keep wolves out.'

'Wolves? Lordy me!'

Her father's spice-shipping wealth had bought Sanda fine gowns, a title and a place at court when in Adaban, but not courtly manners. Jatta usually smiled at Sanda's rough curses, but not today.

'Then it's true—is your brother all right?'

Jatta began to nod, then shook her head miserably. 'He looks awful. All slashed up.'

'Not his face, though?' Sanda had gone pale. She made it no secret that she thought Arthmael handsome. Half the girls in the room agreed.

Jatta managed to roll her eyes.

'Hey, well that's good. I mean, it's not good he's—ugh, just thinking about it. I overheard my parents this morning. There are rumours he's been attacked. Wolves from the forest, right?'

Jatta whispered in Sanda's ear, 'Not *our* wolves.'

9

'*Dark Isle* wolves!' gasped Sanda. 'What about your almighty secret amulet?'

Several faces turned toward them. '*Shoosh*,' groaned Jatta.

Sanda, though, was horrified. She leaned in close, wide-eyed. 'The wolves—do you figure they'll be back, you know, to kill you?'

'Art says so. Tonight.' Jatta's hands started trembling. Her needle dropped in her lap. 'Father tells me nothing.'

'Find out, dormouse! *Make* King Elisind tell you. Or ask Prince Steffed.'

'Steffed would only pat my chin and say, "*Trust to Father and me.*"'

Sanda snorted in exasperation. 'What else did Prince Arthmael say?'

'That—that there was just one wolf, though Father said there were more. I don't really know.'

'So where were you in all this?'

'I had a fit. One moment I was at my desk after supper, the next I was lying on the tiles. Sanda, it looked like a massacre. The wolves attacked Art instead of me.'

'Lordy me, that's disgusting. Aren't you petrified?'

Jatta stared back, feeling helpless, not knowing what to say.

Sanda stopped any pretence at needlework. She glared at Jatta with disbelief. 'How can you just sit on your behind waiting to be torn apart? Your family feed you crumbs, like a pet mouse in a sumptuous little cage. Why hasn't the King told you the wolves'll be back? Why doesn't he ruddy tell you anything? Why does Prince Arthmael know more about your fate than you do?'

Jatta wanted to tell her friend that everything was under

control, that Lord Redd would listen, that she had only to trust her father. But his face that morning, his tears . . .

Her body started shivering. She felt weak and dizzy. The room swayed.

Sanda rose, pulling Jatta firmly up by her waist.

'The Princess isn't feeling well,' she announced to the room. 'She'll rest now.'

Jatta struggled in her grip. 'No, it'll pass—'

'*Shoosh*,' growled Sanda in her ear, dragging her toward the door. 'We're going to get some answers.'

CHAPTER FOUR

'Cheer up, Jatta. Just think how lucky we were to get King Elisind's keys.'

Jatta scowled at her friend as she unlocked her father's study, knowing deception, not luck, had got them inside his private chambers.

They had gone straight from the tapestry room to the Cabinet chambers. As she waited in the chambers' anteroom Jatta had recovered enough to recognise her own name spoken through the mahogany-panelled wall, and voices raised in argument.

Her father had smiled wearily from his throne when she was summoned in. The Cabinet, seated at their horseshoe-shaped table, had examined her suspiciously, almost as if she brought the plague.

'Father, I, um—I'm a little unwell,' she'd stammered into his ear.

'Hasn't Pharmacist Yeemans been called?' There had been dark circles under his eyes from a night without sleep.

'No, Father. I just need to rest.'

'Your chambers?'

'They're crowded with workmen.'

'Still? Ah, of course. Then we shall find you fresh—'

'Father, I . . . may I rest in Mother's chambers?'

Her father's kind eyes had searched hers, and she'd blushed

with fresh guilt. 'Of course, Jay. This has been an ordeal for you, I know.'

He had pressed the keys into her hands—keys to his chambers, his private study, living rooms and the rooms that had once been her mother's. It had been as easy as that. She'd hesitated before leaving, fighting the impulse to confess her pretence. If ever he discovered what she'd done with his trust she would lose more than the unquestioned right to his keys.

Rainbow-coloured sunlight shone through the magnificent stained-glass windows in the King's study. Bookshelves stretched from floor to vaulted ceiling. The ancient texts in them rivalled the crown jewels for rarity.

'Smells musty, like old cloaks,' said Sanda, settling straight into her search.

A portrait of a young woman with two small children hung behind the King's desk. Jatta had studied it before, when visiting her father. Still she felt drawn to it. The woman's large, laughing eyes also blazed from Arthmael's face. He was uncannily like her, resembling his father only in his tall, powerful build. Jatta searched for some likeness to herself in this beautiful woman. The height, of course. She had inherited her mother's petite frame, though if anything Jatta was tinier. Even now, days before her fourteenth birthday, Jatta was still sometimes mistaken for a child. When this picture was painted she had yet to be born. The boy holding her mother's hand, standing rigid in his regal pose under his miniature crown, was Steffed. Arthmael was the gorgeous large-eyed baby in her arms.

Jatta searched her mother's face for something more. Some connection, some warm recognition in those effervescent eyes. Nothing. Jatta dropped her gaze, her cheeks hot, feeling suddenly foolish. The painting could no more tell her it loved her than it could reach out and hold her.

'Hoy! Little dormouse, what are you gawping at?' Sanda's arms were stacked with books. 'Stop your dreaming. We'll need his diary, any Dark Isle stuff too.'

Jatta slid down from the desk and fumbled with the keys. With a fresh wave of guilt she opened the first drawer. It was filled with inks, blotting paper, candles, wax and royal seals.

Her father's diary lay under a pile of parchments in the second drawer.

In the third drawer, cradled in satin, was her mother's journal, filled with bedtime stories and her own exquisite illustrations. Jatta trailed her fingers through the apricot suede of its cover before opening the last drawer.

Here were more diaries, stretching back to long before she was born. Jatta chose one from the year she turned three.

'I—I've found something,' she called softly.

'Come on over. So have I,' answered Sanda from an armchair by the window, bathed in the stained-glass tinted sunlight. Jatta chose two diaries and squeezed down beside her friend.

'What have you got?' Sanda wriggled, settling more comfortably into the tight space.

'Father's diaries.'

'Let's have them first. What's today's entry?'

Jatta's heart was beating fast. 'Ready?' she asked. A slight tremor invaded her voice. Sanda gave her arm a gentle squeeze.

2nd of Lunasept, 3029
The night I believed could be averted has arrived. Innocence has ended for our precious little Jay. Dear Rosserlea, I can't bear to tell

her the truth. Nor of the cruel fate, worse than death, that threatens. My darling, has your sacrifice come to nothing?

Lord Redd's amulet has failed. Sartora will beg him for another, but last night has unnerved me.

These past eleven years Cabinet have kept our family's secret— but they're frightened. They argue Lord Redd will forsake the Sorcerer's Pact now and leave Alteeda defenceless. They're already clamouring for Jay to be delivered to King Brackensith. They say his wolves and Undead will destroy us if she stays.

I couldn't bear it if the Dark King took her, too. While I live I will defend her against that wicked union. Rosserlea, how I long for you now . . . your understanding, your strength, your brilliant mind. I am adrift.

Jatta closed the diary. She stared at its cover, almost wishing she hadn't opened it. Whatever her *family's secret* was, whatever *cruel fate* threatened, something else in that page scared her just as much: her father's sense of helplessness. He'd always been her rock, her sanctuary. She ached for that security.

'He speaks in riddles, Jatta. What's this ruddy "wicked union"? I thought Brackensith wanted you dead, like your poor mother.'

Jatta shook her head miserably, tracing her fingers over the cover's gold embossing.

Sanda wrapped an arm around Jatta's shoulder. 'Hey, don't fret. Your father'll mend things, right? Lordy, he *is* the King . . .' Her voice trailed away and she shrugged. Both girls knew Sanda had faith in no-one except herself. 'Anyway, Princess, you've got me. For what it's worth.'

Jatta looked into Sanda's warm eyes and a grateful smile spread across her face.

Sanda grinned. 'That's better. Look, I found something about Dartith. *Dartith*—that's the Dark Isle, right?'

Jatta nodded.

Sanda chose a heavy volume, not ancient like the others, from the stack at their feet and squeezed back down. The page fell open at a macabre picture. In it, one man was biting into the neck of another as they stood on a moonlit cliff. Blood spurted from the wound. Jatta pulled back in disgust. The caption was handwritten in an ornate script, and Sanda read it with difficulty.

'Our Undead feed on our living. They roam throughout Dartith's extended nights, for long ago Andro Mogon's magic reduced our days to six short hours.

'Disgusting, right?' Sanda started leafing through the pages. 'But it's not what I wanted to show you.'

'Wait—wait a moment.' Jatta slid her fingers in to mark the Undead page. 'I've never heard of magic changing day to night. Andro Mogon must have been incredibly power—'

The book slammed shut on her fingers.

'Ouch! What was that for?' said Jatta.

But Sanda had frozen, her eyes on the study door. A chink of light from the corridor had fallen across the floor. As the girls watched, the door creaked open and a black muzzle poked through. Jatta breathed again. 'It's only Father's dog.'

The great dane paused halfway through the door, watching them. His nose twitched. Then he growled, low and threatening.

'What's wrong, boy? Come here, Rufud,' coaxed Jatta.

The great dane's hair bristled.

She struggled up from the chair with reassuring words, but her movement only aggravated him. He bared his teeth, snarling, inching toward them.

'What is it, Rufud?' Jatta peered nervously around for the danger. But the animal was snarling at *her*. Suddenly he snapped into frenzied barking.

'Lordy!' Sanda jumped up. 'He'll bring the guards!'

Rufud was momentarily distracted. Sanda dived for his collar. She wrestled him out of the study as he snapped viciously at Jatta.

From outside the King's chambers came frantic knocking. 'Highness, are you hurt? Open up!'

'Open the front doors, or they'll break them down!' yelled Jatta, tossing the keys to Sanda. As her friend struggled through the corridor with Rufud, Jatta scrambled to the desk. She stuffed the diaries inside. Whirling back, she seized Sanda's books. From beyond the study came muffled voices and Rufud's whining. She shoved Sanda's books wherever she could find shelf space. Her heart was thumping as she rushed out of the room, not stopping to lock anything.

Sanda was in the King's sitting room, flustered by the captain's interrogation. Guards tramped from room to room calling Jatta's name. As she entered the sitting room they caught sight of her and came running. Rufud began snarling.

She collapsed yawning onto a sofa. 'Can't somebody keep that rabid beast quiet? I'm trying to rest,' she moaned.

'Highness, you're unharmed!' cried the captain. One guard grabbed Rufud's collar and pulled him from the room.

'That deranged canine's given me a splitting headache,' she whined, lying back with one arm draped theatrically across her brow.

'Highness, we've never known Rufud so agitated. We feared for your safety.'

'And yet, here I am.'

The captain bowed. 'As indeed is Lady Crewingburn. With respect, Highness, has she permission to be in the King's private chambers? In possession of his keys?'

'Ah, I was just leaving,' offered Sanda.

The captain cocked an eyebrow.

'Leaving—after reading at my bedside.' Jatta wiped her arm across her brow, then let it flop over the sofa where she lay like a tragic heroine. 'Last night's crisis has left me vexed and fatigued, as you may know.'

An unreadable expression flicked across Captain Naffaedan's face. 'Indeed, Highness. I was there.'

Jatta sat straight up, immediately dropping her pretence. This man knew things about her ordeal that she did not. She searched his face, but he endured her scrutiny with professional blandness.

'I . . . don't, um, remember much,' she faltered.

Naffaedan nodded to his men, who left the room. He turned to Sanda, stretching out a broad palm. She placed the keys in it with a cheeky grin.

'Sanda, could you please wait for me outside?' said Jatta.

'I can't tell you much,' he said once they were alone. His honest, strong face had relaxed.

'Naffaedan, um, how many wolves were there?'

'Highness, I cannot say.'

'You must know. At what point did you arrive?'

'As soon as we heard the Prince's cry. There were twenty of us and as many hounds, but the wolves snapped our swords. Your brother defended himself brilliantly, hurling lamps even after sustaining his wounds. Without his fire and our hounds and nets, we could not have hoped to dissuade the cursed creatures.'

'Did you wound any?'

'Indeed not, Highness. But we lost eight good hounds.'

'Will they return tonight?' she pressed.

Reluctantly he nodded.

'Could you capture them then?'

'Highness, our wise King has devised a different strategy for tonight. You will be safe. Trust him.'

Blind trust? *Still?* Her frustration swelled. 'What sort of an answer's that? Don't treat me like a child, Naffaedan! How many wolves? What strategy? What is the *cruel fate that threatens*, the *wicked union?*'

'Highness! Who dared tell you this?'

She bit her lip. She had exposed too much.

Catching her discomfort, his eyes narrowed. He glanced in the direction of the study. She blushed crimson. Naffaedan bowed and left the room.

'You've told me nothing!' she blustered, following him to the study door. He tested its handle. It swung open. The withering look he gave his Princess was one no palace servant had the right to use. Jatta tried to feign indignation, but the weight of her father's disappointment was already pressing on her.

In stony silence he locked the study door as Jatta examined her bracelets.

His voice, when he spoke, was surprisingly gentle. 'Highness, this won't be in my report to the King.'

Her body flooded with relief.

'But I beg you, trust your father. And don't betray his trust in you.'

'Thank you, Naffaedan,' she said humbly.

He bowed again. She nodded and left.

*

Sanda was propped against the wall, anxiously kicking it with her heel, when Jatta emerged.

'So, what did he say?'

'Not to go back into the study.'

'How'd he figure that—did you *tell* him? Lordy, we're in hot soup now.'

'He won't tell Father, Sanda.'

'Why not?' she demanded. Then she shrugged her shoulders with a laugh. 'Well, that's good news, anyway. Can you get the keys tomorrow?'

'Sanda, I don't think—'

'Don't go all limp on me again. You were impressive back there, with your *rabid beasts* and your *vexed and fatigued*.'

'I feel so guilty.'

'*And yet, here I am!*' pronounced Sanda with a regally pompous flourish. 'You've a hidden talent for this. What an act! Anyway, we've *got* to go back. There's something you need to see in that Dartith book.'

Jatta sighed. She could never match wills with the hurricane that was her friend.

Satisfied that she had consent, Sanda linked their arms. 'Now let's visit your delectable brother.'

'Tomorrow perhaps. Father says only family today.'

Sanda shrugged. 'Then tell King Elisind you want to sleep in the Queen's chambers tonight. That should give us access. And give the Lion a kiss from me.'

CHAPTER FIVE

Jatta found Arthmael propped up on pillows. His heavy chest rose and fell as he slept. Everything in her brother's appearance was heavy, she thought, like a lion, the palace's affectionate nickname for him. His face with its square jaw, thick eyebrows and tangled lashes. Tanned skin, sandy blond hair. His shoulder-length mane spread over the pillows. His eyes, large and green like hers, opened as she watched him.

They shared an early supper. His mood had improved. He'd smiled when she ate every selection on her trays and emptied the gravy boats and butterscotch sauce jug too. While attendants fussed about and Pharmacist Yeemans ground medicines, she eyed his custard.

He managed his usual lopsided, wry grin. 'Where's all this disappearing to, little mouse?'

She shrugged. She'd missed lunch, but that wasn't it. She was still famished.

'Then feed me before mine vanishes too.'

She plopped herself down by his pillows. He winced in pain.

'Your Highness must please be more gentle,' urged the pharmacist.

'Sorry, Art. How are you?'

'I'm bored,' he said between sips of custard. 'So let's play a game. *Nine Phrases.*'

Jatta grinned at his request. 'You're too old.'

'No. Well yes, but I insist on a Jay story, even though it'll be soaked in fairies and fluff.'

She fought the impulse to shove him for his insult, delighted that he seemed as pleased to see her as she always was to see him.

'All right, I'll oblige my patient. But then it's your turn.'

'I don't think so, Jay. Steffed and I could never remember nine phrases, let alone weave them into anything like you can.'

She grinned broader, her cheeks flushed.

'Ready, little sister? Let's see what fairy floss your sugary inventiveness can spin from these: I choose *poisonous black spider*. I choose *heel*, and *dying breath*, and *envy*, and *crocodile teeth*, and *ugly grub*, and *tra*—' He scowled in concentration. He groaned, and Jatta realised with an unpleasant jolt that it wasn't the remaining three phrases that absorbed him, but his agony. Catching her grimace, he grinned weakly. 'Don't worry about me, Jay. It comes, then passes. Are you ready? I choose *trap* and *torn entrails*.'

'T—torn entrails! You're revolting. Delirious too, because I've only counted eight.'

'All right, a ninth. Something sweet . . . a *butterfly*, though I expect I'll regret it later.'

Jatta handed the custard bowl to an attendant. She sat still for a moment with eyes closed, threading together his phrases, weaving in scraps of daydreams and fables till her story formed. She began.

'*There once was a wicked witch whose magical potion made her beautiful to all men. Night-long she stirred warty toads, crocodile teeth and newt eyeballs into her bubbling cauldron; in her sea cave above thunderous waves she drank that potion.*

In all the land there remained one woman, only one, whose natural beauty outshone hers: the fair young queen. The envious witch crept into the palace to cast a powerful spell, which shrank and shrivelled the queen into an ugly grub. But then, before the witch could destroy her beneath her heel, the grub morphed into a shimmering green butterfly.

Oh, the poor king and his children! They were heartbroken by their queen's disappearance, thinking she had deserted them . . .'

Jatta paused, imagining the king calling in despair, sweeping through every chamber. Her eyes were luminous, her stammer had gone. Arthmael nudged his sister to continue.

'All right, Art . . .

'The king and his children never realised, but the butterfly that flitted into their lives was their queen, watching over them as best she could. As years passed they learned to care for the little butterfly. She never left the children while they played and ate and grew, and at night she slept on a miniature silk pillow beside the king.

The witch's dark magic also grew with the years until one day she was as beautiful as the queen, and she returned to the palace.

Thinking his wife had come back to them, the king proclaimed a feast. The royal children saw inside her black heart, though. They pleaded with their father to reject her, and he was torn. The furious witch then set a trap: she hid in the children's bowl of sweets as a poisonous black spider.

The little butterfly fluttered frantically to warn them, but how could they understand? Just as the children reached into the bowl the butterfly queen attacked her enemy, and was bitten instead. Her agony was as if her entrails had been torn from her.

The poor queen! One last time she appeared before them as their mother. With her dying breath she promised to watch over them still, to always be in their hearts.'

Arthmael grunted softly. 'That's clever,' he said. 'But it's a sad little tale.'

'Not for me, Art. It makes me feel warm, like a hug.'

'Because the butterfly watched over her family even after she died?'

Jatta smiled sheepishly, looking down to fidget with her ring.

Arthmael sighed. He nodded to the pharmacist, saying, 'I'll rest now.' His attendants collected their trays and bowed from the room.

'It's a story about Mother, isn't it?' he said gently.

Jatta nodded.

'I don't understand, Jay. How can you miss someone you don't even remember?'

'I miss her bedtime stories ... Remember when Steffed used to make us sit straight-backed among our pillows to read the fables she had written? And when we p—played her games, like *Nine Phrases*. I miss her when I watch Sanda with her mother ... and, um, sometimes, when I've caught Father reading her journals. I want to remember that she loved me. Just like she loved you, and Steffed, and Father. But—but there's nothing there, Art.'

'She loved you, Jay.' He snorted. 'More than any of us.'

She glanced up, startled. Something she'd said had infuriated him; she didn't know what.

'She sacrificed everything for you.' His jaw clenched. His voice grew hard. '*And now, it seems, for nothing!*'

Was he blaming her for her mother's death? She stared at his face. She hadn't seen that anger since they'd been little, when she used to follow him and tattle on everything he did. They'd been enemies back then.

'It's n—not my fault!' she cried.

'Maybe not. But you're here—' He winced in sudden agony.

'And she's gone. She should have just let him take you. Then everything would be all right now.'

'Let who? King Brackensith? Tell me! His wolves want to drag me back to Dartith, don't they? To my cruel fate. Tell me, what's my cruel fate?'

He glared at her, jaw clenched, tight-lipped.

She hated that look. He knew the secret. Arthmael was keeping it from her, too. 'You're so smug,' she said. 'You think I—I don't matter. Well maybe he's changed his mind. It's you his wolves mauled. Maybe he w—wants you.'

'Brackensith doesn't want *me*!' he snapped, his face contorted in pain. 'It's you he wants, you freak!'

Her eyes filled with tears. Her father's words flooded back. *I cannot bear to tell her the truth.* The truth was, she was a freak and she belonged to Brackensith. Arthmael was right. If Brackensith had taken her, their mother would still be here and her father and brothers would be happy. But she didn't deserve to be happy. Or here, with them. Arthmael's words had torn a hole in her, and her own happiness was seeping out.

Arthmael shut his eyes against his pain, against her misery.

'Lord, Jay! Forget it. I'm sorry, all right,' he said through gritted teeth.

'What am I?' She crouched on the bed hugging her knees, smaller and more fragile than ever. 'Tell me why I'm ... a freak.'

He opened his eyes, sighed, then with painful effort patted her shoulder. 'Listen, I was being a real toad. It was just my nausea talking. Glory, you know I've been shredded to within an inch of my life ... You won't tell Father, will you? That I made you cry?'

She shook her head, managing a quivering smile.

'Jay, you're not a freak. You *are* a daydreaming, vague, useless twit, though.'

She laughed weakly, sniffing back tears.

'Everything's going to be fine. You'll get a fresh amulet.' He grinned, but it was too bright.

'You're such a bad liar.'

His face softened back into her favourite crooked smile. 'So, I admit I don't know that. I'm happier not guessing. I'm tired now, Jay. But listen. Whatever happens—*whatever*—you're still my little sister.'

He closed his eyes and she got up to leave.

The door opened and King Elisind crept to the bed. He looked from the bed to her, and sighed heavily. He gravely wiped away her tears.

'What are these for?' he whispered.

Arthmael's eyes opened and he struggled to sit up. His face crumpled into a grimace of pain.

His father felt his forehead. 'Better, I see, since this morning.'

'I expect I'll be well enough—' Arthmael paused to stifle a groan, '—to go to next week's Festival.'

The King cast a sideways glance at Jatta. 'I see you're already well enough to be reducing your sister to tears.'

'I—it was only—I'm sorry.'

'We're friends again,' offered Jatta.

'It's just as well. You two should remember that there are no stronger bonds than family.'

They nodded dutifully. It was a lecture they'd heard before.

'Remember, the palace is jittery with rumour. Now is a time when your loyalties will be tested.' He fixed them both with his gaze.

They nodded again.

'As for you, Jay, it's almost dark. Shouldn't you be in bed?'

'But the wolves—' Suddenly this room with its lights and her father, and the guards outside, seemed safer. She didn't want to leave.

'Precisely, the wolves. I'm not having you wandering the palace when they come.'

'My—my chambers aren't ready, though.'

'Tonight you sleep in your mother's chambers. Pharmacist Yeemans shall ensure you drink your sleeping potion.'

'But the wolves—'

He sighed. 'Jay, child. Go to bed.' He bent down, smelling of sweet spice. He cupped her face in his broad, scarred hands and kissed her forehead. 'Leave the worry to me.'

CHAPTER SIX

Jatta woke to pounding on the front doors. For one groggy moment she thought she was back in the study and the guards were breaking them down. Then she remembered she was in her mother's bed. The sun was high in the sky, so she must have slept through the night . . . and half the morning. Nausea rolled through her belly as she remembered the blue bottle by the bed. Ten drops mixed in honey. It had tasted sweet. That was the last thing she could remember.

Till now. Till that terrible banging, hammering in her head, churning her stomach. Whoever it was had neither decency nor fear of the King. She dragged herself out of bed, but her stomach lurched into her throat. Dropping to her knees, she vomited over the tiles.

She hauled herself through the corridors and unlocked the doors. Sanda shoved past. 'Lordy, Jatta! I thought you were dead in here.' She did a double-take. 'Lordy me, you half-look it. Skin and bones, too. Don't you ever eat? Never mind, why aren't you dressed? We've got work to do.'

Jatta leaned against the wall, wiping dribble from her chin. 'That was you breaking down the door,' she groaned. 'You'll have half the palace guards onto us.'

'No worries. I waited till your captain friend went off duty, then told his guards the King sent me. Urgent Secret Wolf Protection Business.'

'You what!'

'Listen, don't worry about it. Did your wolves come back?'

'No. So maybe we should just trust—'

'I see King Elisind left you the keys. Good—let's get down to it.' Sanda grabbed Jatta's keys and dragged her past her mother's chambers. 'Lordy, what's that stink?'

'That was me. I think the potion's too strong. Listen, Sanda, we don't have the right—'

'Of course we've got the right,' growled Sanda in exasperation. She'd stopped outside the study, one hand on her hip, the other dangling the keys in front of Jatta's face. 'Lordy, you're limp. Do you want to know or not? Don't pretend you don't.'

Her nausea was fading. Jatta felt a burst of resentment, directed not at her friend, but at her father, Steffed and Arthmael. This was *her* life, *her* cruel fate, they were hiding. She took the keys and inserted them in the door.

Retrieving the eleven-year-old diary from her father's desk seemed easier this time. They squeezed down together in their armchair, bathed in warm rainbows.

Sanda started leafing through the Dartith book.

'Here it is.'

She was pointing at an illustration of a monster. Half wolf, half man, bigger than both. It stood upright on a wolf's hind legs with broad, muscular, human-like shoulders and chest, and hands that ended in claws. The face was more beast than human. Mangy fur covered the body. The eyes were almost human in shape, though there was nothing of human intelligence in their manic gaze.

Jatta glanced at the creature. Her heart stopped cold in her chest.

She was a toddler again, paralysed with fear.

This wolf, this thing, was the wolf of her nightmares. Its vicious eyes were alive. They glistened and turned to fix on her. Its face grew monstrous and broke free of the page. Its lips twisted up, quivering. This wolf snarled for her blood.

The room spun. Terror rose in her throat, a strangled scream.

Sanda slammed the book shut. 'Jatta, stop!' But the toddler Jatta screamed still. Hoarse, stifled croaks.

'Jatta, wake up! It's me!' Sanda flung her arms around her unseeing friend, clutching her tight. The book thudded to the floor. With all her will Jatta fought the thing back. Back to the dark crevice in her mind where it slept. In her friend's grip the screams faded, the panic too.

She slumped like the bones had been ripped out of her.

Shocked, Sanda unwrapped her arms to peer close.

'Lordy, what was that about?'

'That's *it*. The wolf,' Jatta tried to whisper, trembling.

'What? The wolves that attacked your brother?'

Jatta stared vacantly.

'The wolves that attacked your mother?'

She nodded.

'You put on quite a performance there, Princess. Do you still want me to read this?'

Jatta nodded and turned her face to the wall, squeezing her eyes shut. Sanda offered a reassuring peck. She hooked a loose strand of Jatta's hair back behind her ear.

Jatta forced a fragile smile. 'I—I'm coping.'

Sanda leafed through the pages. 'All right, well here's a chapter on wolves. Several chapters.' She read.

In our tenth century A.M. the great Sorcerer Andro Mogon created a final punishment for our Isle's traitors: the wolf curse. Of all his curses, this be most terrible. His wolf continues in human form except on the three nights of the full moon. With the setting sun he transforms, having a wolf's instinct to hunt and a madman's passion. He kills throughout the night, first devouring his family and all who once loved him. All men detest him and drive him, if they can, from their midst. Even so, many fear a wolf's bite more than being devoured for, if King Brackensith commands it, the victim might also be cursed.

Sanda leant her head back against the chair and let out a long, exaggerated whistle. 'Imagine monsters like that, loose in the palace. And they want to eat us and curse us. And drag you back to Dartith. Lordy, once one of us is infected ...' She shuddered. 'Hey, I'm coming with you. I'd rather *your* fate.'

But might the palace already be infected? In that moment Jatta realised others in the palace had known of the wolf curse. Cabinet had glowered at her as if she was plague-ridden.

'Art and I were both wounded,' she whispered hoarsely, her skin clammy and cold. 'I think we're—we're cursed wolves.'

Sanda shook her head. 'No, that doesn't count.' She turned the pages. 'Here. Here's how it's done.'

In his murderous, bestial state, the wolf has neither voice nor awareness to utter the curse. He must stay guarding his victim till dawn, till he returns to human form. Only the mature wolf has developed such control of his murderous instincts. With the dawn he must recite the words, immersing his palm in his victim's blood. If the victim survives, he shall also be cursed.

31

'See? The surgeon was with Prince Arthmael. Your father was with you, right? You're both safe. But what this doesn't tell us is, why you?'

'I'm not sure I can handle more answers now,' said Jatta quietly.

'Sure you can.' Sanda was already leafing through the King's eleven-year-old diary. In its seventh month his elegant script became messy, like a child's, or as if written with the wrong hand. 'Doesn't seem he's written the day your mother died. No entry for another . . . another week. Only a page.'

8th of Lunasept, 3018

Today we bid our Rosserlea goodbye. Our procession to Lake Adaban was bleak misery; I cannot remember such crowds, such weeping. My stout-hearted Steffed helped me light the pyre. Little Art, not yet seven, was inconsolable. I am grateful, in all this, that poor Jay is too young to remember.

I burn for my Rosserlea. I burn with revenge, but I'm powerless. Sorcerer Andro Mogon's Undead protect Dartith, just as his wall of fire protects its long shore. Brackensith takes from other kings whatever he covets. We have all been powerless to refuse him—and our Sorcerer Lord Redd stands idly by!

Brackensith stole Sludinia's Princess Noridane as his bride, and her sister Princess Noriward before her. Last week their brother King Norisinid and I assembled every king and queen in secret, to stand united against Dartith. We argued through the night.

With the approaching dawn Brackensith and his wolves appeared in his portal. Brave kings fled. Others of us stayed to battle against his dark magic, and we bear the wounds of swords that turned molten in our hands.

That night Brackensith chose our little girl for his son. He seized Jay from my Rosserlea's arms and she, wonderful fool, grabbed his own dagger to stab his throat. Oh, Lord.

Would that she hadn't. Would that she'd aimed truer.

My darling Rosserlea defied Brackensith and paid with her life . . . as I may have too, without Lord Redd. But now we have his commitment.

Brackensith's heir shall not wed my Jay. She is too tender, too sensitive, to survive in that dark—

'Please stop,' whispered Jatta.

'Lordy, you look awful. Listen, though—this says you get to be queen. What's so *"fate worse that death"* about that? A big arranged marriage sounds more fun that being eaten or cursed. Right?'

'No. I mean, yes. I mean, I'm tired.'

'But you've just slept the morning away.'

'Not that sort of tired, Sanda.'

'All right, you useless lump, but I'm keeping the Dartith book. Make sure you finish this diary page.'

Jatta returned to her own chambers, dragging open her new iron-bolted reinforced door, and flopped down on her bed. She couldn't bear to read more of her mother's death now, or more painful truths, she told herself, sliding the diary inside a freshly embroidered pillowslip.

Life had been so much happier safe inside her cage. But it had all been a confection, her father's spun-sugar lie. Like fairy floss, too, her father's rock was dissolving away.

He came to sit with her while she ate her early supper, and she insisted everything was fine. Two, she decided, could play at his game.

Jatta lay still among her pillows, feigning sleep, tensely listening for familiar sounds. There was Pharmacist Yeemans's cough as he packed away his bag, the women's hushed whispers, their footsteps across the tiles, and the heavy closing of her door. Then followed the new and disturbing clatter of bolts and locks.

Only then did she dare open her eyes.

Beyond her bars, beyond her garden, clouds glowed orange in a darkening sky. Beside her bed lay the blue bottle. She'd protested it made her sick, but Pharmacist Yeemans had insisted on ten drops in his spoon of honey. She'd then pretended to swallow, spitting it instead into her handkerchief. This, she counted with growing resentment toward her father, was the third time she'd defied him.

The potion could wait. She pulled her father's old diary from inside her pillow and sat with it open on the quilts. With a long, jagged breath she read.

Brackensith's heir shall not wed my own Jay. She is too tender, too sensitive to survive in that dark isle.

In my nightmares I still see Brackensith pull the blade from his wound. I hear his words, cold as winter: 'When next you see me, Elisind, you shall be grateful to surrender your daughter.'

I hear him command his wolves. 'Kill the mother. Curse the child.'

Though his wolves have cursed her, I shall never let my Jay taste human flesh.

I shall never surrender my daughter to Dartith.

Though his wolves have cursed her—
The awful truth thundered in her brain.

'Please. Not me,' she mouthed.

The diary dropped. She collapsed into the pillows. Her room spun. The wolf was not outside this barred sanctuary, clawing to get in. It was inside this barred prison, clawing to get out.

Inside her.

She fought to focus, shot a terrified look at the sky, at the white moon rising. Her face tingled. Her arms and legs, too. Her last desperate thought, her last memory, was reaching for the bottle. For drugged sleep. Oblivion.

Too late. Her body was bulging now, flesh stretching and pulling. Sharp edges poked her from inside; the agony was like slashing knives. Something sinister was clawing at her innards. Scraping and snarling. A vicious beast bursting out. Hairy claws slashed out, spilling potion over the floor.

Her furious howl sent a chill through the palace.

CHAPTER SEVEN

Arthmael woke with an awful jolt. It seemed the creature was right by his ear, howling her unearthly song.

Jay. Again. Oh, Lord.

He waited, every muscle tense, the sheets wet with his sweat as her howl trailed into silence. By this time two nights before he'd been at her door. He'd burst in, sword in hand. Impetuous dolt.

No, that wasn't fair. No-one had guessed.

Suddenly something massive crashed against Jatta's wall, sending mortar crumbling to the floor. He sat bolt upright. Pain seared through his slashed chest.

Down the corridor came shouts and the pounding of boots. Outside his glass doors, men raced through the gardens with blazing torches. It was an eerily graceful sight, their fiery procession. Arthmael could hear Captain Naffaedan shouting orders from the ledge above. Steffed was outside his door, shouting too. Jatta howled again, drowning all else out.

He eased his legs gingerly out from the sheets and reached for his sword. As he rose he leaned on it, ignoring his pain, remembering how she'd plucked his blade from him like she was plucking a blade of grass. He managed a wry grunt, hoping his sword would serve him better as a cane than it had as a weapon. Glass shattered next door. Something had been hurled through her garden doors. The wardrobe perhaps. He only hoped her bars had held. He took his first shaky steps, gasping at the pain shooting through his chest.

Naffaedan and his father shouted for nets and hounds from the ledge.

But Jatta seemed to have lost interest in the garden doors.

Boom—boom—boom.

Splinters flew as Arthmael shuffled on his sword along the corridor wall. She was battering her bolted door. Steffed was in the corridor, positioning men with long spears.

Spears won't stop her, thought Arthmael, scowling. Steffed will need fire.

Boom—boom—boom.

More guards were racing past him with torches. Arthmael glimpsed a nervous crowd gathering further down, behind a barricade. Beyond them a family scurried toward the exit.

He hobbled past the guards to the door. She'd slashed a hole, but its four bolt bars—one across its bottom and one across its top, a third at waist height and a fourth at head height—held fast.

'Art! What in blazing heralds are you doing out here?' yelled Steffed. 'Get back to bed.'

'Can't do it,' said Arthmael, poking his head through the hole. 'Can't sleep with this racket.'

Inside, not a thing was left standing. Dimmed lamps flickered over Jatta's four-poster bed lying broken against the wall. The massive wardrobe, which had taken the strength of two dozen men to right, had been dragged toward the glass doors, gouging deep tracks in the tiles. It hung at a strange angle against the bars. Gowns and petticoats lay strewn along its route. Beyond the bars, in her rose garden, guards gathered with blazing torches. Jatta was nowhere to be seen.

'Art! Get your infantile head back out here where it belongs!' shouted Steffed.

Arthmael ignored him. He looked up at a flicker of movement. There she was, clawing her way upside-down among the beams.

'Jay, silly girl,' he sighed. 'Why in glory's name didn't you take your potion?'

To his shock she twisted her snout toward the door. Wolf ears swivelled forward and eyes—Jatta's green eyes—looked into his. They glimmered, seeming almost to recognise him. But in the next moment they grew hostile and narrowed. Jatta snarled, exposing gums. Her teeth jutted over her chin, too many and too big to fit in. Whatever they were made of, they reflected like black glass. A mouthful of shards.

Instinctively he recoiled.

She leapt to the floor, landing on all fours, and rose up howling. Her body was immense, easily taller than a bear, but almost human. Mangy black hair was tufted over her powerful chest. A mane ran the length of her spine. Massively muscled arms ended in human hands and deadly claws. Her hind legs were wolf-like. Her head was, too, with its low forehead. The intelligence had gone from Jatta's eyes; instead they shone with fury. They flicked to the bars, to the beams, then back to Arthmael. With a roar she lunged at the door.

Steffed jerked him back. They toppled together as her massive head burst through the hole. Her teeth snapped shut on Arthmael's nightshirt, shredding it. His veins pounded with terror. She pulled her head back inside the hole as guards reached to grab the princes. Suddenly an arm thrust through. Claws swiped, and pain seared in Arthmael's thigh. Flaming torches jabbed. Jatta yelped and wrenched her arm back.

'Stop!' cried Steffed. 'Don't hurt her!'

Even though it felt like his stitches had torn open, even as he clutched his thigh to staunch the bleeding, tangled there in the corridor with his brother, Arthmael started to laugh. 'Glory, Steffed, what do *I* have to do to get sympathy from you?'

'You can start by not poking your head through her door,' he snapped. 'What is it with you? A death wish?'

Startled, Arthmael tried to laugh off his brother's words. But on top of everything else, he was starting to feel ridiculous.

'Sorry, sorry. But did you see? Just for a moment I thought she recognised me.'

Steffed was staring at the hole. The guards were, too.

'Keep talking,' whispered Steffed.

Arthmael followed their gaze. He gaped. Jatta was peering through, recognition again flickering in her green eyes.

He swallowed hard. 'Remember me, Jay? I'm the titbit that got away last time . . .'

Her ears flicked back. She began a rumbling, uncertain growl.

'Keep it soothing,' whispered Steffed.

Arthmael started again, softly, as if chiding a mischievous puppy. 'Tut-tut, naughty girl, Jay. Just look at this mess, just look at your chambers . . .'

Her nostrils emerged through the hole, sniffing his scent.

'Just look at the mess you've made of *me*. Yes, I'm a patch-work from your needlework class. Naughty, naughty Jay. You're not coming out, not till you've cleaned up your mess.'

One of the guards chuckled nervously.

Instantly she burst through—arm, head, shoulder. The brothers got no warning. No time to disentangle their limbs. To roll away. Claws gouged Steffed's shin, scraping the bone.

Even as Steffed yelled, guards hauled the princes back by their necks. Jatta's frenzied snarling drove them all against the corridor wall. Spittle sprayed their faces.

'Calm down, Jay, calm down!' ordered Arthmael.

The spell, though, could not be re-spun. Her massive shoulders fought to wedge through; armour plates clacked under her pelt. She howled. Pulling back, she tore at the door in frustration, sending splinters flying. Its four bars rattled; they were almost all that remained.

Boots raced along the corridor: the King's own. 'Get them to surgery! Get away from that door!' he boomed.

Jatta bounded around her chambers. She hurled chests like papier-mâché and ripped gowns as if they were tissue. She clambered up her wardrobe, her snout wedged through the bars, howling at the moon for deliverance.

Guards dragged Steffed up. Arthmael propped himself casually against the wall.

'I shall go.' Steffed arched an imperious eyebrow at Arthmael. 'But that jester is leaving with me.'

'Save your commands for the surgeon,' said Arthmael. 'This jester's staying for the show.'

King Elisind suspiciously eyed the remnants of Arthmael's blood-soaked nightshirt and his seeping stitches.

Arthmael shrugged, staunching his thigh with an inconspicuously pressed palm. 'The blood's mostly Steffed's. Listen, Father, Jay knows me. Just let me stay a few minutes.'

The King nodded tightly. 'Don't leave the wall, understand?'

The corridor grew eerily silent, apart from the torches' splutter and Arthmael's irregular soft calls. He flattered himself it was his magic that soothed the rabid beast.

By his tense face, King Elisind didn't agree. 'I don't like this,' he muttered. He called to the rose garden. 'Naffaedan! What do you see?'

'Not much!' came the reply. 'Torch reflection from the glass!'

King Elisind scowled, then gestured two guards to approach the door. Each edged either side. Arthmael shuffled along the corridor's far wall and propped himself there, directly opposite Jatta's door.

All three peered through, finding no movement along Jatta's walls. A thrill pricked Arthmael's scalp as he searched, imagining eyes that would brighten with recognition. The guards slid down on their haunches to look through the bottom hole.

'Nothing, Your Majesty,' one whispered.

No warning came. No-one could have seen her waiting in ambush above the door.

She dropped. Her feet swung through the centre hole. Her legs and torso stretched into the corridor. As her hind claws pierced his ribs, Arthmael's body flushed hot with the memory of last time. He was ripped off his feet. Hooked. Reeled back.

His hips slammed against what remained of the door and she dropped him. He crumpled with a thud. His heart thumped painfully against his ribs. Tumult erupted as men sprang for him. There was no time to recover, to drag himself away—a fractured second, no more, before an arm reached to fish her prize back through the hole. Again her claws hooked his ribs. He flopped in her single bound to the wall.

What happened next probably lasted only moments. In each ghastly one he thought he would die. She jerked him to her face, eyes wild with bloodlust. Her lips quivered, pulled

41

back from jumbled teeth. Her hot breath blew in his gaping mouth.

'Argh . . . argh . . . remember me, little sister?' he pleaded, pinned in her grip as her jaws opened. 'You'll regret this later.' His voice broke at the end.

Some ghost of uncertainty flickered in her eyes.

Then it was gone. The seething hatred returned.

'Don't do this, Jay . . . Jay . . .' he whispered, knowing it was pointless. His nausea welled as her jaws gaped impossibly wide, wide enough to enclose his whole head. *This will be quick*, he thought with courage and sadness.

Another part of him refused to die. It was a hopeless, hopeful act to reach out behind. His fingers felt wall. They swept a wide circle. They brushed glass as her jaws wrapped around his skull. He stared into the dark, dripping cave of her mouth. Even as shard-teeth closed to puncture his eyes, he ripped the lamp from its wall-stand.

He smashed the lamp over his sister's snout.

Bright orange and yellow flashed outside his cave. It roared open as she tossed him away. Jatta jumped back, shaking her flaming jowl, then pounding its fire.

Arthmael slammed into a bedpost and fell to the tiles. Dragging himself up by the post, he staggered dizzily to the wall, then dropped to his knees. On wobbly legs, Arthmael lurched to the door.

She got there first.

Torches, too many to count, were thrusting through. Jatta swiped at their flames. Realising he still held the lamp, Arthmael swung it. He edged closer to the door than she dared. Frustration drove her rabid. She snapped at his flame and swirled to snarl and lunge at the torches. Burning air cooked his back, but he knew she'd have him the instant he stepped from the door. Torches crackled. Men were shouting. His father was calling something, but Arthmael's brain was a jumble.

Jatta danced close. Lord, was she growing bolder?

She sprang, swiping at his lamp. It flew, spraying fire, to smash in a pile of debris. Drawings flashed alight.

Lord yes, bolder.

She sprang back from the heat. Purpose had replaced the wildness in her eyes. She half-crouched, poised to launch. Her eyes narrowed, locking on his.

In blind faith he twisted to the door and dived, head first.

Torches pulled back through the hole. Many hands grabbed his arms and yanked him through. He heard Jatta's snarl as she threw herself after him, felt her claws scrape his heels. Hands dragged him unceremoniously along the corridor. His chest sagged to the tiles and more stitches tore. He expected her to come bounding at any moment to claim him back.

Behind him the bolts rattled. Jatta's snarls changed to a howl. Her plaintive song didn't follow him, and he allowed himself to hope. As the guards laid him down he rolled over to look. The corridor was deserted except for his father, white faced. Arthmael could only guess what watching his own children's mortal combat would have cost him.

King Elisind's furrowed forehead seemed not frightened, merely pitying, as Jatta struggled with one shoulder and one arm through the door. Arthmael understood why. Her howls were frustration. Her armoured chest had wedged so that she could move neither in nor out. Arthmael also noticed the bald, livid flesh on her snout. *Sorry little sister, that may well scar*, he thought. *But you and Father would have been considerably more sorry if your ugly fangs had crunched down.*

Mortar crumbled as she battled the door. Arthmael grunted with dark humour, wondering which might give first: the beam-thick bolts, or a section of wall.

His father breathed deeply, then let the air out in a great gust, probably considering the same thing. 'Guards, we need barricades, anything that burns, both ends of this corridor.' His voice sounded weary, resigned. 'And inform Naffaedan to evacuate the palace. Tell people they may return safely with the dawn.'

Long after Arthmael had gone under the surgeon's needle, long after the rose garden's torches burnt out, the guards listened in dread in the deserted palace. Heraldic stars faded. Night, too. Still Jatta howled, wedged in her door.

Dawn light pierced the sky. Jatta yelped as if some tormentor's teeth had pierced her spine.

Her legs quivered. They buckled, useless, and her haunches thudded on the bedchamber tiles. Fury drove her to twist and strain, but there was no getting back through her wedge to her attacker. She tore chunks from the door.

Her great chest shuddered, then sagged. Arms collapsed. Her massive head dropped to the corridor floor. Snarls lay paralysed inside her throat.

Jatta's eyes fought on furiously alone. They glowered uncomprehending as her body shrank. Bones and armour plates splintered. They jabbed and poked and tumbled with muscle under her pelt. Her hatred seethed while the dark miracle pummelled her pelt back to soft, coloured curves.

A whisper of wind caught the painted-on white lace at her ankles and lifted it from her skin. It teased the lilac colour from her legs and fashioned a gossamer cloth from it, which danced in the wind's breath while the rest of her nightgown re-formed. Bracelets shaped themselves from the gold- and ruby-coloured skin of her wrists. Redd's amulet emerged from the opal skin of her throat, under her delicate chin and heart-shaped pixie face. Jatta's furious, agonised eyes closed.

CHAPTER EIGHT

Jatta woke soaked in sweat. The nightmare was retreating deep below the throbbing in her head.

She lay draped through a door in a smoky corridor trampled with blood. Ceiling-high barricades burned. Beyond, guards peered through, their expressions a mix of resentment, loathing and fear. Behind her, metal scraped on tile—if it was her garden bars opening, they had warped. She eased backwards into her chambers, wincing as she discovered fresh bruises over her chest.

Her father came half-running from the garden. Seeing the devastation, seeing his heartache, her anguish welled in her chest, threatening to boil over. Without a word she let him help her up, breathing in his sweat and the smoke in his hair. She didn't ask what had happened and he didn't offer her lies. He hugged her and she clung tight.

Her voice, when she spoke, was calm.

'Who did I hurt?'

'No-one, not really.'

'No more secrets, Father. I know what I am.'

'No more secrets.' His long, jagged sigh sounded like relief.

'I've done wrong. I spat out the potion, that's why I transformed.'

She'd thought he'd be angry—he deserved to be. And shamed. And revolted, like the guards. But he just nodded as if it didn't matter any more. 'The potion is for sleeping. Jay child, only the amulet can stop your transformations.' He released her and gently turned her chin to examine her cheek. She hadn't noticed before, but it stung burning hot. He daubed on gel from a flat jar, and its burning flared.

'Sit still, child. This is Yeemans's concoction. Lord willing, your face won't scar.'

'Who did I hurt?' she repeated.

'Ah, well . . . your brothers.'

Her stomach tightened unpleasantly.

'Nothing too serious, don't be uneasy. It was partly Art's own foolish fault.'

I know what I am.

Those five words had been painful to say. Wrapping her mind around their meaning, as she perched on her broken four-poster bed, was agonising. Almost impossible.

Wolf. Her memories of wolves brought panic surging. Slashing claws. Tearing flesh. Her mother's hoarse, strangled croaks . . . How could she forgive her own instincts? How, if she couldn't bear to gaze at the Dartithan book's picture, could she bear to picture herself?

'Freak,' her brother had called her. Cabinet had believed it too, and demanded her surrender to Dartith. How long till the entire palace learned to despise her, as the Dartith book warned? As she deserved, for what she was.

Her muscles started to ache again. And she was so hungry.

The door scraped open. Jatta glanced up anxiously, but it was not her ladies, as she'd expected. Nor Sanda, as she'd hoped.

Guards brought food and she scoffed down three trayfuls,

cursing this hunger. Then chambermaids trickled in with buckets. They snorted and groaned at the mess till, spying her, they tensed. Jatta retreated behind the remnants of her bed's drapes, feeling their eyes flit to her as they worked.

She waited in misery for her ladies.

Carpenters traipsed in. They bowed abjectly low, then fumbled with pencils and nervously dropped rulers as they measured her bed.

Her ladies never came.

In humiliation she struggled up, scooped scattered clothes into her arms, and sought refuge in her bathroom. Here was less destruction. The marble bath lay cracked on its side. Rose petals, mineral salts and towels soaked in puddles of water. She dumped her clothes on the bath, fighting back hopeless tears. Never once had she dressed herself.

While guards next door heaved the wardrobe from her bars, Jatta scrubbed off her sweat with sodden towels. She dried herself with a remnant of velvet sleeve. One petticoat was not very tattered; she tied its string at her waist. Her gowns had rips, but she would have rather sat in tapestry class naked than call to the chambermaids for another, or return among the frightened men. She struggled inside one gown's layers, confused at the assortment of sashes, clips and buttons. Lacing up the back proved impossible so she wriggled it around back-to-front. This arrangement seemed almost practical, though uncomfortably tight across her bust. She laced it with a triple knot. Mystified at styling her hair, she instead combed it long and added jewelled clips where she could. She threaded more hairclips through rips in her skirt.

Jatta steeled herself. Chambermaids were sweeping up scraps of her drawings; men were hammering her bed. As she hobbled back through her chambers they stopped, like birds on a lawn ready to take flight.

Sanda wasn't in the tapestry room, nor the reading room. Jatta limped toward the south wing, where the Crewingburns had chambers.

'Wh—where is Lady Sanda Crewingburn?' she asked one of the guards.

He shifted nervously. 'Your Highness, the baron and his family left last night for his ship.'

Jatta felt a gloomy, sinking sensation in her stomach. The Crewingburns had fled. Perhaps her wolf was too disgusting even for Sanda. But perhaps—was it too much to hope she'd left a message?

Jatta limped across the corridor to the music room. Two noblewomen at the harps gasped and didn't rise. She nodded nonetheless.

Jatta wandered to the window, fiddling with the drapes, noticing the harps now played badly out of time. She glanced over her shoulder to see the women whispering and glaring at each other. Her impulse was to run. Instead she pretended to drop a clip from her hair, then crouched to clutch along the drape's hem. Her heart gave a little leap. She could feel Sanda's note. Jatta squeezed her fingers through a hole in the stitching and drew out a scrap of paper. Scrawled on it were a few hurried lines.

Jatta, sorry. Parents found the Dartith book while I was visiting your brother. Mother burned the book, superstitious old cow. Said it's evil. Then Father ranted, made me spill about the wolves.

But now there's one in your chambers and they're saying it's you.

Lordy, how GRUESOME'S that! Poor thing, Jatta, with wolves messing up your mind like they do.

Father's not furious now. He's petrified. Dragging me off abroad and I'll miss your birthday. What a ruddy mess. Don't want to leave you alone with all this—take care. Really. Saved what I could, usual spot.

Wish I was there.

Jatta gave a little groan, aching for her friend.

The harps had stopped. She glanced back, catching the women's look of disgust. She got up and stumbled out of the room.

The guard had been peering in from the corridor. He tensed as she approached.

'Guard, I, um—I want to see inside Baron Crewingburn's chambers. Could you fetch me th—the housekeeper?'

The housekeeper came, but the door was already unlocked.

The distinctive odour of fire met Jatta as soon as she stepped inside. Fireplaces burned continually in winter, the smoke permeating their clothes and hair, but this was summer. The grate was full of ash. Cheese and figs were left half-eaten on the table. Cupboards were emptied, their drawers open. Jatta hurried to Sanda's bench bed. Under its mattress lay the Dartith book, its charred covers and page edges crumbling to ash as she touched them.

She turned to leave. By the door lay the baron's cloak, and from beneath it peeped an ebony trinket box. Jatta knelt to examine the box. Inside were precious deeds and documents, and under them, the baroness's jewels. They had left in an awful panic to forget these. Jatta slipped the book under the documents before gently closing the lid. She would safeguard the Crewingburns' jewels till their return. They would return, she was counting on that. She escaped back through the palace, through the gauntlet of stares, back toward her chambers and the sanctuary of the dragon fountain in her rose garden.

Jatta slid noiselessly past her reinforced oak door. Men were sanding grooves from the marble tiles. Chambermaids sat gossiping on the floor in a half-circle, some resting their backs against her bed and some lounging against the wall as they unstitched gems and lace from tattered gowns. Jatta limped toward the garden, willing them not to look up.

One woman, plump and young, laid down her scissors and held out one of Jatta's bodices. 'Look at them teeth marks, Mrs P.'

Jatta froze.

All eyes glanced up. Jatta panicked and dived behind her bed.

The chambermaid was wriggling her pudgy fingers through myriad punctures in the brocade. 'Lord, I wouldn't care to be inside this, eh? Not when Her Royal Ruddy Wolfness sunk her fangs in!'

'Ha!' scoffed a bony-faced, haggard woman, with a flick of her wrist like a queen at court. 'You squeeze inside? Fat chance of that, Martina.'

The others chuckled.

Martina sucked in her stomach. 'Still, sends little icy shivers down your back, don't it? I mean, we're none of us safe. Why, Mrs P—didn't your own Mr P hear tales how one of them guards got bit? And who was it bit *her*? This place is infested, mark me words.'

The women had all stopped their work. Jatta pressed her

face into the bedpost, cheeks burning, wishing she was any-where but here.

'Nah. This place'll be clean once she goes,' said Mrs P. She brought one scrawny finger to her lips, winking. They all huddled conspiratorially close. Jatta's stomach gave a sick lurch.

'You all know my Panya is chambermaid to the Ambassador ...' Mrs P's theatrical whisper carried clear to the carpenters. 'Well, she overheard his family last night in all the panic, saying Lord Redd already agreed to fix the Princess's curse. Yeah, long ago—the Dark King was wanting her, still does.' Mrs P nodded significantly. 'Seems as though Lord Redd's changed his mind, though. Changed his mind on the Sorcerer's Pact, too.'

'He wouldn't!' cried Martina.

'Has before. Doesn't care that we're suckling pigs here, without an army or real weapons. And don't kid yourself the Dark Isle's been fooling around with swords all these cen-turies, like *we* agreed. Them Undead have got blast rods what'll rip a hole through you, what shoot fireworks powder and glass shards down the barrel. Lord Redd wants the Princess gone, or he'll open our piggy bellies to Brackensith.'

'Poor, doomed child,' murmured one woman.

Martina shuddered. 'Don't pity her. Pity us poor, chewed-up corpses if she stays.'

The women huddled even closer, their eyes flitting nerv-ously around as if wolves might still be hiding in ambush. Jatta crushed her forehead to the bedpost, wishing it would swallow her inside.

'Ha, we's safe enough.' Mrs P looked from face to anxious face. 'We'll wait tight till the Dark King comes for her. Won't be long, eh? Now that Lord Redd's letting him. Good riddance to the plague. Everybody's happy, see?'

Jatta's tears glistened. *'Everyone except me,'* she mouthed silently.

'Everybody 'cept our beloved King,' said an elderly chambermaid.

'Ha! He's got two good sons, eh? Prince Steffed's clever like his father. The Lion, too, he's full of charm, such a dear. Excels at riding and swordplay—'

'Always got a smile for us servants. Real tragedy, what her wolf did to him,' chipped in Martina. There were murmurs of agreement.

'The Princess, though, what's she? Ha! Nothing, really.' Mrs P snorted. 'Vague and useless. Timid. No personality. Lord knows why the Dark Isle has marked such a drab, scared little mouse. But her father'll have no choice 'cept to let her go.'

Jatta's anguish rose. Loneliness and shame overwhelmed her. She clapped a hand over her quivering mouth and dropped to her knees. She crawled on her stomach under the bed. Sandwiched there between the boards and the tiles, Jatta sobbed stifled tears. Her chest shook.

What was she? A plague by moonlight. A *nothing* by day.

Finally Jatta's tears were spent. She lay cramped, her cheek cold and wet on the tiles, aching and starving after her dreadful wolf night. The women gossiped on.

Exhausted, wrung dry, she slept.

When she woke it was late afternoon and the chambers were silent. She dragged herself painfully out from under the bed. Fresh lavender had been arranged on her pillow, fresh flowers by her prison bars. She unlocked them and limped out to her enclosed garden. Its paved paths and maze of rose bushes converged onto a central pond, where a bronze dragon rose from the pool and trickled water from its snout.

Jatta's reflection in the dragon pond was making faces. It scowled fiercely back at her, forehead creased, eyes narrowed, lips pressed tight. *Freak creature*, it mouthed, as if forcing the ugly truth into her brain.

'You're vicious,' she told it, hating what she saw. 'Evil, like the wolves that killed your mother.' Her voice grew hard with disgust. 'You've attacked twice. They'd better drug you or you'll do it again. You'll kill. *Hide away, cursed freak.*'

Jatta snarled at the creature in the pond, her nose crinkling. Two rows of small teeth snapped shut in pale imitation of the beast's gruesome fangs, prompting one blond wisp to fall over her shoulder. Her reflection rippled.

Jatta wound the wet strand back behind her ear. As the ripple stilled, her mouth dropped open in disbelief. Her neck tensed, for there were two faces peering up from the pond. Beside hers, a familiar and transparent child's reflection smiled sheepishly . . . perhaps in apology for startling her, perhaps for being away so very long.

Slowly Jatta turned, wary that she might frighten Dragongirl away. But the imaginary friend of her childhood was there, translucent as frosted glass under the rising moon and heraldic stars. The six-year-old was kneeling and leaning on the wall, as Jatta was, with her chin nestled in her hands.

Dragongirl turned her gaze from the pond to her friend; her face was round, her features flat and sweet, unlike any in Alteeda. Her almond eyes fixed on Jatta's face, warm and curious as always.

'Thank you for coming,' Jatta whispered with a tentative

smile. She stretched down a hand to touch Dragongirl's cheek, but her fingers slipped right through its translucent flesh, quite visible inside. Her hand whipped back and she chided herself for hoping. Hadn't she always known Dragongirl was this way?

The apparition got up and turned to the glass doors. The transparent toy wings she wore flapped with just the slightest encouragement from the breeze. She started to fade.

'No, don't leave!' cried Jatta. 'Not yet.'

The fading child glanced back. 'I be near, Jatta.'

'Where?'

'I always be near.'

Her friend had gone. Jatta's hollow ache returned.

'Jay?' Her father's anxious voice came from within her darkened chambers.

Her impulse was to hide.

She heard his rapid stride, saw his face peering around her doors. 'Jay, are you out there?' Spying her kneeling on the grass, he came to sit on the pond wall.

'Who were you calling to?'

'No-one, Father.'

His raised eyebrows rebuked her. It hadn't been a lie, though.

'Dragongirl, Father.'

He searched Jatta's face before his brow slowly relaxed. But it was such a daydreaming, childish admission—why would she make it up? He patted the stone beside him and obediently she joined him.

'I've had Naffaedan and his men out searching for you. Where have you been?'

'Hiding. People don't want me. They want me in Dartith

with the wolves and Undead, where my wolf belongs, but—'

'You belong with us. You and your brothers are worth more to me than all Alteeda.'

'*Why?* I'm a wolf. And a nothing. I don't matter.'

'*A nothing?* Why would you think such a thing?'

'It's true, though. If it was Art, or Sanda—or anybody else—people would care. I want to matter, really I do, but I'm just a drab, scared . . . Please let me hide; don't surrender me. Don't let Cabinet make me go.'

He took her chin in his scarred hand and brought his face down close. 'No-one's sending you anywhere. When Ambassador Sartora returns, Cabinet will back down. Soon this whole mess will be forgotten.'

'No! It's Lord Redd who's forgotten, Father. If he really cared, he'd never have let Brackensith come and curse me the first time. That broke our peace, it broke the Sorcerer's Pact. Why didn't Lord Redd just smite him dead then?'

'He will, next time. I have his oath.'

'You can't know. His amulet's failed.'

'I know because he's sent you Dragongirl again.'

She blinked in surprise.

'Child, how could I tell you before?' Her father looked at the fountain and sighed as if steeling himself. He smiled down at her; it seemed effortless, except for the moistness of his eyes.

'The attack that ended your mother's life, and that left you cursed, with gashes down your thigh, scarred you in another, deeper way. I had hoped you would forget, but . . . witnessing your mother's mauling, being tossed and buffeted between the creatures as they gorged . . . these things wounded you more. You cried for her for three days, then you lapsed into silence. You gave up play, you recognised no-one except little Art or myself. You stopped eating, slept too much and wasted away. Yeemans warned me your body's growth was retarded, but I feared worse. I feared I'd lose you as well. I begged Lord Redd to help.

'The night I returned I came to your nursery to coax you with sweets, and she was there. Dragongirl was three then, jumping all over your bed pretending to fly. Those milky-clear silk-and-wire dragon wings had you mesmerised, and you were propped on pillows actually complaining you wanted a turn.'

Jatta's skin was tingling. 'I always thought I'd made her up.'

'Surely not, child. Not when I'd sit on this wall, watching you two clamber over your bronze dragon. You'd inform me you were up flying among the stars.'

'Don't tell me the dragon was real, too.'

'No, just Dragongirl, your guardian angel.' He smiled gently. 'I am telling you Lord Redd remembers you; he works in ways we don't understand.'

Grateful tears brimmed. She clung to his words as if they were arms reaching under her bed, dragging her out from that cramped, miserable place to hold her tight.

She would cope till Redd's amulet came. She would face people proudly, would win some of them back. She'd show everyone, show the chambermaids, show the palace, show Arthmael too, that she was more than a drab, scared little mouse.

CHAPTER NINE

Jatta leaned out over the highest balcony for a better view. The Festival procession rode through the courtyard below like a carnival, with minstrels and flags, and toffee apples for the children who ran alongside it. Clattering hooves, music and holiday laughter floated up on the breeze. Steffed glanced up as he passed under her balcony. He waved a majestic goodbye.

A group of Arthmael's friends squinted up, calling something, and she waved back gratefully. One cupped both hands to his mouth. 'Where's Arthmael?'

Oh. Silly, nothing girl. They were wanting Arthmael, not her.

'Jay. I thought I'd find you up here.'

The voice, close behind, surprised her. Arthmael was limping grumpily along the balcony toward her.

'Art, they're already leaving—why aren't you down there?'

He thumped the stone wall. 'They think I'm a freak Dartith wolf!'

His words stung. She opened her mouth to object, then saw the disappointment in his eyes.

'Art, no. That's awful,' she said instead.

He made a resentful sounding *hmpf*. 'The Festival organisers don't admit it, of course. They just say they've no physicians to tend to a royal invalid.' His voice took on a sarcastic tone. '*Profuse apologies, your Royal Highness, but we suggest your health is as yet too delicate.*'

'But that's so unfair. And ignorant. I mean, even *if*—and you *aren't*—because I *couldn't* . . . But even *if* . . . well, we'll have a fresh amulet before wolf-moon.' She watched him take a deep breath, then sigh out his frustration. Her brother could never remain angry for long.

'Listen, Jay, don't rely on that amulet. Sartora's delegation still hasn't returned.'

'But Father's sending another.'

'Lord Redd could be sick. He may have changed his mind.'

'But he remembers me.'

'Listen, your amulet's failed and it's up to us. People are terrified of some epidemic. They just need reassuring, that'll stem the palace desertions. Father's convinced Cabinet—those who are left—to observe me next full moon, and they'll send out a proclamation that I'm normal. We just need to prove we're taking full precautions with you. Maybe Cabinet could watch you asleep then. That shouldn't prove *too* gruesome.'

'*Full precautions? Too gruesome?* For who?' Was he trying to be funny? She'd been so full of sympathy for his Festival snub, and he couldn't even pretend to have sympathy for her wolf.

'Glory, Jay, I didn't mean it like that.' He shot her a guilty grin. 'I know things haven't been easy; there've been unpleasant rumours. But Father dotes on you—'

'*Unpleasant rumours?* Rumours I've mauled my ladies, that I ritually devour little children, rumours I'm not Father's, I'm— I'm *Brackensith's* unnatural spawn! Do you think just because I've stopped crying or hiding or complaining, I don't feel?'

He stared, confounded at her outburst. Then, shaking his head, he relaxed into the same self-conscious grin.

'Sorry, Jay.'

He leaned forward over the balcony, watching the

procession snake through the gates toward the city hall and banking district. She sighed and leaned out too.

The minstrels returned to noisily enjoy an ale in a courtyard. Arthmael's friends were a line of flags winding through city streets before she spoke again. 'Lord Redd hasn't turned his back on Alteeda, and he's not letting Brackensith near me.'

'Jay, I never said he would. Not exactly.'

'If Brackensith does come, I'll escape.' It was just a fantasy. She wasn't even sure why she was telling him, except that Sanda was gone.

He chuckled.

'I'll fly on dragon wings far, far away. It'll be a quest through foreign lands for a proper wolf cure.' She pointed to the distant ocean. 'And Brackensith will never catch me.'

He grunted, then chuckled louder. 'He won't need to. That's Dartith you're pointing at, little sister.'

Jatta read the Dartith book, or all that was still legible, bathed in rainbow sunlight in the study's armchair while her father worked at his desk. The first and last chapters were so badly charred that Jatta could only guess at their meaning, but five paragraphs remained on the crumbling inside front cover.

Long before our own time was the blessed Age of Sorcerers, an age of prophecies, of magical tools and spells. Sorcerers unified our languages, guided our inventions, ended slavery and war and cured disease. All Aerth's kingdoms prospered.

Little be recorded of the Age's first Sorcerer, though before he died—as all mortals must do—he chose an heir. Thus began a long line of Sorcerers and Sorceresses that ended with our own Andro Mogon.

We in the Isle of Dartith learned to curse Andro Mogon, for as he grew old he also grew to fear death, to search for the elixir of eternal life. Indeed he discovered and drank such an elixir, but at a terrible price. He became not dead, but neither alive, for he could survive only on the blood of others.

This terrible price was paid by all Dartith. As the Undead Sorcerer waxed more powerful he also waxed evil. Thus ended the glorious Age of Sorcerers. For three thousand years his merciless rule made prisoners of us all.

Andro Mogon be finally gone, but for these last two hundred years our Dark Kings continue his legacy.

King Brackensith had claimed her to continue this same bleak legacy.

She read further. The book's early chapters described grotesque animal hybrids created by Andro Mogon. This fascination was not unique, for Sorcerers before him had created gargoyles, lizard creatures and dragons. Yet nowhere did the book describe *wolves* as animals, for they did not exist except during the full moon, nor reproduce except by curses. They had no gender, no age, and practically no impulse except fury to devour. It was wolves that Dartithans feared most.

Andro Mogon had intended as much, taking inspiration from the monsters of his people's nightmares. His wolves' jagged, jutting teeth mimicked those of the sharks that once patrolled Dartith's shores, and, like his Undead's teeth, they were made of *obsidian*—a black volcanic glass both useful in magic and infinitely sharp. The armour plates beneath his wolves' hides mimicked dragon scales. Their instinct for tracking, their hind legs and faces, too, were wolves'. Wolves had inspired their name. However, the Dark Sorcerer's own contribution was deadliest, for the hatred that consumed his wolves was his own.

In her sun-warmed armchair Jatta had shuddered reading this, feeling snow packed in her chest.

As Jatta read further, there were other creatures who chilled her almost as much. The Undead. These could not reproduce at all, being not alive. And alone, one commonly didn't kill unless its victim was ill or a child. Unlike wolves, however, they mostly hunted in pairs.

Undead were nobles who'd drunk Andro Mogon's elixir. They preyed by night, draining Dartith's population of happiness and hope just as they drained them of blood. Always there would be nobles—ill, aged and fearful of death—clamouring for their taste of eternity.

Sometimes Jatta's father came to sit on the armrest beside her, and she'd breathe in his spices. 'Andro Mogon was powerful,' she said once.

'Because of his elixir? Because he found a way to exist after death?'

She nodded. 'By the end he even stopped needing blood.'

'He brought shame on the Sorcerer tradition, Jay. He was a tyrant.' Her father sighed heavily. 'His wolves and Undead terrorised those desperate people, and his wall of fire around the Isle held them hostage. His long nights kept their crops meagre and most went permanently hungry. Under Brackensith they still do.'

'Why do you think he died? The book said he simply dissolved away.'

'Why did he stop existing? I don't know, Jay. Maybe someone finally destroyed him. Or maybe his mind, like our bodies, simply grew tired.'

CHAPTER TEN

The magic show really had nothing to do with Jatta's birthday. It was, after all, held the night before, a public holiday. But no-one except a long-buried Sorcerer could claim it, so she secretly did.

She sat in her ruby-studded velvet gown with her father, Arthmael and Steffed—newly returned from the Festival—at their royal table in the Great Hall. Somewhere at the back of the Hall a flute began to play. Jatta felt a delicious tingle in her spine. A lute followed, then a drum picked up the beat. A hush fell over the audience. They craned their necks to see. The trio of costumed minstrels wove down the aisle to wait beneath the stage, in front of the royal table. As a drum-roll sounded, all eyes rose to the stage.

Red smoke billowed from an earthen urn, and out from its cloud stepped the magician. His layers of robes were spangled with suns and moons. His beard trailed to the ground. The crowd cheered as he spread both arms in welcome.

'Your Majesty! Royal Princes and Princess!' He bowed to the front row. 'Great nobles! Palace servants!' He bowed with a broad sweep of his wand to every table, and to the sprinkling of loyal servants along the back wall. Rainbow sparks shot like fireworks from his wand. 'Welcome to our show. Are you prepared for magic?'

The Hall cheered.

'For fun? For mayhem?'

The Hall cheered louder.

He grinned down on the captive faces, flicking his wand to his skullcap. Fireworks shot from it to the ceiling. Purple smoke puffed. The drum sounded again.

Out from his hazy halo fluttered four pygmy owls, dipping among the tables to gasps of admiration before flitting back to roost on his head. The audience exploded into laughter and applause. And then—

It seemed innocent at first.

Something heavy thudded under the stage, then clanged along the floor. Jatta wasn't the only one to hear it through the applause. She looked down to see the drum rolling towards her table, the minstrels backing away. It was their faces that warned her. Staring. Aghast.

Magic was happening.

Real magic.

Between her and the minstrels two columns of air were shimmering, condensing into a translucent, sparkling arch. People behind her stood, clapping, to admire. The magician froze mid-spell.

Crowded in and around this portal arch were the shifting shapes of men.

Applause trailed away. The King staggered up. His chair banged to the floor. Jatta turned in astonishment from the apparition to his stony white face. The hopelessness in his eyes scared her. In that instant she knew that Lord Redd had deserted them.

'Go, Jay,' her father said in a choked voice she hardly recognised. 'Run now. This palace can no longer protect you.'

Her pulse surged. Not stopping to think, she clambered

onto the table. One shoe snagged in her skirts and she toppled forward off the edge. She fell face-first onto the tiles and tasted her lip's blood. The arch was buzzing eerily; she felt its vibration in her ribs. Beside her shoulder shimmered half-formed boots. She dared not glance up. Kicking off her shoes and gathering up her skirts, she scrambled to her feet and ran.

Out of the corner of her eye she saw others were panicking and pushing forward too. She rushed through a door as guards burst in. Blindly she ran down the corridor. Captain Naffaedan was a blur, bounding past her toward the Hall. She spun around, almost calling his name, not knowing where to go. The Hall doors banged shut and she groaned. Inside, people were screaming. Feeling sick, aching for her father and brothers, she wiped the blood from her lip and raced back toward her chambers.

In the Great Hall, the last feeble clap died. Wide, confused eyes turned from the apparition to King Elisind. He stared as if watching his kingdom in flames.

People started clambering over tables to follow the Princess.

Shocked, Arthmael struggled to comprehend what he saw. Blue sparks were flickering, radiating from each shifting shape. Up to thirty men crowded in and around the arch were becoming solid. Such men had never been seen in Alteeda, yet he knew them. Broad, grim faces with almond eyes and noses squashed flat. Black plaited hair. Tall and lean, a head higher than most Alteedans. He'd seen them in Jatta's pictures. Dartithan soldiers.

And others. Arthmael knew them by their bloodless skins and black mouths. A thrill of terror shot through his veins. Undead.

Elisind dragged his eyes from the portal to his sons. 'Go, boys.'

'No.' Steffed stood resolute. 'My place is with you.'

'Go then, Art. Protect your sister. Don't let me down.'

Arthmael nodded. He leapt onto the table and pain seared through his chest. Cursing his wounds, he eased himself down to the tiles. He hobbled urgently. A frightened, clamouring crowd was already at the door. They pressed against its narrow opening.

Dartithans were bounding toward it. The King's guards waited with swords raised. Several nobles stood ready for battle. Arthmael fought his way through, grappling with the pain as elbows and shoulders shoved into his wounds.

'Guards! Nobles!' called King Elisind above the din. 'Throw down your swords!'

Arthmael squeezed through. Moments later the doors slammed shut.

'Throw down your swords, I say! Every weapon! Every man!' shouted King Elisind.

The walls echoed with the clang of steel on stone. All around the Hall, faces turned to their King. Brave, incredulous faces. Frightened, half-panicked faces, too. A hush came over the crowd. Those close to the front saw the portal had gone, dissolved back into air.

Dartithan soldiers shoved people to the ground and locked the doors, as up on the stage the granite arch re-formed. It buzzed, painfully loud this time. People clutched at necks and fingers, feeling their jewellery vibrate.

'Return to your tables!' called the King.

People started to obey.

One man screamed in agony, then another.

Both dropped red-hot swords to the tiles, grasping their wrists above bloody, blistering hands. Around the Hall, discarded weapons glowed red-hot, then white-hot. They melted like wax, burning black shadows on the tiles. People shielded their faces from the intense heat. They drew back, huddling.

Elisind had seen melted swords before—eleven years before. Brackensith's portal had all but destroyed fearless kings when they'd refused to lay down their weapons. Now, flanked by Steffed and Naffaedan, Elisind turned stonily to the stage. Blue lightning flickered as a lone figure formed inside the arch. Elisind watched, his breath deep and ragged, seething with hatred.

Brackensith's body solidified. He stepped forward.

He seemed hardly changed from eleven years ago. The Dark King looked younger than his fifty years. His hair was less black, his build more solid than others from his Isle. His face was a blend of races, a legacy of generations of stolen brides. He might have been handsome except for the coldness in his strangely pale grey eyes.

Brackensith surveyed the assembly with an air of authority, as if he himself had gathered them. Eventually his gaze came to rest on Elisind. He snorted, his top lip twisting in contempt.

'Elisind, you sentimental idiot. You have hidden her.'

Elisind glared. His knuckles were white where they leaned on the table.

'Fetch her now,' said Brackensith. 'Or, damn you, I shall do it myself.'

Elisind nodded stiffly to Naffaedan.

'Majesty,' bowed the captain before striding out of the Hall.

The Dark King watched with a thin, satisfied smile.

'Your co-operation has saved you and your wretched sons

much grief,' said Brackensith. 'It be a pity that pretty little fool you married was not so compliant.'

'You have taken my wife from me, and now you would take my daughter!'

'Tragic Elisind, my heart bleeds.' Brackensith lifted his face to his own men. 'He will mourn his cursed daughter. Shall I offer him mine?'

One of the Undead sniggered.

'Yes, a swap.' One corner of Brackensith's handsome mouth curled nastily. 'Perhaps I shall leave her for you one day. No doubt you shall warm to the wretched creature. She be unnatural, too.'

'You're a sadistic monster,' growled Elisind.

'No, tragic King. My firstborn, Riz, be a sadistic monster, but not me. I take no pleasure in pain. I be merely . . . ruthless. And you, Elisind? What be you? Pragmatic, say I, to surrender your daughter this time. Now that her brother be mauled, now that your palace disintegrates. Do you agree?'

Elisind stared back in defiance.

The unpleasant smile faded from Brackensith's face; his eyes narrowed in suspicion. 'No, Elisind. I see what kind of king you be. Not pragmatic. Not even clever. You be fatally sentimental.'

'Men! We be betrayed!' called Brackensith. 'We be left waiting while our prize escapes. Search the palace!'

He leapt from the stage, seizing and overturning the royal table. He struck the King's face with a powerful blow. Elisind staggered back against his son.

Brackensith's voice was icy. 'I shall leave you vicious Riz. Understand this kingdom be ours till she be found.'

CHAPTER ELEVEN

Jatta careered down the deserted corridors to her chambers. The guards had gone, all fled to the Hall. Wheezing loudly, she unbolted the door and fell inside, then rammed the bars back across. She scrambled through the room to her wardrobe. She dived inside. It felt safe in there. Wedging her finger inside the keyhole, she pulled the doors shut. She jerked her gowns off their hangers and over her body, burrowing deep under their mass. She lay still, frantic for breath, her heart pounding like it would burst through her chest. She listened. Nothing.

Footsteps hurried down the corridor. A single pair, limping . . . Arthmael. Furious, she willed him to hurry past, to draw the evil men away from her hiding place.

His fists thumped on her door.

'Jay, this is stupid! Let me in!'

She shrank deeper into her den of clothes.

'Jay, we have to escape to Lord Redd's!'

'Go away!' she yelled. She listened with dread for more footsteps.

'What's that? I can't hear you! Listen, you're not safe. These bolts won't keep them out!'

The heat under the pile was stifling. Her back was clammy with sweat. Reluctantly she fought her way up till her head broke through and into the darkness, knowing her brother was right. Her chamber fortification had never been intended to keep the Dark King out. Only to keep her in.

She shouldered the wardrobe open and tumbled onto the floor. In moments she had the door open.

Sweat beaded on Arthmael's forehead too. His eyes were wide with alarm. 'Right. Grab your potion and let's go.'

She whirled around to snatch up the blue bottle, then dragged the Crewingburns' box from under her bed. She tucked the charred book under her arm.

'What's this?' he said, digging his hands into the baroness's jewels.

She snatched back the box. 'Not yours!'

'Is now.' He dragged it from her. Her bottle and book too, which he stuffed inside. 'We'll need jewels to pay the Sorcerer,' he said. He shoved a pair of shoes at her and pulled her to the oak door. Angry voices came from the corridor.

'Lord!' he cried.

She thrust her keys at him. 'Out through the garden!'

He shoved the box back in her hands, then hobbled toward the barred garden doors.

Voices snarled in the corridor beyond the oak door; she struggled to draw its bolts across. Wasn't Arthmael through yet? Behind her, the garden doors swung open. She slammed the bottom bolt shut as something massive rammed the oak door. She squealed and jumped. It rammed again as she fled. She raced past Arthmael into the garden.

'Go, go. Forget that!' she pleaded, dancing beside him as he fiddled to re-lock the garden door. He ignored her. An explosion sounded. She glanced back as smoke seeped around its frame. A louder explosion boomed. The door's oak splintered. Smoke billowed through. She whimpered as hands reached through for the bolts. Arthmael's key clicked, and they ran.

Jatta was faster, despite her load. Her brother's breath came in sharp, hissing intakes and she knew he was in pain. They raced for the stables, further from the palace than she'd ever ventured.

Naffaedan had already saddled two big geldings.

'I can't ride. I don't know how,' cried Jatta. The captain grabbed her waist and hoisted her in front of a saddle.

'Forgive me, Princess,' he grunted. He helped the Prince up behind her. 'Now, there's a map and compass in the saddle-bags. And my purse, also.' He handed Arthmael the spare horse's reins.

'You're a brave man, Naffaedan,' said her brother. He kicked their horses into a gallop. Jatta clung to her brother's arm around her waist. As they fled, more footsteps were tramping toward the stables. Their father's loyal captain disappeared back into the shadows.

CHAPTER TWELVE

The moon was a sickly pale sliver. The three heraldic stars each outshone it, bathing the countryside in an ice-blue light too dim to read their map by, but bright enough for Jatta to read Arthmael's watchful face. They rode west through the night. Arthmael spoke little, his arm tensing around Jatta's waist at every sound. Her skin was tingling with nerves. The danger only heightened her sense of wonder at this strange new world.

The picture book pages she rode through were impossibly real. Ever-changing. Sometimes her head swam and her eyes scrunched up in giddiness. There were the comfortingly familiar smells of chopped grass and fruit trees, and wood stoves as they rode through the towns, while the smells of a tannery and a slaughterhouse were as unpleasant as they were unfamiliar. Once their path crossed under a forest canopy which smothered the sky. Here Jatta breathed in darkness and damp earth and more unfamiliar scents. The undergrowth rustled and squeaked, owls hooted, and something strange screeched far away. She listened intently to pounding hooves as a herd of deer took flight. Arthmael heard it too, and she felt his heart quicken against her back.

They paused to drink at a brook and change horses. The brook gurgled and tugged at her fingers and for a delicious moment she almost forgot the Dartithan soldiers, or that in eleven nights it would be wolf-moon.

As they rode on, Jatta's imagination turned to their crusade, to Lord Redd. The same breathless awe she'd felt as a child, when she had imagined soaring on a dragon's back, opened inside her again. Would Lord Redd set three seemingly impossible tasks, as in her mother's fables, to test her resourcefulness? Or would he demand still more jewels? When she begged for her wolf's cure would he answer, 'My child, I've waited eleven years only for you to ask.'

After again watering and resting their horses they found the highway. Her birthday dawned as they rode on.

'Listen, Jay,' said Arthmael at last. 'Redd's hall is hidden somewhere in his forest. It shifts, apparently. There's a gatekeeper, a dwarf called Driddle and, well, it can be hard to find. The next town has directions if you know who to ask.'

By the time they rode into town Jatta had missed breakfast and lunch. Arthmael tethered their horses in the crowded shopping district. She tried to get out of the saddle. 'Ouch,' she complained. 'I'm bruised all over.'

He shot her a look to remind her others were suffering more, and the accusation stung. *Selfish little mouse.* She slid to the ground and her legs buckled beneath her. She collapsed in an untidy Princess heap.

That broke the tension, almost made the indignity worthwhile. He chuckled as he dragged her up. 'We need food,' he said, handing her a saddlebag and Naffaedan's purse. 'Make yourself useful while I find out about Redd's hall.' He limped off.

The street was smelly. Jatta waited patiently for help, two fingers pressed to her nose. No-one approached. Confused, she tried to catch a shopper's eye. One woman returned her tentative smile before disappearing in the crowd. A few others stared. Jatta wondered whether to announce herself. 'Off the road, sweetheart!' yelled someone and she jumped back in fright; a cart of chickens trundled by where she'd stood. A child eating a meat pie gaped up at her from the kerb. She knelt down beside him.

'Hello, little man. Could you show me where you bought that lovely pie?'

He pondered her question, then pointed a grubby finger down the street.

She laughed. 'No, I meant could you please take me there? I'm on a quest for food.'

But the child shook his head.

As Jatta walked down the crowded street, locals made way for her and her entourage of skirts. She nodded, though disconcertingly no-one bowed back. Some stared curiously. Were they admiring her finery? Were they surprised to see her wandering lost and unchaperoned? Only then did it occur to Jatta that no-one recognised their Princess, and her anonymity both thrilled and intrigued her. Her adventure had begun; her wolf and the palace's pity and shame were left far behind.

As she opened the bakery door a bell tinkled. A soft-faced woman greeted Jatta. She smiled and her eyes half-disappeared behind full, pink cheeks.

Jatta nodded back. 'Would you please sell me bread?'

The woman gestured expansively toward the dozen different loaves on the wall. Jatta pointed to one.

'For yourself, M'lady?'

Jatta nodded.

'Maybe choose another, then. That's bran meal. Gritty. Rich folk like yourself, they prefers white bread. Or seeded, perhaps.'

'Whichever you think.'

The woman chose a long stick with poppy seeds. 'Will that be all, then?'

Jatta hadn't heard her. She'd discovered trays of sweet pastries along the counter.

The woman smiled again at the young noble's childlike delight. Her eyes squashed to slits again. 'Something sweet, M'lady?' she asked.

Jatta creased her forehead, unable to decide.

'Pear turnovers, marzipan pastries . . .' The woman pointed proudly to each in turn. 'Custard tarts, toffee nut clusters, strawberry wafers . . . and cherry pies.'

'Please sell me two.'

'M'lady? Of which?'

'My brother likes pastries very much. Two of each, please. No, will you sell me four?'

The woman grinned broadly as she deftly packed the lot into the saddlebags. Jatta wondered how she managed to see past those cheeks at all.

'Six pennings sixty, M'lady.'

Jatta grinned back, uncertain how to respond.

The woman continued to smile expectantly. Finally she nodded at the purse in Jatta's hand.

Jatta blushed. The woman must have thought her a fool. She rummaged through it, trying to imagine what a penning might look like. Silver coins, copper coins. One gold coin shone, big and very heavy. She placed it in the woman's waiting palm, confident that she had not offered too little.

The woman peered at the coin in surprise. Then she held it up to her face, examining both sides.

'Is something wrong with it?' asked Jatta.

'Wrong? I guess not, M'lady. But I can't take it.'

Jatta's blush deepened, and the woman's expression melted into warm pity. 'Dear girl! Have you any idea what a kroun is worth? Why, a year of my wages, to start.'

'I, um . . . I'm not used to money.'

'Dearie! Here, don't get in a flutter. Let's just empty this out.' She upturned Naffaedan's purse onto the cabinet. 'See, now, this tiny silver one's a penning. Ten of your coppers, here, make one penning. Ten of your pennings make up a square silver coin, one of these.' She counted six of the pennings and six coppers into her palm. The rest she swept back into the purse, then popped Naffaedan's kroun in last.

'Got that, dearie?'

Jatta nodded gratefully.

'Good girl. You take good care of that kroun, see. How old are you, eleven?'

'Fourteen.'

'Well, dearie.' She grinned. 'Tell your mother you're plenty old enough to learn the value of things.'

Arthmael was already waiting by the horses.

'It seems there's a giant fig tree in Redd's forest, and the hall sometimes appears above that,' he said. 'Only the dwarf Driddle knows where to find it.' He lifted Jatta's saddlebag back onto the horse. 'So, what did you get?'

'It's a surprise. Don't squash it, Art.'

He opened the flap.

She looked up at his face and her smile died.

'What's this?' he growled. 'Where's the real food? No fruit, no cheese, no meat. Glory, Jay, we're fleeing the Dark King, and you pack for a picnic.'

She could say nothing. He lifted her roughly into the saddle, then swung up behind with an annoyed snort. As they rode he took deep breaths, trying to relax. 'Sorry, sorry, Jay.' He gave her shoulder a pat. 'It's not your fault. It's not as if you knew. Happy birthday, all right?'

Ignorant little mouse.

Hardly had they ridden five streets when they heard panicked cries. They looked sharply back. Crowds were yelling, emptying the street. Children were screaming as their parents grabbed them and fled for cover. Mingled with the wails was the pounding of galloping horses.

'Brackensith's soldiers,' breathed Arthmael.

The crowd pressed against their geldings, driving Arthmael and Jatta against a shopfront in their panic to clear a path. The geldings were scuttling, wide-eyed. Threatening to rear.

'Let's go!' whispered Jatta.

'Can't. Too late. We'd trample the crowd.' He pressed her shoulders down onto the gelding's trembling neck. 'Lie low, Jay.'

He was stroking its neck. 'Whoa, whoa,' he reassured. The first Dartithan horse thundered past, its rider's face grim. His black plait had unravelled and hair streamed behind. Five more soldiers thundered past, all lean and long and uniformed in red chain mail. Then followed another thirty.

The crowd clung silently together, but when no more soldiers followed they ventured out from the walls and shops and alleys. Stall holders began taking stock of damage.

Arthmael and Jatta again picked their way above the crowd.

'They weren't looking for us,' she whispered.

'They will be. They know where we're headed and they'll

set up road blocks. Or they'll find Redd's hall first.'

'What can we do, Art?'

'We'll take back roads. Disappear, take our time.'

CHAPTER THIRTEEN

Naffaedan's map was invaluable. The lanes they took were almost deserted and the horses found plenty to drink under bridges and from streams. That night they slept in a haystack, worn out after a night and a day in the saddle. They woke with the dawn to find their geldings eating the bed out from under them. For their own breakfasts they chose cherry pies.

Arthmael decided to give Jatta a riding lesson. 'Try not to be too hopeless,' he said, grinning.

So she tried. She concentrated on mimicking him precisely, from his ease as he strode to her gelding and scratched its chest, to his straight-backed, loose-hipped elegance in a walk. When she fell in a canter he came rushing. 'Grip his shoulders with your knees, then you won't be pounded around the saddle like tough old mutton,' he said, chuckling as he brushed her down. 'You're not hurt, right? Little people don't fall very hard.'

Maybe, but they still fell just as far. Every palace-soft muscle complained, her thighs most of all, but she was determined he'd never know. She practised till he was satisfied.

'Lord knows there's a whopping lot you don't know. But you're a fast learner,' he said, mounting his own gelding.

That made it all worthwhile.

There was a delicious freedom in controlling her own horse. Arthmael let her canter ahead. She could feel the wind on her cheeks and the lope of the gelding's powerful body. Nodding at an old man gathering kindling and at a shepherdess, the only souls they passed, she soaked in the sounds of bells and bleating. There were moments when she almost forgot the danger or Arthmael's sacrifice.

Her brother seemed more relaxed, too. He guffawed, almost falling off his horse, when she fled wide-eyed from a stray cow.

By midafternoon the pastures fell away. They stood on the edge of Redd's forest.

There were many paths in, but Arthmael chose the one the townspeople had recommended. As their horses trod deeper, stepping over fallen trees and across streams, late afternoon shadows stretched across their path.

'We'll stop here for the night,' said Arthmael, and they collected firewood. They ate pear turnovers. She asked him how money and taxes and towns worked, and he didn't scoff. Afterwards they lay listening to the night creatures rustle, watching the fire.

The next morning they set out early and, after barely two hours, caught their first glimpse of Driddle's house.

Nestled amid the tall pines, it was the strangest of concoctions. The elegant building was two storeys high with a sandstone veranda and sandstone roof. Every detail was so intricately carved that it seemed the entire facade might have been crocheted in lace, then turned to stone. Most enchanting of all, it was, like their childhood nursery, two-thirds full size.

They tethered their horses and Arthmael knocked on the chest-high door. After a few minutes' wait he knocked again. Only then did they hear footsteps inside. The door opened to reveal a sour-looking man no taller than Jatta's waist, with legs too short for his fat body. His child's nose seemed out of place in his bearded, aged face. In one stubby hand he held a wooden spoon. Something gluggy dripped from it onto his dressing-gown.

'What?' he spat. 'Me breakfast's burning—so if it's lost you are, youse two brats can stinking wait.'

The young royals had never been so rudely addressed. Jatta smiled awkwardly, edging behind her brother. Arthmael drew himself up to his full height, till his head brushed the veranda ceiling.

'Certainly we have come to ask directions,' said Arthmael, eyes flashing. 'However we are not lost.'

Driddle's expression changed abruptly. With a sleek smile he beckoned them to enter. 'Come in then, come in. You're looking for the great Sorcerer. Why didn't you say?'

Inside, Arthmael was forced to stoop. The dwarf led them, waddling past a grand but child-sized staircase, down a sand-stone-lace corridor lined with portraits and busts of himself, and into a kitchen. He bid them sit at a low table, then returned to stir a great pot on the stove.

'Have youse had breakfast yet? I'm making oatmeal porridge.' He got out three golden plates and plopped in spoonfuls without waiting for their answer. 'Charcoal, fetch our guests some spoons.'

A blackbird swooped out of his carved sandstone nook and down into a stone shelf. He emerged with a silver spoon in his beak. Hopping back along the table, he dropped the spoon into Jatta's hand. As Driddle placed their meals before them the clever bird returned with Arthmael's spoon.

'Tell us all about yourselves, why you've come. Then when you've eaten, Charcoal'll show you the way.'

'Has Charcoal taken other visitors lately?' asked Arthmael cautiously.

'Nope. None have passed this way.' The dwarf was already shovelling down his porridge.

Arthmael and Jatta exchanged glances. Ambassador Sartora, then, hadn't made it this far. The news, however, was mostly good. It meant the Dartithan soldiers had also failed to find Redd's hall.

They helped themselves to jugs of milk and molasses. But with their first mouthfuls they screwed up their faces. Driddle's porridge was as salty as cured fish. Jatta politely gulped her mouthful down. Arthmael spluttered his out. The dwarf looked up angrily.

'You don't stinking like what I dishes out? Well, begone with you!' He spat on the ground himself, then got up off his chair and scooped their porridge back in his pot. 'You bratty ingrate nobles!' He grabbed a dishcloth and started scrubbing porridge from the table, cursing under his breath. 'See that, Charcoal? Noble scum, mine's not stinking good enough for 'em, is it?'

Charcoal flapped his wings, swooping off the table and into the corridor. Jatta scampered after the blackbird. Arthmael, hurrying behind, bumped his head across the ceiling.

Charcoal was waiting for them on the veranda, tilting his head. No sooner had they caught up than he swooped toward the trees. They grabbed their horses' reins and cantered in pursuit, only to find the bird preening his wings on the first high branch. He tilted his head at them again, yellow eyes blinking. After a long minute he resumed preening under his wing. Their horses chomped among the ferns.

Arthmael chuckled. 'All right, Charcoal, let's move on before nightfall.'

The bird blinked, then began tearing at the bark. He tugged at a grub, hopping around on the branch for better leverage, while Arthmael rolled his eyes.

'Go!' shouted Arthmael with a loud clap of his hands. The horses flinched and looked up. The blackbird blinked down without releasing his prize.

'Do you think we might have followed the wrong bird?' suggested Jatta. She reined her horse off through the trees.

Charcoal, though, had abandoned his grub. He warbled for Jatta's attention and swooped to the ground. He picked his way among the ferns. Arthmael, Jatta and their horses followed step by laborious step. It seemed to Jatta that Charcoal was as contrary as his master, for the more Arthmael urged him on, the more distractions he found among the leaves. The sun was climbing high through the trees before they glimpsed their goal. Beyond the pines they spied a patch of sunshine and a sea of colours on the ground. From its middle rose a giant fig tree. They broke into a canter, leaving the blackbird warbling indignantly behind.

CHAPTER FOURTEEN

They found themselves in a meadow so thick with tulips that it seemed a shallow lake, rippling red and yellow and purple in the breeze. Anchored in its middle was the giant fig tree. Their horses waded in, cutting a narrow wake. The perfume was intense. Only in her daydreams had Jatta seen such a magical place. Above the meadow floated a crimson cloud, pillows of fairy floss lazily folding in on each other. And nestled in among this was a magnificent hall. Golden, with roof glinting in the sun. The giant fig stretched up several storeys to tickle the underside of this fluffy fantasy.

Jatta tethered her horse and lay down in the rainbow lake to soak it all in. Two unicorns were chomping close by. They whinnied in greeting and wandered over to investigate. Jatta offered up her hand which they nuzzled, snorting. Their breath smelled deliciously horsey. Arthmael's wounds had defeated his attempts to climb the tree so he eased himself down to lie beside her and scowl, perplexed, up at the cloud. 'No way up, Jay. Hmm . . . lend us your wings?'

She reached to shove him, reached—astoundingly—through shimmering golden dust. Something unnatural was happening. Arthmael struggled to his knees.

'Lord Redd!' he called to the canopy. 'Lord of Light and Knowledge, we beg an audience with you.'

They stared as shimmering dust condensed into an ancient

face with golden flowing beard and eyes that examined them intently. Trumpets sounded and the leaves shook. Jatta scrambled up from the tulips to kneel beside Arthmael as the face spoke, a voice like liquid gold.

'What are your names, young ones? And why have you come?'

Arthmael bowed. 'Great Lord, we are Prince Arthmael and Princess Jatta, second and third born of Elisind, King of Alteeda. Our kingdom is threatened by the Dark Isle. We plead for your help.'

'Ah! I have been expecting you, son and daughter of Elisind. You have brought payment?'

Arthmael unclipped his satchel with nervous hands. He dug in deep, pulling out the tangle of Crewingburn jewellery. The Sorcerer's face peered down, pleased.

'Indeed, very good. Climb onto my pets.' The golden vision faded and was gone. Arthmael rubbed his neck, surprised.

He glanced around. 'I suppose he means the unicorns.'

To Jatta everything about this place seemed magical. Yet she felt uncomfortable. She had imagined the great Lord of Light and Knowledge would recognise them.

Arthmael helped her onto one glowing-white beast. No sooner had he also mounted than their unicorns trotted to the very centre of the meadow. Stamping their hooves, they sprouted great feathered wings.

They climbed with powerful flaps in a slow spiral toward the cloud. Any suspicions quickly dissolved as Jatta leaned along her unicorn's neck. Tingling pleasure flushed through her as, little by little, the tulip lake was retreating; already she'd drawn level with the forest canopy beyond.

The unicorn moved with reassuring rhythm beneath her

and she was soon lost inside the cloud. From somewhere behind came Arthmael's voice. 'Jay?'

'Yes, I'm here.'

'Let me do the talking, all right?'

They surfaced from the cloud into the golden hall's courtyard; they recognised it as such by a crystal well. Crowded inside the courtyard's golden walls was the densest of exotic gardens. Jatta slipped from her unicorn to golden pavers. Date palms loomed overhead. Cherry trees, quinces and tangerines, groaning with fruit, thrust up through beds of strawberries. The air was thick with their scents and Jatta's mouth watered.

Arthmael was by her side. 'Hungry?'

Her answer was drowned out by screeching from the date palms above. A tribe of squabbling monkeys in striped purple waistcoats descended on them, tugging at their hands. They pulled the visitors toward a doorway, then escaped back to their palms. Jatta and Arthmael stepped inside.

At the far end of the cavernous hall were steps and a high throne, where the aged Lord Redd sat in golden robes that cascaded to the floor. He beckoned with one crooked finger.

Arthmael gave Jatta's hand a reassuring squeeze. His palm felt as clammy as hers.

How magnificent! Nothing in her father's palace could have prepared Jatta for this. She sneaked glances to both sides as they approached. The walls teamed with sculptures, like ghostly figures frozen in stone the moment they emerged. Marble nymphs leapt into the room. Marble huntsmen chased stags through forests of gems. Her head swam with the riot of detail. She lifted her eyes to the ceiling for relief. There, though, swarmed more scenes. As she stared they seemed to enact themselves, like pantomimes, for her entertainment.

She tore her eyes away, back to the Sorcerer.

He sat majestically above them, his ancient face shining with serenity. In one hand he massaged a purple ball, plum-sized, that twinkled with stars. Arthmael and Jatta knelt on the steps before him. When they raised their eyes he was pointing to a silver tray at his feet. Then at Arthmael's satchel. Jatta nudged her brother. He crawled forward to empty their treasure, clanking, onto the tray.

'Now tell me your troubles, O children of Elisind.'

Arthmael cleared his throat. 'Lord Redd, first we humbly ask that you renew the magic in Princess Jatta's amulet.'

'My magic is powerful. Do you worry that it weakens, child?'

Ludicrous question! Jatta flicked her brother a quick, troubled glance.

'Great One, not weakened . . .' Arthmael shifted awkwardly on his knees. 'The amulet has failed.'

Jatta caught the startled, aghast expression that flashed across the Sorcerer's face. In the next moment he recovered and nodded wisely.

'Do not despair, Elisind's son. My amulet has protected your sister these last eleven years, and I shall replace its spent magic. Yet such a powerful spell will be costly. First find me a more worthy gift.'

'But Lord Redd, we can't.' Arthmael swallowed hard. 'Forgive me, we thought you knew about the wolf. We thought you sent a sign, Jatta's guardian angel . . . the apparition . . .'

Jatta watched the golden face closely, finding no recognition at Dragongirl's mention, finding nothing at all except patient indulgence as he waited for Arthmael to reach his point.

'I mean, yes, Lord, normally we could get more payment. But now Brackensith has invaded—'

There. That same startled blink. Frightened, almost like the carpenters after her catastrophic wolf night. How could he not have known? Had the old man grown senile?

Arthmael must have seen it too. He faltered. 'Er, that's another matter, Lord. Now that Brackensith has invaded, we reverently petition you to honour the Sorcerer's Pact.'

The Sorcerer leaned forward to Jatta, his benign smile again fixed in place. 'I am not uncompassionate, child. I shall renew your amulet, for Alteeda's treasury is hardly your father's to command.' He turned to Arthmael. 'But patience, young Prince. Do you assume only Alteeda requires my attention?'

Jatta unfastened the pearl string from her neck, rising to offer it even as she wrestled with the Sorcerer's excuse. Was this the diplomacy of refusal? He took her amulet and held it to his temple, closing his eyes in concentration. Even now, he squeezed the ball.

'Oomba-goomba, Fidey-fie-fum, fidelly-folf.
I command you, amulet, to banish this wolf!'

Scarlet sparks shot from his temple, arcing through the amulet, making it glow.

Jatta eyed the great Sorcerer sceptically. *Fidey-fie-fum?* But the child's nonsense rhyme wasn't what worried her most. It was a new suspicion. Perhaps the amulet had *never* worked. She couldn't explain it, but a chasm had opened between the evidence of her senses—indeed, all she'd been taught to believe—and the Sorcerer's apparent ignorance.

'Lord Redd,' she challenged him. 'You swore to devour Brackensith with fire if ever he entered Adaban. Perhaps his magic is greater than yours?'

That same startled expression. Surely he wasn't afraid of them? Of Brackensith, perhaps? Or of discovery . . .

'No magic is greater than mine, Princess!'

He stood up, glaring now, towering over her. Both hands pumped the starry ball. 'Here is your proof. Watch and be awed!'

Arthmael shot her a quelling look. 'Are you determined to insult him?' he hissed under his breath. Jatta's confusion doubled. If her brother still had faith . . .

The tribe of uniformed monkeys again came shrieking. They dragged platters heavy with exotic fruit and mouth-watering sweets and cakes.

'Now eat,' Arthmael warned. 'Whatever his lapses, he's our sole hope.' Arthmael popped a creamy coloured fruit into her mouth. Its texture was like banana. Its taste, a burst of all fruits at once.

'Amazing.' Arthmael grunted, rolling a piece around with his tongue.

She sneaked an anxious glance at the Sorcerer, who still scowled at her. She cast her eyes back down to the sweets.

Jatta knew the names of only some of these delicacies. She chose a white square dusted with powdered sugar, filled with cherries. It felt soft and tasted heavenly sweet, but unlike anything she had imagined.

Lord Redd snapped his fingers. A fanfare sounded. Servants appeared, and with them came fresh delights. The hall filled with animals.

Bears paced, restless, to the sound of drums. Lions leapt through flaming hoops at the command of women in leopard skins. The Sorcerer's monkeys swung like acrobats from sculptures on the walls. Ostriches raced in crazy circles while dark-skinned children danced on their backs. Jatta recognised these creatures from picture books and gasped despite herself.

In front of them, so close that its trunk almost brushed her face, an elephant swayed. This great beast of fables captivated Jatta most of all, but she'd always pictured it bigger. She imagined it now. To her astonishment, the Sorcerer's elephant grew. An absurd idea leapt into her mind. It thrilled her.

She closed her eyes, concentrating hard.

'Jay!' Arthmael's voice was urgent. She opened her eyes. With a gush of delight she saw her elephant had grown massive. Its head pressed flat against the ceiling. She flicked a glance at the Sorcerer. He was gaping wide-eyed at the beast. Both hands pummelled the ball.

And she understood. Jatta returned her concentration to her elephant. For it was hers to command now. She shrank it back. Then further. While the circus played on around them, the Sorcerer struggled to control the elephant. Jatta imagined its hide fluorescent green. Green it became. She imagined it smaller. As tiny as a dormouse. With a chuckle she added miniature dragon wings.

The Sorcerer's jaw dropped. Her elephant flitted into the air. It darted straight for the throne. And into Lord Redd's open mouth.

In that moment Jatta sprang to her feet and up the steps. She seized the starry ball.

The green elephant slowly dissolved. The circus too. The hall, the cloud . . . the Sorcerer, as well.

Jatta and Arthmael found themselves in a vast shed with screaming monkeys, beneath a rough wooden throne. On it stood the dwarf, prickling with fury.

'Stinking thief!' He jumped down, landing sprawled beside

her. 'Orb's mine! Give it back here!' He bit her thigh through her skirts. Jatta kicked back, her foot connecting with his fat stomach. Like a bulldog, he bit deeper. Arthmael seized his collar and dragged him, cursing, off her. Driddle tumbled into the platters, rolling in what was left of their feast. Arthmael stood bristling over him. 'Impostor! Deceiving vermin!'

The dwarf struggled to his feet, wiping porridge from his beard. He spat on the ground. 'Deceived you, did I? Too right, and many other willing morons besides!'

Arthmael's hand was on his sword. 'What have you done with Lord Redd?'

Driddle spat again, a sneer on his nasty face. 'He's in that orb.'

Arthmael wrested the orb from Jatta, turning it in his hand, peering close as if to discover some magical seam. He squeezed. Its insides sparkled while odours—of camp fires and custard tarts—seeped out. His eyebrows pulled down in confusion. He handed it back. 'You try, Jay. Try letting him out.'

Jatta pressed, and stars sparkled inside. Beneath the orb's shiny surface it felt soft as jelly. Silently she asked Dragongirl to guide her, prayed to the Sorcerer himself for inspiration. She closed her eyes, kneading the squishy ball, but calling on him didn't feel inspiring at all. A sacrilege, really. She visualised him anyway, picturing the golden statue of him that stood between her parents' thrones. In the statue he was younger, his beard close-trimmed. Her eyelids flinched as Arthmael's sword clanged at her feet. Then she heard him kneel, dragging Driddle down too. She peeped.

The throne room's golden Sorcerer stood with arms spread toward her, smiling down in serene gratitude. She blushed and knelt. But as soon as she stopped kneading he began to fade. An awful understanding threatened, one almost too enormous to contemplate. Frightened, she kneaded the orb.

Lord Redd continued to hold her gaze. Not her faith, though. Shouldn't a real Sorcerer smite Driddle dead? Or thank her for his rescue? Or at the very least query what they were all doing in a shed?

Driddle sniggered.

She understood, then. Lord Redd would wait forever unless she fed him his lines. Jatta fed him his lines.

'Art?' said the Lord, his voice mellow and smooth as honey, as he sat on the step beside Arthmael. 'Art, I don't think there was ever a Lord Redd.'

'Pardon?' Arthmael's face lifted in confusion to the Sorcerer, then, incredulous, across at Jatta. And finally, aghast, to the Great One's serene face. 'Jay?'

Lord Redd spoke low. 'Yes, it's me. Tell me, has the dwarf always been Lord Redd's gatekeeper? Has he always quizzed visitors about their backgrounds and petitions first? Does some helper always take them on a merry chase while he sets things up?'

Arthmael just shook his head. Desolation contorted his handsome face.

'Art, I think Lord Redd's always been inside the orb, along with the circus and the golden hall, and anything else you can imagine.'

Jatta let her Sorcerer fade. She could only stare forlornly around. Oatmeal porridge. The platters were laden with oatmeal porridge. They had been eating Driddle's cold breakfast, imagining it a feast. For fifty years Aerth, every nation except Dartith, had put its faith in an illusion. For eleven years her family had imagined themselves safe. There would be no cure for her wolf now. No defence against Brackensith. The dwarf had reached into her chest and torn out all hope; it lay cold and seeping through his stumpy fingers.

Jatta turned wearily to Driddle. 'Why?'

He snorted, then jerked his head toward their jewels.

'Lord,' growled Arthmael. 'If we'd only known.'

Driddle scoffed. 'And done what? Eh? Every ploughman's son knows there ain't no cure for what she's got. You're a royal cretin, to think you can buy her salvation with jewels. You can't change the freak's curse. There ain't nothing can be done, I say. Surrender the pampered brat.'

'Vermin!' Arthmael turned on the dwarf, his face livid, his teeth clenched. 'You hold life cheaply.'

'It's youse royals what hold it cheap. How many lives is one princess worth? Two? Ten? A thousand, eh? One wolf's too many. If Brackensith's come, he'll set his wolves among us and there'll be no end to the killings.' He spat on Jatta's hems. 'And every last one'll be at her diseased feet.'

Arthmael's frustration boiled over. 'I ought to wring your neck!' He grabbed Driddle's throat.

'No, Art!' yelled Jatta.

'Bobo—fetch—ball!' rasped the dwarf.

With a fearsome screech a monkey swept down on Jatta. He snatched the orb.

Suddenly the barn disappeared and a shadowy, blurred jungle pressed in on them. Bobo hooted in triumph.

Arthmael's heavy hand tightened, his expression terrifying. 'For every life that's ruined, you'll pay. For every life that'll be lost!'

'Bring—ball—' choked Driddle, purple faced.

'Art, stop!' cried Jatta. She hooked into the monkey's

illusion, scooped up a wad of porridge, and a fat orange pawpaw appeared in her hand. Squeezing still, Bobo swept down to snatch it. He hooted in fresh victory, and bit.

Jatta hooked in harder: out of the fruit roared a great orange tiger head.

Bobo screamed and fled.

The ball dropped to the shed floor as his jungle faded. Jatta pounced on it. 'Please, Art. Killing him won't help us,' she pleaded.

But as the dwarf's struggles had weakened, so had her brother's rage. Arthmael's eyes now narrowed in disgust, whether at the dying dwarf or at his own lethal grip, Jatta had no idea. He scoffed and released him. Driddle staggered coughing behind the throne.

'That weasel deserves to be locked up,' he growled.

Jatta sighed. 'So do I.'

Arthmael scooped up the Crewingburn jewels and they emerged from the shed into sunlight. The courtyard garden was gone, the crimson cloud too. They stood instead on a plateau rising like a giant tree stump from the meadow. The monkeys rushed out behind them to scale the few spindly trees.

'Those would be our date palms,' said Jatta sadly. She ventured past the squabbling tribe to walk along the plateau's edge.

Arthmael wandered past her, not answering. She peered over the cliff, an almost sheer drop. A dangerously narrow path wound down its face to the meadow. Their geldings grazed under the giant fig, but the tulips had transformed into a field of weeds.

'I imagined we'd climbed higher.'

'And I imagined we'd flown,' muttered Arthmael miserably. 'I just can't work it out.'

Two mules waited by the shed. They mounted the beasts and began the precarious descent. It was Arthmael who eventually broke the silence.

'Jay, about the Sorcerer. It had to be real, at least in part. I mean, we ate real fruit. We flew through the sky.'

'Illusions, Art. All we saw, and heard, and smelled. And tasted.'

'And what we touched?'

'No, not touched. The mules, the monkeys . . . we felt them because they *were* real. Remember, even the Sorcerer. Those were Driddle's hands taking my amulet, like, um—like from inside a Sorcerer handpuppet. Remember how the porridge-fruit felt soft in our fingers? On our tongues? The porridge-sweets too.'

'But Jay, we really did fly.'

Jatta took the orb from her pocket, and closed her eyes as her mule rocked beneath her, picturing herself riding a unicorn inside a crimson veil of cloud.

'Feathered wings are more traditional, Jay.'

She opened her eyes.

Her imagination had captured much of the dwarf's illusion. The most obvious differences were the absurd dragon wings her unicorn had sprouted. She stretched out, wondering whether her hand would touch rib and leather membrane or pass through, like air. Like Dragongirl. Her fingertips disappeared inside. The wing felt gritty as sand. She closed her eyes, imagining herself flying lower, under the cloud. She looked down. The rock beneath her had disappeared—had dissolved into an illusion of meadow far below. From this height it looked like she was flying.

She stopped squeezing and the meadow illusion faded back to rock.

Jatta kneaded again, craning her neck past her unicorn's wing to see its hooves. It trod on still, down their invisible path. It occurred to her that the mule must still see its path, even though Bobo had been fooled by her pawpaw illusion. Monkeys must be particularly clever, she concluded, or mules particularly dim. She stopped kneading, then began again. The mule trod on regardless.

'Stop it, Jay. You're giving me a headache. I still don't get it, though. The monkeys were real, right? And the mules are unicorns. What poor creature was the elephant?'

None. Just sand. Pure fantasy, like her Sorcerer and so much else they'd seen but not touched. She massaged the orb, concentrating hard on the curve in the cliff wall ahead. Her forehead furrowed and an ominous rumbling began. She liked the sound of it, and made it crack like thunder as the cliff crumbled before her. Her mule trudged on.

'Lord!' came the cry behind her. Rocks blasted past Arthmael's face and an elephant trumpeted, warning them both that it was rounding the bend. Arms plucked her from her mule and to her brother's chest. He was spinning around as rocks hurtled ahead, wild for escape. Behind, his mule stubbornly blocked retreat. She was sure he considered knocking it off the trail.

'It's all right!' she tried to call out over the din. She'd grant him one thing, his reflexes were sharp. Arthmael didn't hear. He flung her around to the rock wall, squashed her between it and him as his sword swooshed out to face his unknown foe. A boulder rolled through his legs and he gaped at that. But his eyes bulged wider still a moment later.

Her elephant crashed through, too immense for more than one foot to fit on their trail, carving a wide highway with its shoulder where the wall had been.

It was fluorescent green.

Jatta struggled to poke her face out from behind his ribs to direct her performance. 'It's just a show,' she called, stifling her giggles, sandwiched between his pounding heart and sharp rock edges in her back.

The stampeding elephant bore down on them. Feeling just a little smug, she made it stomp through her waiting mule. Arthmael relaxed and moved off her, just a little. She thought she heard him swear. The elephant tore through them both. The sensation was like being sprayed with sand. She let the elephant wreak havoc all the way around the bend behind them. For good measure, an ostrich pursued it, squawking as it ran in crazy zigzags.

Arthmael glared at her with the full force of his disapproval. It disconcerted her. She had thought he'd be impressed. She was. Hadn't she answered his question? Indeed, she was guilty only of extravagance in her demonstration.

She pocketed the orb. The demolished cliff mended itself. Without a word Arthmael pulled her from the rock and dusted her off. He carried her under his arm to her waiting mule and plopped her unceremoniously on top.

'Very entertaining,' he said flatly.

CHAPTER FIFTEEN

'Art, talk to me. What are we going to do?' Jatta sat among the fig tree's giant roots, arms folded in frustration. Neither of them had felt like chatting since the dwarf, but Arthmael seemed particularly, uncharacteristically, sullen. She'd been a heavy responsibility for him these past three days, she knew, though he'd been cheerful enough. They'd had hope. A plan. Now their options all seemed dismal.

'We'll camp here tonight,' he growled.

She winced at his tone. With so much else unravelled in her life she ached sometimes for his reassurance. Her brother was already busying himself stomping on logs, cracking them for firewood, intent on avoiding her eyes.

'Art. I wasn't talking about tonight.'

'I know. I told you, I haven't worked that out yet.'

'We could return home.'

'No!' He dumped his load and looked at her for the first time. 'I promised Father. We're not going back, understand? If we set foot anywhere we're recognised, Brackensith will swoop like a ravenous dragon.'

'So we're fugitives?'

He let out a long sigh. 'That's right. Now get off your royal rump and help with the fire.'

'You require a fire?' Jatta reached into her pocket and massaged the orb.

Immediately his logs burst alight. Arthmael leapt back with a curse.

His tension broke and he laughed. 'Cute, Jay. All right, come here. So how's it done?'

'I can't say exactly. I just imagine. Try.'

She walked over and slipped the orb in his hand. Her brother creased his forehead in concentration as he massaged. Stars sparkled within.

Nothing else happened.

'Close your eyes, Art.'

He kneaded the starry orb hard against his forehead. A speck of red light appeared between her and him, visible only in the darkening evening. Screwing his eyes tight, his whole body tensing, he coaxed it to a candle flame that danced uncertainly in the breeze. He opened his eyes and disappointment spread across his face. His meagre flame spluttered.

'Keep feeding it, Art.'

'That's easy for you to say.' His candlelight faded to a tiny red cinder. Jatta hooked in while he squeezed and a sword appeared in his hand. Fire burst down its length. He stared in amazement.

'How did you do that? You stole the dwarf's illusion, too.'

She shrugged, grinning awkwardly. Her theory was the orb performed best for vivid imaginations. To use Arthmael's words, for *daydreaming, vague, useless twits* like her.

'Pity it can't rid us of your wolf.' He touched her shoulder with his sand-sword. Jatta clutched her wound and squealed, reeled around twice, staggered groaning in death throes, then collapsed. To Arthmael's amusement flames engulfed her.

'I'm hungry,' she said, rising on one elbow. The flames dissolved.

Arthmael stopped squeezing and tossed back her orb. 'I can only offer you two-day-old pastries. I'm so heartily sick of pastries.'

'My dear uninspired brother! I can transform our marzipan slices into a feast of cold lamb, and toffee nut clusters to pork crackling, and custard—'

'My fanciful little sister! I don't think so. I've had enough of conjuring for one day, thank you all the same.'

The moon rose, a sliver no longer. Its fat crescent had been feeding on the sky.

Despite their game, despite her new toy, dread of a bleak future was seeping through Jatta's heart. Now only Yeemans's potent sleeping potion would keep her from murderous rampages. She took the Crewingburns' jewellery box from the saddlebag to check how much precious potion was left.

She groped inside the box and her heart stopped. The velvet was sticky wet. Her fingers found only the tiny glass stopper.

Pastries or crackling or lamb roast, no supper could have tempted them after that. Arthmael found the bottle tangled in sticky wet bracelets in his satchel. Afterwards they lay beside their horses on a bed of weeds. But sleep wouldn't come. She thought about Dragongirl, who, despite her translucence, was more real than the Sorcerer or any other illusion of the orb. 'Who are you, Dragongirl?' she mouthed to the sky. 'Can you cure my wolf?' No response came. 'I guess not. You would have already, if you'd been powerful enough. But you're here, though? You said you'd always be near.'

There was no sign. Jatta watched the heraldic stars creep across the sky, despising the hateful moon, missing Sanda, missing her father and Steffed and the palace, missing fourteen happy years.

'We can't just hide,' she whispered to herself.

'I know.' Arthmael's voice beside her was soft and sad. Perhaps he also was missing home.

'Art, what will happen now?'

Her brother took a long time before answering.

'Brackensith won't be denied. He always expected we'd reject you. Maybe we were proving him wrong. I don't know— the palace was relying on Redd. That's all irrelevant now. After next moon, if Brackensith sets his wolves among us, many Alteedans will turn against Father. We're rabbits in a hutch to Brackensith's creatures. Your own wolf . . . your popularity will reach new lows. Eventually no-one will offer you sanctuary.'

How many lives was one royal freak worth? The dwarf's words had been spat out with venom, yet she couldn't dismiss them. Knowing her father's dedication to save her at all costs, she shuddered at the carnage her flight would cause. At the carnage *she'd* cause without potion, to Arthmael first. He was careful to avoid mentioning that.

'Perhaps I should surrender to Brackensith. It might be for the best.' Perhaps she'd be better managed among her own kind. She struggled to keep the dread from her voice. 'It mightn't be so terrible. I'd retain the privileges of royalty, and one day I'd be Queen. You could even visit in the portal, sometimes.'

'Glory. How can you be so naive, after all you've read? Listen to me. No-one who's visited that barbaric isle has returned. Nothing decent can survive there.'

'But eight generations of Dark Kings have chosen brides like me.' She propped herself on one elbow, watching his eyes glistening as he lay staring at the almost half-moon. 'Other princesses have survived.'

'Not many.' He turned his head to face hers. 'Do you think you'd stand a chance? Sludinia's Princess Noriward bore Brackensith five sons in misery. Then one day she was left unattended. She was found broken on cobbles beneath his tower. Then he snatched her sister Noridane, who bore him a daughter before slipping into depression, wasting away. It's all in your book. Only death brought their releases.'

Jatta shivered, despite the mild night. It wasn't easy being heroic. 'I don't want that. I don't want to die.'

'No, Jay. I don't want that for you, either.' There was kindness in his voice.

'But death is my only release from Brackensith?'

'Jay . . .' His voice trailed away.

His silence was her answer. She lay thinking for a long time.

'Then so be it, Art. I'll offer myself as a sacrifice to save Father and Alteeda. Brackensith will watch me die.'

'Jay—'

Suddenly they weren't alone. A third body lay between them. Arthmael tensed, slipping his sword from its sheath.

The stranger, a girl, sat up, and the blood drained from his face. She scrambled to her feet, laughing in the starlight. 'Look at your face! Like you've seen a ghost, Art.'

The figure turned to gaze at the fig tree, now a fiery inferno. 'Farewell, loathsome Dark King!' she cried, and raced toward it. Her face blazed orange. Baby-fine hair and skirts whipped around her in the fire's fierce wind. She flinched, protecting her face with raised arms. Still, she flung herself inside the inferno. Her clothes were alight. She flailed and moaned in agony. The flesh on her elfin face melted. With a scream that tore through him, she dropped to her knees and was consumed.

'Art, could it work?' Jatta's voice came close beside him, jolting him out of his wide-mouthed horror.

'Lord, Jay, there are scary things lurking in that mind of yours.'

'Yes, but could—'

He laughed nervously. 'Maybe. Your illusion needs some refinements.'

'Yes?'

'Well, you were too heavy on melodrama for my taste. *"Farewell, loathsome Dark King"*—that has to go.'

Jatta grinned self-consciously.

'And burning flesh actually stinks, not like the roast chicken smell that wafted over from the blaze. Also, I appreciate that you need to be able to see what you're doing, but, well, it spoils the illusion to see you here in double.'

'Mmm . . . Anything else?'

'I think I'd prefer you to fake an accident. Not suicide. If he believed you'd deliberately defied him in death there might be retribution on Alteeda.'

'Is that all?' she asked tentatively.

'We'd have to surrender to Dartithan soldiers. You do understand we may never return?'

'It might work, though?'

'You're a strange one, little sister. But you're definitely growing on me.'

Jatta grinned up at the stars. Her brother approved of her plan . . .

'You know, Jay, it was smart of you to see through Lord Redd. No-one else has. Not in fifty years.'

. . . and of her.

CHAPTER SIXTEEN

Naffaedan's map was again proving invaluable. For many miles a deep river ran between Redd's forest and the road, and only one bridge crossed it. This bridge was a strategic point, Arthmael concluded, where Dartithan soldiers would have set a trap. They would ride into that trap.

They set out early next morning, riding till long afternoon shadows lay across their track.

'We'll stay here for the night,' said Arthmael, stopping in a ferny clearing by a stream. 'There's kindling here, but we'll need more. Real firewood for a real camp fire, not your purple ball tricks.' His wry smile creased one cheek. 'Do you think you can manage that?'

'I'm not completely useless,' she retorted, but he was already leading the horses to drink at the stream. She turned back toward the trees.

She'd grown to love the forest in the afternoon. Sanda had often described its deep, rustling shadows and the sun shining in golden ribbons through the trees. Squirrels chased each other high above her head and shy deer grazed. She found mostly rotted logs near the clearing, so she continued down a gentle slope, then up another. The deer lifted their heads to watch, then edged a safe distance away. One doe followed as Jatta collected branches, though when she turned to coax her shy companion it backed away. Jatta was imagining Arthmael's face when she returned with her firewood, plus her first pet, as she reached down for sticks by a mound of dappled brown earth.

The mound quivered.

Jatta jumped back with a squeal, dropping her bundle. The mound scrambled up, shaky on overlong legs, and took off with its mother. Jatta chuckled. So much for her new pet.

She gathered up her firewood and headed back. After a few minutes the way seemed somehow unfamiliar. The oaks were gnarled and massive, and the ground more open. 'Art!' she called. She waited holding her breath, but her only answer was the rustling of the forest. She put down her bundle and cupped her hands to her mouth.

'Art! Where are you?'

The forest fell silent. After some moments the sounds returned. She plopped down among the leaves to think. All her life she'd stayed in the palace. She'd memorised every door-knob, every tapestry stitch, but this forest was immense and confusing. The sun was low, a bright ball through the trees.

'Which way to our camp?' she called to the squirrels. They ignored her. But if she could climb high, like them, mightn't she see Arthmael's fern clearing, or at least the stream? She took off her shoes and headed for the most gnarled oak. The first branch was higher than her shoulders. She grabbed it with both hands and jumped up. Wriggling forward on her stomach she struggled to hoist one knee over the branch, then the other, to lie along its length. She looked down, suddenly nervous. She'd never climbed, except with Dragongirl, and then Sanda, on her dragon fountain. She twisted her head up to see the next branch and her nerve failed. For the umpteenth time Jatta wished for her fearless friend. Feeling the orb in her pocket, she kneaded.

'Hey! Jatta, you dormouse! Come on up.'

High up with the squirrels, legs dangling, sat Sanda. Jatta grinned.

'Okay!' called Jatta. Gingerly groping her way up the trunk, she rose to stand. She lifted one hand to the branch above. 'It's, um . . . it's a little scary, though!'

'Scary?' scoffed Sanda. 'Well, get moving. It'll be a ruddy lot scarier come nightfall.'

Jatta definitely needed two hands. She stuck the orb between her teeth, gnawing gently into its soft, shiny skin. Stars sparkled beneath her nose. She reached for the second branch, swung a leg over, then eased her body up.

'That's it!' called her friend. 'Lordy, you're a ruddy squirrel.'

Jatta's grin broadened. She climbed and Sanda encouraged, harassed and bullied. Finally Jatta had climbed high enough to see the stream. Her fingers were white where they hugged the trunk. Her heart pounded. Sanda's feet swung so close above her that Jatta might almost have touched them. Almost.

'Don't look down,' said Sanda.

Jatta peeked down and her stomach did a queasy flip. It was terrifyingly far.

'Lordy, I *told* you.'

Jatta shook her head, squeezing her eyes shut, starting to tremble. 'I can't go higher,' she mumbled through a mouthful of orb. 'What can you see from up there?'

'How should *I* know, Jatta! You're scripting this thing.'

Jatta laughed nervously, almost spitting out her treasure. 'Sorry,' she mumbled. 'I forgot.' Reaching for the next branch, she willed her shaky legs to climb.

She'd made it. Jatta spat out her orb, wiped its spittle on her skirts and absently kneaded. The friends sat together in the canopy, surveying the forest. Beyond the ancient trees, to the right of the setting sun, was the clearing, a flicker of flame at its centre.

'There!' Sanda pointed. 'There's your brother.'

'Uh huh. Ready to go?' Jatta poked the orb back between her teeth and they began the long descent.

They collected more firewood as they walked back in the fading light, and Jatta told her friend about Lord Redd and their terrible disillusionment.

'So, Art stole your mother's jewels. To pay Lord Redd,' said Jatta.

'Mother'll be furious.'

'Then we stole them back from the dwarf. They're yours to take, now.'

'Jatta! Troll-brain.'

'Sorry,' grimaced Jatta. 'I forgot again.'

They emerged into the clearing. 'Last one back gets to kiss your brother!' said Sanda. They raced back to the campfire, Sanda straggling behind.

Arthmael turned to gape.

'Glory!' he cried. 'Where did *you* come from?'

'That's not a very princely welcome,' Sanda retorted. 'Your sister invited me, and your ruddy sleeve's on fire.'

'Glory,' he said again, beating at his flaming cuff. The linen, though, hadn't even been singed. Sanda stifled a giggle.

He glanced suspiciously at them both. 'Jay, did you do this? Is that the ball thing you're squeezing? I'll have to confiscate—'

'Hey, be chivalrous and take my bundle first,' interrupted Sanda. 'My ruddy arms are dropping off.'

He jumped to his feet with an apology and hurried to help. Instead of wrapping around her load, though, his arms trailed through Sanda's stomach. 'Argh!' he cried, leaping back.

'Ha!' guffawed Sanda, bending double. 'You look like you've been dropped in a den of dragons!'

Jatta chuckled. Arthmael started laughing too.

'That prankster phantom is a bad influence on you, Jay,' he grinned, reaching for his sister's bundle. 'Will it be staying for supper?'

Sanda shrugged. 'What are we having?'

'Sweet pastries,' said Arthmael, groaning. 'We've been ploughing our way through a mountain of them.'

'Actually,' said Jatta. 'We can provide whatever you fancy.'

When her brother insisted he'd had quite enough of cherry pies Jatta imagined one a beef and bacon pie, and transformed strawberry wafers into cheese biscuits. They sat around the fire retelling star tales and legends of sorcery till the red cinders turned black, dusted with ash, and their last warmth died. Jatta had heard Sanda's tales often before, but the gruffness of her voice and her face lit by the firelight made Jatta happy again. For a long time afterwards the girls lay gazing up at the heavens.

'There's mine—there's Ganus,' whispered Sanda, pointing to a moon-sized star just above the horizon. She, like thousands of other fourteen-year-olds, fancied it her private omen of greatness, for Ganus had first appeared a few days after her birth. 'There's Manus.' Sanda's finger lifted to a halo of light behind wispy black cloud. The heraldic star winked at them as the cloud shifted. Sanda pointed at the sky's brightest pair. 'And there's yours.'

Jatta's star, Aedossus, gleamed high in the heavens beside

tonight's half-moon. She might almost have confused them if not for Aedossus's ice-blue colour. Tonight she didn't want to be reminded of the moon's tug on her. She slid one hand over her eyes and peeked from between two fingers. There. Aedossus shone alone.

'I've missed you, Sanda,' whispered Jatta.

'Me too, dreamy dormouse.'

'I watch Ganus sometimes. It reminds me of you.'

'Me too—I watch the ruddy moon. Aroooo-oou!' Sanda unleashed an otherworldly howl.

The undergrowth rustled nervously. Arthmael grunted under his horse blanket and rolled over.

A swell of quiet misery washed over Jatta.

'Do I scare you, Sanda?'

'Don't be daft. You're my best friend, right? And friends don't tear each other to pieces ... Is it true, though, you ate your attendants?'

Arthmael's drowsy voice came from under his blanket. 'Quiet, you two. Let me sleep.'

'Good night then, Sanda,' whispered Jatta. 'Will you ever come back?'

'I don't know. Will you?'

Jatta sighed.

'All righty. Good night then. Good luck.'

'Goodbye,' whispered Jatta. She slipped the orb back in her pocket and slid two fingers over her eyes again.

The next morning they set out in drizzle. By midafternoon they were sodden and almost within sight of open land. Even Arthmael's spirits were low.

'Perhaps we won't find soldiers at the bridge,' said Jatta

without conviction. 'Don't you hope they've given up and gone home?'

Arthmael scoffed. 'Pretty fantasy, little sister. The most we can hope for is a dry prison cell and a change of—'

Suddenly alert, Arthmael scanned the trees. Branches cracked. Jatta, too, glimpsed movement through the rain. Arthmael's hand tensed on the hilt of his sword.

'Who's there? Show yourself!' he called.

From behind the trees came a horse with two riders, rain-drenched boys of about ten. They rode up, each pressing a finger to his lips as if fearful of waking the forest.

'Are you the royal Princess?' they whispered, awed. 'And the royal Prince?'

Arthmael nodded. 'And who are you, to be following us like thieves?'

'We're Nirin and Neel. Our folks got a farm this side of the river. They sent us to fetch you here in Redd's forest, if them Dartithans didn't catch you first. There's a reward on your head, Princess. And there's a gang roams these parts to collect it any ways they can.'

'We intend to be captured,' said Arthmael.

The boys' eyes widened in disbelief. 'No! Strewth, no— Oops, begging your pardon, Majesty. But you don't. Follow us, let our folks tell you.'

Shadows moved ominously, stealthily, to their left. Jatta grew nervous. Perhaps this was not the place to surrender.

The boys whimpered. They whipped their horse around and galloped back through the trees.

Two masked riders broke cover. They bore down on Jatta and Arthmael with swords high.

Any uncertainty evaporated.

'Whoo! Whoo!' The riders whooped a strange war cry.

'Whoo! Whoo!' came replies far behind.

'Go, Jay!'

Jatta took off after the boys, terrified for her brother. Arthmael tightened his reins and drew his sword.

CHAPTER SEVENTEEN

The first rider came with sword swinging.

Arthmael's blood pounded. Every heavy muscle tensed. Pain seared through his wounds as their swords clashed. Their horses circled, white-eyed. Arthmael wrestled with the pain, assessing his opponent. Strong. Practised. Swords clashed again while the second rider charged.

'Whoo! Whoo!' came the war cry, closer now.

Arthmael cursed. *Too many men to battle.*

He rose in his stirrups, both arms high. The man saw his chance and lunged. Arthmael's sword crashed down mightily through the blade, snapping it, its hilt flying from the man's grip. Its broken blade wedged deep in Arthmael's saddle and his gelding bolted.

Too late Arthmael saw he'd bolted into the second rider's path. Too late he saw the second sword swinging at his chest. No time to block it. Arthmael swooped horizontal underneath its swipe, his pain stabbing. His foot flew from the stirrup as he slid half down his saddle. Both riders kicked into pursuit.

Arthmael struggled up at full gallop, leading them away from his sister. Accomplished at the hunt, till now he'd never been prey. They seemed to know every low branch, every fallen tree. Hooves thundered behind his. He glanced back to see the two riders pressed against their horses' necks. Murderous eyes gleamed above scarf masks. Fly as he did, they were gaining.

'Whoo! Whoo!' his attackers called.

'Whoo! Whoo!' came replies from the trees behind.

His mind racing, he groped through his saddlebag for the Crewingburns' box, grabbing a handful of jewels. He dropped them. Then more. Still more jewels scattered back along his path till he let the box fall, too.

He galloped on. The gang continued to call. He allowed himself a slow, sly grin, for his two attackers no longer replied.

The gang's calls came all around as Arthmael stealthily walked his gelding back through the trees. He spied the two tethered horses first. Then the two men, combing through ferns. They'd found the box and squabbled in hoarse whispers while they dropped precious baubles inside it. Rain fell, dripping from Arthmael's hair as he crept behind them. Neither man looked up till the second rider felt sharp steel on his nape.

Arthmael pressed a finger to lips that twitched with humour. 'Quiet now, men. I won't trouble you for long. I'll just be needing your remaining sword.'

The second man shakily untied his swordbelt, which Arthmael wrapped around his waist.

'Thank you. Your jacket and mask, please.' He bowed to the first swordsman, who pulled off his scarf to reveal an Alteedan face no older than his own. Arthmael chuckled softly in surprise, then more deeply with the effort of struggling one-handed into the too-tight jacket. He tugged the mask down his face.

'And of course my jewels. I must congratulate you on such diligence in collecting them.' He plucked the box from their laps. 'Oh, I ask one more tiny favour. That you refrain from your charming war cry till I'm well gone. Agreed?'

The youth and his companion nodded warily.

'Good. Because if I was captured I'd be obliged to explain how you naughty boys let me slip away.' He shook his head in mock disapproval. 'How you're so bad at sharing.' He swept into his saddle and was gone.

As Arthmael rode back to the river, the gang scoured the forest around him. He silently thanked his meagre disguise and the worsening rain. He headed along the riverbank in the direction the boys had fled, spying farms ahead. At last he shook the tension from his shoulders, pleased that his wounds had settled down to a dull ache. He entertained himself by rehearsing his treasure-hunt tale for Jatta. She'd appreciate the cleverness of it.

'Art!'

He was more relieved than he'd imagined to see Jatta and the boys cantering out from the trees.

'Art, we hid. I was so worried.'

She leaned precariously across her saddle and hugged him. He offered her bony shoulders a pat, knowing she'd like that. She let go, seemingly satisfied, then tugged off his mask. He'd forgotten he had it on. The skies rumbled; rain pelted their faces like gravel as the boys led them between unripe wheat-fields to the farm.

Dogs were barking as Arthmael dismounted to open the gate. Through the rain he saw a man and woman on the veranda aiming their bows at his heart.

'Ma! Pa!' called Nirin. 'We found 'em!'

The woman lowered her bow. 'My, it's the poor Princess.' Then she called to her sons, 'You two, go hide them geldings in the shed!'

Jatta and Arthmael trudged through mud to the veranda

while the farmer scanned the forest. 'Your Majesties, have you been followed?'

'I believe not,' said Arthmael.

'Scar's gang gave us chase. But we was too quick by half!' called Nirin as he led their horses away.

'These're rough times, dear,' said the woman, smiling reassuringly at Jatta. 'My boys here'll keep a lookout.' Then, seeming to remember the nobility of her guests, she attempted a curtsey. 'I ain't humbly introduced meself, though. I'm Marta and me husband's Nasseem. Would your Majesties be so very gracious as to come inside our wee place? It ain't much to look at, Majesties, begging your royal pardons.'

Jatta grinned at the woman's awkward formality. 'We're grateful, Marta. And we're not Majesties at all, nothing so grand. We're just Highnesses.'

They followed the couple inside to a house filled with squeals and laughter. Several children were chasing each other through one large room that seemed to serve as kitchen, dining and living quarters. Their laughter and the aroma of fresh-baked bread welcomed Jatta and Arthmael as cheerfully as Marta had. Several loaves cooled on a long, rough table. A pot of something meaty bubbled on the kitchen hearth, next to piles of washing-up. Marta clapped her broad hands once. The game of tag stopped as if someone had yelled 'Freeze!' Yet another child, an infant perched cross-legged at Jatta's feet licking a bowl, looked up, his face streaked with batter.

'All right, you lot. Out. Go play in the shed,' barked Marta.

The children filed past, gaping. Arthmael winked and the younger ones giggled.

Marta glanced up to the ceiling. 'You too, Naralea.'

Till now Jatta hadn't noticed the mezzanine floor above

their heads, nor the eleven-year-old face peering down over its edge. Naralea's face withdrew, then moments later she was scampering down a ladder, gathering up the batter-faced baby and hurrying out the door.

'Your Majes—Royal Highnesses—please sit, sit,' offered Marta, sweeping vegetable peelings from a long bench at the table. Her guests perched there, dripping mud onto a pile of dirty washing. The strewn chaos reminded Jatta of her own chambers.

Nasseem closed the door. 'Right. I'm afraid the two of you can't afford to be Majesties, nor Highnesses neither, from here on. We'll have to get you plainer clothes, with that brute Riz about.'

'Riz?' said Arthmael.

'Yeah, his men've been terrorising the villages hereabouts. Figuring you'd go to Lord Redd. Looking for you, Princess.'

'But who's Riz?' insisted Arthmael.

'Brackensith's son,' said Jatta. 'His firstborn.'

'The heir, Jay! The one who wants to marry you.'

'No. That's Drake, fifth-born.'

'Yeah, we hear about it from Riz's men,' said Nasseem. 'Cold, calculating brutes, every one. Riz reckons he's heir by birthright, but he never was Brackensith's favourite. Fell right out of favour when he torched his castle wing.'

'He burned down his own chambers? Why?' asked Arthmael.

'Twisted spite, no more. His father had him grounded for taking pot shots at slaves. They was carting water, see, and he was on the parapets above. *Whizz!* with his arrows. Yeah, his brutes don't seem to have no humour normally, but they reckon that were rather funny.'

Marta shuddered. 'They say they'll torch any village what hides you, just the same as he done to his castle wing, 'cept with everyone in it.'

Nasseem reached an arm around his wife's shoulder and squeezed.

Arthmael watched ruefully. Jatta pressed her sodden shoulders to her brother's chest for warmth and murmured, 'The sooner I give myself up, the sooner this ends.'

'Don't do that!' Marta and Nasseem shouted.

Arthmael blinked. Jatta flinched in surprise.

'I mean, think about it,' continued Marta. 'Why would Riz want you alive? If you was returned to the Dark Isle he'd be finished here. He'd have to follow you home, like. Princess, I don't think it suits him to find you alive. Course, if you were dead ... well, that'd be his secret. He'd be happy to search for you forever, looting and plundering, and with wolves too, like he's been threatening. Brackensith'd be none the wiser—'

'Doesn't Brackensith know? Or care?' demanded Arthmael. 'What's happening to Father?'

The farming couple exchanged awkward glances. In the silence that followed, Nasseem studiously cleaned his fingernails. Eventually Marta spoke. 'Your Highnesses, Brackensith's gone. Prince Riz has got all Alteeda as his plaything. Your father and his whole court is ... well, they're hostages in the Great Hall. Riz feeds 'em nothing but peelings, slowly starving 'em all to death.'

'No!' Arthmael jumped up, every outraged muscle tensed. 'We'll raise a revolt!'

Nasseem shook his head sadly. 'Neither swords nor trickery's any use, 'cause the Dark Isle'll only keep sending troops.'

'I won't stand by and do nothing!' shouted Arthmael, thumping his fist on the table.

'Riz has our hands tied,' answered Nasseem quietly.

'Garbage! How could you, *Farmer* Nasseem, presume to know the recesses of Riz's mind?'

Nasseem sighed. 'My cousin's a palace cook, Highness. In these bleak times we all share what we can. Brackensith intends just to teach us a lesson and take the Princess back. *Riz*, though, he's vermin, another type of creature altogether. He's found hisself giant lizard birds as pets. A dragon too, and he's giving it a taste for human flesh. Already he's brought over a thousand men, and five Undead with their blast rods, and harangues his father to send wolves. He's opened the dungeons, offering pardons to any murderer or thug what'll do his bidding.'

Marta continued. 'Riz figures he's been done-over for his own Dark Kingdom, see, and he's just itching to claim our throne for hisself, permanent-like. All he needs is an excuse. Think it through, Highness. King Elisind would be blasted to scraps, moment there's trouble.'

'Marta's right, Highness.' Nasseem leaned across the table, pleading with gleaming eyes. 'The Sorcerer's Pact is all we got now. Go on. Visit Lord Redd and hope he takes pity on us all.'

'It's all my fault,' murmured Jatta. Arthmael sank back to the bench beside her. It was their turn to exchange disturbed secret glances.

They sat down that night to a simple feast of fresh-baked bread, ham and lentil stew, apricots and sticky raisin buns.

'Eat up! Eat up!' urged Marta, who was progressively relaxing with her guests. 'Lord knows when you'll next get a meal as sound as this!'

Certainly they'd never experienced a meal as chaotic. Marta's tribe of children hardly waited for their guests to start before clamouring for this or that dish. The littlest boy, perched in his father's lap, spat his lentils into the butter and grizzled throughout. Young Nirin swapped raisin buns with Jatta. The boy nibbled hers, decided it was after all the smaller, and swapped again. A week before, such discourtesy would have scandalised Jatta and Arthmael, but tonight their minds were on more painful matters.

Marta chided them as she did her own little ones, and her Mother Hen cluckings gave Jatta some comfort. She and Arthmael allowed themselves to be bossed into second helpings, and complimented repeatedly on their father's wise rule.

They sat in a corner whispering while the children were read stories in bed.

'Lord, it's all hopeless,' groaned Arthmael. 'If we surrender, you'll be quietly murdered. If we fight, Riz will assassinate Father and Steffed. If we wait . . . I can't do it, Jay. I can't wait and do nothing while Alteeda is strangled.'

And while my wolf erupts in seven nights, she thought bleakly.

'Jay? Did you hear? I said we can't wait while Father and Steffed starve. I just didn't have the heart to tell our generous hosts about Redd. There's no Pact, no higher power.'

'Perhaps there is a higher power,' said Jatta slowly, wrestling with a new idea.

Arthmael grunted. 'No Sorcerers, Jay, just one dwarf's twisted joke.'

'Not Redd. Brackensith. We could appeal to him.'

He lounged back with sceptically raised eyebrows. 'And how do you propose convincing Riz to take us there?'

'We can't, of course . . . we'll have to go direct. To Dartith.'

'Glory. But no-one's ever gotten past the firewall. How do you intend—?'

'I haven't figured that out yet. Any ideas?'

'Me? No, Jay. You're the one with the ideas. Some that work and some, like hiding in your wardrobe, that don't. Think fast on this one. I'd rather we weren't stranded on some Dartithan beach come wolf-moon.'

CHAPTER EIGHTEEN

In the end they told Nasseem and Marta about Redd. At least, they confessed they'd already visited him and warned that Alteeda could expect no help from the Sorcerer. It seemed unnecessarily cruel to explain how the dwarf had made fools of them all. They also didn't explain where they were headed, and their hosts didn't ask.

Jatta had convinced Marta to let her wear one of her own taffeta petticoats under Naralea's coarse woollen dress, though the bodice still rubbed.

Marta glanced up from lacing Jatta's work boots. 'Don't scratch, dear,' she chided.

Jatta and Arthmael both itched, though. Arthmael's baggy trousers and yellow ochre tunic appeared to cause him even greater discomfort, but Marta had the good sense not to fuss over the towering youth.

The sun was peeping over the wheatfields when Marta hugged Jatta goodbye. 'Remember, cross your horses at the sandy bank, where the river's shallowest. Riz's men guard the bridge. And try not to talk to people, dears. Those grand noble accents'll betray you, quick as an arrow.'

Their saddlebags bulged with Marta's hazelnut cookies and fresh fruit. Arthmael and Jatta set off for the port of North Straefordshire, and Dartith.

They had ridden through back roads for only ten minutes

before a youth about Arthmael's age rode up beside them.

'Hey! Are you crossing the river?' he asked with a good-natured grin. 'Might I join you?'

Jatta flicked Arthmael a quick, reassuring glance. She closed her eyes for a moment, drawing on the memory of Marta's rough dialect.

'Nah, be gone with you,' she drawled.

The youth ignored her. 'I reckon your girlfriend here is a mite unsocial,' he nodded at Arthmael.

Arthmael and Jatta both scowled at him.

'If it's talk you're wanting, me cousin's mute as a mite.' Jatta hoped her tone might discourage the youth, but he was determined to make conversation.

'Poor dumb blighter. Deaf too?'

'Nah, so it'd pay you to keep a civil tongue,' she said. 'Or better yet, go.'

'So where you from?'

Jatta struggled to remember anywhere local from Naffaedan's map, but her mind went blank. Beside her, Arthmael was mouthing something.

'... Ampville!' she guessed.

'Ambville, you mean?'

She nodded.

'Thought so. Are you family of Marta's? She's got family in Ambville.'

'Have others told you that you're a meddlesome plague?'

He shrugged. 'It's just I saw you this morning saying your goodbyes.'

'And here's another goodbye I'd be happy to say.'

The youth grinned, riding on beside them in silence till they came to the river.

'Best to lead the horses,' he said, slipping to the ground. Arthmael also dismounted to take Jatta's reins. Jatta started to climb down.

She screamed as rough hands jerked at her waist. They dragged her to the sand. Her back thudded hard. Arthmael whirled around, his sword ready.

But the lad's knife was already at Jatta's throat. 'Drop it. Drop your sword. Hands high,' he snarled.

Jaw clenched, Arthmael threw his sword to the sand. Jatta fumbled one hand toward her pocket.

'Your hands too, Princess!'

She obeyed. The lad lifted his chin and whooped. 'Whoo! Whoo!'

That same chilling war cry. From the other side of the river came whooping replies. A band of wild youths emerged from the trees and came thrashing through the water. They rampaged around Arthmael and Jatta like a pack of hounds at a kill.

One youth dismounted and swaggered over to Arthmael. A scar stretched across his stupid-looking face, from the corner of his mouth to his ear. He tore the satchel from Arthmael and threw it to the sand, on top of the sword. 'Tie him up, mates!' he said, and four bandits descended on Arthmael. Others descended on the booty.

He swaggered around Jatta like a prize-fighter in a ring. 'Princess. We've come to rescue you. Haven't we, mates?' His friends whooped. 'Back to your groom. He's waiting for you, back in the Dark Isle. And our reward's waiting for us, back at the bridge!'

The others broke into howls of laughter. He preened for his audience, pulling open his shirt and puffing out a hairless, battle-scarred chest. Something purple gleamed there too. Jatta shuddered. An amethyst medallion, fist-sized, hung from his neck on a bloodied ribbon. There was no mistaking Ambassador Sartora's medallion of office. She shared a disgusted look with her brother. Scar might be stupid, but he was also brutal.

Scar's hands searched her body. She went rigid, feeling his fingers close over the orb, drawing it from her pocket, examining it. As he pressed, stars sparkled. He whistled low. 'Now let's get moving,' he called, pocketing it.

They tied Jatta and Arthmael to their saddles and led them back along the river. Jatta tried frantically to think of something, anything, to say that might turn the gang back from the bridge, but images of Sartora and his terrifying last moments had hijacked her brain. It was Arthmael who spoke.

'It's a fat reward, is it, that Riz offers for Princess Jatta?' he called out.

'Hey Scar! The mute blighter can speak!' guffawed their riding companion.

Scar ignored him. 'A reward that's fat enough, eh mates?' The gang whooped.

Arthmael spoke again, 'I swear, the King will offer a richer reward. Much richer!'

'Which king?' called Scar. 'Does you mean King Brackensith of the Dark Isle? Or King Riz of Alteeda?' His mates sniggered.

Undeterred, Arthmael tried a different approach. 'I meant, why would Riz honour this offer? You know his reputation.'

'Course we do. Don't nobody got a higher respect for his reputation than us. That's why we're going way outta our ways, so as to get in his good graces. Better in than out. Don't want to end up dragon fodder, do we mates? Whoo! Whoo!'

'Whoo! Whoo!' they chorused.

'Shut up, hear?' called Scar. 'Let me do the talking.'

They'd arrived at the bridge. Six tall, thin men in red mail tunics strode over. All wore black plaits, and bleak expressions on their flat and uniformly broad faces. Jatta turned in her saddle to see Arthmael. Beneath his attempted nod of reassurance she saw he'd run out of ideas.

'Hey soldiers, we've caught your Princess for you!' Scar's bravado was enthralling his mates. 'We've come for our reward.'

The Dartithans coldly surveyed the group. Recognition lit in their eyes as they came to rest on the petite peasant girl and the thick-set lad at her side. Their officer strode to take her reins.

'Your name!' he commanded Jatta.

A stream of options gushed through her mind. She could refuse. Or pretend she was someone else. Or attempt a bribe. Or . . .

She took a deep breath and looked down into those cold eyes. Her voice, when it came, was strong. 'I am Jatta, third-born of Elisind, King of Alteeda. And I demand you deliver us to King Brackensith direct, not to his son.'

He snorted a humourless laugh. 'How, Princess? We each be stranded in this soft-bellied land till King Riz's work be done.'

She charged tack without faltering. 'You know I'm a wolf?'

His jaw tensed as he nodded. From beside her came sharp breaths and creaks in saddles, but she did not break his discomforted gaze.

'You want nothing to do with me,' she said ominously. 'In

125

six nights I'll erupt, gnawing through doors, clawing through bodies, rampaging with the strength of fifty.' She shot a dark look around at the men. They were unnerved, intently watching, so she leaned down close to the officer, drawing in a breath of his hair. A part of her imagined how ridiculous her delicate mouth must look in its sneer, but it was working dark magic on them. 'Soldier,' she whispered. 'I'll remember your scent.'

His hard eyes flinched, but then he turned to growl at his men. 'That be King Riz's gut-ache. We shall deliver her and be gone well before wolf-moon.' He nodded warily up at her. 'Your portrait in the Great Hall does you no justice. It paints you as naught but a nervous pup.' His eyes scanned the frightened horsemen for Scar. 'Well done, boy. Have others seen you this morning?'

'There weren't nobody but us at the river.' Scar's eyes flitted nervously back to Jatta.

'Well done. Follow us for your reward.'

The soldiers led the geldings back through wheatfields to a farmhouse, Scar's gang trailing behind, and the officer ordered the gang be paid. Alone with the captives in the farmer's bedroom, he set about cutting their ropes.

'What now?' asked Arthmael, rubbing the circulation back into his hands.

'Now we find something worthy for the Princess to wear.'

Puzzled, Jatta searched the deadpan face. 'But I have a wardrobe of gowns back at the palace.' She now dared to hope Marta had been wrong. Perhaps Riz did intend to present her to Brackensith.

'You be not returning to Adaban's palace. You be travelling through Vardensen Desert to Goy-an Canyon.'

'What's at Goy-an Canyon?'

'King Riz be there, and it be in your interest to look worthy.'

Jatta nodded hopefully at her brother.

'Your brother be free to go.' The officer gestured to the open door. 'Hear me, Prince?'

'No. I share my sister's fate.'

'So be it. Our journey begins at midnight.' He left, locking the door behind him.

'Did you hear that, Art? That's good, isn't it? Everything might still turn out.' Jatta heard her own words and a slow, dry smile spread her cheeks. Not so long ago the thought of sacrifice to Dartith had horrified her. There were worse things, she knew now.

Her brother wasn't listening. He peered out through the window shutters. She joined him, straining for a view through the slats.

'I see them, Art. Two Dartithan soldiers. Watching us watching them.'

'Look beyond them.'

Jatta strained her eyes further. Eleven tiny figures were digging together in the wheat. Two others in distinctive red tunics were watching.

She chuckled. 'Scar's gang. Perhaps their reward's buried. A pot of gold.'

'Perhaps.' Arthmael rose to test the door. Then he began searching the room. She sat watching as he pulled apart bedclothes and flung clothes from chests.

'Art, I'm not sure we want to escape.'

He ignored her. Like a lion he paced the room. He ransacked it, but found nothing except clothes and needlework, painted bowls and a few cheap trinkets. He thumped the wall. Bristling, he returned to the shutters, staring out for what seemed hours. Jatta joined him, gently squeezing his shoulder. 'Perhaps he won't kill us. He did offer you freedom.'

Her brother continued staring out to the field. 'No. If I'd walked out that door I'd have ended up with *them.*'

Jatta peered out. The two soldiers were now shovelling, filling the hole.

'What, the soldiers? In the field?'

'Sweet, sweet Jay. So clever, yet so naive. No, the gang. Buried *under* the field.'

Ice formed in Jatta's stomach. *All murdered.* Suddenly her quest had grown deadly real: more real than the bloodied medallion, more real than tales of dragon-baiting or suicide plots, more real than rumours of starving hostages. She'd chuckled while they dug. Had she heard Scar's screams? She tried to think back; there had been distant calls. She shuddered, imagining Scar's surprise. His pain. His final terror. Had he still been alive when the first dirt landed on his face? If she'd looked she'd have witnessed it all. Life was fragile. She understood that now.

'How do we escape?' she whispered, shivering.

No weapon, no orb, no real plan. They discussed options till dark, when two flat-faced soldiers brought them food wrapped in cloth. No utensils. Just cold sliced ham, pickled onions, dumplings and Marta's hazelnut cookies.

'They have our satchel,' said Jatta when they were alone again.

Arthmael nodded. 'My guess is they've removed everything from the bodies—everything that might identify them. Scar and his mates were the only witnesses to our capture. Whatever Riz wants with you, he needs it kept secret from his father.'

Jatta's mind, however, was not on Riz. 'If everything was removed, my orb hasn't been buried. Art, the soldiers may have it.'

Arthmael put down his cookie with a lopsided grin and rose to knock on the door. 'Soldiers!' he called. They heard movement, but no reply. 'Dartithan guards! Those half-witted thugs took our possessions—a burnt book and a little purple ball. Will you find them for us? There were jewels too, but Princess Jatta offers them as reward.'

The soldiers said nothing. Beyond their door they heard snorts, as if the young royals were in no position to ask for anything.

At midnight the Dartithans reappeared. Their prisoners' wrists were again bound and they were led out into the drizzly night. It seemed every soldier they'd seen thundering through the market five days before was securing provisions on wagons or hitching horses. Jatta and Arthmael were bundled inside a carriage and heard its lock click before they, and the convoy, lurched on their way.

CHAPTER NINETEEN

The sun rose outside their carriage, the second they had seen since leaving the farmhouse. Sand and rocks stretched out to distant mountains, the view only occasionally relieved by scraggly shrubs. Each trundling, mind-numbing hour took them further from Dartith, further from anywhere. Closer to wolf-moon; only tonight and tomorrow night lay in-between. These were their only certainties.

Arthmael lolled in a corner, humming to himself. Jatta leaned forward with her sweaty forehead pressed on the glass, her mind reaching out for the orb. For the hundredth time that morning she tried hooking in, imagining its white stars in front of her nose. Nothing. The Vardensen Desert heat was stifling.

They'd explored the subject of escape till their heads ached. But without the orb, or a map, or water, and with only shrubs for sanctuary in the inevitable pursuit, they could do nothing. They talked about home, too. Arthmael's anecdotes of his pranks on Alteeda's heir had Jatta giggling so much that soldiers' faces sometimes appeared, frowning and perplexed, at their oven window. Jatta and Arthmael knew they were really saying farewell, though. It was hard not knowing where their journey took them: to their deaths, or Dartith. Thinking of it made Jatta queasy. It felt almost as bad as knowing the worst.

The heat lent a lethargy to even the most critical of

questions—a question Arthmael had long since tired of discussing. 'How is Riz going to cage my wolf?' said Jatta again, half to herself. 'Or, he could concoct me some potion . . .' She recited the blue sleeping potion recipe from her Dartith book.

'There's a third option,' Arthmael muttered to the corner. 'Riz has a taste for baiting dragons. He'll want to fatten your scrawny little hide, too.'

Jatta felt stricken. He had no right to raise that spectre! She pressed her hands either side of her face, pretending to peer out. Feeling dirty, contaminated.

He sat up, sighing. 'Look, I'm sorry, Jay,' he offered, awkwardly patting her back. 'But we'll never get to Dartith by pretending Riz is all fluffy like you.'

Deep down she knew that. Since the gang's murder she had no illusions left. Or maybe just this one. On this, Arthmael might be wrong. She settled back in her corner and silently asked Dragongirl to provide sleeping potion, then reached again for the orb.

It seemed the Dartithans no longer thought a desert escape possible either. When their convoy stopped to set up tents under the midmorning blaze the prisoners were permitted to wander freely. Their carriage windows were ordered unbolted.

The horizon's corrugations had smoothed away by late afternoon and they trundled on again. After her third night curled up under Arthmael's jacket, Jatta woke and stuck her head out the window. Sand, rocks. More shrubs. The mountains crept closer. Eventually even she tired of the monotony and settled against her brother's shoulder to doze. When her eyes opened, a beetle had flown inside their carriage and Arthmael was lazily watching it climb over his wrist.

'So there are things living out there,' she said, yawning.

But he'd flicked off the bug and was straining to hear a distant pounding over the clattering of wheels. To Jatta it sounded like horses' hooves, a great army up ahead. Arthmael grunted and thrust his head out the window as if expecting to see all Alteeda rising up against Riz. Impossible, she thought. Ahead lay only Goy-an Canyon and, beyond, impenetrable mountains.

'It's water,' he decided, and stretched his shoulders out too.

Jatta chuckled sceptically. Water trickled over her fingers. It sloshed from the palace wells. Three days ago at the river crossing it had splashed and swished and surged. This sound rumbled.

'A waterfall. It's Goy-an Falls, Jay.'

She squeezed her head out in front of his. The mountain range loomed close; a canyon snaked between it and Vardensen Desert. Mountain rivers wound down, cascading in mighty falls into the canyon, stealing the desert's rain to create a lush paradise. She'd seen pictures in books, but could never have grasped the torrent's power. Pictures indicated nothing of the thunder that drowned out all other sounds.

The sun was a white blaze when their carriage stopped. Arthmael got out to help her down, but a new face appeared at the door: a youth not much older than herself. His plait was disconcertingly greying, but it was his eyes that made her stare. Hooded like other Dartithans', they were handsomely large and wide set. Their almost-black pupils were flecked a startling blue. The youth must have been used to such attention for he waited, grinning smugly, till she remembered her manners.

He said something which the canyon falls drowned out. She smiled politely. 'I be Kristith. Time to dress!' he shouted. He laid a court gown and shoes across her lap and left a bucket of water, perfumed soap and towels before shutting her in. Jatta blinked in surprise. Did he expect her to climb sheer cliffs inside a cocoon of taffeta, brocade and velvet? To what inane purpose?

Obediently she knelt down on the floor, dunked her head in the bucket, then started to lather her greasy hair.

Scrubbing off caked grime and sweat, she began to feel more like a princess again. She imagined orb stars while wriggling into her bodice, but to no effect. Polite rapping on the door hurried her along. She considered the courtier's shoes with their high heels and pointed lace toes, but decided her farming boots would be immeasurably more sensible. No-one would notice under her flummery of skirts if she took dainty steps. The door banged harder and she opened it. Kristith stood there examining her admiringly. She blushed. He turned her around to lace up her back, his hands unpractised but unexpectedly gentle.

He led Jatta through the camp to join Arthmael at the canyon edge. Log ladders had been attached from ledge to ledge down the cliff face. The soldiers were carrying supplies down into the jungle while others, swaggering Alteedans with villainous faces, helped.

'Prison scum that Riz pardoned!' shouted Arthmael in her ear before he swung onto the ladder. She nodded, recalling Nasseem and Marta's warning. Ominously, this part was true.

Waiting her turn to climb, Jatta reached for the orb. Still nothing. If the orb was travelling with them, its new owner wasn't experimenting with its powers.

She peered down the cliff and felt dizzy. Far below, trees seemed to swim. Blood pounded in her ears just as the falls pounded all around. She willed her eyes down to the first ledge. Arthmael was there shouting up to her. She couldn't hear, but his arms stretched up as if to catch her fall. Despite her fear she grinned. Valiant Arthmael. Any attempt to save her on that narrow ledge would send them both hurtling to the jungle floor.

Jatta remembered her climb down the great oak with Sanda, and suddenly the distance didn't seem quite so dreadful. Kristith was placing her hands on the ladder. She nodded, manoeuvring herself backwards onto the first rung, her legs trembling in their prison of skirts. Imagining Sanda coaxing her on, she stretched down for the second rung. It felt firm against her boot, not impossibly far, and for the first time in her life Jatta imagined herself brave. She ventured to the third rung, breathing heavily. 'That's the way,' whispered Sanda's voice in her ear. 'Look at you now. Not a dormouse, you're ruddy Bobo scaling a palm in his striped purple waistcoat. Why did you reckon you needed me?' Jatta giggled nervously. With white knuckles she lowered herself to the next rung.

She stepped shakily onto the ledge. 'Good girl, Jay!' Arthmael shouted in her ear.

Once on the canyon floor they trekked away from the falls, following a path beneath the cliff. They were met by another man, an officer. His blue-flecked eyes were shrewd and compelling; his plait was white-grey, though he was not yet forty. As he gripped Kristith's shoulder in greeting Jatta concluded they were father and son. Their manners, however, could not have been more different. 'I be Commander Fand,' he said with a curt nod, looking Jatta up and down. He picked up a damp tangle of hair, scowling. 'We shall have to do something with this.'

Kristith strode on with Arthmael while Fand followed close behind Jatta, keeping a mirthless watch on all she did. The dark rainforest teemed with giant ferns and insects and ugly hybrid creatures. Even her dragon books had described few of them. Soaring above their heads was an ugly lizard-bird with leathery bat wings and an obsidian jagged-toothed beak. She recognised it as a pterodactyl the Sorceress Ambro-An once created for her own amusement. It swooped down past her face, snatching a snake. She squealed and jumped back into Fand as the python writhed skyward.

The commander grimly put her back on her feet. 'Not to worry, Princess. We be as strange to them as they be to us. Prey be plentiful here. As yet, most haven't noticed we be tasty too.'

Eventually the dense forest soaked up the falls' thunder. Jatta could hear the felling of trees and glimpsed Alteedans with axes through the understorey. Somewhere ahead came another roar, one that both thrilled and chilled her. It was a sound she had always imagined. The Dartithan in front of her tensed.

'Dragon,' he murmured.

They approached a bustling camp site, eight long tents in a row. Behind the tents stood a half-built cage as wide as a room and twice as high. Alteedans swarmed over it, securing a steel bar in place and ramming rivets through. Others drew red-hot metal from a blazing fire and hammered it into more rivets.

A pot bubbled over a campfire; a Dartithan sipped its broth from a ladle. At his feet two Alteedans chopped giant slabs of meat. A moment's glance told Jatta why neither was helping on the cage. One was old and stooped and the other, with his leg in bandages, appeared to have recently lost a foot.

Fand issued orders and Arthmael was put to work carting supplies. The stooped man was brought before Jatta.

'Old barber, can you do naught with this hair?' said Fand.

The man ran practised fingers through Jatta's tangles, teasing them out, piling them on top of her head. 'Captain, I reckon I need combs, clips and ribbons,' he said.

The grey-haired commander tossed him a lace drawstring bag, then turned and left. The barber took off his jacket. He laid it across a decaying log and, with a professional flourish, he gestured for Jatta to sit.

'Would your Highness care to please describe for me the latest palace styles? I admit to being somewhat outta touch, these last fifteen years.'

'Were you in prison?' she asked.

'I admit as much, your Highness.'

'Then use your judgement. I guess Riz would be ignorant of our palace fashions, too.'

As his fingers worked on her hair, he chatted. 'Why were I in prison, your Highness? I do admit I made mistakes, one being how I slit one fool feller's throat. Weren't me fault, a mere slip of me razor ... mostly, any rate. And I would've stayed rotting in prison if not for King Riz. He offered us all jobs terrorising the villagers or plundering at court, or this work here. Well, I ain't much at terrorising, but I wish now I'd tried me hand at plundering, or else even stayed put.'

'Why?'

'Well, Highness, King Riz enjoys feeding his dragon, don't he?'

He fixed the last jewelled clip in her hair and stepped back to admire. 'I'd have liked to have a mirror for you. You looks all grown up, a right queen.'

Commander Fand had reappeared.

He grunted approval. 'Come. King Riz waits for us in his hide.'

Jatta was led forward along a narrow track.

'In his hide?' she asked.

He pointed up into the canopy. 'Yes, Princess. Where he can watch without being watched.'

They stopped by an immense pine tree where two Dartithan soldiers waited. Jatta followed Fand's gaze high into its canopy, to a log platform there. Ropes and pulleys ran back down to the ground where a waist-high wicker basket sat.

'It be a spectacular view,' he said, lifting her inside the basket. He squeezed in beside her and the soldiers hoisted them up. With every lurch past the undergrowth Jatta's view improved. She saw a clearing as wide as a field, its far side bounded by the canyon cliff. A cave four storeys high was cut into the cliff and around its entrance were piled broken bones, some so long she imagined their owners had been giants. Bolted into the cliff was a massive chain.

On the other end of the chain, resting its forlorn chin in the dirt and snorting little puffs of dust, lay a hatchling dragon no bigger than herself. Its silver scales glinted like mirrors, dazzling her eyes. As she squinted, the misery in its face tore at her heart.

They'd almost reached the platform when Fand leaned down to whisper in her ear. 'I be saying this once only, Princess. It be in your interests to please the Prince.'

As the basket jerked up past the floor, a coronation cape came into view. It trailed along the platform. With surprise she recognised the maroon velvet and polar bear trim. Next she saw a pair of white satin slippers embroidered with pearls, and leggings too short for their wearer. Riz stood in profile, leaning over the railing to watch the clearing. Jatta recognised his crown. Like the slippers, leggings and cape, it was her father's.

Fand leapt neatly onto the platform, then lifted Jatta out.

'Sire,' he bowed.

Only then did Riz turn around. He looked nothing like other Dartithans. Certainly his brown, beaded hair was plaited in the Isle's fashion, but his nose was finer and longer, and his face less pale and broad. Jatta might almost have thought him good-looking except for something disquieting in his face. Perhaps it was the smarmy smirk that twisted one corner of his mouth. No, she realised, as he lounged against the railing languidly nibbling his ring. It was in his eyes. Something dangerous, unfocused, mercurial—like a malevolent child.

'Yes, elegantly dressed, the green suits her eyes. I like the hair. Your idea, Fand?'

The commander nodded.

'Trim little figure, not exactly pretty. You promised me pretty—but no matter.'

A plaintive whimper, like a puppy's, drifted up from the clearing. Riz turned again to lean over the rails and giggled, a most disconcerting laugh from a man in his mid-twenties. 'Come, come! Jatta, see.'

Jatta joined him. Two men in Dartithan battle armour had entered the clearing. A couple of things struck her as odd. The first was the way the men stumbled around, clanking, as if they had never worn armour before, dragging their weapons through the dirt. Also, they wore no Dartithan helmets. By their nervous, thuggish faces she saw instantly that these were not soldiers, but two of Adaban's criminals.

Beside her, Riz grinned stupidly. 'I like to see their faces. Yes, that be the best part.'

She realised what would follow, and her sympathy switched from the forlorn baby to the men. 'Call them back,' she whispered, her throat dry. 'Please—it's *barbaric*.'

Riz's eyes hardened at the word. He twisted to her with undisguised hostility, the dragon forgotten.

'Get on your knees,' he hissed.

Jatta blinked.

'You will beg forgiveness, or join them.' His eye twitched.

'Sire,' interrupted Fand blandly. 'She merely recognises the man from this morning. Barber Reek.'

'Oh . . . Barber Reek.' She grasped at the lie, and swallowed twice to wet her unco-operative throat. 'Majesty, might you let him live?' She worked a demure innocence into her green eyes. 'He styled my hair delightfully, and he understands fine hair . . .' She stole a glance at the clearing. One ashen-faced criminal stood guard outside the cave, his spear trembling. The other used his sword to prod the poor hatchling. Its puppy whines grew louder. She imagined she could also hear the man's knees clanking. 'And he didn't jab with the clips. Sometimes they jab.'

Riz snorted out his sudden anger and settled for petulance. 'Your hair suits you, Jatta. It be pretty, almost as white as Fand's.' He scowled at Fand. 'It be unlike you to squander talent.'

A dragon roared, distant inside the cave. Jatta stifled her flinch. 'Then, Majesty, you'll let me keep Reek? Keep them both?'

Riz bestowed a bountiful smile and patted her cheek.

A terrible roar rose from the cave mouth and Riz's eyes lit.

He whipped back to the rails. 'Too late,' he said. 'We shall try your hair long.'

An adult dragon bounded into the sunlight, blazing silver. Short limbed, long necked, she towered a full storey high at the shoulder. Jatta screamed. The thug at the cave's mouth screamed too. He overbalanced and tumbled onto his armour-clad back, flailing like a beetle. Monstrous jaws swept low as he groped for his spear. He thrust. It splintered as her jaws snapped shut. For one moment their eyes met: his terror, her hatred. He forgot to scream. She snatched him up in her jaws. She tossed him high, like a juggler's club, then caught him, crunching down on steel. She screwed up her face in distaste and spat out the metal wreck. It hit the ground with a clanging thud.

Riz was giggling. In that moment, Jatta despised him.

The dragon turned her attention to the second armoured thug. He was stumbling away to hide. She bounded after him, making the ground shake. In four strides she blocked his escape. He reeled around, back to the hatchling. Again she tried to outstrip him—but he dived onto the baby. The poor creature was dragged onto its side. It struggled to be free. But he, equally terrified, wrapped himself around it.

The mother towered above them both, cocking her head to one side, brow creased. She viewed the awkward dilemma from left, then from right. The hatchling thrashed in the dust while its passenger sobbed.

The mother's face relaxed as she seemed to make up her mind. She called to her little one, a soothing, bubbling, dove-like coo.

'This bit be good,' said Riz.

The dragon drew a deep breath while her baby tucked its

wings beneath a scaly spine ridge and curled into a centipede roll. The man clung sobbing to its back. Next a fire burst over them both, so intense that it melted the poor man's armour. His head was blackened and he no longer cried.

The hatchling uncurled, whining. The mother peeled off its passenger like a dry cicada, then tenderly gathered her baby into her jaws. As soon as she lifted her head, the hatchling started choking. The mother, remembering, hastily returned it to the ground. She attacked the chain with fire and teeth again and again. Eventually, whines from within the cave drove her reluctantly from her baby's side.

'I win! Yes, I win!' Riz was shouting in the commander's impassive face. He turned to Jatta. 'Fand here bet that armour would save their wretched hides.'

'As always, Sire, you have judged correctly.' Fand bowed.

'I win, you lose! That means you be next dragon fodder.'

'Sire!' he protested.

'Only teasing, Fand. Still, we be needing another. Find me a fresh volunteer for her breakfast.' Again he examined Jatta, and not only her face. 'Will you be joining me for breakfast? And supper? It be our little secret, we shall not tell Father. And what be your age?'

Jatta stared dumbly, an awful dread rising at Riz's words.

'Fourteen years and eight days, Sire,' Fand answered when she didn't.

'Surely not?' Riz playfully made a wide-eyed, aghast face, as though inviting Jatta to refute such a claim. When she continued to stare he turned to Fand. 'Your son be that age; she be half his size.'

Fand nodded. 'True again, Sire. Remember, it need be

in name only. Unlike your brother, you have not the luxury to wait.'

'Unlike my *brother*!' screamed Riz, suddenly furious.

Jatta flinched.

'Unlike my *brother*! I deserve all my brother has, and more! I be heir! *Me!* Not the blessed, beloved, *perfect* Drake!'

The commander bowed low with dignity. 'You shall have what your brother was promised, Sire, plus a legitimate claim to Alteeda's throne.'

Jatta's heart thundered—*she* was what Drake had been promised. So Riz intended not to return her, or kill her, but wed her! Her claim to the throne followed after her father's. After Steffed's. After Arthmael's. Her life's price was her entire family: for her to reign they must die. Her last illusion exploded into horror. Vicious, sick Riz! How would he murder her family? She had little doubt he'd feed them to his bride.

Riz's fury had vanished like a toddler's tantrum. He beckoned her.

'Come closer, Jatta,' he simpered, attempting charm but managing only his twisted smirk.

She stepped forward, trembling as she curtseyed, understanding that to expose such plans in her presence he must think her either stupid or utterly powerless.

'Say something.'

'Majesty, how are my father and Steffed?'

'Happy and well, sweet Jatta. They send you their love.'

Stupid. Riz thought her stupid. She played along, hope stirring, forcing a pretty smile. 'May I visit them, Majesty? May I say goodbye before we leave for Dartith?'

'Perhaps you won't have to leave. Would you rather stay on with me at the palace?'

'Oh yes, Majesty! But mustn't you send me through the portal?'

'Ah, the portal ... the damnable portal. If it were destroyed, Jatta, you need not be prisoner to Dartith.' His dangerous eyes held hers while his voice dripped honey. 'You could stay here as my queen.'

Jatta's mind was racing. So the portal was the key. With it destroyed, Brackensith could not return. His treacherous son could run amok in Alteeda. Riz would have her wolf dispatch her family then.

Two elegant silk tents nestled in jungle behind the hide. Fand returned Jatta to these, not the camp, after the dragon's feeding hour.

He nodded at the larger, guarded tent. 'That be King Riz's ...' He opened the second tent's flap. '... And this be ours.' Inside were four hammocks and Arthmael. Fand nodded elegantly, then left.

Jatta's tension broke and she ran to her brother.

'He sickens me!' she spat. 'He's disgusting and vicious!'

Arthmael blinked, then broke into a perplexed laugh at her fury.

'Stop it! This isn't funny. Riz means to kill you. And Father. And Steffed.'

Her news didn't seem to surprise him.

'Probably he'll marry me first.'

That did.

'Fand's behind this,' she said. 'Riz has only half a brain, and *that's* addled. If he thinks I'll thank him, he's mistaken!'

'Who, Riz?'

She scoffed. 'No. Riz understands nothing more than

torture and killing. It's Fand who wants legitimate succession, with his *"It be in your interest to please the Prince,"* and his hair clips and bows!'

'Then let's thank Fand we're still alive.'

Suddenly her anger collapsed. Her lower lip trembled, her eyes grew moist.

'Hey, Jay. We're not dead yet.' His palm drew circles on her back. 'Listen, think of something else. Reach out for your ball.'

She nodded miserably and closed her eyes. Stars danced in front of her nose.

'Fantastic work! Now send up a signal.'

She imagined a shower of fireworks exploding from the orb. Arthmael raced outside and down the track to the camp. It was some time before he returned, unsmiling.

'It's stopped now,' she apologised. 'Whoever it was has stopped squeezing.'

'That's okay. It's here, Jay, and we'll find it.'

Arthmael spent the afternoon with the Alteedans, discovering whatever he could. Kristith brought Jatta strange robes, courtly clothes for her brother, and invitations for supper with Riz.

Jatta dressed herself. The Dartithan robes were neither heavy, nor fitted, nor layered. The slippery, ice-blue silk draped around her bust and hips, drawn tight by criss-crossing ribbons around her waist; it rippled down to her ankles like liquid. Kristith returned with another pair of heeled shoes, and his smug grin. She ignored him, and he left while she unlaced her boots.

CHAPTER TWENTY

The others were already waiting when Jatta and Arthmael entered. Riz's royal tent had been festooned with hundreds of candles and layers of gauzy drapes. Alteedan musicians played, not particularly well, in the corner. A low table was laden with delicacies. In the night's breeze the drapes danced, the flames too. The effect was intimately romantic. The assembled guests, however, inspired no romance in Jatta. Commander Fand sat at the low table rigidly ignoring an Alteedan to his right. Jatta didn't recognise the man, but by his brocaded cloak and accent as he attempted banter, she took him for a Southern noble. And of course there was Riz, jitterish as an over-wound toy. He had changed his cape for a cream satin coat embroidered with gold and topaz, smelling vaguely of spices. It fitted loosely on his tall, lean body, though the leggings were again short at the crotch. Jatta remembered her father wearing the outfit with considerably more poise a few weeks before.

The Alteedan's name was Baron Randall. He confessed quite freely to having been imprisoned after torturing his chef. The poor man had burned his supper. Tonight however, the baron was at pains to compliment Riz on his meal. 'Majesty! Your roast in truffle jus is, dare I say, breathtakingly piquant. Gamey, indeed. Decadently so!'

Riz was enchanted with the man's praise. 'Very nice, agreed? I can tell you our roast be a lizard-bird thing, but what sort I cannot say. Cook has worked marvels, especially as we fed an apprentice of his to the creature yesterday.'

Everyone laughed politely, not sure whether their host was joking. Jatta left the rest on her plate.

'Now begins the fun part of our night,' said Riz when the meats were being cleared and a fruit platter offered. 'I hear you in Alteeda enjoy gambling for high stakes. As we do.'

Jatta and Arthmael exchanged puzzled glances.

'Oh yes you do, Jatta, do not deny it.' Riz giggled blithely. 'Be that not so, Randall?'

'Majesty, yes indeed. Among the circles into which I have tragically fallen.'

'You see, Jatta? So we shall play a Dartithan game. Each of us shall pose a riddle. He whose riddle remains unanswered gets to keep the wagers.'

'We have nothing,' breathed Arthmael in Jatta's ear.

Riz's eyes darted suspiciously to Arthmael. 'Eh? You *did* remember your wager?'

'Sire, here be the Prince's wager.' Fand laid Arthmael's gem-encrusted sword on the table.

'Huh!' scoffed Riz. 'Have you conjured something for Jatta, too?'

Fand placed the orb on the table. Jatta and Arthmael breathed in sharply.

'That's mine!' cried Jatta, grabbing for it.

Riz rapped her fingers with his knife, snatching the orb. 'What be this, then?'

'Magic, Sire,' said Fand. 'Squeeze it and smell.'

Riz held the orb to his nose. Stars sparkled inside. 'Smells like cheap women's scent.' He tossed it to Randall. Jatta's head reeled with half-formed ideas for escape, even as she blushed at her outburst.

'Mmm ...' moaned Randall rapturously. 'Crisp-skinned roast pheasant with chestnuts.' He sniffed again, lips quivering. 'And brandy butter sauce.'

'Please Majesty, may I try?' Jatta held Riz's gaze with innocent doe eyes.

'It be thine, Jatta,' he said coyly, taking the orb to hold it under her nose. Then as she reached up he snatched it away. He giggled coquettishly. 'If you can fool us all with your riddle!'

Fand grunted. He produced the Ambassador's bloodied medallion as his own offering.

'My wager,' announced Baron Randall, smugly throwing down a heavy purse. 'Here are my winnings from several such games.'

Riz smirked slyly around the table as he offered the crown from his head. 'I warn you, friends, no-one has ever bettered me at riddles.'

'Indeed,' said Fand. 'Shall I go first?' He took a moment to collect his thoughts, then began.

'*It reaches for the sky.*
It burrows into the ground.
In spring it leaves,
But it be always around.'

'You be a natural poet,' giggled Riz, and Fand nodded in deference.

'It goes but it stays?' asked Baron Randall.

Fand glanced at him without comment.

'It be a bird, a digging sort of bird,' said Riz. 'Birds fly off to warm places in spring, yes?'

Jatta spoke quietly to Arthmael. '*Leaves* is a pun. It grows leaves in spring.'

Randall shot a furtive look at Jatta. 'I have it!' he exclaimed. 'Tree. It's a tree.'

'I knew that!' chimed in Riz.

Fand nodded. 'Of course, Sire.'

'Yes, I won,' crowed Randall. 'So, shall I go next?'

He picked ten grapes from the fruit platter and arranged them in a row along the table. 'Ready? Ten flies are on our table here. With one *swat*—'

He slammed down his open palm. Jatta jumped.

'—I kill three flies. How many flies are left on the table?'

They all stared down at his hand, and the remaining grapes.

'You must think us simpletons with such a riddle,' scoffed Riz. 'There be seven left, seven!'

Arthmael laughed. 'Except real flies wouldn't wait around.' Arthmael swept up the seven grapes and tossed them toward the tent flap. 'There are only three flies left on the table.'

Laughing too, Randall lifted his hand. There lay what was left of three grapes.

Fand was studying Riz intently. Jatta turned too. There was fury brewing in Riz's set jaw and a nervous tic in one lower eyelid as he struggled with the humiliation of their laughter, of being proven wrong. In that moment Jatta realised how dangerous their game had become. She must lose. She would forfeit the orb. And more, besides, if they were not all careful.

'A very tricky question!' exclaimed Fand with uncharacteristic enthusiasm. 'And trickier, cleverer questions to come!'

Riz managed a strained smirk.

Jatta flashed Riz an ingratiating smile. 'I have one.'

All eyes turned to her.

'What am I? I don't have legs, but I travel to my kingdom's limits. I am two-faced, but I only show one. Men find me hard and cold, yet sacrifice what they love for me. I have greatest power when given away, yet lust for me keeps me locked up.'

The table stayed silent as all contemplated the riddle.

'I give up,' said Arthmael.

'I too,' said Fand.

'It is . . . no, it can't be a woman, or a bride, because she'd probably need legs, wouldn't she? I'm wrong, aren't I?' Randall looked to Jatta for inspiration, but she gently shook her head. 'No, I'm afraid I can't quite imagine this one,' he sighed.

Riz snorted. 'Ha! Jatta, thine be an impossible riddle.'

'I'll try to think of a clue, Majesty,' she said, smiling angelically. She absentmindedly withdrew a kroun from Randall's purse and tossed it between her palms.

Recognition dawned on Fand's face. On Randall's too. Arthmael grunted approvingly.

'I be waiting for my clue, Princess,' growled Riz.

'Kings leave their imprint on me,' she said. Seeming to grow bored of the coin, she rolled it across the table to him.

Riz flicked it back at her in frustration. 'Kings leave their imprint! What sort of clue be that?'

'The answer's *coin*,' announced Arthmael. 'That was Jatta's clue.'

Jatta rebuked her brother with a scowl. He stared back, confused.

'No, it be not fair!' said Riz, whining like a hatchling. 'I would have got it, but she told her brother the answer. I saw their secret glances. These two be conspiring to win!'

'Majesty, of course it isn't fair we both play,' Jatta said. 'You're right, disqualify me.'

'Jay, what are you—'

Jatta gave her brother another sharp glance. He glared back.

'Yes, cheaters must be punished,' whined Riz. 'Your brother be disqualified, too.'

Jatta took Riz's hand in both of hers. Peering up through her fringe of lashes, she kissed it humbly, though she'd rather have licked poison toads. Arthmael grimaced. Fand watched with careful indifference as Riz's anger dissolved.

Riz patted her cheek in gracious forgiveness. 'I shall permit you both to attempt my riddle, though it be too, too clever for you. Friends, all listen.

'Two kings go to battle. Five times they do, and every time there be a clear victor. Yet both kings win and lose the same number of battles as each other. How can this happen?'

Riz smirked smugly at each guest in turn.

After a minute Fand announced the riddle was too difficult for him. Jatta agreed. Waiting for the others to admit failure, she toyed with the question. Of course it was logically impossible to win two and a half battles. It was equally impossible for each king to win one battle, or two or three. Unless—

'I have it!' exclaimed Arthmael.

Jatta and Fand shot him the same withering look. He stopped, then realisation dawned. 'Uh, I mean ... I'm not good at numbers. Majesty, could you repeat the question?'

'I'm embarrassed to say, but—it's tragically obvious,' said Randall. 'Yes, your riddle's even simpler than Fand's. I'm afraid these kings don't battle each other. They battle *other* kings. I'm correct, aren't I? Yes, I do believe I am. As I've answered two riddles, and as Prince Arthmael's disqualified, I suspect that makes me the winner.'

Randall pocketed the orb and the Ambassador's medallion

of office, then reached for the crown, grinning up at Riz.

The grin froze. Riz's eye was twitching madly. Fury contorted his features.

Randall withdrew his hand hastily, blood draining from his face. 'Of course my purse is yours, Majesty. The crown too, obviously the crown.' He rose, edging around the table to the entrance. 'I'll just take ... the sword.' He snatched it to his chest. 'I beg you forgive me ... abject apologies ... I'll—I'll remove myself from your sight.' He bowed and stumbled from the tent. Arthmael slipped out behind him, chasing the orb in the pocket of another doomed man.

Riz turned to Fand. The commander bowed and strode out.

Jatta edged around the table to slip out too.

'Sweet Jatta,' came a syrupy voice behind her.

She took a shaky breath and turned around slowly. Riz's fury had vanished once again. He was beckoning her, wearing that same twisted smirk that passed for charm. Against all her instincts she returned to his side. He took her hand, stroking it, and a shudder of loathing passed through her. He didn't seem to notice.

'Naughty Jatta, to have cheated at Riddles.'

She forced an apologetic smile.

'I shall forgive you. I be very generous. You think me generous, Jatta?'

She nodded.

'I have a present for you. A lifetime of happiness, this gift. Guess what it be.'

Jatta was through with riddles for now. Nonetheless she forced herself to gaze up into that twisted face with innocent anticipation.

'No, don't give me that sweet Jatta smile. I know you.' He

took the betrothal ring from his pinkie and placed it on her middle finger. It hung there loosely. She stared down at the Dartithan family crest, an Undead face in a full moon, carved in precious jade. Beneath it, his initial. Fresh dread mixed with her loathing.

He lifted her hand to his nasty mouth and kissed it. Her flesh crawled. It was all she could do not to wrench it away. He had her ring on his little finger now, stuck on the first joint.

'Happy?'

She nodded up at him.

'I too, Jatta.'

It was after midnight when Arthmael sneaked back into their tent. Jatta was lying awake in her hammock while Fand snored and Kristith breathed slowly.

'One of the Alteedan thugs has it, I don't know which one,' he whispered.

'The orb?'

He nodded in the dark.

'What about Baron Randall?' she whispered.

'It was sickening. Riz's men woke the Alteedans to offer a bounty: all Randall's possessions to whoever found him. They're animals, Jay. I know you don't like fox hunts, but that's what it was like. Riz's men were the nobles and the Alteedans were the baying hounds. They chased poor Randall through two tents and into the forest. I watched them almost tear him apart.'

Jatta shuddered. 'Is he alive?'

'Till the dragon's next feed.'

CHAPTER TWENTY-ONE

Riz was in love. His conquest of the Alteedan Princess filled him with giddy power, power he hadn't felt since that day shooting slaves from the parapets.

Indeed, his was a triple conquest. In winning the fair Princess's heart, Riz had defeated his rival, Drake, and won a kingdom as well. Riz the Magnificent, the Invincible, the Wise. Riz the great lover.

He summoned Jatta to the royal tent the following dawn. There he showered her with gifts and wooed her over breakfast with stories of his wit and heroism.

Jatta's downturned eyes he took to be shyness. Her questions about his father, and Dartith, and his plans for Alteeda, he saw as evidence of her insatiable thirst for his opinions. And her demure admission that she thought him unnaturally handsome confirmed her good taste.

He told her secrets, too. He whispered of his father's daily portal visits. How he, gallant Riz, risked Brackensith's rage for his darling's sake, how only the portal stood in the way of their true love's union. How he would mastermind the portal's destruction and sever Dartith's link with Alteeda. How Fand nagged him about it daily.

Jatta listened to all this with wide-eyed innocence.

Then the hour of Brackensith's visit arrived. Riz had her escorted from the tent, though afterwards he summoned her and described its success. She begged to catch a glimpse of his father, to wait in hiding next morning. Her reckless hero agreed.

He took Jatta to watch his other great love. They stood hand in hand in the canopy as his dragon was fed last night's guest. Jatta buried her face, sobbing, in his primrose suede waistcoat, and he consoled her tender heart. A king among kings, sharing one of the finest, happiest moments of his life.

Though her tears were real, he would soon discover his beloved was not what she seemed.

CHAPTER TWENTY-TWO

Arthmael was still awake when Jatta crept into their tent that second night.

'How goes young love?' he whispered.

She crawled into bed. 'Please, I'm in no mood for your jokes. I've been walking a dagger's edge all day.'

'Seems *someone's* having second thoughts. Admit it, Jay. He's not the shining prince of your dreams.'

She groaned. 'Creature of my nightmares, more like. But listen. I've found a way to reach Brackensith direct.'

'How's that, little sister?'

'Riz gets a visit every morning through the portal,' she whispered. 'I've convinced him to let me hide and watch.'

'Clever Jay. So Brackensith will sweep you and Riz back to Dartith ...' Any humour drained from his voice. 'And we'll hear nothing of either of you again.'

A heavy silence followed, broken only by Kristith's slow breathing and Fand's snores.

'No, Jay. Not alone. What about our original plan? I can find the ball, I know I can now. Then we can fake our deaths. Please, we work well together. Have you thought how to get past the firewall?'

'I've run out of time.'

'Wolf-moon. That's what's panicking you, isn't it? Has Riz planned some sport for you tomorrow night?'

She nodded in the dark. 'He won't tell me what.' She'd witnessed enough dragon feeds to imagine, though.

'All right, the portal. But I'm coming with you, Jay. I'm hiding too.'

Jatta sighed. She had dreaded this moment, promising herself she wouldn't waver. She would be strong, as he would have been, if it had been his choice to make.

'Art, please, I've thought it through. What if you're missed? What if you're found? I can't afford risk. I can't fail.'

'No,' he whispered fiercely. 'I won't surrender you to that dark place. You won't survive there alone.'

A lump of bittersweet affection formed in her chest. His words were hugs in the night.

'Jay, listen,' his whisper pleaded. 'You'll risk a slow, lonely, miserable suffocation in Dartith . . .'

'Yes.'

'. . . but you won't risk killing here.'

'That's right.' She'd guessed where he was heading. She curled inward, clasping her chest.

'Jay, that's crazy. Riz disposes of these prison scum daily. Why martyr yourself for the sake of—?'

'Don't let me kill! Not like they killed Mother!' Her desperation came out in whispered croaks. Panic clawed at her insides; wolves flashed in the blackness. She wrestled them back. 'I'm telling you I can't cope with tomorrow night.'

There was another long silence. 'All right, Jay.' His voice sounded hoarse and cracked. 'At least let me find your ball. Tonight in the mess tent I overheard something, a couple of thugs bragging they'd scored it.'

'You know I'm going, with or without it?'

'I know. I wish I could do more.'

CHAPTER TWENTY-THREE

She'd missed her chance to tell Arthmael goodbye. When she woke for breakfast he was gone. She vaguely remembered him rustling about in the night, maybe sneaking out for the orb. Her insides ached. She'd sat on her hammock and rehearsed all the embarrassing things she wanted to say, things he'd suffer through and pretend weren't important. He didn't return. She wrote a note. *'Thank you for keeping me alive and sane.'*

The distant crack of axes forced her through the flap to her fate.

She hurried to the royal tent, and her wide-set eyes assumed their innocence. Her small mouth set itself into the vulnerable, shy smile that the mad Prince found so appealing. On this last morning she could afford no upsets.

She paused between the soldiers outside his tent. Inside, music played, and several voices murmured while heavy papers rustled. It reminded her of a drawing workshop.

This didn't bode well for a morning date with Brackensith, she thought uncomfortably.

One Alteedan voice spoke louder than the rest, something about crowns.

'Make it all diamonds, then, you imbecile,' answered the familiar whine. 'It must match our wedding gowns, ice-blue and silver. I be not wearing this broken old thing!'

She slipped inside to see Riz swipe his crown at an Alteedan kneeling before him. The man—weedy, bespectacled, not much older than Steffed—flinched, but took the assault. Riz settled Alteeda's crown back on his head. He was seated on the low table amid a jumble of manuscripts. Wedding plans, illustrations of crowns and processions. Wedding outfits too, the groom's even more extravagant than the bride's. Two Alteedans sketched more designs while soldiers laid out King Elisind's costumes as inspiration. The supper party's musicians played harp, flute and oboe in their corner. Practice had not improved their performance.

Riz looked up at the open flap and squealed in delight. 'Such a treat! The gentle bride herself!' It jarred Jatta's teeth even as her shy smile broadened and she glided to him. He patted his knees but she settled demurely by his side, a defiance that made him pout till she pulled a picture across both their laps. He slithered an arm around her waist.

'See what a procession we be, returning through Adaban's boulevard? This be you, and here be I . . .'

He pointed to the picture: two riders on horseback preceding the dragon's cage. At least she assumed the ridiculously costumed beasts were horses. Each was enshrined inside decorative silver plates, like scales, with a stuffed dragon tail trailing behind. Ribbed silk wings stuck out behind both riders' knees.

'Dragons, see?' he prompted.

'Brilliant. You spoil me, Majesty. Such discerning attention to detail. Such a feel for the theatrical.' Her big, innocent eyes looked adoringly into his. Then those big eyes grew wounded, accusing him through thick lashes. Her chin dropped to her chest and her bottom lip trembled.

158

'I am rebuked! What have I done?' he protested in mock horror.

Her voice was tragic. 'You promised we would spend this morning together, Majesty, just you and me.'

'Oh, that? No, your tender heart must wait, darling. We have much to plan. Kristith be leaving tonight to organise our wedding.' His eyes flicked to the back of the tent. Jatta's followed.

She'd missed him earlier, lolling against a tent pole. Kristith's usual smug grin twitched with humour. Let her flirtations entertain him. Tomorrow would find him languishing with his father in Dartith's dungeons.

She leaned in so close to her betrothed that her breath blew warm in his ear. His own breathing stopped. 'But Majesty,' she whispered, 'you promised you'd show me your father.'

'Be patient, little Jatta,' he whispered. 'Today he came early. Been and gone.' His lips left her ear to kiss her forehead. He didn't notice all pretence drain from her face, the empty devastation left there as he reached for another manuscript.

She hardly heard his words after that. Wolf-moon. Too late for escape, no place to run. What hope remained for her soul's salvation, now that her wolf was in this monster's custody? All she loathed and feared was even now crouching inside her, tensing for the setting sun. She reached for the orb. Nothing. 'Help me, Dragongirl,' her heart pleaded. 'I'm not asking for a cure, I know that's too much. Just help me, somehow, just—'

Riz's fingers around her waist pinched her ribs sharply. 'Be you bored?' His voice was suddenly malicious. She tensed and sucked in a breath, then focused in surprise on his irate face.

'My efforts be entirely on your behalf, Jatta,' he snapped.

Stupid girl. She needed her wits now more than ever. Had

he just asked her something? Her eyes dropped to the menu in her lap. She swallowed hard, forcing back the fear.

When she looked back at him her expression was all puppy-dog remorse. 'Was I daydreaming, Majesty? How remiss, I'm half asleep ... my constitution is so delicate ...' She pressed a hand to her breast with a fluttery sigh. 'I need rest tonight.'

'Not tonight.'

'Oh, but mightn't we put off the entertainment, just till tomorrow?' Her liquid eyes pleaded. 'Please, please, might I have something to help me sleep? Would my King be so very peeved?'

'Indeed I would. What shall *I* do tonight? Without you I be bored.'

'Oh ...' As her charade faltered, her pretty face fell. 'Would you at least grant me one tiny favour? Tonight, just tonight, don't feed me what you ... what you feed the dragon. Feed me whatever else you want, anything from the jungle, anything ...' Her voice trailed away.

'Enough,' he growled. 'Now I be the one growing tired.'

He was losing patience. He'd give her nothing, she knew that. She lost all control. 'Please, I beg you!' She slid off the table onto the floor, knowing it would not work even as her plea tumbled out. 'Don't make me eat! Not people! I can't stand what I am, what I do. Don't blacken my soul!'

Wrong. Stupid. Destructive move.

His eyes narrowed. One twitched. Hadn't he been subjected to hysterical grovelling all his vicious life? Where was the shy naivety that had kept her in favour, and her brother out of the dragon's jaws?

Under his seething gaze she shakily got off her knees and

wiped her eyes. As she accepted the inevitable, a measure of self-control returned. She stroked his hand, which had formed a tight fist on his knee, tracing patterns across his knuckles till it relaxed. She forced a trembling, pretty smile from under her wet lashes.

The twitching stopped.

She took in a long, hopeless breath and let it out in a gust. 'I'm sorry, Majesty. I don't really mind. It's just ... I'm ... deadly tired.' Her words were so drained and flat they sounded true.

'You be a selfish little thing, Jatta,' he said, churlish. 'I have needs, too. Not everything be about you.'

She mechanically reached for a diagram—was it Adaban's banquet hall?—and laid it across her betrothed's lap, settling at his feet and asking him, please, to unfold his grand vision for their seating plan. He seemed satisfied to forgive her.

She played her part without conviction. Perhaps he believed her uninspired questions and subdued admiration were indeed due to exhaustion. She laboured through menus and festivities with only one comfort: numbers. Her safe delivery to Dartith would save more lives than the one—or several—she would end tonight. That was what tonight was about. Not brutalised, half-eaten bodies, but numbers.

It numbed her heart.

Jatta's withdrawal didn't seem to bother her betrothed. As the afternoon wore on he became increasingly buoyant. Jatta noticed nothing. When another pair of hands eased the guest list she'd been cradling from her lap she gazed up, dully annoyed to see Kristith above her. Smiling again. Didn't that boy have a second expression, she wondered.

Day was fading. Suddenly the reality of this surreal nightmare pressed in on her, immediate and deadly. Today had been long and painful, but she'd never willed it to end. Let her stay in this frightened moment forever.

Riz was giggling, a sound no longer absurd but sinister. He was above her, jittery with anticipation. He reached down both hands, dragged her to stand. Her legs were weak. Boneless. She'd fall if he released his grip.

'Finally. She be awake,' he said. 'A game, Jatta! Do you fancy a little game?'

She nodded. Her throat had gone dry.

'Here be how we play. You choose someone, any man here.'

'Wh—who? Why?' she croaked. Shouldn't she be leaving for her cage? How much time had she left?

Shaking her hands free, he swept to the corner where his musicians played. Her knees buckled. Strong hands gripped her elbows from behind, steadying her. She glanced up, confused, to find Kristith's grin.

'Choose now. *Why* does not matter.' Riz almost sang the words, his spirits were so high. 'That be the beauty of this game. Why? Because you like his baby-face . . .' Riz pinched the young harpist's cheek. 'Because he be useful . . .' he paraded past his soldiers, brushing their coats with an expansive sweep of his arm.

'Because now he be not.' He pranced to pat under the weedy jewel-designer's chin.

They were wasting time, weren't they? She needed to be locked up. Now. Jatta blinked around at the men. Some shrank back, trying to blend into the tent wall. Others stared back like nervous sheep. The harpist played several suspect notes in a row.

'Who? *Who*, Jatta?' Riz was losing patience.

Her face tilted back to Kristith's smile. 'Um, I choose Kristith.'

Kristith's eyes tensed slightly.

Riz spluttered, then twittered. He clutched at his mouth, giggling like the entire gaggle of her tapestry class. Jatta tried to look suitably amused. The tent waited tensely.

Riz wiped his eyes, sniffling. 'Not Kristith, I cannot give you Kristith. Fand be most cranky with me if I do.'

Slow realisation spread. She was choosing supper. No, no. Her eyes brimmed. Her legs were water too. She sagged back into Kristith's chest.

Kristith whispered into her hair. 'Choose now, or tonight you be sampling this entire tent.'

The thrumming in her ear made it hard to hear. Cloth stuffing had replaced her brain. She stared through tears at the tent pole, unwilling to meet any eyes.

Riz made an impatient hiss.

'Just point,' pleaded Kristith.

She couldn't.

Her slack hand rose. Strange ... she wasn't aware she'd made a decision. She couldn't have, for her arm was as watery as her legs. It was Kristith's firm hand that guided her elbow. She did not resist. Numbers. She was trading one life, one future, one family's suffering for several. Reluctantly she dragged her eyes to witness whose death warrant she and her puppet master had signed.

His face swam in her tears. The jewel designer, seeming more puny than before. Their eyes met. He looked down in misery, she in shame.

'That be cheating,' whined Riz. 'Kristith helped you. Choose another, choose more.'

A familiar voice was at the tent flap. Fand was there, unhappy about something. He strode to Riz and she caught snatches of his words. 'Pointless pomp ... destroy portal first ... if Brackensith discovers ...'

Riz's good mood had evaporated again; he ordered everyone out. For once he seemed to be defending himself. Kristith swept up the wedding plans and pulled Jatta past, grinning at his discomfort.

It was happening now. Her nightmare. The designer was being dragged along the trail behind her and she could hear him pleading that he'd done nothing wrong ... he wasn't meaty enough ... he had wonderful sons. He started sobbing as they drew close to the cage. She called to Dragongirl, to her orb. She tried to shut it all out, imagining dragons flitting through blue ...

But real dragons were nothing like fantasy. They tore at their victims like wolves ... there was no escaping.

A wolf vision flashed in her mind. She was teetering on a canyon's ledge, dirt crumbling beneath her toes, trying to shuffle back into an army of Rizes. *It's not my fault*, she told them, knowing it was, even as the ground dissolved under her soles. She fell. The cliff face was a streaky blur. Her scream twisted to an unearthly howl. It streamed up and away, never reaching her ears. She didn't hear the thud.

She woke inside darkness, inside a heavy wet mass pressing on her chest so she could hardly breathe. That confused her. Was she still locked in her vision? Or had she woken early in the night? Then she realised she was buried. Alive. She panicked, she clawed to be free. The mass didn't crumble like dirt; bits lodged under her nails, too soft for coffin wood. It flopped and rolled, and dripped on her face like warm, sticky rain.

Her victims.

Blank terror engulfed her. They were too heavy, too many. She'd have given her soul to be dragged out from under, but it was worthless now.

'Jay! Jay, are you all right?'

The familiar voice jolted Jatta out of her waking nightmare, though her mind couldn't move past its dread. Blank-faced, she hardly registered the fading daylight, or Kristith and the others collected around the chasm.

'Jay! Say something, will you!'

Not a chasm but a deep animal pit. Her pit.

'Jay!'

And Arthmael calling up from inside.

No! Too much!

Suddenly she had energy. She struggled to wriggle free, to run from her brother. Kristith pinned her to his chest with one arm. She clawed his fingers and bit his chin.

'Ow!' he growled.

'Jay, listen! Calm down, they're letting us up!'

She flopped in Kristith's arm. Tears welled again, grateful tears for one small mercy. 'Unhand me, I'll stay,' she pleaded.

Kristith released his hold and walked away. She dropped to kneel over the edge, blinking tears to see clearly. Arthmael was with other Alteedans, all muddy from digging, being hauled up in a basket like the one at the hide. She flung her arms around him before he'd climbed out. He dragged her back from the edge, and the gathering crowd of Dartithan spectators.

'Listen, Jay, we don't have much time,' he whispered, pulling a mug from inside his tunic and thrusting it into her hand. 'They caught me rummaging through tents before dawn, so no orb—yet. I found this, though. It's what they put on arrows.'

'Poison. For me?'

'Glory, no. Sleeping paste, you twit. It's for the dragon, but it should work. I'm not sure how much to use, though.'

She started sobbing gratefully again.

He rubbed her shoulders. 'Shush, shush, they might hear.'

Sniffling, she dug her fingers into the mug, withdrawing a wad of blue paste.

'Lord, Jay. Not that much.'

'You said you don't know.'

'Yes, but there are worse things than waking up early.'

'No there aren't!' Panic, so close to the surface, welled again. 'That stuff's dangerous. I do need you to wake up . . . eventually.'

'I'll take that chance.'

'Don't be absurd.' His face soured. He scanned the pit's assembly with disdain. 'What's a few thugs, thieves and embezzlers, eh? Glory, these lot are mostly murderers and Dartithans.'

'They're people!' She glared at him, the blue wad poised at her tiny chin. Her lips parted.

'I said no!' He seized her fingers, wiping two-thirds onto his muddy jacket. He tossed away the mug. 'Lord, don't you *want* to save Alteeda from Riz? Just don't fret about it, all right? It's not as if you'll remember.'

But she'd know. Exhausted, defeated, she glanced into the pit. Numbers, that was what mattered. The last of the diggers were up, and the puny jeweller was on his way down. Tears for his boys dripped. Her tongue poked at the paste.

There was a sudden *whoosh*, then cold steel pressed on her tongue. She flinched back.

The sword blade belonged to Kristith. He stood grinning at her shock. Arthmael stiffened beside her.

How long had this strange Dartithan been eavesdropping? Had he heard them talk of saving Alteeda from Riz?

She heard Riz now, whining about Fand as he came down the track. His mood was not good. If Kristith told, Arthmael would be thrown back into the pit. Without doubt.

She needed an ally.

'Kristith.' She paused to honour him with a delicate, if teary, smile. 'May I count on your . . . *discretion*? When I am Crown Princess of all Dartith I will remember my friends.'

He chuckled. 'Crown Princess? Of all Dartith? Then you do intend surviving this night?'

What was this riddle? She, alone in Goy-an Canyon, was assured of surviving wolf-moon. Her smile didn't waver as she waited for him to explain.

'Which be your aim? Sleep—or suicide?' His eyes flicked to the paste on her fingers, then returned to her charming but uncomprehending face.

Arthmael grunted. 'Sleep, *obviously*.' He turned to Jatta. 'Jay, I think he actually wants to help.'

Kristith bowed to them both. His sword rapped like a schoolmaster's cane on her palm till she opened it out flat. Expertly the blade scraped along her hand, then flicked the excess paste to the dirt. He scraped most of the blue from between her fingers. Finally he tilted her palm left, then right, gauging his dosage.

'Size?' he asked.

'Pardon?'

'Brown bear? Black bear? Sloth bear?'

'She's huge, terrifying,' answered Arthmael. 'Bigger than a polar bear.'

Kristith chuckled softly, as if Arthmael was a proud parent exaggerating his daughter's first steps. Nonetheless, he scraped a smidgeon back on.

Riz had entered the clearing.

'Jatta!' he called, short-tempered. 'My darling, should you not be down your pit?'

She licked at her fingers.

'We're grateful,' whispered Arthmael. 'Why, though?'

For a moment Kristith's smile drained away. 'Not all Dartithans be as vicious as Riz,' he said, then left.

If her soul hadn't been at stake Jatta probably wouldn't have finished licking her fingers. They tasted bitter as poison, which wasn't surprising. As it was, she didn't get as far as sampling the streak down her thumb. The dizziness hit within heartbeats. Her stomach heaved. She wobbled and toppled into her brother. After that she remembered very little, except the world—ground, faces, sky—pitching wildly, and a vague triumph as Riz wailed in horror.

CHAPTER TWENTY-FOUR

'Stop shaking her, she's not a salt-cellar!' shouted Arthmael.

He was not heard over Riz's wails. But eventually Riz stopped shaking the limp Princess and, with a strange tenderness, pressed her against his heaving chest. The wailing degenerated into a series of self-pitying whimpers. 'My darling, my darling, don't leave me, my darling.'

Arthmael grimaced at the faux tragedy. Riz's pain might even have been affecting if he'd had so much as a rudimentary interest in the girl he cradled, in anybody except himself. What did disturb Arthmael was seeing his sister manhandled.

'Majesty, she's not dead,' he said with thinly disguised impatience.

Riz registered Arthmael for the first time. He stared, measuring the Alteedan's expression, then sniffled. 'What have you done to my darling?' he whined.

'Nothing. She swooned. Girls are tender and fragile creatures. They do that.'

Arthmael studied her sleeping pixie face, its cheek crushed against Riz's shoulder, and he smiled ruefully. There was immense power latent in this frail girl.

As if to demonstrate this, her gown rippled. It grew fine as organza, then settled and was absorbed into her skin. Its jewels and velvet painted her figure but hid nothing.

It was happening again.

Her delicate chin was distorting. It gouged Riz's collarbone till he squealed. He dropped his bride as he leapt back. She thudded to the ground, sprouting black tufts, already his size and expanding. Muscle and shards of armour did frenzied battle, bubbling her pelt.

Riz squealed more, but the tone had changed. He giggled too, in nervous delight. His hands clutched his wide open mouth as he crept forward. 'Monstrous ... impossible,' he breathed.

Arthmael stared too. She lay on her back with wolf legs akimbo. On her massive barrel chest, black fur was matted and sparse, like tufts had been torn out. The last of her transformations was happening. Obsidian teeth, too large for her terrible snout, were growing, jutting out at odd angles. She was ferociously ugly, even in sleep, but Arthmael hardly registered that. What he saw was his sister, and what he felt, now that she wasn't trying to crush his head or disembowel him, was the painful urge to protect her. He grunted, bemused. She'd hardly need his protection from physical harm. Her armour did that. But from herself.

Arthmael tore his focus from Jatta. Soldiers pressed forward warily, and he guessed now why Kristith had doubted him. His sister's size was a novelty for Dartithans, too.

One Dartithan alone was showing presence of mind. Fand's fury could be heard from the trail. 'What mean you, she be not in the pit? Use the basket, man!'

Soldiers sprang to action. It took twenty men to haul Jatta to their shoulders from the dirt. Arthmael alone supported her head. His companions were nervous, and that was hardly helped by Riz, who took command of one of Jatta's leaden hands and used it to play-claw at their faces. Arthmael wished his sister would rouse just enough to swipe him once. They poured her inside the basket. Splits opened and it tipped dangerously to the side. The ropes groaned, as did the labouring men while they lowered Riz's prize. Then, halfway down, something ripped. Jatta dropped out the bottom and fell a full storey, landing on her back with a thud. The jewel designer scrambled to the pit's far corner. Arthmael stood sentry above.

The forest surrounding their clearing had grown shadowy. The moon rose white and two heraldic stars already shone their cool blue. Soldiers lit yellow torches. Riz waited with legs dangling over the pit, aggravating Arthmael again. The mad Prince was staving off boredom by dropping pebbles onto his bride, complaining that she should have revived by now. Arthmael gritted his teeth and entertained himself by imagining Riz being helped over the edge. Supper came, spicy minced lizard or something, in pancakes. Arthmael scoffed down three helpings, watching Riz winding himself up. This, Arthmael thought, might not end well.

For once he was pleased to be wrong. Riz merely made soldiers leap across the pit till two fell in, scrabbling at the wall on their way down. After that he got up, whining, and went to bed.

Arthmael stayed. He'd expected the two soldiers to be helped back up, but nobody moved. Only the little Alteedan called to be let out. Arthmael settled, ankles crossed, to watch the two Dartithans dig a tunnel through the soft dirt. Its purpose confounded him till sometime before dawn they judged it deep enough and crawled inside, dragging dirt to block the entrance. Apparently they didn't share his confidence in Jatta's sleeping through. After that he got up, stretched, and dusted dirt crusts from his trousers.

'See you, Jay,' he whispered to the scruffy black mass, watching its chest rise and fall, then sauntered off to the Alteedans' tents in search of her orb.

His footfalls had barely grown quiet before his sister stirred.

CHAPTER TWENTY-FIVE

Jatta's wolf was in a foul temper. Her head was groggy, stupid with sleep and too heavy to lift. It ached with too many sounds and smells, with the taste of mud and something bitter, and she still hadn't opened her eyes.

The sounds were an aggravation, fresh meat clamouring and calling above. Squealing, too. Her chest heaved a great breath to sample the smells. Heavy-lidded eyes opened. The clamouring above rose to a crescendo.

She was lying under a slate pre-dawn sky, at the bottom of an earth shaft rimmed by fires. Rimmed by faces, too. Excited faces—but that would change soon. So many scents. Her head rolled to look around. One meat was pressed into the corner a mere lunge away. Two others cowered, buried in dirt. All three smelled of panic. Above, far beyond, she caught the scents of a hundred more. She staggered to her feet and the meat fell silent. Her nostrils flared with two delicious scents. One she remembered from before, the meat that had escaped twice, the almost irresistible scent that aroused something unfamiliar, something disturbing. His scent was fading now, moving away, mingling with a hundred more. The other had just approached the shaft. He smelled of spice. Her snout jerked up and found him, legs dangling, above. He squealed.

That woke her primal hate. Jatta's hair bristled till she

seemed impossibly big. She would make him squeal differently. She coiled her massive haunches and launched.

It was more of a drunken lurch. She fell back, floppy-legged. In frustration she jumped again, pathetically colliding with the wall. Her claws dug deep trails as she slid back to the mud. Frustration only served to clear her drugged veins, to feed her fury. She shook her head wildly to clear it. She leapt high, and clawed at his dangling heels.

Others dragged the squealer up out of reach and she howled her frustration. Her haunting note modulated up and down for a dozen heartbeats before fading to the grey sky. The squealer was clapping his puny, bird-boned hands. He dropped pebbles.

She would crush his eggshell head. She unravelled in frenzied flipping and twisting. Landing on meat, she launched off it. She gouged out walls. His delight only frustrated her more. Come closer, she snarled. Peer over the edge and let my jaws tear out your feeble chest. And he giggled. The soldiers stood rigid and the forest hushed.

As if answering her dare, the squealer shuffled forward, dragging something. Other meat, pleading. Baby-faced, clinging.

Jatta dropped to the mud. Her moment had come. With self-control that was the limit of a young wolf's endurance, she waited. Both were at the lip now. Struggling. Giggling. Her haunches springing slightly, she readied herself.

He bit at the clinger's arm. A mistake.

As the clinger fell, she uncoiled. She was in flight, passing him halfway. Earth streaked by till the squealer's white chicken legs filled her sight. She stretched up to grab.

One clawed hand grabbed air.

One closed on legging. Yanked. Silk ripped. She snarled, falling back empty-handed.

Above her the squealer toppled. Her snarl turned to victory as they plummeted one above the other, flailing in a wild vertical dance. She thudded like a sack of bolts, armour plates scraping. The squealer landed on top, rolled off. Then arrows hailed.

They were hailstone stings, piercing her pelt. She sat up, shook them out. Some tips stuck out, like hedgehog quills. She grabbed handfuls, plucked them.

Then the fires dropped. Her enemies.

They blazed down from a pale grey sky. Her ear was alight. She bounded to her feet, snarling and belting at her ear. She battled the fires, leapt at them. Bashed them. Let them know how ferocious she was.

They lay vanquished in the mud, sizzling suns under a morning sky. All here at her feet.

The squealer, too.

He had two in each puny hand, pathetically poking at air from his corner. His ugly slit-mouthed face was distorted with fear. The scent filled her lungs and her blood-lust surged. She leapt, swiping all four from his grip with the back of her arm. He wasn't squealing now, just pup-whimpering, so she jerked him up by his leg and rattled him upside down. There, that had him squealing, just as she imagined he should. Now she would rip off each spider limb. She wrapped claws around a second leg and pulled.

Agony. The attack came from behind. Had her spine split open? She yelped as her legs quivered. They crumpled, useless, and Jatta fell to her haunches. Her prize swung. She twisted around, blindly seeking her tormentor. She snapped in a frenzy. She dragged useless legs. Her prize dropped, crawled away. She didn't care anymore. Still the invisible thing was there, murdering her, making her chest shudder, sapping the strength from her arms. She fell backwards, mud splattering into her snout, and snapped her last. Her tongue lolled. Her eyes glowered, furious. Her body shrank, lashed by armour that splintered under her pelt.

The squealer sidled, crab-like, from his corner. He crouched, hugging his chicken knees. He insolently poked at her wrist's pelt as it softened to turquoise brocaded skin. He stroked the organza film as it thickened to green velvet.

As her eyes closed, Jatta's last furious, impotent urge was to scrape that pasty, awed face from its skull.

Jatta let the wolf's memory fade. She didn't fear it like before, knowing in a few heartbeats it would be gone. One breath. Two breaths. On the third breath she opened her eyes.

She lay looking at early morning sky from the base of a shaft . . . her animal pit. Dartithans peered curiously over the edge. Curious, not vomiting or horrified. That, she assured herself, was a promising start. She wanted to vomit herself. She counted again, letting the sleeping paste nausea roll up from her stomach. She was mucky and wet and famished. And sore. That didn't matter.

She gritted her teeth and tensed to turn her head to the left. No blood. No body parts. That was wonderful. Arrows wounded the mud, and torches burned in it. Arrows stuck out of her singed skirts, too, and holes riddled her bodice. Two soldiers were crawling on elbows out from the wall. Peculiar. She'd work that puzzle out later. She could scarcely believe it, but *two* Alteedans—yes, the harpist and the jewel designer— were mostly intact in the corner. A small miracle. She'd slept through the night.

Some insect or creature was nipping her right hand. Instinctively she flinched away; she whipped her head to the aggravation.

Bad move. The insect was none other than her betrothed. His lips pursed petulantly at this rejection. He dragged her hand back and pinched harder as payback. She adopted a wounded innocence of her own.

'Majesty, how do I deserve these hurts?'

'Oh, *now* she be all virtue. After she dragged me over the edge, and bruised me, and slashed at me.'

'Pardon?'

'And almost murdered me.'

Her expression froze in place, seeing him for the first time dishevelled and caked in mud, his dressing gown singed, his leggings bloodied tatters. Yet miraculously, unfathomably alive.

'Bad, bad Jatta,' he whined. 'Perhaps I shall punish you. Perhaps keep you down here till tonight.'

Please, no. Brackensith. Her wolf. Her stomach plunged painfully.

She could rescue this. Jatta's tangled lashes swept shyly, remorsefully down. Then, after a suitable pause, her liquid eyes searched tentatively for his. Their tender pleading melted his nasty gaze. 'Majesty, you mistake my wolf's attentions. There could be no greater expression of my love.'

'To single me out for your supper?' He scoffed, then scowled down, flattered despite himself, digging his fingers through the mud.

'You know it is,' she whispered. 'Doesn't a wolf track down those she loves? Doesn't she lust for their blood?'

'You didn't attack your *brother*.'

That was one small mercy.

'Because it's you who fills my thoughts, Majesty. I *have* attacked him, though. Oh, I can't bear to think about it . . .' A delicate quaver invaded her voice. 'One slash, one hundred and seventy-four stitches.'

'So many?' Riz scowled down at the mud.

'Yes, the first time. But, oh, two wolf-moons later . . .' She left the sentence hanging, watching his macabre curiosity do battle with his rejected heart. For a long time he wavered, still concentrating on the mud. Finally he spoke.

'Two wolf-moons later?'

'Two wolf-moons later I tore through a bolted door for him. My hind claws plucked him mid-flight. I—' She debated whether tears were too hammy. No, not for this audience. One teardrop trickled to tremble on her lip.

'Mid-flight? You flew?' Reluctantly, Riz at last lifted his eyes to her face.

'Almost. Oh, Majesty, to think I might have hurt *you*. I tremble, just imagining . . .'

'No trembling! No more swooning!'

Swooning? His fervency surprised—and inspired—her. She raised one arm to her brow, dangerously close to swooning, while her lashes fluttered. 'I'm too weak to talk. Majesty, I'm faint with hunger.'

'Then eat.' His eyes flitted over her body. 'You be scrawny from a wolf-moon without meat.'

'Yes, Majesty. Breakfast. With you?'

He nodded. 'In the hide. And you shall tell me every detail.'

'Oh, let me change gowns first. Later, Majesty, while we wait for your father.'

He nodded assent.

'Yes—but oh, no, it is too, too brutal!'

'Nothing be too brutal,' he urged tenderly.

CHAPTER TWENTY-SIX

Arthmael's task was daunting.

In the pre-dawn he sneaked into the camp site. Seven tents, not counting the mess tent, slept a hundred men; yesterday he'd searched little more than the stores. He had no idea which tent held the orb's new owners, although one man, he remembered distinctly, had lost an arm.

Body odours flooded his nostrils as he slipped through the first flap. He held a candle to each sleeping face, barely daring to breathe. It was a pity, he thought, gently prodding their blankets for missing limbs, that he'd paid such avid attention to the man's deformity and not to his features.

The second and third tents slept Dartithans. In the fourth he didn't find the man. He did however find weapons. Many criminals slept with daggers in their hands. A few had let theirs slip and he took one for his own belt. Arthmael also recognised the Ambassador's amethyst medallion, hanging from its bloodied ribbon around one rogue's neck, a trophy that so far had brought ill fortune to three men. He sliced its ribbon and pocketed it, hoping it might serve as a bargaining tool.

In the fifth tent men were rousing with the dawn, washing in basins and stepping into their work tunics. He wandered around casually, trying to look like he belonged, but even those who'd not seen him around the camp site eyed him, with his noble bearing, suspiciously.

In the sixth tent men were already filing out for their camp site ration of porridge. He began to fear he had missed the one-armed thug. After only a brief investigation, he hurried toward the final tent.

Most of its men had already left but, even from outside, Arthmael spied something that made his heart beat fast. He'd seen white sparks.

Four men were clustered inside with their backs to him in what looked like a game of darts. The fifth, a thick-set thug, sat at a table pummelling Jatta's orb. Arthmael took a deep breath and entered, attempting a murderer's swagger.

'Well, well! If it ain't a pretty, poncing dandy come to join us,' sneered the thug.

Arthmael quickly dropped the pretence. He held out the Ambassador's medallion. 'Good day, man. Let me swap my booty for that starry ball.'

'Lad, you can keep the ball and bauble both, and all these, besides.' The thug jerked his head at the table. There lay Arthmael's sword, a nobleman's watch, a silver belt and Randall's own bloodied cloak. 'That is, if you can throw straight.'

The other criminals had stopped their game to stare. He saw now that it was not darts but daggers that they hurled at a tent pole. Three knives already stuck out of the wood, just below a white chalk cross.

'All right,' said Arthmael.

'Oi, lad!' shouted a man with one arm.

Arthmael recognised his face immediately.

'You haven't asked what prize you gets for losing,' smirked One-arm. The others laughed.

'Don't nobody tell him, neither,' said the thug, with a sly wink. 'Might spoil his aim, if he sweats over that.'

One-arm walked up to a line drawn in the dirt. He took aim, and the knife *whooshed* through the air, flipping like an acrobat. It thudded inside the white cross.

'Well thrown,' said the thug.

It was Arthmael's turn next. He was no stranger to this game, but he hadn't played it since he was a boy. Arthmael held the dagger tip between thumb and fingers, poised above his head. He glanced at the others, recognising a stooped old man wiping sweaty hands. He guessed it was this old barber who'd so far thrown poorest—and wondered what was at stake, besides these six stolen treasures. He drove the thought from his mind, imagining he was twelve again, and his fingers remembered too. With feet apart he began to sway forward and back, his dagger also picking up the rhythm. He flicked, and it flipped somersaults through the air. It stuck, *thump*, in the cross centre.

One-arm strode to the pole. 'Mine's closer!' he said triumphantly.

'No. The lad's is dead centre,' said another.

The old barber said nothing. He looked sickly pale.

The thug placed his orb on the table. He stood at the line, casually shuffling one foot across it and, without looking down, redrew it closer. Those who noticed said nothing. He kissed his blade, spread his feet and confidently took aim. But the knife flipped high. It hit hilt first, clanked down onto Arthmael's, and landed in the dirt.

Arthmael's dagger wobbled loosely, then dropped.

'Oi! I won!' whooped One-arm, bounding to the table.

'Who's lost?' stammered the barber.

The thug was back at the pole, nudging Arthmael's dagger through the dirt past his own. He looked up to wink at the others. 'The lad lost. His were the furthest.' They went silent.

One-arm grinned. 'Bad luck, lad. We hopes your running skills is better than your dagger skills.'

'Pardon?' said Arthmael.

'You lost, lad,' said the thug. 'You just volunteered as next dragon fodder.'

'What? But mine was closest! You all saw that!'

'It ain't now,' said the thug. The others laughed. Only the barber was silent. 'Now say your prayers, 'cause King Riz is itching for another show.'

Arthmael spun around, blood thundering through his brain. Two men blocked his exit.

'The lad needs a guard of honour!' The thug prised knives from the pole. Arthmael's dagger *whooshed* across the tent.

Arthmael leapt onto the table. He kicked a knife as it was tossed toward One-arm. It thudded into the treasures at his feet. He snatched it up. Snatched his sword, too, into his left hand. He scanned the room, every muscle tense. All had knives. He'd never fought, not for real. Only in the forest. Only Jatta's wolf. Never hurt a man.

Clutching the orb, Arthmael ran on shaky legs for the royal tent, hoping desperately he wasn't too late. Four soldiers blocked his entrance. 'Let me in! I must see the Princess!' he demanded.

'You shall wait, Highness,' came the flat reply.

'This is urgent! She'll want to see me.'

'It be the *King's* wants that matter. Come back later.'

'When?'

'Later.' The four Dartithans stared ahead, signalling an end to argument. Arthmael's frustration boiled over.

'Jay! Jay!' he yelled. There was no answer.

'Jay!' He rushed for the flap, ducking between their bodies. They spun around, jumping on him, knocking the breath from his lungs. He was dragged wheezing back along the ground. One soldier gave him a swift kick. 'Highness or not, you shall wait!'

Arthmael got unsteadily to his feet and staggered back into the jungle. When he was no longer in sight he slipped under cover to the back of the tent. He listened at the silk for Jatta's voice. The long silence disturbed him as he waited, imagining all manner of horrors. Finally he could wait no longer. With his dagger he ripped a long gash in the tent and stepped through.

It was empty.

The soldiers rushed in, swords drawn.

'Where's Jay?' he said.

Commander Fand knelt to examine the rip, his other hand absentmindedly massaging the orb. Arthmael stood flanked by soldiers. His sword and dagger lay bloodied on the low table.

'King Riz will not be happy with your handiwork, Highness. We who understand the King endeavour to keep him happy.'

'Where's my sister?'

Fand grunted. 'Be *that* your worry? Your sister be break-fasting in the hide.'

'Give me back that ball.'

'What be its secret?' Fand rose to face Arthmael, inscrutable as always.

Arthmael stared back defiantly.

Fand grunted again. He turned the orb in his hand,

massaging still, watching its stars. He closed his eyes and green sparks shot out through his fingers before showering to the ground. The soldiers gasped. Arthmael, too.

'It be a magic toy, right?'

Arthmael nodded warily. Here stood another like Jatta and the dwarf, or at least with a germ of their imagination.

'*Wrong.* It be more. What be its powers?'

'It's just what you see. Your fireworks are nothing, an illusion, not warm or real.'

'How came you by this sword and dagger? Understand you be forbidden arms.'

'I won—' But Arthmael had suddenly gone white, a nightmare flashing through his mind. That sickening *squelch*—that moment when he'd sliced into One-arm's heart.

Fand examined him curiously, his gaze lingering on Arthmael's blood-drenched sleeve. 'You won them? From Alteedans?'

Arthmael wrestled with the vision and his legs trembled again.

'Be you unwell?' said Fand.

It was all he could do to nod.

Fand sighed. 'Highness, you leave me no option. You be under house arrest.'

The soldiers each took an arm. Fand tossed them the orb.

'The ball! Please, Fand, give her the ball.'

'I think not,' said the commander. He turned to another soldier. 'Hurry, mend this rip before King Riz returns.'

Jatta's nerves were playing perverse tricks on her stomach. She could keep nothing down. Finally, pressing her forehead against the hide's railing, squeezing her eyes shut against this morning's slaughter, she forced both nausea and hunger into the deep recesses of her mind. Brackensith, she promised herself, would feed her a full lunch in Dartith.

CHAPTER TWENTY-SEVEN

The commander was waiting outside the tent when Jatta and Riz returned from breakfast.

'Has Arthmael been here?' she asked.

'Been and gone, Highness.'

'Did he leave me anything?'

'Don't dawdle, Jatta!' Riz pulled her playfully through the flap, dropping it closed behind him. 'Now, where shall I hide you?' He swept around the room, his coronation cape trailing theatrically behind. 'Under here?' He crouched beside the low table. 'No? Behind these?' He batted his lashes coyly at her through the gauze drapes. 'No? Then in here?' He lifted the lid of a chest, stuffed with rich clothes. He giggled, delighted at his game.

Jatta looked around. There really was nowhere to hide. She moved close to Riz, reaching up to unclasp the cape at his neck. He looked down at her, his breath on her upturned face. She shuddered.

'You be trembling, Jatta.'

She forced a modest smile and took the cape from his shoulders. 'Let me hide under this.'

'Anything to please you. It be time now. Lie still.'

Jatta crouched and he flung his cape over her. She waited, peeking out from under its fur trim. From behind, Riz seemed almost as nervous as she was. He fussed, adjusting his crown, assuming one regal pose then another, before settling on feet planted apart, one hand confidently behind his back, the other thoughtfully stroking his chin.

The air between him and the tent shimmered, like transparent grains catching sunlight. She stared, mesmerised, as grains merged into a sparkling arch.

It began to buzz. Jatta felt it vibrating through her chest. Blue sparks flickered, radiating from a human form now growing distinct. The arch hardened, its black granite carved with ancient symbols, and its passenger stepped out.

Like his son, Brackensith's face was less flat, a blend of races with a long Sludinian nose and pale grey southern eyes. The overall effect was striking.

'Remove that ludicrous crown,' he demanded of the stiffly posed Riz.

Riz hurriedly dragged it off, holding it in clammy fingers by his side.

'Father, all goes splendidly. Tomorrow we drug the dragon. In six days we shall parade it through the capital, that all may fear and revere your name.'

'Six days! Did I not tell you to abandon this charade? Where be Drake's Jatta?'

'Father, this expedition be mounted for your greater glory.'

'Utter dragonrot. It be to satisfy your perverse lust for carnage. I give you a simple task and you turn it into a bloodsport. How can you find Jatta from here? How can Fand run Alteeda from here?'

Riz's hand behind his back started twitching nervously. 'The palace be safe! I have left my Undead and four hundred men at Adaban.'

Hardly daring to breathe, her back wet with sweat under the heavy cape, Jatta waited for her moment. But Brackensith's words were making little sense, snagged in the tangle of regrets in her head. No goodbye for her brother. No rehearsed speech for the Dark King. No hope of return, with the orb still lost.

Angrily she dragged her mind back to the moment. Brackensith was speaking.

'And who be out searching for Jatta?'

'I have only one thousand men, Father. Bring me more. Bring me my wolves. Bring me an army, that I may subdue these infidels and fetch your prize.'

'You think me a fool, Riz.'

'But Father, you promised me wolves!'

'Haven't I given you Undead and blast rods? I shall bring you wolves when I be satisfied with your progress.'

Her heart pounding, Jatta seized the moment. She scrambled up, tangled in cape, struggling to drag it off. 'King Brackensith! I'm Ja—'

Riz's crown thudded to the dirt. Like a hound on a hare, he was upon her. In the next moment he had the cape back over her head and his hand clenched on her mouth.

'I'm Jatta! Jatta!' she tried to scream. But only muffled groans escaped. His fingers crushed her nose too. She couldn't thrash, couldn't scream, could hardly breathe. So she bit. She had his finger, the velvet too, and ground both mercilessly. At first he held fast.

'Riz!' thundered Brackensith. 'Who be that?'

She frayed a fabric hole.

'Argh!'

His hand was gone. She gasped a breath. 'I'm J—' she

screamed before he stuffed velvet back into her mouth. She was gagging as his fingers closed over. Then it got worse. She couldn't breathe at all.

'Jatta's . . . little chambermaid, Father.' Riz's voice trembled. His body trembled too, where he clamped her to his chest. 'Father, just a wench from the palace I took a fancy to.'

'You useless rake! You squander time on dragons and wenches while my prize wanders free!' Without warning he struck his son violently. Riz reeled back, dragging Jatta with him. She struggled, sucking urgently at cloth.

'Riz, you will return to Adaban with me.'

'But—but the dragon—'

Brackensith's eyes blazed in anger. Riz argued no more. He called for soldiers. 'Guards, I be returning to Adaban now.' Riz spoke low. 'Bring the dragon as planned, but first feed it this bundle. I can have no further use for—'

'Bring the wench with you,' Brackensith said coldly. 'If you be tired of her, at least let her family have her back.'

'Father, she has family here among my men.'

'As you wish, but let her go. You revel too much in bloodshed.'

Her lungs were empty. She prayed to Dragongirl. She pleaded to the orb. She willed Brackensith to understand her half-word, to question the desperation in Riz's voice, to uncover her. He was so near, a velvet curtain away, but she had only thoughts to reach him with.

Then she saw her error. One little thing could reach him. Brackensith would know its significance. Her finger wore it like a noose.

She shook her wrist. Riz's betrothal ring fell to the dirt. Squeezing the last air from her lungs, she kicked his ring. It was through. She heard it ping on pebbles as it wobbled a path to Brackensith.

Dizzy now, she slumped . . . and hoped he'd hear it too.

Riz did.

He craned his chin over her velvet head. As the evidence rolled to Brackensith's feet he squealed. He jumped onto the ring, dragging her. They landed awkwardly, swaying like dancers.

'What mad game be you playing?' Brackensith growled, barely enduring the absurd charade. 'Step back from your bundle and let me see her face.'

'Father, do not look!'

'What be you hiding?'

'I—her face be burned . . . just a little.' Riz's words trailed away. He let Jatta slip, and she crumpled at his feet as he read his father's deadly expression. Whimpering, he half-knelt to retrieve his bundle. Brackensith raised one hand. Riz surrendered completely and shuffled back, clutching his ears.

Jatta was crouched on all fours, sweat-drenched, spitting out cape.

'Stand up, girl, so I may unravel you,' growled Brackensith.

She struggled onto one knee, wheezing for air. 'Ja—Ja—' Her gratitude swelled for her guardian. For Brackensith, too. She reached up her arm and felt his grip through the cape.

But neither guardian nor dark king had heard her prayer, though it seemed Fand had heard Riz's.

'Majesty, Highness! The Princess be found!' Fand's gasped shouts preceded him into the tent. He bounded to the King, carrying a royal sword like a tribute, and Brackensith dropped Jatta's arm.

The King took the sword, peering close. Satisfaction twisted his lips.

'No! I'm Jatt—' she cried before Fand's hand clamped tight.

'A rebellion, Majesty! She be in North Bradfirth, our messenger says.' Fand bent over, clutching her to his heaving chest, genuinely out of breath. Had guards fetched him from the camp? 'The Princess's forces fight on, but her brother be captured. There be his sword.'

Jatta bit and struggled, hearing Brackensith stride to the portal. Leaving her.

'Come, idiot son,' said Brackensith. 'I shall deliver you to North Bradfirth. Capture the Princess without burning her, without killing her. Can I trust you at least to do that?'

She heard another pair of feet scrunch to the portal. Blue sparks flickered and they were gone.

Fand removed his hand and Jatta gasped for breath. 'Fand!' she cried. 'Don't throw me to the dragon! Take me back to North Bradfirth. To Brackensith.'

'And risk a traitor's fate? A wolf's bite?' Fand dragged off the cape and his men set about binding her wrists and ankles. 'No. We would rather be dragon fodder ourselves.'

'Then I beg you, let my brother go. He's done nothing wrong.'

'Princess, you know better than to ask. He shares your fate.'

'Take me to Brackensith, please. Let me plead your case. He'll show mercy for your crimes under Riz.'

'Mercy?' A wry smile formed at one corner of his mouth while his men scoffed. She had never before seen him smile. He hoisted her over his shoulder and they strode out of the tent toward the clearing. 'Mercy? This be an Alteedan word, not ours.'

CHAPTER TWENTY-EIGHT

It was no use struggling. Jatta lay over the commander's shoulder, her face crimson with blood, bonds cutting into her ankles and wrists, jolted with every stride. She'd offered him jewels and lands then begged again, reminding him of his own young son. Nauseous from the jolts and from fear, and with blood throbbing through her temples, she reached out for the orb. Again and again. Hoping against hope that Arthmael had found it. Then, as she caught her first whiff of sulphur, praying that he might at least escape.

The men trod quietly now, eyes alert, hands tensely gripping their swords, though none would stay and fight if they could run. They filed onto the edge of the clearing and the commander laid her down.

For the first time she could look around, and what she saw terrified her. The dragon watched at the cave mouth, flicking her tail.

Fand was whispering in Jatta's ear, his grey plait brushing her throat. '... Riz needn't know ... painless ...'

Hope rose again. 'Pardon? I ... What did you say?'

He breathed, 'I be saying I could dispatch you here first, if you like. A little slice, just so.' He demonstrated, running his blade lightly across the back of her neck. She shrank back.

'No, Princess? As you prefer. Should not be long, now, either way.'

He nodded to his men and they backed silently along their route. Jatta was left bound and alone. Desperately, she called to the orb. The dragon tilted her snout, nostrils twitching, savouring Jatta's wolf-moon scent in the breeze. Hungry eyes met hers, and Jatta's last feeble hope died. Wolf or girl, she was prey. The dragon swallowed, a ripple of movement down her long, ribbed throat. Jatta pleaded to the orb. The dragon rose. Bones crunched underfoot as she lumbered across the clearing.

Stars flickered weakly before Jatta's eyes.

Wonderful Art!

Her mind raced, wildly searching for the right illusion, praying illusions might work on a dragon. She hooked in, knowing the one creature this mother would not attack.

Halfway across the clearing the dragon stopped. She blinked at the hatchling lying helpless where the human had been. She sniffed the air, nostrils flaring. Suddenly confused, she stepped back. Stretching up her great snout, she sniffed high, then slowly swayed her neck, sampling Jatta's hatchling smell from all angles, growing increasingly agitated.

Jatta concentrated harder, refining her dragon odour, nervously watching the display.

Suddenly, the dragon made up her mind. She rose like a mountain on hind claws, wings beating, roaring sulphur at the Jatta-hatchling. She swung her neck in great arcs, tracing out a streaming plume of flame. Jatta felt the heat on her face.

The display was fearsome. A threat—there was no mistaking it. It was Jatta's turn to be confused, for dragons had no predators. Another dragon! Instinctively, fearfully, she glanced behind. But she was alone.

Then it dawned. Jatta-hatchling was the intruder.

Whatever she looked like, she'd unwittingly drawn odour from the adult. What was a hatchling smell?

Too late to find out. The mother attacked. She thundered to Jatta. Her towering bulk raged. Gaping jaws swung down from the sky.

In that moment Jatta switched odours. The jaw canopy froze open. Jatta quivered within it. It pulled back. The massive head tilted. Reptile eyes blinked, trying to make sense of the smell of hazelnut cookies. A great tongue reached out and licked Jatta-hatchling from chest to face. The sulphurous stench was overpowering.

The dragon seemed not to like the hazelnut cookie taste, or perhaps the gritty texture. Screwing up her snout she shook it, snorting. But hazelnut had masked Jatta's own fresh meat odour. Her heart thudding painfully, she attempted a hatchling whine. For the dedicated mother this final evidence was overpowering. She cooed back, then rolled the Jatta-hatchling over, nudging her up inside massive jaws. Great wings beat, bearing them to the sky.

Petrified, Jatta peered down from inside a row of deadly teeth. Treetops whirled below. She gasped; sulphurous stench filled her lungs. Nausea rose as the mouth swallowed mucus, squashing her between spongy tongue and ribbed roof. The great head tilted down, and Jatta fell against teeth. Her face hit hard. The clearing lay a horrifying distance below; only her teeth-cage stopped her plummeting.

The mother dived; the clearing rushed up at Jatta's face. Forgetting to whine, she screamed.

The dragon swooped into the dark cave. Jatta forced back her panic, whining as claws touched ground. She was laid in a nest, feeling glassy-smooth bodies pressed against hers. The mother offered soothing purrs, then returned outside to her captive baby.

While Jatta's eyes, and nauseous stomach, were adjusting in the dimness she felt a painful nip on her elbow. She kicked her bound claw-feet at the aggressor but it bit harder, drawing blood. Frightened, she matched her odour to her three nest-mates', but it made no difference. The bully hatchling had taken exception to her. It lunged. This time the teeth sank through sand-scales to tear a strip from her skirts. She struggled, rolling from its jaws onto the others. They nipped in annoyance. In desperation she dragged herself over the edge. The bully turned to pick on its brother.

In the gloom Jatta changed back to human shape, though she dared not relinquish her odour. Bound and cut, lying in a sharp pile of bones beneath ravenous baby dragons, she started shaking. She should have died, would have died horribly like Randall and the armour-plated thugs, if not for the orb. If not for Arthmael. Gratitude and relief flooded her body as she sagged onto the bones. Gratitude for her brother. Relief that dragons didn't find hazelnut cookies tasty, and that they had minds. Her dragon might not be as clever as Bobo, but at least she had more imagination than a mule.

Jatta took a deep breath. She felt among the gruesome refuse and found a broken bone. Convincing herself it was the wrong shape to be human, she reached down to scrape across her ankle ropes. Beetles and grubs writhed into her skirts.

In minutes the ropes had frayed through. She wedged the bone between her knees to attack her wrists.

Jatta tested whether Arthmael was still squeezing. Stars sparkled. His fingers must be cramped by now, it occurred to her, shaking her own. There in the dark, her mind wandered over a bright landscape of ideas. One, in particular, excited her. She'd thought it first two days before, after witnessing the armoured thug's nightmare: fire had blackened him, but the mirrored hatchling had miraculously survived.

Jatta now imagined herself and Arthmael sprouting their own scales and dancing inside a wall of fire. Well, not dancing, not literally. Not sprouting either. Here though, in this nest, squabbled a fire-proof treasure of mirror scales.

Never for a moment could Jatta imagine *killing* a baby, even the bully, for its scales. Other reptiles moulted, though; Arthmael had once chased her around the rose garden with a snake skin on a stick. Perhaps somewhere in this cave were moulted or broken scales. She peered around in the semi-darkness. Nothing. Just bones and grubs. She shuddered—the armour also lay here, picked clean like lobster shell.

She crawled out from the bones and away from her nest-mates before she dared to slowly stand. Then, sweeping with her feet for discarded scales, she headed deeper into the cave. *Clink* went something against her heel. She scooped up her first piece, grinning.

Deep ahead shone a pinprick of light. Perhaps she would have more luck there. The light might also be a second exit, an escape. As she gathered scales into her pocket, Jatta left the nest far behind. The light ahead was her beacon, glowing green-blue through the blackness. She groped along walls, finding hers was just one of many passages.

Jatta at last drew close to her destination, and her mouth fell open. She'd discovered no exit, but an enormous lighted cavern. She stepped inside, and gasped at its beauty.

There was not one light, but millions. They twinkled over the roof and walls like a night so saturated with stars that there was no room for even one more. Their soft blue-green light was reflected back to the roof by a thick carpet of broken glass. And littering the floor, half-buried in glass, lay hundreds of giant skeletons.

Not glass, but mirror scales. Jatta had stumbled upon a dragon graveyard.

Her spine tingled. Her whole body flooded with awe, knowing she was the first person to witness this sacred place. She wandered, slipping and scrunching through scales till she sat in the very centre, inside a magnificent rib cage. There, bathed in flickering light, she imagined what it would have been like for each great dragon. Old or sick, perhaps wounded, aware it was dying, it had followed the light's beacon. She wondered, as it lay down on the bones of its ancestors and looked up to the stars, if it had felt the awe she felt now. Perhaps Jatta would be the last creature ever to witness this place, now that Riz's men had arrived.

That thought reminded her of pressing needs. She slipped off a petticoat, drawing the waist cord very tight, and knotted it to make a sack. When her sack was heavy with scales, some orb-sized, some bigger than her hand, she stood. 'Thank you,' she breathed to the long-gone dragons, her eyes luminous. She hoisted her load on her shoulder and trudged out.

The way ahead was black. It had never occurred to Jatta that the nest's light would be too dim to guide her back. Nervously she began the trek, feeling her way along the wall. When she came to a place where the passage forked she would grope both honeycombed walls, and take the straighter of the two.

As many minutes dragged by, and nothing but blackness greeted her, her tension grew. Her arms ached from their burden. She looked back over her shoulder to the graveyard's beckoning blue-green glow.

The walls grew wet as minutes stretched into hours. Her shoe sloshed in a puddle. She looked back and saw nothing. Blackness lay all around.

She had taken a wrong turn. The trouble was, she did not know where.

Jatta's breathing had grown shallow and quick. She retraced her steps in the blackness till she came to a fork. Should she take the left? Or the right? With trembling hands she stuffed some handfuls of scales in her pockets. She would lay them at intervals behind her; then if she needed to retrace her steps the scales' scrunch underfoot would guide her.

After several minutes she came to a three-way fork, her arm screaming to be free of its load. She left her bundle there, venturing several paces up one passage, then returning to try the second, then the last. Everywhere the walls seeped. Everywhere was blackness. Jatta's eyes brimmed with tears.

No creature could find its way back through the graveyard labyrinth, she realised. Till this day none had tried.

She picked up her load in trembling arms. She stumbled back to find the left fork. For an hour or more she trudged, leaving her trail, making decisions at forks, till the passages grew too narrow.

Her tomb was so narrow. So silent. So wet. And black.

'Let me out!' she screamed as her panic rose. Terrible, absolute blackness pressed in on her, squashing her chest so she could hardly breathe. A mad impulse overwhelmed her and she threw down her bundle. She ran. She thudded into stone and stumbled away. She thudded again, fell in a puddle, struggled back up and stumbled mindlessly on. Her forehead slammed into stone. Pain seared through her skull.

CHAPTER TWENTY-NINE

She was lying on her back in blackness, shivering and wet, imagining her ladies would lift her out of the bath, as they'd done once before. Her ladies never came, and her mind slipped back into blackness.

She was lying on her back, shivering, not sure if she had been sleeping or awake this long time. Was this her first day, or her second, in her tomb? Had her wolf come and gone, like a stranger passing in darkness?

Her thirst wailed. She rolled onto her stomach to suck from the puddle, tasting its mud till her stomach filled. Her head throbbed. She touched a finger to it and felt a fat bruise. She tried to stand, bumping up against the cave roof, and remembered. She'd been running into walls like a lunatic. She slumped back to the puddle.

'No-one will find me,' she whispered to the blackness. 'Riz's men think I'm dead. Arthmael does too.' Her heart ached for her brother. He could not still be alive.

'Art,' she cried. 'They've already killed you, haven't they?' As if to prove herself right she reached for the orb.

Nothing. Not even a spark.

She drew her knees to her chest and buried her face. Tears welled. Great jagged sobs convulsed her.

After minutes or hours her sobs quietened. Then finally

there were no more tears, no will left to drag herself out of the puddle. *Let me die, let me die.* Her mind looped the thought, but death in the dark might take a very long time.

Something—not death, but something tingling and much less welcome—was invading her limbs. She surrendered to its sensations, to sparks of pain. She could harm no-one here. Not tonight . . . not ever again. The thought was vaguely comforting as magic pummelled her body. Memory slipped away. The urge rose. To kill, to spill blood. She could almost taste it.

Jatta, creature of the Sorcerer's perverse imagination, heaved her chest from the puddle and shook water from her snout. She sniffed the blackness for prey. Damp rock, damp fur, dank water, nothing more. Her bloodlust burned. Her superior sight scoured, finding no moon, only baffling black night. Her ears swivelled, picking up little more: malice in her breathing, power in her heartbeat and slow dripping from her fur. A low, threatening growl told the walls she was not happy.

She bounded to her feet. Something slammed into her skull, knocking her back to the puddle. In sudden fury she launched, spinning around to her invisible opponent, only to be smacked in the forehead. She landed on her back with the thud and grind of armour plates. She shook her head, then flipped defensively to crouch. Her shoulders quivered with tension.

Her attacker waited, too. Moments dragged on too long. Fur spiking, she growled her challenge.

The enemy seemed to have fled.

She rose warily till her head bumped into something solid. She twisted to snap, scraping off a chunk.

Rock.

Dull realisation formed as she straightened her thighs, letting her neck and mane scrape along the ceiling. Her senses had been right: there was no enemy. She sniffed again.

No prey, either.

Her head jerked up to howl her frustration. It hit hard. Again pain shot through her skull. This last insult was too much. She lurched forward with arms outstretched to half-stagger, half-run from this tube.

Jatta hurtled into the labyrinth's bowels, ricocheting off stalactites. She tore at their columns with teeth and claws. Dismembered her enemies. Ground their soft limestone bones to chalk. Sought revenge for too many nights without human flesh. Through the night she never tired. Formations that had outlived the age of Sorcerers lay vanquished, rubble under her feet.

Her frenzy eased as dawn approached. Still the yearning for blood was unsatisfied. She hugged the last unbroken stalactite and howled in frustration, eyes closed, throat stretched to vibrate her song. Only her wounded chamber, and the maze beyond, heard its echoing beauty.

Far above her prison, dawn light touched the canyon rim.

Abruptly, Jatta's song cut off. Pain spliced her spine. Her legs spasmed, then lost all strength. They hung as her arms slid, clawing tracks down the column, till she dropped through blackness. With a thud she hit rubble; plates jarred and grated.

She dragged herself away on her hands, snapping at every broken stalactite, snarling at phantoms, never fathoming that the attack had come from within. Paralysis invaded her shoulders. As the great trunks of her arms shuddered, her hands slid through rubble. Her face collapsed onto broken stone. Jatta's eyes closed and consciousness slipped away.

*

Just how long she'd been awake Jatta wasn't sure. There'd been the body ache, like she'd been bounced off every boulder down Goy-an Falls. That came first. Then came hunger, growing ravenously insistent. Finally the other ache arrived, the realisation—the disappointment—that she was indeed awake. Alive. She groaned and rolled over. This would take time; there would be many more pointless hours to endure.

'Hello, sleepy Jatta,' whispered a familiar voice.

Jatta's whole body froze, except her eyes, which shot open. Dragongirl was sitting cross-legged by her shoulder, curiously watching the play of shock, disbelief and relief over Jatta's face.

Jatta's heart thumped and she started shivering. A dozen urgent questions swamped her brain, but two words rushed out. 'Don't go.'

'You wish to stay here?' asked Dragongirl, incredulous. She giggled and scrambled up.

'No, no.' Jatta staggered up, too. Everything ached more. Her legs wobbled from starvation and fatigue. Dragongirl skipped ahead. Her strange robes glowed a faint white and the rubble was dimly lit under her sandals.

'Wait.' Jatta wove drunkenly after her. 'Do you know the way out?'

Idiot question, really. If this apparition really was Dragongirl, then getting out shouldn't be a problem. But mightn't she be a trick of Jatta's overwrought, starved mind? If so, then they would never leave. Jatta preferred the first option.

'Wait! I have to look for my brother.'

Dragongirl turned around, hands on hips, with an impatient frown. Jatta called to her orb.

The faintest of stars spluttered from so far away.

Shocked joy spread through her chest, as if Arthmael had lit a spark there. He was alive! And he had not given up hope. Neither would she.

Dragongirl rolled her eyes and ran ahead.

Jatta hobbled to catch up, every part of her complaining. She was in no mood to listen to complaints, though; Arthmael would be waiting and anxious. The way was littered and she stumbled, tagging close behind her childhood friend. Keeping up helped: in Dragongirl's halo she could see where rubble lay. A fresh, delightful question occurred. How could her friend be a hallucination, or some quirk of Arthmael's orb, when her light was as real as the rubble that stubbed Jatta's toes?

And then in Dragongirl's glow Jatta glimpsed fresh hope: the edges of fresh-broken stalactites. Her breathing quickened. Wherever they were heading, she'd passed through here in the night.

Her legs trembled with weakness. The passage again grew wet and narrow. When a scale scrunched underfoot Jatta squealed. Dragongirl stopped, beckoning with an impish smile. Jatta's discarded bundle, faintly illuminated, lay by her guardian's knees. Jatta lurched to pick it up, laughing.

Try as she might, she could not get answers from Dragongirl. Why hadn't she answered her other prayers? Might she *please* save Alteeda from Riz? The child would wait, giggling, till Jatta hobbled close, then skip teasingly around a corner for her to follow.

Jatta turned one corner to find her guardian angel gone. There, miraculously, was the familiar dim light of the dragon's nest. With a whispered *thank you*, she hobbled toward it.

She didn't glance behind to see a second milky figure. Dragongirl had returned with an old man. The child tugged on his fingers till he smiled down.

'Well done, my Dragongirl,' he said. His voice was gentle and weary, compelling in its gravelly depth.

His eyes lifted to watch Jatta; the pain in them was unconcealed. He whispered, too low for Jatta to hear. 'I worry for you, little Jatta. I do what I can, yet I be no angel. You would curse me if you knew my dark side.'

CHAPTER THIRTY

The three hatchlings bobbed excitedly to smell the wolf meat limping toward them. Jatta stopped short.

She had a new idea. She and her brother might escape if she could free the chained hatchling. Hadn't Riz's men relied on the dragon staying close to her baby? Lord help them if the dragon had no safety to consider except her own.

To reach the baby, Jatta would need to distract the mother. She would need her nest-mates. She hobbled closer with her bundle and leaned into the nest, dangerously close to the snapping jaws.

'Lunch, my pets. Come and get it.'

The babies tumbled out, ravenous. She limped toward the sunlight, turning back to see. Good. They were waggling and whining behind.

Jatta kept to the wall, out of the clearing's view, and laid her bundle just inside the cave mouth. Hardly breathing, she edged toward its opening. She peeped.

The mother was close. She had her back to the cave, her wings spread as she bobbed in agitation. The sun was high, and a lot had happened since yesterday. Riz's cage now stood at the clearing's edge. Men sat on top, training their blue-tipped arrows at the dragon. Jatta dropped to her stomach and wriggled into sunlight. Here, hidden among megalith bones, she glimpsed archers in the hide. Still more concealed themselves among foliage. The chained hatchling lay whining, barely a jump away. Seeing Jatta, it shuffled to sit up. Its head tilted in puzzlement; reptile eyes blinked.

Arthmael knelt in the centre of the clearing. His ankle ropes were a half-unpicked tangle. His wrists were still bound; they kneaded something sparkling.

She ached to hug him.

The dragon seemed not at all interested in her tormentors' latest offering. Like Jatta, she recognised the waiting danger.

In that moment the nest-mates came whining into the sunlight. The mother whipped her head to them, then let out a fearful screech. She thundered back to the cave as the first arrows *whooshed*. Jatta chose this moment to morph.

Purring, Jatta-hatchling dived for the baby in chains. It purred back in pleasure.

'Poor baby, you're starved for company,' she whispered.

The heavy chain was welded like the bars in her own chambers. Jatta-hatchling examined the baby's iron collar. Its neck had worn raw. Still, she couldn't believe her good fortune. The two circular halves of the collar were not welded. It was held in place by two fat screws.

Jatta-hatchling snatched a broken scale and twisted. The first screw dropped to the ground.

But the baby wanted to play. It was nipping lightly at her bodice-scales and whined when it couldn't snag hold. Jatta struggled with the second screw till she was painfully head-butted. Reeling, she glanced back nervously. The mother had swung all three nest-mates up onto her spine, where they clung by hooked claws. Another round of arrows *whooshed*. Most glanced off. Two stuck in the mother's tender belly. She was heading, somewhat groggily, to collect Jatta.

The baby was nipping Jatta's wing. Its snout sank through grit till it found her hair, dragging her over. Jatta-hatchling sprouted a second head. Her playmate blinked and tumbled back. Jatta quickly unscrewed the collar. At that moment, monstrous jaws wrapped around her. She was scooped through the air, landing against a dragon spine. She clung to it as her body slid.

The freed baby was purring, excitedly trying to clamber inside its mother's mouth.

She scooped it up, purring too, then slung it up to cling beside Jatta. The mother spread her great wings as fresh arrows *whooshed*. One lodged in her wing. She rose unsteadily into the air, toward the hide.

More arrows flew. Jatta felt the dragon inhale, heard the rush of air to her chest, knew what would follow. Flame shot through the trees. The hide was alight. The archers too. They screamed, rolling around, and one jumped to his death. The dragon lifted her throat to roar. Jatta felt the boom through her own body. Her ears hurt.

The dragon swooped from the sky. Archers stood on the cage, emptying their bows up at her. Two more arrows lodged in her chest and she faltered in mid-air. Still, she scooped the massive cage in her claws. She climbed vertically. Men fell, flailing.

Jatta-hatchling swung helpless. She collided with a nest-mate and lost her grip. She slid down the mirror back, then onto a wing. Suddenly she found herself bouncing high. She was tumbling back, then bouncing again on her wing trampoline. This time she clutched at an arrow embedded there. With every great flap, Jatta was tossed. Her stomach lurched into her throat. But she held on.

The dragon seemed to know where to go. She flew high over the tents as men raced out. With a screech like ten thousand fingernails down slates, she released the cage. It crashed, flattening one tent. She flew low, unsteady. Long streams of flame incinerated anything left standing.

She returned to the clearing. Her body dipped with every laboured beat, grown groggy. Grown heavy as stone.

Fand's remaining men had reorganised. They waited in ambush just inside the cave. But they had not troubled themselves to learn a dragon's powers. She smelled them, their fear too. Rolling low, tail dragging through the dirt, she unleashed an unimaginable white-hot burst. Rock melted. Chain too. No-one inside had time to scream.

She climbed one last time, giddy with the drug in her veins. Momentarily she lost consciousness and swerved. Jatta-hatchling was tossed through the air—she was falling, shrieking. The mother dived, jaws wide, and scooped Jatta inside. But she, too, was falling. Flapping crazily. Spiralling. The ground rushed up. She almost recovered. She flailed out of free fall, as the Princess's heart stopped. Then she dropped, a dead weight. The ground shook.

Jatta was thrown against the mouth's roof. Her mind went black.

CHAPTER THIRTY-ONE

Jatta woke, nauseous. Confused. She was in a cramped, dark, spongy place. A sulphurous wind whistled up from behind. Chinks of daylight shone through—through dragon teeth. She wasn't sure whether to cry or laugh. Flight on dragon wings was certainly not as she had imagined.

She tried to free herself. Lying on her sodden back in the tongue, she pushed her knees against the roof with all her might. It didn't budge.

She sat back down, wondering what to do next. *Arthmael.* She reached out for the orb. Stars sparked. She wanted to laugh.

She pressed her face through a gap in the teeth. 'Art! Art!' She called again and again. Her brother was alive and he would be looking for her.

'Jay!' came a distant shout. 'Where are you?'

She laughed. 'In the dragon!'

Arthmael thrust his wrists through his sister's prison and dropped in her orb. While she unpicked his bonds he teased her for growing so skinny. For the stench too. For leaving him waiting so long. His cheerfulness hardly wavered, though the skin under his eyes was dark from too little sleep. Grunting, he prized the jaws open a slit, but the hatchlings had slid down their mother and waggled dangerously close.

'Ouch! Distract these calf crunchers for—'

Arthmael never finished his sentence. He froze, his gaze fixed on a point above the mother's jaw. The hatchlings purred up at the same spot, and flapped and tail-flicked in their excitement. Adrenaline quickened Jatta's heart, too, for she realised the eye had opened. Praying she wasn't too late, she massaged the orb. Arthmael morphed. His hatchling backed away, unnaturally, on two hind legs.

'Get down!' she whispered. 'Keep your arms tucked in.'

Arthmael's hatchling dropped to all fours. Jatta's cage opened and the great tongue gently rolled her out. The mother's snout nudged them into a line-up with their nest-mates, though her narrowed eyes never left Arthmael. He was too big. His sandiness made her snort. The sulphur stench had him coughing.

Jatta's blood pumped through her veins in hard little bursts. This was not progressing well.

She turned his coughs into whines, but still the mother seemed uncertain.

'Can dragons count?' he whispered.

Whatever her talents, this mother definitely seemed uncomfortable with six. She eyed each baby closely in turn. The bully hatchling beside Arthmael took the opportunity to nip; its jaws sank through sandy scales to his chest. Arthmael's hatchling-jaw tensed. The bully lunged again and Arthmael rammed its shoulder, sending it sprawling.

Instantly the mother's head flicked to him. Her eyes narrowed. Her next move showed deadly strategy.

She cooed to her babies.

As the four hatchlings to their left curled into centipede rolls, Jatta battled rising panic. Jaws nudged her into a ball, too. She obeyed, much too weak to run.

Arthmael groaned. 'Not good, right?'

Jatta nodded minutely. The mother heaved in a breath.

'Can't you turn us into rocks? Disguise us?'

Jatta shook her head. They'd still fry. Flames shot to the first hatchling, engulfing it. She squeezed the orb harder.

A roar like colliding mountains rose from the rainforest.

The mother's jaws slammed shut. Her face whipped to see a golden dragon crashing through blackened pines.

'I hope that one's yours!' cried her brother. Two heavy hatchling-arms seized her waist. Her arms hugged his sandy neck. He ran. She changed him back to Arthmael, peering over his shoulder. Her golden dragon shot flames into the clearing. As she'd expected, as she'd hoped, the mother scooped up one hatchling and flung it onto her spine, then two more. Arthmael was heading for the cave, or the bone piles outside. She wasn't confident either would be safe—or that her brother wouldn't collapse. He wheezed with every laboured bound. It didn't help that she pressed on his wounds.

Time to bring on her intruder. The monster soared into the clearing. Its golden mirrors scattered sun rays. Its flame streamed through sky.

But the distressed mother flung up her last hatchling and ignored the display. *Why?* Her neck flicked to Jatta. For one heart-stopping moment their eyes locked. Then she screeched at the fleeing pair, a choked-out keen almost as if they'd murdered her babies. Jatta had never known a sound so tortured. The ground shook with her pursuit. Jatta's golden dragon was above, snapping down at the mother's neck.

But nothing could distract her.

She had the cave mouth blocked in three bounds, and they had nowhere to run. Arthmael was gasping, knee-deep in bones, by the baby's chains. Trapped, like the armoured Alteedans. Inexplicably, the mother was cooing. A sickening vision flashed in Jatta's mind, of another coo right here, and a blackened Alteedan cicada. Somehow, it was happening again. Jatta prayed to Dragongirl, then scrunched up her eyes and curled against her brother to await the firestorm. The mother filled her lungs.

'For Lord's sake,' wheezed Arthmael. 'Change back!'

Change back?

Jatta's eyes burst open: it was her *hatchling's* silver arms that wrapped Arthmael's neck. She was kidnapped, and she'd obeyed her mother's coo to roll up.

They were out of time.

'Dive!' she cried.

Arthmael clutched her hatchling face to his cheek and lunged head-first inside a pile. Bones rolled and scattered. They were exposed. In those moments Jatta focused on one tumbling hatchling-sized bone.

'Lie dead still,' she breathed.

A fire-burst issued over their heads, then the jaws snapped shut.

The mother was purring. Jatta's hatchling-bone was tumbling to settle on its side and Jatta made it purr back. The mother sniffed, nudged it to roll. She sneezed at its sandiness. It sneezed too, and thumped its tail, but didn't get up. Then gently, protectively, she rolled it inside her jaws. She turned, weary now, to lumber home. Jatta squeezed till the cave swallowed her from sight.

Arthmael laughed. He guffawed. He thought it a deal funnier now than he had a few minutes ago.

She laughed too, giddy with gratitude, giddy from starvation, giddy with the wonder of being alive. And when they'd done, he pulled his sister to him and hugged her. He was not a demonstrative sort, but he clutched her gaunt shoulders for a long time.

He finally released her. His fingers coaxed her chin up.

'Jay, they told me you were dead.'

'But you didn't believe them.'

'I couldn't.'

'That's what kept me alive.'

It was Arthmael who sneaked inside the cave mouth for her scales. Jatta had been scared of the carnage she'd find. She needn't have worried. All that was left of Fand and his men were a few charred bones. Her petticoat sack had vaporised. The scales, however, shone as brightly as the last day they'd been worn.

'All right. First priority is your wolf,' said Arthmael as they searched the Alteedan camp. Very little was left here either. They saw two villains looting bodies and another five, disfigured by burns, sitting in shock. The store of sleeping paste was ash. Arthmael shrugged and grunted as if he wasn't bothered. He was being too careful with her. She must look as fragile as she felt.

'Bad luck about the paste,' he said. 'Think you can tolerate another night in the pit?'

'Um, I can get out. I woke up last time and dragged Riz back down.'

That broke through his charade. His mouth dropped in shock. 'And you let him *survive*? Glory, Jay. Worse luck.'

She stifled a shudder. He was right to be disappointed. Crunching up Riz would have done everyone a service. Except herself.

'I mean, not for you,' he backtracked. 'Good luck, fantastic luck for your conscience, Jay. So . . . what stopped you?'

She shrugged.

'Don't you remember anything?'

'Soldiers in tunnels . . . torches burning in mud . . .'

'Torches? Your wolf still doesn't like fire?' He laughed, shaking his head. As one hand rubbed his exhausted face, his laugh trailed into a groan. 'Leave this to me. I've more-or-less done it twice before.'

The royal tent and their own had escaped the carnage. Arthmael found the Dartith book, a spare sword and Naffaedan's purse among Fand's things.

Jatta took a minute to wander back through the royal tent. It felt eerie. The cape lay where Fand had torn it off her, a coil of rope beside it. Underneath, ground into the dirt, was Riz's betrothal ring. She scraped it out. Her father's crown had rolled under the low table. In a chest she found the Crewingburns' jewels and Baron Randall's purse. She took the crown and jewels. The rest—chests of Adaban fashions, cage designs and wedding sketches—she left for the jungle to claim.

Randall, Fand. Nearly everyone she'd met over these past four days was now dead. Scar, their desert escort, many Alteedans and almost every Dartithan—with one regrettable exception.

'What will Riz do now?' Arthmael's voice at her side startled her. 'Kill Father and Steffed?'

'Not yet, I don't think. Not while the portal remains. But with Fand gone it's hard to guess.' She sighed and threaded Riz's ring on Arthmael's finger. 'Keep this for Brackensith, please. It falls off my thumb.'

'And it makes your skin creep.'

She almost smiled. That, too.

She changed back into her farming dress at Arthmael's suggestion. It swam a size too big, now.

'Riz thinks we're dead. Let's keep it that way,' he said, shouldering the scales. 'We really should be leaving. There'll be horses and supplies on the cliff top.'

'But—' The horses would be terrified of her wolf-moon scent.

'Leave it to me, Jay.'

She'd grown dizzy and weak. As he helped her back to the ladders they heard men's distant screams; the dragon's babies needed feeding. Jatta's skeletal legs refused to run, so Arthmael carried her on his shoulders.

The cliff-top Alteedans had fled, but Arthmael found four horses and a covered wagon, which he stacked with enough scavenged wood for a festival bonfire, plus their scales, water and provisions for the long ride north through the desert.

CHAPTER THIRTY-TWO

'Eat, Jay. That wolf's making you scarily skinny.'

Arthmael laid a bag of sesame biscuits on the blanket by her face. He'd cleared a corner in the wagon for her, wedged between barrels of water, firewood and horse feed. Jatta yawned, too lethargic to do anything except reach inside the bag and drag a biscuit out. She tapped at her mouth till she found the opening. Even keeping her eyes open was a battle.

'Sorry, but I can't do anything about the smell.' He sprinkled powders from canisters, then opened more horse blankets to cover her. It was stuffy underneath, and it stank of camphor, pepper, garlic and horse sweat. It didn't bother her, especially if it disguised her wolf-scent.

'Now I'll go get the horses. Jay?'

She had already drifted to sleep, the half-chewed biscuit still on her tongue.

She woke up lying on dirt as Arthmael roughly shook her shoulder.

'Glory, Jay. You sleep like the Undead. I was starting to think you'd snore right through the night.'

She smiled groggily. If only. She blinked up to see a chest-high, wide ring of debris encircling them. It smelled of lamp oil. A torch spluttered by Arthmael's feet. She struggled up on one elbow. Dizziness threatened to topple her back.

His hand steadied her shoulder. 'Here, eat.' He pressed something sesame-smelling against her lips. She opened her mouth obediently, he popped it in, and she chewed. She was famished, she realised. This morsel tasted delicious. She held out her palm and he emptied more broken biscuits into it. She shoved them in her mouth. When she'd swallowed he poured her a mug of water. She gulped that down and looked around for more food.

'Well, that's a relief,' he said, handing her the bag of biscuits. 'I was worried you'd forgotten how.'

As she scoffed biscuits, she watched her brother. He had a short, forked log propped against his thigh. He was practising winding rope around both forks, his hands efficient and quick. She'd watched kitchen staff truss geese this way for the rotisserie. She glanced around at the bonfire ring. The analogy made her smile.

'Are you stuffing and roasting me tonight?'

He looked up. His face stretched into a surprised, eye-scrunching grin at her improved mood.

'Aw. My little sister just made her first joke. But no, if all goes to my brilliant plan, neither of us will be feasting tonight.'

Inwardly she cringed. She'd asked for that. Her smile stayed fixed as she held out both wrists for him to bind.

'Later.' He took one hand and directed it back inside the bag. 'Think about it—where do your bracelets and clothes and everything go while you're morphing? I've seen it, they're absorbed into your skin. Ropes around your wrists would probably go the same way.'

Later? She didn't hear the rest.

'Art, don't do this.'

'I'll be fine.' He grinned too broadly, pretending nonchalance.

'I took notes last time. Your jewellery and gown go first. Then you morph. I have maybe thirty seconds between when you reach the size of a storehouse and when you start howling. Not much happens in between, at least on the outside. See, that's plenty time to truss your ankles to your wrists.'

'No. Light your fire, but stay away from me. *Please.*'

He patted her shoulder. 'Don't fret. I'm just trying to be thorough. We don't need you raging around like before.'

Jatta lost her appetite after that. She sat with her knees curled up under her chin, and prayed to Dragongirl to lead him away, to make him change his mind. The sun drifted below their bonfire ring; bright rays peeked through its gaps. Beyond the debris she saw an immense stack of timber. Two hundred paces beyond that, under a scraggly tree, stood the wagon and their horses munching feed. He'd thought about this, been very prepared. She admired him for that. She tried to trust him, telling herself no-one knew her wolf better.

As the last rays winked out below their ring, she settled face down and crossed her wrists over the small of her back. She begged Dragongirl to keep him safe.

'Art. My nose tingles.'

'I'm here.'

'I can't . . . move.'

He rubbed her shoulderblade. 'Jay, I'll see you in the morning.'

Her skirt billowed behind her in the still evening, dissolving to gossamer and fluttering to settle over her legs, soaking inside. Its colours stained her skin. Her shoulders bulged, pushing out mounds of dirt, sprouting mangy tufts. Jatta felt her bones shatter and tumble. It was agony, agony. Her scream gurgled in a paralysed throat. Some malevolent fist had got inside her mouth to crush and drag it into a deformed new shape. Glass shards erupted from her gums.

Her massive wolf feet were on her brother's knees and he was binding them. Again and again he wound round. He was saying her name, lying—saying that everything was all right. She groped for his words while she could still recognise his voice. She was losing him now, his name, his purpose here. Something new was growing, clawing. Not her body, but something scraping through its insides. Jatta fought that, fought it harder than she'd fought before, desperate to protect the youth, knowing only that he mattered more to her than her own diseased life. Her last plea was to the invader itself, for pity. Pity not for her—she was dying—but for the fresh meat binding her wrists.

Fresh meat. Her furious green eyes strained to see him knotting her wrists to her feet. She tried to sever *his* wrists. Her limbs didn't obey. Not yet. They would soon, like that time before, with the squealer. Tonight's urge was as strong. No. *Urges.* Two. Hatred battled with something alien, some urge she didn't understand.

The creature glanced up from his work to her face, and he froze. Fear coursed through his veins. Fear fed her anger. He came to life then, scrambling up. He grabbed the fire stick and ran.

Her paralysis ended.

Wolf snout twitched. Nostrils breathed in the taste of him. Hate-filled eyes watched the creature vault over his barricade. Arms tensed inside their bonds, strained apart till ropes groaned and snapped. Hands brushed coils loose, then braced against the dirt to lift a massive chest from the ground.

Jatta rose. Flame was spreading in a crescent around her;

the creature raced before it, poking with his stick. She launched after him.

Or tried.

Her hind legs wouldn't separate. She overbalanced, falling on her face. That only made her more furious. She bounded three-legged across dirt to him, awkward and slow, then stood face-to-flame. Her old enemy, fire, licked her snout and sizzled her pelt. She snarled through it at the creature. He flickered orange, standing there, staring up. Stupid, strange prey. She reached her arm through. It burned, it hurt, it smelled bad. His eyes grew wide. There, she could smell his fear now. He dodged her claws, tried to run, so she back-handed him. That had him reeling. Whining with pain, she groped, found his neck. Jatta plucked him through the fire. But her arm was alight. She dropped him to shake her torched flesh. Orange streaked through the deepening sky.

'Hold still, Jay. Calm down girl, calm down.'

The creature was beneath her, his voice soothing, his yellow tunic wrapping the flame. She didn't shake him off. Her low brow furrowed, for it wasn't his fear she smelled now. It was some instinct that didn't make sense, not here, not offered up to her.

He busied himself attending to her throbbing arm, chattering away. Scarred, pale brown. Naked to the waist, weak, as all his kind were. He unwound the tunic to examine her wound. He picked off singed fur clumps and poured water from a small barrel over it. That soothed the heat. She settled to sit in the puddle. He tore the yellow cloth into strips to tenderly bind her arm. The sound of his voice pleased her. She cocked her head, contemplating whether there was some way to eat the creature and still keep the voice.

He had patience, more patience than she did. Beyond the fire, other creatures were whinnying their fear; her predatory hatred was again bubbling up. She debated whether to risk the blaze to dismember all four, or to tear apart this perplexing one here.

For either attack she would have to free her legs. As she hooked claws under her ropes the creature complained. He slapped at her fingers.

That decided her mind.

She grabbed him by his neck and ankles. In one sweep she had him wrapped around her face, his belly in her jaws. His terror filled her nostrils, but he was entreating again, not shrieking or sobbing as his kind should. She hated that he divided her even now. She was head-sick of confusion. She would end this. She willed her jaws to crush down.

He was rubbing her shoulder. Pelt rolled under his palm. Peculiar, pleasant. Disturbing. Vague half-memories that weren't hers taunted her. One in particular: she was a runt lying face down in dirt and pleading with a faceless monster. It was too much.

She pulled the creature from her jaws. Threw him away.

She lifted her throat to the moon and howled. Her note of frustration rose, then hung under the stars. The whinnyers answered as it trailed away. Jatta sniffed through the fire. They were rearing and stamping the ground, calling to her. Her bloodlust surged. Her fury too, freed from the seductive voice. She ripped claws through her bonds, took one bound to the fire. She leapt through flames that now stretched toward the sky. Her mane trailed a comet of flame. She landed rolling in a cloud of sparks and dust, stinking of burning fur. She was up and flying, ten strides in one bound. She pounced on one rearing back. Her victim fell to its side and she rode its thrashing. Frenzied after five tortured nights without a kill. The others broke free. She didn't care. The chase was part of the thrill. But the meat was tasteless. She spat it out.

Nothing like flesh of her natural prey.

Her snout lifted, twitching. The strange, delicious, weak creature waited inside his fire, smelling of anxious . . . affection. She snapped the air in his direction while memories taunted her brain. Too complex, too difficult. She turned and bounded after the whinnyers.

Arthmael wished he had a heavy jacket. And a better handle on his sister. He crouched with his head tucked between his knees for protection from his firewall, and cinders settled on his broad, bare back. They stung. He listened for his sister, but all he could hear was the fire-wind roar and the cracks of heavy logs settling.

Suddenly his back shook. His chest convulsed with laughter.

'Glory, Art. Who else could foul things up so spectacularly, and still survive Jay's wolf?'

His words whipped away in the fire wind. 'What were you thinking, slapping her fingers? Imagining *anything* might hold her? And then you manage to roast yourself inside your own barbecue. Huh. *And* lose the horses . . . At least she'll get one good feed tonight, take the edge off that nasty temper, fatten up those bony arms.'

Midnight passed. As the blaze settled and the heat on his back grew less raw, his head settled heavily into his arms. During three wolf-moons he'd slept less than his sister.

'Sleep? Yet another bad idea,' he mumbled, staggering to

his feet. 'It's not your snores that'll charm Jay when she returns for dessert.'

He stretched. 'Jay! You there?' he called warily. Only the crackling wind answered. He waited and listened.

One section of barricade collapsed in a spray of cinders. He took a running leap across. There were bits of horse decorating bushes. Their wagon had been thrown against the sole tree and both had split open. Horse feed and provisions were strewn over the ground. He began cleaning up, in part to ward off sleep. Thankfully much was salvageable—obviously not the horse, which he buried to spare Jatta's feelings in the morning.

Manus slipped below the horizon. He allowed himself to consider that Jatta mightn't return tonight. The nervous nausea he'd refused to acknowledge eased.

Heavy dread took its place. She was out there after another body-draining episode, without shade or water and, judging by the bits he'd buried, she'd probably not eaten either. The sun would shrivel her by midday. He tried to think of a positive perspective on this development, but there wasn't one. *If* he could find her, they'd need barrels of water to get through the desert, but they had no way to carry them.

One of the horses returned, a minor good omen. He called her Lucky. He spent the hours before dawn lashing together a makeshift cart, two wheels with boards tied across their axle. He stacked it with water barrels, food and essential supplies, the scales, her book and the purse and jewels. He stuffed a compass and maps inside his pocket. The sky grew royal blue. He paced; if he sat down now he'd sleep through the dawn.

Dawn found him standing on the overturned wagon, searching. Birds circled out west. Otherwise nothing moved.

Dry shrubs dotted a pale grey plain; any one of them might be hiding his sister. His eyes returned to the west and his heart beat quickly, unevenly. He wasn't sure whether to be grateful or sickened. The birds were dropping from their circle to congregate on the same spot on the horizon. They were big. Too big for anything except predators, or more probably carrion eaters. Why hadn't he noticed before? He was sleep starved, that was why.

He offered the mare oats and water, hitched her to his cart, wet her down, and swigged all he could manage. She baulked at leaving the shade. He slapped her haunches and they walked together into the already overheated Vardensen Desert.

Sweat stuck Arthmael's shirt to his chest. It soaked a second shirt he'd tied around his forehead to protect his neck. He blinked sweat out of his eyelashes. Lucky struggled beside him, suffering as her haunches lathered. She stopped often and refused to continue till he offered her water. Seeing the last carrion birds drop from the sky, imagining Jatta alone with them, he cursed the minutes it took for Lucky to gulp from the bucket.

Staying awake got harder. His head felt like it had been stuffed with rice. Someone had poured in water and it was expanding, cracking his skull. He checked his compass, never sure if his legs were wobbling beneath him or if the ground itself was up and moving. There were periods when he blacked out. Had he been sleepwalking? But the vultures were close now, massed on a body, hopping and bickering. Their ugly, naked heads tugged at flesh. It made him sick. Lucky refused entirely to approach. He left her, waving his hands like a madman, weaving drunkenly as he yelled.

The vultures scattered, leisurely. Indignant. One snapped

half-heartedly as he stumbled through the black carnage. Arthmael thought he recognised his sister in the pieces. Her black mane. Her massive ribs.

But it occurred to him that, dead or alive, wolf bodies existed only within wolf-moon. He collapsed to sit untidily. 'She's alive,' he whispered, though a part of him knew this was not the most logical, not the only, conclusion.

Lucky had turned around and was trudging back to the memory of shade. 'Come back,' he called, but his throat was dry and she ignored him. Only her ears flicked in recognition. The vultures hopped closer.

The dirt looked so inviting. If he could just catch a few moments' rest . . . He fought its almost irresistible pull and forced himself to look around. The vultures were back, so far giving him a wide birth. He scanned the horizon and his heart lurched again. West, further than he could have seen before, more vultures hovered. They'd found another meal.

He was too late! He lurched to his feet, torn between the impulse to stagger to his sister and the impulse to draw back, to not witness. Offering his heart a minute's reprieve, he scanned further north.

There, on the horizon! Blue lights streaked upwards to suddenly bloom, difficult to see in the bright sky. A red firework fizzed in spirals.

His heart stuttered, then pounded in double time. Joy and adrenaline rushed through his veins. Abruptly, vibrantly awake, he lurched after the cart, caught Lucky as she picked up into an exhausted trot, and dragged her around. 'If you've got that much energy you can use it to rescue a princess, you stubborn mule,' he grumbled in a delighted mood. 'Just remember, I'm the water keeper. There's nothing for you back there.'

They stumbled on, stopping to drink only once. Then the fireworks stopped. They were close though. Arthmael dragged the mare.

'Jay!' he called. His eyes swept bushes. His chest hurt, imagining the worst.

He saw them only as he passed, yellow sparkles spluttering along the ground. The burning in his chest flared agonisingly. He dragged the horse to his sister, unscrewing the bottle with his teeth. She'd covered herself in branches as meagre protection. Branches tumbled off as he lifted her wasted shoulders. He dribbled water onto her swollen tongue. Her throat swallowed. Then again, and again.

'Jay.' His voice broke.

Her eyes fluttered half open, then closed. He wasn't sure she'd recognised his face. He recognised hers, but it was changed. Clear, pale skin stretched tight over her skull, a grotesque parody of the pretty elfishness he remembered. He leaned over to keep her in shadow. His offering dribbled in, but it was slow work. She choked easily. She was too dry to perspire, burning hot. The horse nuzzled him, impatient for drink. He elbowed her sharply.

Jatta's eyes opened, enormous and innocent in their gaping sockets.

'Drag . . .' she rasped.

He pondered her question for a moment. 'Did your little friend guide me here? No, Jay. I found you myself.'

Her smile flickered. She seemed to like that answer.

'Home . . . now?'

Maybe she was delirious. Maybe she just meant their camp. 'No. Right now you need shade and I'm tired. Vardensen Ruins are close, we'll rest there till dark.'

She smiled at that, too. So accepting, so fatalistically placid. So fragile. The skin on her upper arms was wrinkled and her elbows were the thickest part. He gently lifted her. Her lightness terrified him. Like a soul, she might fly away. Arthmael swallowed twice to dislodge the dry lump in his throat. He draped her on the cart and smacked Lucky's rump. They trudged north.

CHAPTER THIRTY-THREE

His blurred vision could no longer read the map. Through the corrugated haze he thought he saw it ahead, the ancient city of Vardensen with its untidily crumbling sandstone fortress walls. It, like the desert, was a dead testament to Andro Mogon's magic.

Vardensen's main entrance was more of a stone tunnel than an archway, because the fortress wall it cut through was five paces thick. Arthmael made it no further. The sudden drop in temperature was such relief that he decided then and there to stop for the afternoon.

With mammoth effort of will he settled Jatta on a blanket on the pavers. He filled her mug and crumbled sesame biscuits into it to make a sort of soup. He had to feel his way because his dried brain couldn't focus his eyes. He fumbled and dragged off Lucky's load. She was nudging him, thirsty again, and he overbalanced against her neck. It felt nice there, warm and soft like a pillow. He didn't remember sliding.

Arthmael woke breathing in the pleasant smell of oats. His throat was parched again, and he was hungry, but miraculously awake for such an impromptu nap. He'd somehow settled to sleep with his head on the horse feed. Jatta's face was beside his. Its sickliness shocked him again, her ball-like eyes watching him placidly, her cheek wrinkled rather than flattened against the sack. Poor kid, it must have cost her to crawl over the cobbles. Her tentative smile twitched, and he grinned back as convincingly as he could.

'Hi there, little sister. Hungry? Thirsty?'

Her mug was empty. That was good. He poured fresh water for both of them. They shared dried fruit. She sucked on hers, had trouble swallowing, so he dissolved more biscuits in her water. It gratified him to see how greedily she drank.

He examined her burned arm. The blistering was not bad, not like he'd feared, though her woollen sleeve had completely burned away. The dress was singed in many spots. All down its back, where her mane had caught alight, was burned off, though thankfully not her reddened flesh. A peculiar magic, her wolf.

She tried to talk. He leant close.

'I knew ... you were ... alive,' she croaked.

'Did you know I'd find you?' he asked.

'No.'

Her voice was accepting, calm. She'd lain in the sun sending up fireworks, waiting serenely for death. She had more horror of killing him than dying, he knew that.

'How did you know you hadn't eaten me?' he said, working hard to sound casual.

Her eyes dropped to the bandage she still clutched, the tunic he'd torn up and wrapped around her wolf burn. It had probably fallen off when she'd morphed back.

'My wolf and you ... friends, now.'

He chuckled. 'Sure, Jay. Bosom buddies.' He patted her shoulder gently. She closed her eyes, looking not like a wolf, but a puppy. A half-starved, grateful stray.

But the sun was setting. It was time to leave. He scooped up the sack of feed and looked around.

Lucky was gone. Why didn't that surprise him? He took a deep breath and sighed it out in frustration.

'Jay, did you hear where the horse went?'

She raised a limp hand, pointing to the city's north.

'When, Jay?'

'Last . . . night.'

That rocked him. He stared blankly.

'No! Tell me we haven't wasted a day!'

She blinked, suddenly wary.

Lord. He'd slept away their chances of survival. How pitifully, selfishly weak. Lucky would be dead, or near enough, and then how would they get out? He might manage to carry his sister on the cart, might even manage to fatten her up on the way, but how could he ever carry enough water for their long trek out of the desert?

Her face twisted when she read the expression on his. He forced a grin. 'Listen, Jay. I'm off looking for Lucky. Will you be all right?'

'My fault.'

'That's daft, it's mine. But I can fix this—do you believe me?'

She nodded uncertainly.

'Good girl.' He poured out a handful of fruit. 'I want these gone before I'm back.'

The fruit had disappeared an hour later when he returned in the dark. He woke Jatta and made her eat and drink. It frightened him that he'd let her go twenty-four hours without a meal. He woke her twice more in the night, then at first light he left her cheese and water, and set off again to look for Lucky.

Arthmael followed horse tracks in the heavily layered dust,

passing blocky, flat-roofed buildings crammed tight together. All were honey-coloured sandstone, all surprisingly intact. Arthmael searched inside a few, but found nothing except urns, bronze farming tools and Dartithans' bones.

This was a place founded by Dartith's refugees. They'd thrived here for a few short years, Arthmael's professors had said, had grown grapes and oranges. A river once meandered down from the hills and through these streets. Like the hills, the river, vineyards and orchards were gone, flattened and dried into desert by Andro Mogon. 'Why?' he'd asked. To punish their leader Vardensen, his once-favoured great-grandson, for ever leaving Dartith. There'd been no escaping the vengeful Sorcerer. This had been the lesson of Vardensen's destruction.

Arthmael returned outside, seeing the one thing he'd dreaded.

Birds circled above the city's north.

There he found the mare, already dead. Andro Mogon's desert forgave no error. Lucky's luck had run out as, probably, had theirs.

It was midmorning when he got back. He woke Jatta and while she ate he told her what he'd seen, that they would stay now till she had more strength. Though he didn't say it, they'd stay till he'd figured out what to do.

It was after midnight, their sixth night in Vardensen. His sister lay propped up against their tunnel, staring as usual up at the desert moon. Physically she was much stronger, though she slept too much, grown sombre. She never played with her ball. She'd told him about Dragongirl in the labyrinth, and he'd chosen to believe, although the phantom seemed to have forgotten them since. She said she'd let go of life in the caves. They were both still alive, though, so why was she this sad? He didn't push. Maybe he should have, but then she'd bury him under a dump of misery and he didn't have the words to dig them out.

Besides, he had his own unpleasant memory to protect.

'What a waste.' She turned to him, her eyes as empty as her voice. He settled beside her to wrap an arm around her skinny shoulders.

'What's a waste?'

She laid her head on his chest. 'Us. Our deaths.'

'We're not dying . . . not yet.'

'How much food do we have?'

'We'll run out of water first. Listen, Jay, I've been thinking. We could leave, make it back to camp. Then we'd try for the canyon. That's maybe another two nights' walk. With your ball we could survive the dragons quite some time . . . maybe one day fresh explorers would come.'

'Can't we get out of the desert?'

He'd known she would ask. 'We'd have to hand-pull the cart, ditch the scales and most of the provisions, load it with every drop of water. We'd travel by night, ditch the cart by the end. It'd probably take a couple of weeks, and chances are we'd still shrivel up with thirst. I recommend the canyon.'

He waited, hoping her chin might pull up with his favourite shy smile. His confidence wavered to doubt, then discomfort when her back started trembling. She was crying.

'Oh, Art! What about everyone else?' She punched the words out in sobs. 'What about Father and Steffed? The whole court starves whether we die in the desert, or make it out, or—or to the canyon, and every day we're not delivered to

Brackensith brings more carnage. With the scales we might have saved everyone. Instead our Grand and Noble Sacrifice is withering away. That's the stupid, ridiculous waste.'

Arthmael rubbed her back in silence. She kept her cheek pressed to his shirt, wet through with tears. When he judged she'd calmed down enough, he answered.

'You know, Jay, you look like a kid, you cry like a girl, but you think like a wizened old soul. Thinking's good, normally. When it changes things. Right now it's just making you miserable, and that isn't helping us. You can help, though.'

Eventually he was rewarded by a tiny, muffled, 'How?'

'By growing fat and strong and happy, so we can try— *try*—to get your scales out. The cart's going to be heavy, so you'll have to help me pull. We'll leave tomorrow afternoon.'

She lifted her face with a brittle attempt at a smile. He grimaced at her pain. With some effort he managed a roguish grin.

'That's better, Jay. Supper and a story, then.' He'd taken to re-telling their adventures since she'd been sick.

'The one where you win back my orb,' she whispered.

Both understood she meant the story of his house arrest. He'd never answered her question about the first time, about the one-armed Alteedan.

'You eat, I'll talk.' Arthmael scooped oats and a biscuit onto a brass plate he'd scavenged. This story was comic; it worked best with a demonstration. He held out his hand in a flourish; she offered her orb and the dwarf's useless amulet. He waited till she had the biscuit in her mouth, then he tucked her amulet inside his sleeve.

'You might think, little sister, that your brother lacks your prodigious imagination. Maybe so, but he has more wits than the apes who pass for Fand's soldiers,' he began, drawing her in with a sly wink.

'I'd just slashed Riz's tent and you two were up viewing the dragon's breakfast in the hide. There I was, watching four of Fand's finest fool around with your ball. They were trying for fireworks but getting mostly smells. One managed venison on a spit, another got battle odours—blood, guts, burning. One conjured Riz's girlie giggle and got everyone sniggering. Nothing spectacular, Jay, not like Fand's fireworks . . . or my candle sparks.' He demonstrated with a red flame on his thumb. A second flame lit, then a third, fourth and fifth on his knuckles as they kneaded the orb.

Her smile flickered. 'Impressive.'

'Indubitably. I rival you. Are you tempted to surrender your ball?'

He laughed as her puffy eyes tightened defensively. 'Glory, Jay. Where's your sense of humour?'

She tried harder to smile.

'Good girl. So I told them, "You have to caress the ball and coax it just right. Then it turns into its true form—not a conjurer's toy, but a purple gem fat enough to buy your own army, and dragons and kingdom as well." They liked that idea. I got them stroking and tickling and kissing the thing, even fed them tender lines.' He was hamming it up, his enthusiasm taking over. 'But of course . . .'

'Nothing happened.'

'They were more persistent than I'd hoped, though eventually even they got bored. Then I said innocently, "Twiddle your fingertips. Here, like this . . ."'

'And they gave you the orb.'

'Right. I had Ambassador Sartora's fat amethyst waiting up my sleeve. Are you watching?'

The orb dropped from his cupped hand to hide in his lap. The amulet slipped, with a flourish, down his sleeve to his cupped hand.

'Magic,' she said.

He displayed her amulet blazing with five flames, just as he'd displayed the grand amethyst blazing to his soldier guards. Grinning, she reached for the orb. He surrendered it only when she slapped him.

'And you kept on squeezing,' she said. 'All day. All night. All the next day. Your hands must've dropped off.'

'I'm no martyr. There were times my hands cramped, like that time you despaired. And I dozed a bit through the night. I guess you were too busy remodelling caves to notice that.'

He yawned at the mention of sleep, squeezed her shoulder and got up to stretch. 'Right, I'm off to the guardhouse. Pleasant dreams, little sister.'

'No, stay, please. You never used to talk in your sleep.'

'I do now.'

'It won't bother me, Art.'

But his yells and night sweats might. His grin tightened. It strained him, leaving her alone. 'Good night, Jay. It bothers me.'

CHAPTER THIRTY-FOUR

In the end they packed the crown, book and jewels, too. They weren't heavy. Arthmael hitched himself to the cart like a horse. Jatta pushed it from behind along Vardensen's dust-covered highway. She wasn't helping much, but at least she wasn't sitting inside as he'd since offered. She'd believed him before; their chances of survival weren't good.

He was cheerful to be doing something again. He called back as he trudged. 'So, Jay, we're off to see Dartith. Tell me about our new friends.'

'Mmm . . . well, you'll meet Undead.'

'Andro Mogon's "*Chosen*," right?'

'Uh-huh. An Undead has unique status. He's above the law, allowed to kill anyone—except the King.'

'Can this creature be killed?'

'There's a death penalty for trying. But yes, with a shard from the obsidian slab he sleeps on. That's where his soul resides, inside the obsidian. You have to slice right through his four pulse points—heart, throat and both wrists. Then his soul seeps out of the slab and . . . well, it goes wherever souls go. He needs his soul.'

'It's a bit gory. Isn't there another way to dispatch the thing? In case I ever choose the wrong drinking companion.'

'The other way's gorier and it's not quick. You have to prevent him getting back to his soul at dawn.'

'Sounds easier.'

'Well, he'll start to decay and he won't be happy. He might take two or three days to rot away and in the meantime he'll enlist help. Undead aren't sociable, but they band together under threat.'

'Delightful place we're holidaying. A good choice, Jay.' As he trudged, Arthmael twisted back to toast Jatta with a guzzle from his water bottle. His wink teased her. His sandy mane was already streaked with sweat.

They hadn't shared sleeping space since that first night in Vardensen. Today they slept on sand pillows under their cart, on an oven-hot desert plain.

Muffled groans woke Jatta. It was Arthmael, slicing an imaginary blade through the air. His eyes were wide open but they saw nothing.

'Don't—make—me—do—it.' His hoarse whisper frightened her.

'Art! Wake up.' She nudged him urgently.

He blinked, then squeezed his eyes shut. When he opened them they were filled with misery. He lay staring at the boards.

'Jay, I killed three men.'

She didn't know what to say.

'We threw daggers for your ball. They said I'd lost, I'd be dragon fodder. I said I'd won.'

'So—so you killed them?'

'There was a fight. They started it. But yes.'

'Then they were trying to kill *you*?'

'The look on their faces, Jay, the moment I thrust. The *shloosh* of my steel through their hearts. I can't get it out of my head.'

Jatta let the silence hang, imagining what killing might have felt like for Arthmael. It wasn't hard. She'd imagined it for herself so often.

'I'd feel the same,' she said quietly. 'It can't be wrong to hate killing people.'

He snorted, and she felt the contempt in that sound was for himself.

'Maybe not back home,' he said. 'Back home we didn't face impossible questions about who should die. And swordplay was a sport, a display of manhood, just a *game*. Everything felt stable and safe—well, till your wolf reared its head. But my conscience was safe. Out here, though . . . it's might, not right, that matters. I can wield a sword well enough, but now . . . I'm no longer sure I can kill. And I can't afford to be girly, not weak, not fraught. Not with you depending on me. I can't afford memories that make my hands shake.'

They'd stopped for another rest, always thirsty. After two weeks of night-trekking the moon was bloated three-quarters full. Jatta lay on the dirt. She squeezed her orb and rewound its face to a crescent. Who was she fooling, though? Only herself.

Arthmael came and lay back on his elbows, his thick throat stretched to the stars as he watched. She felt guilty feeding her misery with the moon, so she put on a show for him. She exploded its yellowed face, showering sparkles through the sky and over them like an heraldic falling star.

He smiled as if he could read her thoughts, and swallowed. His Adam's apple moved under his beard.

'What's it like when you're a wolf?'

'I don't know really, don't want to. I'm not supposed to remember anything yet,' she answered.

'Yet?'

His easy question would be difficult to answer. She took a deep breath. 'The book says that after something like twenty-five years I'm supposed to remember flashes. The highlights. The taste of my kill.' She grimaced. 'A mature wolf remembers everything, carries all that bloodlust and hatred and fury around screaming in her head every day. Art . . .' This was the hard part. 'I'll change. Someday you're not going to like me anymore. Promise me if we're still in Dartith you'll leave. Alone.'

'I won't forsake you.'

'The me you know will be gone.'

'No. Your wolf is different.'

'That's what scares me. Maybe it *is* different, because it's started. Art, I woke in the desert remembering . . . things. I remembered morphing, losing my self . . . the pain, mostly.' Her body tensed, and her eyes screwed up with the memory of splintering bone. Taking deep breaths through her nose, she coaxed the pain back, coaxed calm back into her muscles. Arthmael examined the stars till her eyes reopened. 'I remembered you, too, telling me everything would be all right.'

'It will be.'

Was he humouring her again? No, his voice had pleaded. He needed this—fearless Arthmael, who'd never before shied from unpalatable truths.

'See, you're only remembering your *Jay* self. The rest isn't going to happen, not for a generation. Not ever.'

She wanted to believe, like him.

'You think too much, Jay.'

He was right. Thinking wouldn't change a thing.

*

After their fifteenth night they trudged on till the blaze forced them under the cart. Jatta licked the last water from her mug. There was no more after this, and another night's hike stretched ahead. Maybe two. They'd discussed dumping the scales; they'd get further now just on foot. But that had never really been an option. Getting out had always been a gamble.

That afternoon Arthmael didn't cry out in his sleep.

It was others who woke them.

The thunder was like Goy-an Falls: hooves pounding too close. She glimpsed them through the wheel, past Arthmael's shoulder. Glimpsed enough to stir old fears. Arthmael's sword was unsheathed but he lay still. His eyes flicked to her skirts, his finger pressed to his lips, and she understood. The soldiers were almost upon them. Twelve, too many to fight—even if Arthmael could rouse a bloodlust to match his prowess. She reached into her pocket for the orb.

Gone. She groped among her skirt folds. It must have dropped out as she slept.

Dartithan horses fanned out to circle their meagre cart. Arthmael's face rolled to hers, slowly, so that the movement attracted no attention. She mouthed, 'No'. They were exposed. Only their unlikely position and good luck had blinkered the soldiers, and now that they'd swung down from their saddles they need only look down to discover the fugitives. Boots shuffled dirt while she discreetly scrunched her skirts and Arthmael prodded around. Her breath felt too loud.

The Dartithans ransacked the cart above them. Her frightened eyes watched their faces through gaps in the boards. They bickered and swore. They divided up jewels and passed scales around. The officer guessed what the scales were and slung them onto his own pack horse; no-one guessed their purpose. They went suddenly, uncomfortably quiet when someone found the crown.

'The King will be wanting that back,' growled the officer's gruff voice.

'He will not miss it. He be not surviving the week,' said one.

Pain twisted Jatta's insides. She froze.

'Not him, you weevil wit. *Riz.*'

'King Riz be gone within the week, too, I think,' said the other. 'And us. Rumour be he found the Princess.'

'Has he now?' growled the officer sarcastically. 'That be confounded inconvenient for him. You shall find her escaped soon enough. Again.'

'But she led a revolt in South Saeth. His Undead torched the town yesterday.'

'I hold no doubts they did,' growled the officer. 'And I wager these scales that he danced and giggled while it burned. But you think these mainlanders have guts for revolt? They be spineless as worms. Now torch the cart. Hand back the jewels too, and I shall personally see our beloved *King* gets the lot.'

While the men objected, Jatta's arm desperately swept the dirt. Her orb must be lost. She'd last used it leagues back, exploding the moon.

'You're leaving,' Arthmael whispered grimly.

Two words. They gave her the most tearing feeling of loss. 'No,' she pleaded.

'I'll be following right behind.' He grinned tightly. 'I'm no martyr, Jay.'

Yes, he was. Her eyes grew moist.

'Listen, Jay, I'm no army, either. I'll catch up if I can.'

'No. I'm fighting with you.'

He gave her a pained look.

Why make this worse for him than it already was? She nodded, knowing that if he scooped her into a saddle with the scales, she *would* desert him. In that moment she almost wished it was wolf-moon.

'Good girl,' he mouthed, his neck banded with tension. He twisted smoothly out from under the cart. Horses side-stepped away. Jatta wriggled out, casting one longing glance back, catching movement. The orb was there, rolling out from under her hem. As Arthmael's arms scooped her up, she snatched it.

Even as she morphed, she knew it was a bad choice. But she was already in the air halfway to a horse's back before she'd thought of anyone else.

Arthmael looked appalled.

It was too late to change. Riz's voice screamed down from the saddle at thirteen aghast faces. 'That treasure be mine! Mine! Give it back!'

The cynical officer looked incredulous. She could appreciate that. Why would Riz hide in a desert, under a cart, with a feral fugitive-prince?

'So! You speak treason and think I do not hear?' she yelled, circling them, hemming them in. 'Think I be stuck in South Saeth? Remember my father's portal, you cretins.'

'The *King* be here?' The officer sneaked a frightened look under the cart.

'*The* King? We be two Kings, two!' Her fist punched the air above Riz's head, feeling its sand. Was she also wearing Alteeda's crown? Too late, again. 'Father and I be hunting dragons in the canyon. Yes, a reward for finding Drake's bride.'

Father and I? What was she thinking? She'd seen Brackensith just once, for a few moments, and this charade was confusing even her. The men gazed around, terrified. Some peered into the sky. Arthmael had recovered, and grinned crookedly up at her.

'You cannot *see* him, treacherous cretins!' she squealed. 'No, he be off riding our dragon. Now hand me my treasures and be gone. Go, or else, um . . .'

'Or else join me as supper,' added Arthmael cheerfully.

The officer blanched. Evidently he was aware of Riz's canyon diversions. He hurried to obey, handing her the sack.

She should have refused, should have made him deposit it in the cart. She should have remembered how heavy it was.

'Let me, Majesty,' said Arthmael, dodging past soldiers to her. But she had already reached down from the saddle. She'd taken the sack.

Its weight dragged her. She felt herself slide sideways in slow motion. Too late, she dropped the scales. As she continued her path to the ground Arthmael grabbed for her. His arms disappeared somewhere inside.

Men leapt back as if from a striking snake.

Riz's head trailed down through her brother's chest, hips and legs to hit the ground. The jolt stole Jatta's breath. The horse backed away, wide eyed. Arthmael quietly drew his sword.

'Why stare . . . rank wretches?' Her Riz leapt to his feet, taking breathless gasps. One eye twitched. 'Have you any notion . . . how that hurt? How my skull aches from his belly?' She wheeled on them, coronation cape rippling. She caught enough breath to scream, 'Think this shall never happen to you? Let this be warning, one portal trip too many, and—and you shall grow immaterial like me.'

Some blanched white. Several hands gravitated to swords. In her peripheral vision she caught the officer's cold nod.

The sky screeched like fingernails down slates, breaking the impasse. Everyone looked up. From south came a dragon to the rescue, with the Dartithan King riding her neck. Twelve pairs of believing eyes turned to Jatta.

The officer dropped to kneel, pleading, 'Majesty, we beg you.'

'Oh, so now you expect deliverance,' she whined. 'You steal my spare crown, you call me impostor, you ... you *stare*, and still you plead not to be eaten. Well, we shall see. You shall have a sporting start before my dragon hunts you. That be more than fair, yes?'

Not one had the courage to answer.

'Go.'

The soldiers scrambled for horses, swung up and fled. Their dust settled over Riz's cape as his sour expression drooped to grief.

'That proved entertaining,' said Arthmael. He had one arm draped across the pack horse's neck, absently patting it as he grinned up at the hovering dragon.

For once his humour was completely unpardonable. She flung the orb at him. It flew wide, but he still reached and caught it. He laughed at her in surprise.

'Don't!' She glowered miserably. 'He's almost dead.'

'Father, you mean? I find that reassuring,' he said blithely, then his grin faded. 'To be frank, I'd imagined worse.'

'Pardon?' she demanded.

He busied himself unpacking the horse. 'I figured they both were dead, but I didn't know, all right? Jay, I can't worry about things like that. Not crises I can't control, not tragedies I can't know. Unlike you, I just don't have the energy.' He tossed the sack onto the cart, then strolled over to rub her shoulders. 'I need all my energy to deliver you to Dartith. Father's alive, Jay. We'll keep him alive. Yes?'

'Yes.' She smiled weakly.

'Good girl.' He flashed her favourite wry grin, then jerked his head toward Straefordtown. 'And we *will* make it, now our Dartithan benefactors have provided water and a horse.'

CHAPTER THIRTY-FIVE

They emerged from desert to cottage farms and the outlying suburbs of Straefordtown. Rain sprinkled their faces, streaking desert mud into their lashes.

By midday they'd tethered the horse and found the city square, an open market bounded by grand public buildings. The police station here, and council chambers too, were burnt-out shells; it disturbed them, even more than the dozen ransacked shops or the shanty town being hammered together in a schoolyard.

There was no explaining the almost festive vibrancy to the square. Mounted constables waded through the crowd. Storeholders nodded up at them while children patted their horses. Shoppers gossiped in impossibly long queues outside bakeries and vegetable stalls.

Above the crowd, above the constables too, and towering over the council chambers' steps, was Straefordtown's famous landmark. The life-size bronze dragon—the shire's emblem— spread a long protective shadow over the stalls. There was a commotion under its column now: a woman's voice shouting, an elegant voice nonetheless, and constables gruffly arguing. Jatta and Arthmael joined the crowd gathering on the steps. What they saw jolted Jatta's stomach with unease.

'Come,' growled Arthmael through clenched teeth. He drew her out of the crowd and up the council chambers' steps.

They peered out from behind its charred doorway. The woman's groceries were in baskets at her feet. Three small girls clung to her skirts while she tore at papers plastered all over the dragon column. Reward posters.

'Shame! For shame!' she cried, lean, tall and formidable. Indeed, some of the burly uniformed men did avert their eyes.

One officer worked his way along the buildings. She turned on him. 'Tobin, don't you have vandals to round up? Don't you have highways to protect?'

Ignoring her anger, he jumped the steps to the council chambers and glued posters to the very door Jatta and Arthmael hid behind. If he'd bothered to peer inside he may have recognised their faces from his posters. He'd have earned himself forty krouns.

The crowd below seemed to be polarised. A trio of aproned apprentices climbed to tear off the wet posters even before he left for the next facade. Unlike the woman, they were arrested at once.

A mounted officer arrived and the crowd parted for him. Balding and unimpressive to look at, he had dark bags under his eyes and a stubble beard. He swung from his horse to hit the ground wearily. While the woman argued at him, he wordlessly lifted the children from her skirts and into the arms of three constables. To Jatta's confusion the girls clung there. Perhaps they, like their mother, were familiar faces to the force.

'Do not betray King Elisind's love for his children. Tear off these symbols of our oppression with me!' their mother called as the officer chained her wrists and pulled her through to the steps.

Arthmael only just managed to drag Jatta behind an over-turned desk before the officer and prisoner stepped inside.

The woman's eyes were narrowed and fearless. Arthmael and Jatta got soot in their hair as they peeked out.

The officer groaned and rubbed his eyes. His hand slid down his stubbled chin, then dropped. 'Stay out of politics, Porsha Prentis. You've no notion, so quit provoking Riz. Do you want us sacked, like North Bradfirth? Burnt to the pavers like South Saeth? Look around the market—half the faces are Bradfirth's. Here we've got food coming in. Gas. Law.' He plucked a poster that was still stuck to her skirts and held it to her face. 'Paper. Ink.' He released it to float to the soot. 'Won't you just play along?'

'Play along with that vermin?' she scoffed. 'Will you betray your King? Surrender his children?'

'Will *you* let him starve?'

'I'll trust in Lord Redd to rescue him, not vicious Riz.'

'Like Ambassador Sartora did? Like South Saeth? Porsha, even now Redd's forest is swarming with petitioners.'

'The Lord won't betray his Sorcerer's Pact.'

The officer let out an exasperated gust of air. 'He's dead, Porsha,' he muttered, and leant to unlock her chains.

She ignored the comment and gazed around the blistered ceiling, then lower. Arthmael grabbed Jatta's head to his chest, but he was less fortunate.

Porsha's eyes locked with his. Their confusion changed to recognition before she quickly looked back to the officer.

'Soon enough, Porsha, someone will find that girl's selfish, sacred little hide. Alteeda will survive without its Princess. Not without its King.' The officer turned and left.

Arthmael and Jatta stayed hidden, listening for Porsha to leave, too. She didn't. She picked her way through the debris.

Jatta admired this woman who championed her, so she

squeezed. She moulded Arthmael's nose thicker and made his eyes smaller, a less strikingly handsome upper face. His strong jaw was already hidden behind beard. She reddened both their hair. Her own face she modified just a little.

They rose together. Porsha peered first at Arthmael, suspicious, and Jatta wished she'd padded out the planes of his cheeks. Porsha bobbed down to examine Jatta. Jatta had flattened her bust and thickened her petite waist, repaired burns in her dress and cleaned off dust. Her cheeks and forehead were rounded like a nine-year-old's. For the first time in her life Jatta looked to be tall for her age. She watched Porsha's expression relax; she imagined it must be one thing to defend a Princess, quite another to give her asylum. She smiled shyly and Porsha returned it with her own motherly, encouraging smile.

'Why were you hiding, child? Are you in trouble?'

Arthmael's jaw tightened. 'We're not in trouble, just humble refugees in town for supplies.'

Porsha straightened and eyed him sceptically. 'Not with that noble accent, you're not, young man. Nor that Dartithan ring. Who are you, with your farmer's dirt and trousers and tan?'

'He's my Uncle Lionneller. We *are* refugees,' said Jatta. 'Please help us. We fled the palace but Riz still—'

'Jay,' warned Arthmael under his breath.

'Please, Porsha. We need a place to stay tonight. Just a barn, we're used to sleeping rough. And maybe something to eat and grass for our horse.'

Porsha's kind eyes were fixed on Jatta. She chewed her lips in contemplation. Her eyes flicked to Arthmael. 'Do you have money for bread?'

250

Arthmael nodded.

'Good, that will help. Now let's go rescue the constables from my girls.'

Porsha bought turnips and lentils with Arthmael's silver coins. At the bakery she bought cheap bran bread. Her five-year-old eyed the cream tarts covetously. She tugged at her mother's skirts. 'May I, please?'

'You know the answer, Pippa,' Porsha whispered. 'Maybe next week.'

Porsha led them back through the markets.

'We also need to buy glue,' said Arthmael.

'For what purpose?' Porsha asked.

Jatta pulled a handful of scales from her pocket. 'We want to attach these to clothing.'

Porsha took one, turning it, smiling at her own reflection. 'Gracious, it's a mirror. But it's hard as steel.'

They bought a toffee-coloured glue block Porsha recommended. Ten-year-old Patra and seven-year-old Lana rode on the cart home. Young Pippa rode on the dusty horse.

'Stable him with the others, girls,' Porsha said when they reached the family's three-storey townhouse. 'And tell Grandfather we'll need his gluing skills.'

Arthmael and Jatta followed her along a wide hall to a living room furnished with plush antiques and a harpsichord. An old man sat reading a book, and Porsha gestured for her guests to sit also. They exchanged puzzled glances. How could such an elegant household not readily afford bread?

'Jay. Lionneller. Let me introduce my husband's father, Gile,' said Porsha.

Gile peered critically over his book at them. 'Jay?

Lionneller? What odd sort of names.' When no-one responded he continued. 'So what is it you youngsters intend to glue?'

Jatta again produced a scale. Gile turned it over, bit it, flicked it close to his ear, and leaned back in his sofa with a perplexed snort. 'I'll be a wolf's supper! Mirrored like a dragon scale, but stone hard. What in gremlins' grotto is it?'

Arthmael's smile twitched. 'You might have guessed right.'

The old man eyed him sceptically. 'Where'd you find them, then?'

'A graveyard.'

'Right, young fellow. If you're wanting these *dragon scales* to stick, I recommend leather.'

Arthmael groaned. 'Come on, Jay. Back to the market.'

'Wait,' said Porsha. 'We have trunks of old clothes in the attic.'

'We'd want to pay you for them,' said Jatta.

For the first time the old man smiled. A gold tooth gleamed. 'Missy, that'd be grand. Every penning helps.'

They formed a work group in the living room. Jatta yawned often, missing her day's sleep while her feet massaged the orb under her skirts. She and Porsha sewed leather hoods with slits for eyes; Pippa and her sisters sorted scales into sizes. Arthmael brushed each with the glue that Gile had boiled up, then the old man carefully positioned each overlapping scale on the outfits.

'What's it all for?' asked Pippa.

All eyes turned to Arthmael and Jatta. Jatta stole a peep at her brother, whose head shook minutely in warning.

'Guess, Pippa,' said Jatta. 'If you guess warm, we'll tell you.'

The girls liked this game, and Porsha joined in too. Gile

worked on, growing increasingly ill-tempered. 'Right, we've learnt what these outfits aren't. Kindly end our suspense. Tell us what, by the stars, they *are*.'

'They're coolsuits,' said Jatta. 'They keep us cool no matter how hot it gets.'

Gile snorted, as if despairing of a straight answer.

When Arthmael asked, though, Gile did tell of their own troubles. In the five weeks Riz had held Alteeda's palace, no-one in the King's service had been paid.

'I'm a history professor,' said Porsha. 'I'm still lecturing, but others are off seeking paying work. They have families to feed.' She sighed in resignation. 'We teachers aren't essential. If students aren't memorising Sorcerer reforms, towns won't crumble.'

The same could not be said for others on the King's payroll. Those who lit the night's streets were running out of oil. Widows and the poor had received no pensions.

Most crucial of all were the constables. As they left their posts for paying jobs, escaped prisoners had taken to robbing along the highways. There'd been rioting and looting too, as food failed to reach towns. A neighbouring shire, where the sheriff had been stabbed, was under siege as rival gangs battled for power.

'My husband sheriffs North Straefordshire. His men still earn half pay—we offer it from our own savings. To set an example we live off the same. But one life's savings won't last long among a hundred men.'

The children went to bed. Jatta's mind had numbed from conjuring and her toes had cramped before they finished the suits. Porsha leant close to stroke her hair.

'Past bedtime, squirrel. Do you need a bath?'

Jatta's chubby cheeks spread in an exhausted grin. A bath. It had been too long.

She followed, stumbling up stairs to a pantry-sized room. A full-length brass tub and a chair took up half its space. 'Thank you,' she whispered as Porsha left her alone.

The relief as she slipped into the warmth was immense. She scrubbed with scented soap and the water turned murky. That would be tricky to explain. Her eyes closed. Her body grew too heavy to get out, her breathing slow. Now that her guardian had brought her to kind Porsha, she might relax.

Jatta woke shivering. She tensed. Her eyes bolted open to an unfamiliar ceiling, flashed to the door, then squeezed shut. Drat, drat. Surrendering to urges was never safe, never okay. She lifted her goose-pimpled elbows to the tub rim, hauled herself to sit, and looked for the towel.

The chair was occupied.

Porsha was staring. A pained look tightened her face.

Oh, no. One hand fished the tub for her orb while she resisted the impulse to dive back under. She gave up fishing, too. She turned to face Porsha and tried pleading.

'Don't tell,' was the best she could manage.

Porsha slid from the chair to kneel by Jatta's tub, whether in reverence or in sympathy Jatta couldn't tell.

'Highness, how did you do what you did?'

'What, change my face? Please, I can explain everything. Um, not everything but ... Look.' She groped around her shivering legs for the orb, then pressed it for Porsha. Her fine chin rounded out. Porsha blinked, shaking her head a few times as if to clear it.

Jatta stopped squeezing. 'Just let us leave. I'm sorry we've compromised you. Five minutes start, that's all we ask.'

'Highness, it's not me you should fear. How could I, a mother, betray you?'

Nonetheless Jatta read guilt in her face. 'Who, then?'

'The man I argued with in the courthouse, my husband. He's waiting for you below.' Porsha grabbed a towel and wrapped it around Jatta as she stepped shivering from the water. 'When I told him we had guests, he'd heard your pet name. I assured him you were merely a child.'

'Then we can trick him?'

'I hope so. Do others know you have magic?'

'No-one except Art and Redd.' No-one else living.

'Lord Redd!' Shock and hope froze her face. She dropped from her knees to sit. 'Will he save us?'

'Um, not exactly.'

Porsha's eyes locked with hers. Whatever they read in Jatta's, their hope wavered to doubt.

'Redd was an impostor,' said Jatta gently. 'No-one special, just really clever with the orb.'

'Impossible ... but who will follow? Our Age of Enlightenment ... his line mustn't be broken.'

'No-one will follow,' said Jatta. 'Andro Mogon died. His line was broken a hundred and fifty years before Redd.'

'But what's to become of us?'

Finally Porsha accepted. It twisted Jatta's stomach to watch an all-too familiar hopelessness wash through her.

'What are we to do? We've lived the Sorcerers' Code,' said Porsha. 'For seven thousand years we've forsaken armies and kept our weapons archaic. We imagined ourselves a careful, gentle world, but we're infants dumped in a schoolyard. Innocents. Who will protect us from Dartith's playground bullies?'

Jatta knew the answer, though it was hardly reassuring. Only Dartith itself could punish bullying Riz. 'We'll cope. Remember, we haven't had a proper Sorcerer these three thousand years and we managed till now.' *That* was because no-one had dared defy Dartith before now.

'Cope? Jay, how?'

Jatta loved that Porsha called her by name again. She looked down into that motherly, strong face and made a decision. 'Can you keep a secret?'

'Of course.'

Jatta settled beside her on the tiles. Battling through the towel's folds, she slipped her hand inside Porsha's. 'You were right not to trust Riz. Art and I are going to Brackensith direct so he'll leave Alteeda alone. That's what the scale suits are for. They're fireproof.'

Jatta relaxed against the soft rise and fall of Porsha's chest. Finally Porsha leant down to kiss her scalp.

'You're planning on staying in Dartith?' asked Porsha.

'That's likely. Yes.'

'That will be Alteeda's loss.'

Someone knocked on the door. 'Porsha!' called a weary male voice, not one length from Jatta's ear. Her shoulders tensed.

'Patience, Lerrick,' called Porsha. 'Give the child time to dress.'

Porsha waited for his boot steps to retreat downstairs. 'Hurry now, Jay. Let's not keep him waiting.'

CHAPTER THIRTY-SIX

'No, Jay. I'm not performing my Uncle Lionneller act for that Riz-loving traitor.'

Arthmael shouldered the suits, each scale reflecting a midnight moon from the window, creating light patterns on the walls. He'd been marking a map when she entered. Both the crown and the Crewingburns' jewels were left beside Jatta on the bed. She wriggled into Patra's shoes and ran her fingers sadly through the tangle of jewellery. 'He's only trying to save his city,' she sighed.

Arthmael dragged her up. 'Then he can have the jewels. We can't take them. Where's your ball?'

Outside the door a floorboard creaked. They froze.

The door burst open. Sheriff Lerrick stepped in, his sword at his belt. The bald, bleary-eyed man still hadn't shaved. He eyed them suspiciously, then turned to lock them all in.

'What's your hurry, my young fugitives?'

Arthmael shot a glance at his sword by the door. The sheriff followed his gaze, and grimly drew his own. Arthmael stepped to shield his sister.

Lerrick now saw the treasures on the bed, and surprise flickered over his face. He beckoned Arthmael to bring him the crown, but the Prince stood defiant. Jatta picked it up and skirted around him.

'Jay!'

She crossed the room.

Lerrick took the crown, tested its weight and, scowling, handed it back. 'Where did you young royals get this?'

'Riz. Riz stole it,' said Jatta.

'That doesn't answer my question.'

Jatta sighed. 'We were his prisoners.'

'Then you've escaped him once already. You're a self-seeking, slippery pair.'

Arthmael was bristling. 'You imagine Riz will release our father? I tell you on my royal oath, trust nothing, *nothing* about Riz.'

The sheriff ignored him. 'Young Princess, where were you headed with your ludicrous mirror—?'

'Roach brain!' growled Arthmael. 'Whose word do you accept, that vicious viper's or mine?'

The sheriff shifted his weary attention to Arthmael. 'Highness, under everyday circumstances I'd place my trust in a simple royal hot-head like you, but today's stakes are too high. Setting you two free serves no-one but yourselves. Handing you over, on the other hand ... Doesn't Alteeda deserve what little hope Riz offers?'

'What hope Alteeda has rests with us!' Arthmael's face was livid, his jaw clenched.

'Come, now!' The sheriff spat the words, losing patience. 'You may have pilfered your father's crown, but he's not dead *yet*.'

With an agility spectacular for his size, Arthmael sprang. The scale suits were already off his shoulder, flung before him. The sheriff had time only to point his sword and yell. Their weight came crashing, knocking him sprawling. Arthmael's body followed, ramming into Lerrick before his head hit the tiles. It hit tiles a second time as Arthmael's fist slammed.

'Right, Jay. Grab your ball and the saddlebag. We're taking horses.'

Jatta stared numbly at the sheriff's body as her brother untangled its belt and buttons from scales.

'He's breathing, Jay. Go.'

The adrenaline hit. She was out the door and careering down the stairs. Porsha was with her, running out through the garden.

Arthmael's powerful legs drove him past them toward the stables when they heard twin commotions.

Sheriff Lerrick was calling to the street.

Something else was terrifying the horses.

CHAPTER THIRTY-SEVEN

Arthmael drew his sword. 'What's scaring them?'

Porsha had found a weapon, a spade. 'Horse thieves, rabid dog,' she called. 'I don't know.'

He bounded on. Porsha and Jatta crept along behind.

Arthmael burst into the stables. The animals were wide-eyed, backed jostling against the wall. He glanced quickly around. Nothing. Porsha sneaked in. Still the horses glared at the door, their terror rising. Jatta poked her head tentatively around it and they panicked. They reared, pawing at the air. Their whinnies rose to shrill screams.

'Jay,' shouted Arthmael. 'I think it's you.'

The blood drained from her face.

'Just walk back,' he shouted. 'Sit on the swings for me, Jay.'

'No ... it's not time yet,' she protested weakly. But she obeyed.

The horses dropped back to the ground, snorting the fear out their nostrils.

Arthmael slumped back against the stall and groaned.

'What's happened?' Porsha's eyebrows pulled down in confusion. 'Was that some orb effect?'

'No, just Jay.'

She stared blankly.

'Haven't you heard rumours from the palace?'

Realisation dawned on Porsha's face. She leaned alongside Arthmael, shaking her head. 'The poor, poor girl.'

'What is today?' he asked. 'The 27th? No, the 28th?'

She nodded.

'We lost touch.' He didn't blame himself. He didn't have time. 'Sleeping potion . . . Where can we get surgery-strength sleeping potion?'

'Our hospital was looted last week.'

Glory. 'Porsha? Saddle the horses anyway.'

'Jay?' he called. He ran into the starlight, then almost tripped.

She was not alone.

She was on the swing, just where he'd sent her, with Sheriff Lerrick's hand resting on her thin shoulder. Another officer flanked her and two constables, honest-looking young men, sat on the other swings. All smiled amiably at Arthmael, except Jatta, who didn't look up. A tender, fatherly scene perhaps, spoiled only by the chains on her wrists.

Something inside Arthmael ripped. Raw pain and fury burst through. He couldn't protect her from her wolf, but he could protect her from this. His expression terrifying, he bore down on Lerrick.

The men stepped into a line shielding the swings. They drew swords.

Mid-bound, Arthmael scooped up a child's wheeled horse and hurled it. It clobbered one constable, who fell to his knees. Arthmael swerved to the man and kicked the sword from his grip, catching it left-handed as others closed in. Three swords clashed on his two. All experienced. All fearless. The officer, the heaviest, worked his way behind Arthmael. Arthmael was flipping and contorting like a rabid dog. Lord, he was dizzy.

'Use your ball!' Arthmael yelled. 'Help me, here!'

Nothing. No spare head sprouted. No dragon dive-bombed.

Dizzy and whirling. Their swords were everywhere, a confusion of wrist-wrenching blows. His swords swung like batons in defence, but he couldn't work up a good swing. 'Surrender, damn you,' growled Lerrick.

He should. He should be afraid, he knew it, but Jatta had spoiled him for that. No death could trigger such horror as her shard jaws. His opponents' chests heaved. His own magnificent strength was failing.

Help arrived from a different source. When her spade thudded into the back of Lerrick's knee, Arthmael blessed Porsha, his own guardian angel. Lerrick grunted and buckled, and his sword arm jerked. For one precious moment the sheriff's chest was exposed.

Arthmael was furious, but not that furious. He lunged to slice biceps, not quite to the bone. Lerrick howled. The arm hung useless.

Arthmael's jaws clamped at the sight of blood. His adrenaline surged.

His opponents didn't miss a pulse, but two to one were more manageable odds. The officer drew his arms back to chop through Arthmael's neck. Arthmael saw it coming. He ducked, slicing both thighs as he spun around low, instinctively feeling where the constable's sword would be. Arthmael's left sword clashed it as his right sliced up. The constable looked surprised. Padding exuded from a diagonal slash through his vest. Each wound had been surgically shallow; Arthmael couldn't afford more blood.

Both men were wheezing, driven into the swings under the

full force of his assault. 'Will you retire?' he huffed. 'I'm reluctant to kill you both.'

The constable rasped out a 'Yes'. He might not have relented, though, if he'd known how *very* reluctant Arthmael was. The officer hissed.

In that moment Arthmael rammed both swords into the constable's. It flew. The man toppled backwards through a swing and landed, legs tangled above him.

'And you, man?' Arthmael glared, panting, both swords ready for the officer's assault.

'Do it, Tobin. Just surrender,' said the sheriff. 'He's not getting his sister back, either way.'

The officer dropped his sword. Arthmael's eyes fixed on Jatta, still on her swing; her eyes pleaded, so fragile, so shamed by her looming wolf. The first constable, the one he'd bowled over with the wooden horse, nervously held her, his sword to her chest. The orb rolled between his shuffling feet. The constable and officer now joined Sheriff Lerrick behind her. Arthmael shot the bleeding sheriff a deadly glare. For all his swordsmanship, the scene had re-formed.

'If you want her to live, you'll leave alone,' said Sheriff Lerrick.

'I can't save Alteeda without her,' he growled.

Lerrick laughed sourly. 'Since when is your duty to Alteeda? Where've you been cowering this last month while we lose our homes? While better men lose their lives defending their families? Did you even try to reach Lord Redd?'

Blood thundered in Arthmael's brain. He tossed one sword. Brandishing the other, he stepped to the men. They flinched back. He snatched the orb from the grass, though, and thrust it in the sheriff's face.

'*This* is our glorious, omnipotent Redd!' he shouted. 'Not deaf. Not dead. *This* in the hands of a grasping old dwarf!' Flames lit his knuckles as he squeezed. 'Show him, Jay!' He glanced down at Jatta. She'd curled up, scared. His faced contorted in guilt. He placed the ball back in her chained hands and wrapped her fingers around it.

His voice was mostly controlled, and his eyes' fury restrained as they returned to Lerrick. 'Listen hard, man. Your chances of appeasing Riz? Nil. Fluffy dreams. He has no intention of finding my sister.'

Between them a figure formed, a Dartithan clutching a struggling bundle. Lerrick stepped back, his eyes wide and wary.

'Fand!' the maroon velvet bundle was pleading, and Lerrick's eyes widened further, recognising both the voice and cape. 'Don't throw me to the dragon! Take me to North Bradfirth. To Brackensith.'

'And risk a traitor's fate? A wolf's bite?' The Dartithan soldier dragged off the cape to reveal Jatta's flushed face.

The constables flicked incredulous glances to Jatta on the swing.

'No. We would rather be dragon fodder ourselves,' the Dartithan answered.

'Then I beg you, let my brother go. He's done nothing wrong.'

'Princess, you know better than to ask. He shares your fate.' The Dartithan faded, his last words too, as his audience gaped.

Arthmael continued, his voice hard. 'Riz thinks she's dead. And you want to offer her on a platter! Go ahead. She'll be dispatched forthwith—with you and your family, and these heroes as well. Maybe he'll grant you the privilege of digging your own graves, like the last lot.'

The sheriff slid his good hand over his mouth. His shoulders sank, and he looked, if possible, more haggard. 'I—I wanted only what was best for . . . Lord forgive me.'

'You asked what the scale suits were for? We're going through the firewall. I'm sacrificing my sister to Dartith just as you required.' Arthmael scoffed bitterly. 'Duty? Don't think, Sheriff, you have even one syllable to teach us of that. We were reciting the Sorcerer's Code Royal before we could read. Jatta is Elisind's daughter. I'm Elisind's son.'

CHAPTER THIRTY-EIGHT

They refused the sheriff's escort. Jatta mounted a mare nervously, using the orb to disguise her odour. Arthmael and Porsha swung into their saddles.

'Don't fret, Jay,' Arthmael smiled. 'I've a real plan tonight. Ironclad. You'll be safe.'

North Straefordtown's port serviced only the great merchant ships, so they rode into the moonlit fishing village of Little Ilsea instead. Its seaweed and salted fish smells were novel and not altogether pleasant odours for both Jatta and Arthmael. A mongrel dog chased them up its main street, snapping and scaring the horses, till someone called it from inside the tavern. Otherwise, the village slept. 'Too sleepy for constables or posters,' Porsha pointed out with satisfaction.

She said goodbye on the jetty, crouching to stroke Jatta's hair, then offered a wrapped bundle to Arthmael. 'Your Highness, your jewels.'

Arthmael laughed dryly. 'The jewels are payment for your sheriff's hospitality. And the crown—we rely on you to return it, once our journey's completed.'

With dawn came fishermen. 'Will you take two passengers?' Arthmael asked several crews in turn. They shook their heads, though, with any mention of the Dark Isle.

'Dump you on the beach with the fire? Have you barnacles

for brains? Why, I'd sooner dump you out there in the deep,' said one. 'I'll not have young blood on me hands.'

Jatta and Arthmael sat down between the last two boats. She pulled her knees up to her chin. He stared down to the water lapping the piers as they struggled to think up a new strategy.

Something soft was rubbing along Jatta's leg. She looked down. It was a huge tabby cat.

A grateful smile spread across her face. The cat lifted his chin in invitation and she tickled it. He squeezed up into the narrow valley between her chest and thighs. Laughing, she straightened her legs to give him a lap. She stroked from his head down to his tail and he closed his eyes, purring. 'What's your name, gorgeous boy?' she whispered.

'Stinker,' came a rough, warm voice above her head.

She jumped. The cat opened one eye. The voice's owner— the cat's owner too, she guessed—squatted down beside them.

'Ain't many he takes a shine to, lass. Consider yourself complimented.'

She laughed again. 'It was no compliment of yours to invent such an atrocious name.'

'Believe me, lass, Stinker deserves it. He rolls around in prawn heads and sleeps with the fish. Got no sense, and no sense of smell neither. Anyways, I'm Dermott.'

'Morning, Dermott. Do you crew a boat? Will you take us?'

He laughed. 'Lass, in that get-up you're too fine for fishing.'

'For two hundred pennings will you take us back home?'

'And where's home?'

She pointed to a speck on the horizon.

'The Dark Isle! You're kidding me, lass.'

'Not at all. We came with Riz and now we want to go home.'

'Nah, you look like Alteedans. You sound like fine young noble Alteedans.'

'Dermott, have you ever seen Dark Isle folk?'

'No, but—'

'And isn't our offer generous?'

'Very, but—'

'Then *please* take us home.'

He shrugged, then laughed. 'Little lass, I'll see what I can do.' He rose and left.

Arthmael shoved her, grinning. 'Let's see if we can't make more convincing Dartithans than peasants!'

Dermott returned with his skipper, a giant tub of a man with a blubbery neck that wobbled when he spoke.

'So, you're Dark Isle folk. I swear, you look like Alteedans to me.'

Arthmael attempted humour. 'What exactly had you expected? Glass teeth?'

Skipper Pettit didn't laugh. 'Maybe. Show me, then.'

They both provided cheesy grins.

'We're not Undead,' said Jatta. 'Undead decay to soup in daylight.'

Skipper Pettit shuddered. His walrus throat wobbled. 'You might still be them wolf things. How does I know you won't tear us apart?'

His words jolted Jatta's stomach.

'I'm as normal as you or Dermott,' said Arthmael, too breezily. 'But lock us up, if you feel safer.'

Dermott winked at Jatta. 'Stinker has vouched for 'em, skipper.'

Pettit grunted. A single ripple ran the length of his throat. 'Youse two, bring your luggage and follow me.'

*

Jatta sat among the rope coils, feeling the wind whipping across her face and through her hair. Stinker lay purring on her legs. She was watching the beach, saying a sad goodbye to Alteeda. Fisherwomen mended nets on the beach while their children jumped in the waves. Dogs raced along the surf-line, barking.

Jatta soaked in each sensation. The strong Alteedan sun. The *flap, flap* of the sails. The gentle roll of the deck. Even the slight nausea in her head. There was so much she wanted to remember.

Dermott left the nine other crewmen to finish tightening the sails and came to squat beside her. 'Seasick, lass?'

'A little. It's my first time on a boat.'

'What? Then how'd you get to our Alteeda?'

'Um, Brackensith's portal.'

'His what?'

'His travelling machine.'

'Ah, right, then ... but you don't look too pleased to be going back.'

'I'll miss Alteeda.'

'Stay on then, a nice girl like you.'

'Dartith's where I belong.' Alteeda wouldn't miss her.

Pleading tiredness, they took supper early in the boat's only cabin. It was cramped for two, more like an oversized crate perched on deck than a proper room, but Arthmael had no intention of staying the night. Their supper's fishcakes were greasy and the turnips were burnt. Jatta fed her fishcakes to Stinker, having sunk into the melancholy that tugged at her these wolf-moons.

'Eat. For both our sakes, please,' said Arthmael.

She picked at a turnip till it was gone. She brought it back up. Her moist eyes said, '*Sorry*,' then glanced out the porthole at the setting sun.

Arthmael grinned with deliberate cheer. 'Don't fret, we've got chains tonight. Look what I found, just lying around—well, bolted down—on deck.' He leant under the bunk and hauled up the boat's anchor, still attached to a coil of thick chain. The anchor alone was taller than Jatta. He threaded it twice through her bunk's pipe metal frame where her feet would be, then looped its chain into a coil. 'See? I only have to slip this over your ugly paws and tighten. Easy.'

He looped a second coil beside it. 'For your wrists.'

He reached back under the bed, then tossed six palm-sized rings in her lap. 'Look, these boat shackles work just like your amulet clip does.' Grinning, he spring-clipped one ring through two chains. His cheerfulness hardly wavered. 'Clever, right? Let's see your wolf claw out of this.'

It *was* a resourceful idea. Brilliant, so long as the boat didn't need its anchors in the night. She tried to smile back, humouring him humouring her. But then her gaze drifted to the porthole again. Dread grew in her face.

'I'll stay if you want, Jay.' His animation had drained away. She tensed.

'Fair enough. But I'll be just outside.'

She lay on the bed. They waited without speaking in the darkening room.

'Art?' Her whisper was hard to hear, turned away from him as she was. 'Would you have killed my wolf if it was killing you?'

'You *were* killing me. And you're practically indestructible.'

'If you could?'

'No, Jay, don't ask. Ever. Rightly or wrongly, I've never separated you two.'

They waited. Her nose tingled.

'It's happening.'

He patted her shoulder. Something heavy plonked down on her legs.

Stinker. They'd forgotten Stinker. They blinked in disbelief at the purring ball.

CHAPTER THIRTY-NINE

The cat was hissing. Then scratching at the door. Arthmael gazed into Jatta's terrified, pain-ridden eyes as she expanded over both ends of the bunk. Its metal groaned as it sagged. He waited with pounding heart, chatting about nonsense, about how Dragongirl continued to watch over them both. The cat yowled.

Jatta's teeth were erupting—his cue.

His hands were clammy. He threaded a coil over her paws and up her hind legs. His fingers slipped, wasting precious seconds, as he tugged it tight. He threaded the second coil on her arms and tugged. Clipping shackles on, he glanced up. Her hostile eyes were on him.

He'd run out of time.

He threw down his last shackle and scrambled for the door. Stinker dashed out with a yowl. His sister's howl rose in answer.

He shut her in. His slippery hands slid the bolt. Her howl shook the sails, trailing slowly away in unearthly song. 'Shoosh, please,' he whispered without hope.

Her protest began. Steel banged and jangled. Thuds rattled walls. Clang-clanging, that was the anchor being jerked. He'd expected blind rage; things could have been worse. Timber cracked and she stilled.

He crept to the porthole.

She sat in the twisted, overturned bunk, sniffing his satchel. She'd torn her bunk's bolts from the wall. He groaned.

She looked up. Those hate-filled green eyes stared into his. Recognition flickered.

'Jay, can you hear me?'

The ears swivelled at his voice.

'Jay, please. It's me. Art.'

The head shook a few times, as if in confusion. The eyes blinked. He watched in awe as their hatred seeped out.

There were shouts at his back.

'Over here!'

'Blasted stars!'

Arthmael spun around. Drawing his sword, he blocked the door.

'What in blazes is in there?' yelled Skipper Pettit, waddling along the deck like a walrus.

'Nothing to harm you.'

From behind the door came a guttural growl.

'Wolf!' cried someone.

'It's inside with the lass!' said Dermott.

'It *is* the lass,' growled Skipper Pettit.

Now the snarling began. Steel banged and scraped as though she was rowing her bunk across the floor. The small group shifted nervously. Those who hadn't already drawn daggers did so now.

'Kill it!' someone yelled over the din. Others goggled past Arthmael at the door, not nearly so brave.

'Stay clear! My sister has never hurt anyone,' he lied. 'Attack her and she will!'

Abruptly, the cabin went silent. No-one moved.

Something heavy thumped, accompanied by a short jangle,

like chain settling. For three heartbeats nothing happened.

Thump-jangle. Scrape.

That was the bunk being dragged. Arthmael felt an unpleasant tingle down his spine. 'Jay?'

Pause. *Thump-jangle. Scrape.*

Two matted, chained fists shattered the porthole. A monstrous wolf face thrust through, eyes coldly calculating. Jatta licked her teeth. Arthmael stared in disbelief. The men shuffled back.

Her head pulled inside. *Thump-jangle. Scrape.* Her great mass hurled against the door. It shuddered and split.

'Lord. Hurry!' cried Arthmael. 'Find somewhere secure!'

'For the wolf?' said Dermott.

'No, for us!'

'The hold, men!' yelled Skipper Pettit. Crewmen turned and fled along the deck.

She rammed again. Arthmael stumbled back as the door splintered. It tore off. He saw her, chest heaving, still chained. Her head hid above the door frame.

'Jay, calm down. It's Art, you remembered me before.'

Her face lowered into view. Malicious eyes locked with his. Lips pulled back in a snarl, exposing shards that protruded at odd angles from crowded jaws.

'No, it's me. Jay . . .'

She crouched to spring.

'Jay . . .' he pleaded, horrified. Seeing no recognition at all. Mourning—in that crowded moment—for her, waking tomorrow alone.

She launched herself at him. Claws and teeth and chain hurtled through sky. He flinched against the inevitable.

She never completed her arc. An invisible force jerked her

back, while something banged behind her. She crashed at his feet and the deck bounced. Suddenly rabid, she snapped at him, spraying his legs with spit. She twisted behind to yank and bite and snarl at her trailing chain. The cabin doorway clanged like falling scaffolding.

Arthmael's eyes shot there, where both anchor and bunk were jerking, and he understood. His sister was still attached. The door frame cracked; the bunk jerked part-free.

Arthmael fled, too.

Ahead, the crew were disappearing down a hole in the deck. The fish hold. They'd flung open the deck's hatch and jostled each other down a ladder. Someone jumped from the hatch lip in his panic, falling more than a storey, landing hard. But Pettit was wheezing, still on deck. Arthmael slipped his arm around the blubbery waist.

Behind him the cabin wall splintered.

He dragged Pettit, staggering under the dead weight, willing his legs not to crumple. Jatta's bunk scraped in jerks along the deck.

'Here! Take him.' Arthmael guided Pettit's feet onto ladder rungs. The men reached up to help their skipper down.

'Leave the brother out there!' someone spat, slamming the hatch in his face.

Arthmael shot back a glance.

Jatta was snarling, struggling to him on bound hands and legs, hauling bunk, anchor and door frame. It might have been comical if it hadn't been so terrifying.

'Let me in!'

'Surrender your sword.' Dermott opened the hatch a slit.

Arthmael dropped it, his token defence.

The hatch swung open and he leapt down, landing

painfully on his side. It swung closed and the bolt slid across.

Jatta was on the hatch above their heads. Scratching for edges.

'It'll tear off the door!' wheezed Pettit. 'Jam the hatch!'

The men scrambled in the blackness. Terrified, they climbed the ladder to stack shelving planks under the hatch door. They stuffed the space full, several doors thick.

Jatta tore as they fled back to the corner. There they cowered, in a dungeon no wider than four strides, staring up at their barricade. Wide-eyed, like the morning's horses in their stable.

As the minutes passed Arthmael and Dermott ventured under the cracking and ripping hatch. Splinters drifted down through the planks. Chinks of moonlight made dappled patterns on their upturned faces.

'Jay! Calm down.'

Jatta went silent. Arthmael craned his senses, hearing sea splash on the hull. Masts creaked. Men shifted behind him. Her monster shadow lowered slowly, deliberately, to all fours, blocking Arthmael's moon. Her head snaked. Arthmael imagined green eyes searching the dark hole.

'Good gir—'

She growled, wary. Threatening.

Her head lowered to poke among the planks, armoured snout clacking. Sniffing. Arthmael tensed, uneasy about what she'd find. His scent, but more. Old cargoes, the men . . .

Their fear.

Their tentative truce was over.

Her frenzy erupted. Claws gouged. Teeth snapped and stripped planks to mush. Chains jangled as shoulders rammed; the pile of planks cracked. The men drew lots. Their skipper scored the least exposed spot, wedged in the corner.

Jatta's agony of frustration crescendoed. She flung herself skyward, a twisting, snarling hulk. Dappled moonlight returned. Something massive crashed down on the stockpile. Everything smashed through. Logs boomed onto the floor and rolled to the men, chasing Arthmael as he ran. Debris dumped down; a shaft of moonlight lit the haze. The anchor had embedded in the deck; piercing the ceiling like a giant fish hook. The bunk had wedged in the hatch and its chain hung through. Arthmael's stomach twisted. He didn't need to look to know what dangled, tangled in chain beneath. Still, his gaze lowered to slow swaying feet, down a plague-rat pelt to arms outstretched in chains, as if begging. Her head hung at stomach height. Her eyes blinked in the settling sawdust, their confusion so endearingly Jatta's that, despite everything, he called to her again.

She snorted out debris and sneezed. Her ears pricked to his voice, to the undisciplined drums of a dozen hearts, to bodies jostling back, to chests so crushed they could barely catch breath. Saliva glistened on crowded teeth. Twisting toward the men, Jatta flexed her thighs to swing.

The ceiling creaked as she swung from starlight into the corner. Arthmael's head pounded. Black arms reached, and for one dreadful moment claws brushed his shirt. His scars twinged. Then she was dragging back. He dived for the floor. Men stumbled over him to line the walls. Again she came swinging, faster. Further this time. Her wolf stench swept over him. Further. Her murderous stare pinned Pettit to his corner. Her fingers clawed strips from the skipper's heaving waistcoat.

She was dragged back, snarling.

'Get down!' yelled Arthmael.

Pettit was frozen. His face was blank, beyond fear.

'Twice, now, you'll owe me,' growled Arthmael, scrambling on hands and knees to tug Pettit's belt. Still he wouldn't budge. Jatta pushed off the far wall. She came swinging, stretching for them both. In desperation Arthmael punched out the skipper's knees. The monumental man crumpled on top of him. 'Ah!' gasped Arthmael.

Jatta snapped over their backs.

Her veneer of control vanished. She flung wild on her chain, a spiked war flail from her own Dartith book. She banged off walls. The crew dropped to their backs in the debris. Those who could not bear watching cringed on their bellies. Her sweat sprayed. Her snarls blew stench and slobber through their hair.

It rained. The men listened to the anchor's creak and groan, dreading the moment it would tear through the deck. Hearts hammered ribs till they ached.

The sky was a starry deep blue when she stilled. Her lament began, as beautiful as it was chilling.

Arthmael listened to her song, and his hope grew. He sat up to stretch, wary at first, and looked around. He chuckled at the scene: sodden bodies littered the floor as if napping under her stage-lit lullaby.

Their night was not over, though.

Jatta had howled out her frustration. Her focus returned. She twisted up to grab the chain above her feet. She gnawed.

That dissolved Arthmael's grin.

Steel shavings drifted to the floor. They decorated her fur and wedged between her teeth. Arthmael groaned, finally out of ideas. 'Jay, Jay ...' he whispered. 'Lord, is there no stopping you?'

The grinding paused. Her ears twitched.

Arthmael laughed, his voice slightly high. She rotated slowly to blink.

'Jay, listen, your ordeal's almost over. Ours, too,' he said, imagining himself rubbing her shoulders. 'Relax, wait with us. Nobody's dead; don't go spoiling it now. Think about Dartith, you'll be happier there, all the blue paste you need . . .' He chatted while she unfurled herself slowly. She watched upside down. When the dawn came he crawled to wait underneath and caught his sister as she slipped, too skinny, through her chains.

The crew crept all around, drawing daggers.

'Everyone's safe,' he told her.

His overbright smile betrayed him.

CHAPTER FORTY

Skipper Pettit wrenched Jatta up and shook her. The orb dropped.

Arthmael struggled on the floor with a knife to his throat and two men riding his chest.

'I command you, hands off her!' he shouted.

'Shut it, Dartithan,' growled Pettit, not even sparing him a glance. 'We've no quarrel with you.' His livid face closed on Jatta's. She dangled, frightened in his grip. 'Give me one reason I shouldn't throw your wolf hide to the sharks,' he said. 'Eh? And good riddance!'

Jatta pleaded the first thing that came into her head.

'Because I'm Princess Jatta.'

The men roared in laughter.

'And I'm Prince Arthmael!' shouted Arthmael over the guffaws.

'And I'm Lord Redd,' spat Pettit. 'Now get this freak monstrosity upstairs and overboard.' Someone grabbed Jatta's thighs. She screamed as she was hoisted over his shoulder like a tuna.

Arthmael bit the hand holding the knife to his throat. His own hand found the wrist, crushing it till the knife dropped. He bucked off the others, leaping up as more men spun to him. The knife, though, was already at Pettit's flabby neck.

'Put her down!' Arthmael yelled.

'Drop your knife, lad, or you'll join her.' Pettit's throat trembled with rage as he spoke, and the knife cut into its fat.

'I said put her down! Harm her, and I'll see you tried for treason.'

'Oi! Drop her!' boomed Dermott.

The man let go and Jatta fell, sprawling among logs. She thrust into her pocket. Empty! Crawling on her knees, she began frantic searching.

'Fair's fair, lad.' Dermott held out his hand for the knife still pressed into Pettit's flesh. But Arthmael stood his ground, sweat beading his forehead.

'I'm Arthmael, son of Elisind. And I demand you deliver us to the Dark Isle!'

Dermott squinted, looking at him sceptically. 'Prove it, and we might.'

Arthmael lowered the knife. Pettit snatched it and thumped him hard across the ear. With a fresh spurt of anger Arthmael raised his fist, but the knife was already at his chest.

'We're waiting, lad,' said Dermott.

Arthmael drew himself up to his full, indignant height. 'I am Arthmael Juliat Iorwerth Lionneller, Grand Duke of Alteeda, second in line to the royal throne. I have mastered the Classics and swordsmanship, and I recite the Sorcerer's Code Royal. My father is Elisind III. My grandmother, Jatta II. My great-grandfather, Steffed VI. My great-great-grand—'

'Bad luck none of these is here to vouch for you, lad,' growled Pettit. 'Proof. Or over she goes.'

'Um . . .' Jatta snatched something purple from the sawdust between Pettit's boots. She rose timidly. 'Does anyone carry a gold kroun?'

The men's faces relaxed into grins. Some scoffed.

'If we had krouns, lass, do you reckon we'd be out on this sieve day 'n' night?' said Dermott.

'No-one, then? Art, show me your purse.'

From the purse she dug Naffaedan's heavy gold coin. Dermott took it, turning it in his hand as he studied both its face and Arthmael's. After a while he passed it to the others. 'You're a fine-looking lad, I'll grant you that.' He grinned.

Skipper Pettit passed it back to Arthmael with a wary nod. 'I swear, if I'd figured I were carrying real royalty, I'd have asked for one of *these* pretty coins.'

'Take us now, and it'll be yours,' said Arthmael.

'No hard feelings, then?'

Arthmael nodded back. 'None. Not after a good breakfast.'

Pettit relaxed into a throat-wobbling laugh. 'Your royal Majesties, it's a deal.'

Arthmael examined the coin curiously as the men started clearing the hold. On one side was the King's profile. On the other side was the Queen's; the likeness to his own was striking.

Arthmael grunted, then gave his sister an affectionate nudge. 'That was inspired. Glory, I had no idea Alteeda minted two-headed krouns.'

Jatta returned the orb to her pocket. She bit her lip, smiling impishly. 'Then I guess it doesn't.'

At midday the boat weighed anchor offshore. The crew leaned out over the rails, admiring the inferno. Sun shone down on their heads, but it was the firewall that made the air stifling hot and lit their faces like sunset. It followed the Isle's shoreline along sandy beaches and up over cliffs as far they could see, as high as a city wall. It burned brilliant orange with blue flicking tongues, yet it consumed nothing.

When Arthmael and Jatta jangled up to join them, the crew turned to goggle at a sight almost as bizarre. Each mirror was a dancing flame.

'You look like bonfires yourselves, you do,' grinned Dermott.

Arthmael took off his hood and pressed the kroun into Pettit's hand. In return massive arms enclosed him in a blubbery hug, all wrongs forgiven.

'Good luck—though I swear the royal line's inbred, what with two reckless fools like your Majesties. And one a wolf, atop.'

Their tiny boat was lowered. Dermott had volunteered to row them ashore, and he took Jatta's hood and gloves before helping her onto her seat. She was grateful. She'd been gorging herself since just after dawn. Stinker jumped from the deck down beside them. He sat purring in her uncomfortable, silvery lap while Dermott and Arthmael rowed. With every stroke the air felt more heavy and stifling. It dried their throats and stung their eyes.

'The water's hot as a bath,' she said.

'And I'm roasting on a spit, here,' answered Dermott. He was crimson-orange and soaked in sweat. Arthmael bid him stop when the water grew shallow. Jatta nuzzled Stinker's chin one last time, feeling it vibrate, before reluctantly handing him over.

'Stinker here'll miss your little cuddles,' said Dermott.

She smiled. 'But not my crazed attacks.'

'True enough, lass. That'd be a right pain to deal with.'

Dermott returned through the surf while they stood chest-deep. Hearts pounding, they adjusted their hoods and gloves.

CHAPTER FORTY-ONE

Jatta slipped her glove inside her brother's as they trudged through the surf. Like children playing peek-a-boo they had to cover their eyes. What they glimpsed were boiling waves washing over sands that had turned to glass. The immense bonfire roared and crackled. Sand at its edge bubbled like toffee.

They stopped before it, their suits heavy but miraculously cool. They stole one last glimpse, held their breaths and stepped through.

It was like plunging under warm water. A profound silence swallowed every crackling roar. Even their jangling seemed muffled and distant. They strode blindly forward.

What happened next even Jatta could not have imagined.

A voice came wafting through the fire. Forlorn. Pleading. A woman's, distant at first, then intimately close.

'Help me, please.'

Jatta froze, her heart stopped. She willed herself to peek.

This face would return to haunt her through her life.

A woman composed of nothing but fire stood by her shoulder. Her ancient robes whipped around her. Her blazing eyes were tortured. A fire-baby was in her arms, its blanket alight.

'Help me, I cannot get out!' cried the voice. The flames picked it up and sucked it away from Jatta's ears.

'Follow us!' shouted Arthmael. He quickened his pace.

'No! You be going the wrong way,' came the fire-soul's voice.

Jatta peeked again and her eyes burned. The woman was with Arthmael now, trying to tug at his arm, but her hand merely blazed against his suit.

'You know the way,' called Jatta. 'Why can't you get out?'

The fire-soul's mouth opened and closed, but she could not find an answer.

Arthmael strode faster, gripping Jatta's glove. The fire-soul struggled to keep up.

'Why are you here?' called Jatta.

'I flee the Dark Sorcerer!'

'How long have you been trapped?'

'I know not ... Lord help me, I remember nothing!' Her anguished voice trailed behind them. They stumbled forward through the flames.

Arthmael stopped short. He dragged Jatta off in one direction. Then, haltingly, in another.

'I don't know which way is forward!'

Again they were not alone. Other tortured souls crowded close with pleas that tore at their hearts. 'Have you found our father?' wafted one childish voice while another sniffled eternal tears. 'Father! Don't let go our hands,' it called as flames swallowed it back.

'Make it end!' screamed Jatta. 'Let me out!'

'Which way out?' Arthmael called to the voices.

'To your left. To the sea!' came their answers.

Arthmael turned right.

'No!' they cried, in a great forward surge. 'That way leads back, back to savagery and pain!' Millennia of souls surrounded them, so dense a congregation that Jatta imagined they might drag her from Arthmael, that she might open her eyes to find some other hand leading her back. She clutched him tighter, feeling scales dig into her palm. 'Don't let my hand go!' she said, but her words drowned in the tumult. Arthmael tugged her forward. The hopeless cries fell behind.

And as they dwindled one last voice pleaded to Jatta. She would later describe it to Arthmael as wonderfully gentle and life-weary, grown gravelly with age. In its intimacy she felt she was home. Yet, it disturbed her more than any other, for it alone understood what it was. It alone knew her name.

'Little Jatta, my soul be prisoner to the Dark Sorcerer, too. Will you help set it free?' The voice was there, inside her hood.

CHAPTER FORTY-TWO

Jatta and Arthmael burst through flame into grey light. They stumbled jangling across scorched earth till they outran the fire's roar, then further till they fell among thorns.

Arthmael helped Jatta remove her hood. Their faces were crimson, dripping with sweat, their hair plastered to their heads. They looked around and found themselves in a bramble-infested Dartithan field, lit as if by a threatening storm. They looked up, finding only slate-grey sky and Dartith's sickly sun. It sank quickly toward the horizon—they watched without hurting their eyes—though a mere couple of hours had passed since midday.

Not knowing if they would ever return, they buried their suits under a pile of stones. An orchard lay nearby, rows of scraggly trees on a rocky hill.

'We'll need some secure place for you tonight,' said Arthmael.

Jatta nodded. They headed toward the orchard.

They found the farmer and his sons picking peaches. Like Dartithan soldiers, these men were tall, pale and lean. Their broad, flat faces had sunken cheeks, as if their bellies were rarely full, and their ragged trousers hung loose.

'Sir, can you offer us lodgings and—' began Arthmael.

The farmer eyed them suspiciously. 'Get off my land! I be no stinking charity!'

'We have silver coins.' Arthmael held out several of

Naffaedan's tiny coins. The man took one, examined it and bit down.

'These be not proper coin! And I like not the look—nor the sound—of you, stranger. I'll have naught to do with *strangers* on a wolf-moon night.'

Jatta concentrated to rehearse his heavy accent in her head before answering. 'No, not proper coin, sir. Proper silver these be, though.'

The farmer stared down at her curiously. She blushed, realising her accent had been far from convincing. She tried again. 'Our silver be favourable exchange for a dry spot in your barn. Agreed? Yes, safe from the wolves.'

The farmer snorted, as if their safety was not his concern, but he took the coins.

'We won't bother you for supper,' offered Arthmael. 'We'll make do with a few peaches.'

'That be ten extra, then.'

Arthmael reached for extra coins. The farmer snatched them from his hand and pointed through the trees to a brick barn. 'Sleep there. Go not near the farmhouse. Anything, anyone, comes near my kin on a wolf-moon night, I shoot it. You hear?'

Their eyes fell on the quiver across his back and the chipped sword at his belt. They nodded.

The farmer squinted at the horizon. 'Boys!' he called. 'Get we home now!'

Arthmael and Jatta were left alone to gather their supper, but Jatta was too nervous to eat. She slipped her peaches, withered and spotted as they were, into the satchel. They headed toward the barn.

Jatta traced her fingers along deep claw marks in the door.

'I don't think I'm the first wolf to plague this barn,' she said, half to herself.

Arthmael grunted. 'Sure, but I bet no wolf ever got inside. We could have done with one of these last night.'

The barn was built like a brick tunnel, with long slits for windows. Its barrel roof allowed no entry from above. As if confirming Jatta's suspicion, they found its door, made of layers of logs, could be bolted from the inside too. The barn was dry and dark and smelled sweet, of last season's peaches. Arthmael had vaguely hoped for divided rooms inside, but in the dimness they found only straw, rusty tools and broken carts.

'Seems I'll be spending the night outside,' sighed Arthmael.

'Sorry, Art.'

He nudged her good naturedly. 'Better me than you tearing around out there.'

She helped him carry bundles of straw to make a bed by the door. Then he closed her inside and dragged the bolt across. 'Pleasant dreams, little sister,' he called through the logs.

'Good night,' she said miserably.

She crouched in the gloom, reminding herself that she'd wanted this ever since Redd's hall. Not exactly this barn, no, but her father's life back, and Steffed's life, and Alteeda's freedom, too. A fair swap for a youth and a diseased girl. She wrapped her arms tightly around her knees, tensely waiting. Despising herself, feeling for the signs.

Her nose tingled.

'Keep him safe,' she pleaded to the darkness.

Then her arms and thighs ached. Memory was slipping, trickling away. She fought it till she forgot why. And as consciousness faded, the familiar urge rose. To kill. Anything. Anyone.

She lifted her throat and howled.

She lunged at the door, ramming with her massive shoulders, feeling it heave. Testing. She leapt at the walls, gouging. She clawed through the floor, howling to finding bricks buried in its dirt. Two rows, ten rows, many rows deep.

Back to the door. Careering into it, crazed, shoulder-first. Feeling it crack. She clawed and bit deep, ripping off thigh-thick strips till stars poked through. She crammed her snout against frayed wood, smelling freedom beyond. And fresh meat.

Arthmael sat rigidly on his bed of hay, staring at the door. He'd long since tired of pleading with her. His mind groped for wild plans of escape, knowing that in this mood she'd allow him none.

Suddenly, she stopped. He waited in the silence.

Then he saw them. Perhaps she had smelled them. Dark shadows flitted through the orchard toward the farmhouse. The family had gone to bed, or most had—one feeble light remained. For the first time Arthmael felt compassion for the farmer. He took a breath to call out a warning, then stopped. His voice might not carry across the trees. And he, alone in the night, was far more vulnerable.

As he watched, Jatta began pacing. The shadows were surrounding the house and he strained to make them out. Too co-ordinated for wolves. Men. They were men.

He gasped at a sudden blast. Fire flashed. Bricks flew. Then came a tumult of screams and yells and wails. Women's. Men's. Children's. He felt sick. And in the din, Jatta also howled. The candle went out and the screams and wailing went on. Finally only wailing carried across the trees.

Jatta had once said the Undead often spared their victims. Half-believing this now helped control his guilty shudders.

More shadows slunk. Too close. Fear gripped his chest. Tonight hell had opened wide to spill out its horrors. His impulse was to hide. He burrowed under the hay, realising that Jatta had again grown silent.

The men's bloodless faces were white in the moonlight. They drew close, treading carefully. So close that, peering up through the hay, he could study one cruel, haggard face. The man's robes were ancient, relics of some long-forgotten fashion. He wore a blast rod at his belt. The odour of rotting flesh assaulted Arthmael.

'It be trapped behind that door,' the Undead growled. Arthmael shuddered under his camouflage. The man's teeth gleamed glassy black.

'Let it out then, if you choose,' said the other. 'But do not imagine gratitude from a wolf.'

'Gratitude? No, friend, it be terror I like to imagine. The pain in its next victim's eyes.' He stepped forward through the hay. And onto Arthmael's knee.

Arthmael sprang up, wide-eyed, a ridiculous straw-covered scarecrow. He saw the other Undead clearly, saw that half his lips had dissolved and skin peeled from his bloated cheeks.

The second Undead grinned. 'Look at those eyes. There be your terror, friend.'

'And supper, too.'

Both stepped toward him. Arthmael tripped back against the door. In that moment he chose. Chose Jatta. He thrust the bolt across, darting inside. In the darkness he groped for the inside bolt. It wasn't where he'd thought.

Hot wolf breath blew through his hair. Wolf teeth were

being licked by his ear. His heart hammered like it would break through his ribs.

'Jay, it's me. Little sister, it's me.'

Silence in the darkness. Outside, too, as the Undead waited. Then Jatta's rumbling, uncertain growl.

His body flooded with relief. 'Jay, I know you can hear me. Some part of you can.' His voice was soothing, though it trembled too. 'But not my words, right? Well then . . . believe me, I appreciate how unpleasant this is for you, and I know sometimes I've been . . . a tad patronising. But I'm trying, and I'm very lucky to have a sister like you. Really. Well, apart from the wolf thing . . . and the kidnappings . . . and dragons . . . and Undead . . . Anyway, we're in this together—'
His hands swept shredded timbers, not finding the bolt, feeling chilled fingertips poking through instead. His hands flinched to fists.

Her growl rose into an ugly snarl.

'—so please don't eat me, Jay.'

Snarling, Jatta pushed him to the ground. Again she clawed at the door; outside, the Undead shuffled back with eager sniggers.

'Calm down, Jay.'

The door swung open.

'Jay, no!'

She burst out into the moonlight. Lifting her snout she howled. A howl of freedom, trailing to a hauntingly musical note. She sniffed the air. Peaches. Straw. Dirt. Her creature, his fear, too. A town far away, with a limitless supply of fresh meat. And closer . . . She looked down. Standing at chest height were two creatures. They looked like fresh meat but smelled like decay.

They stared up in admiration. One spoke. 'Have you ever seen a wolf so . . .?'

'Magnificent,' said the other.

'Look, its eyes.' The creature's stinking finger reached near her chin. 'They be gree—'

She wrenched off his arm.

'Damn!' he yelled.

He was on the dirt gathering it up. The other one fled.

She bounded for the trees.

'Jay! Listen, stay!'

She stopped. That soothing voice. That most delicious meat tinged with warmth and almost-memories. It calmed her hatred. Her creature was standing beneath her now, panting. She ached to be hunting fresh meat. Yet she wanted the creature with her. With one sweep of her arm she had him, pinned against her chest, dangling.

'Put me down!'

Together they bounded for the town.

CHAPTER FORTY-THREE

This night had dragged on for days, or so Arthmael felt. Still Ganus had not set. Pinned against Jatta's chest, Arthmael's ribs were bruised and he was groggy from two sleepless nights. His head had come to rest in the crook of her arm, but every bound jolted him out of momentary dozing. Hours ago, back when they'd crossed barren fields, he'd grown hoarse from pleading. After that, when she'd found the cobbled road, he'd despaired of her ever stopping to rest. One thing only he felt grateful for. Whatever he was to her now—and he understood little of her wolf mind—it was no longer a meal.

They travelled alone, only occasionally sighting another wolf or a slinking shadow. Of the barrel houses they passed, as many were crumbling as intact, and bricks littered the road. When the road rose up from the valley, Jatta paused to sniff the air.

Ahead Arthmael saw the lights of a great city on a hill, its base protected by a high wall, black against its forest of yellow lamps. Above it all sat a castle. Jatta broke into a run.

She reached the wall and stood whining in confusion. The cobbled road ended here, and a moat and raised drawbridge separated her from her prey.

Arthmael listened to the sounds of a market, to the shouting and clamouring and scraping and pounding, to the complaints of livestock. Inside that wall, Brackensith's capital, Dredden, blazed with light and noise as if the day had already begun. In contrast to the mollusc-like farms and villages, it seemed a place fearless of wolves.

Jatta raised her snout to sample the smells, unwilling to enter the moat, growing increasingly agitated. Arthmael struggled and was let down.

'That's right, Jay. They're inside and you're out. Now don't you wish you'd heeded me?'

Jatta howled at the moon.

'That's surely not going to help. If you'd bothered to eat before, you wouldn't be so hungry now.' He sat down between her legs, his own legs dangling over the moat, and opened the satchel. The peaches and book were mashed together. He shoved at her, overtired, sore and hungry. 'Now how do you expect me to eat this!'

Something large splashed up between his feet, a human head rising from the depths. Instinctively he arched back into Jatta. The head tilted at him with a soft, sensual laugh. A girl. Her hair trailed down her shoulders and floated in the blackness as she trod water, her face hidden in shadow.

Jatta snarled and swiped down half-heartedly. 'Manners!' growled Arthmael, blocking her arm with his. It was like trying to divert a battering ram, and his bones ached to the shoulder. He'd be bruised tomorrow. Glory help him and the girl both, if Jatta had intended real damage.

'You be a brave puppy, boy, to wrestle a wolf, and fuss over your belly when its own be empty,' said the girl. Her voice was exotically accented, not exactly Dartithan, and as melodic as her laugh.

His ill temper melted to fascination. 'Be careful with your cheek, *girl*,' he answered. 'It's you my wolf might make a meal of.'

Jatta, though, had lost interest in the stranger and left to pace up and down the moat, howling.

'Your wolf finds neither of us appealing. It be making the soldiers nervous though.'

His eyes shot up to the wall. Men there were training arrows across the moat.

'Jay! Come back.'

'Jay?' queried the girl.

'My sister.'

'Jay . . . Jatta, mean you?'

He stared down, amazed. But the girl's face was hidden.

'Why come you to Dartith, Arthmael?'

'How—Are you magic?'

'Don't be thick, boy. Your face betrays you. Your accent, too. Harsh and grating it be, none like it in all the Isle.'

'But you know us.'

'I reside . . . beside Brackensith's castle. I hear things.'

'Then you can get us inside. Jatta has decided to marry his heir. We've come to bargain with him.'

'Bargain? You do not know vile Brackensith.'

'He must call back Riz. Riz is terrorising our people.'

'Riz acts on Brackensith's orders to find your sister.'

'It wasn't Brackensith's order to murder her!'

'Murder? But what is to be gained by such betrayal?'

'Our kingdom. Until Jatta's delivered, it's his to plunder.'

'You have proof? That rank reptile!' Her voice was fierce. 'Father will have his black heart on a platter.'

'Father—Brackensith?' Arthmael's brow pulled down in confusion.

She growled in contempt.

'You, a princess! What in glory's name are you doing alone,

in a black moat, exposing your precious neck to the night's foul creatures?'

'Fishing.'

'No, tell me honestly.'

'Be you naming me a liar? Then you can rot in the crypt!'

'Ouch, girl. You're prickly as a bramble. All right, you're fishing. Where are your fish?'

'I've eaten them.'

'Pardon? A princess in a moat gnawing on raw fish?'

'So? Perhaps you'd rather I sucked on your neck!'

'Glory, no. What a perverse thing to say.'

'Do you want my help or not?'

'Yes, yes. But we'll have to wait for dawn. For Jay.'

'Impossible.' She called up to the wall. 'Soldier! Lower the bridge!'

A voice wafted down. 'Highness. Wolf lurking.'

'Shoot it!' she shouted.

'No!' Arthmael scrambled up, his heart pounding. But he tripped. She'd gripped his ankle with ice-cold fingers. In that moment, sprawled there, he realised what Jatta had already known.

He'd been arguing with an Undead.

'Jay! Run!'

Jatta heard his fear. She stopped mid-howl. Something whizzed through the night. She flipped with a yelp. Landed hard. Whined. Then nothing.

'Jay!' he wailed, kicking free.

'Idiot boy,' growled the girl.

Arthmael bolted to his sister. The huge creature lay limp but breathing deeply. His hands raked her fur, finding no blast mark, no embedded arrow, only a trail of silk ribbons from her snout. He thrust past crowded jaws, elbow deep, and groped ribbed wetness till he found it. He pulled the dart from her throat.

The Undead approached, white, dripping and disturbingly beautiful in the moonlight. He drew his sword.

'Do you propose to dispatch me with *that?*' She laughed dryly. Again she lifted her head to the wall. 'Bring a stretcher! And twenty strong men!'

'She's alive,' murmured Arthmael.

'Idiot boy. Did you think Brackensith's soldiers would harm his own wolves? They come to the wall, howling and clawing to get in. They're shot with sleeping paste a few times and learn to leave us be.'

The black-plaited soldiers trooped down. Arthmael helped them lift Jatta onto the stretcher.

'It be a big wolf, Highness,' said one. The man seemed relaxed toward his princess, much more so than he had been in handling the unconscious wolf, and Arthmael began to doubt the Undead-coldness of her touch. He saw she carried no blast rod. Perhaps water instead had chilled her fingers.

'Go on ahead,' she said to the soldier. 'Wake Father and tell him Noriglade has a surprise.'

The man flinched, looking decidedly less comfortable.

'Don't dawdle, man. He shall thank you for it.'

The soldier seemed somewhat sceptical, but bowed and loped back toward the drawbridge.

'Wolf!' cried someone as the stretcher entered the night market. Frightened crowds shuffled from their path.

As the princess led their little procession through Dredden's emptying streets her body flowed with a sensuality that matched her oboe voice. The slippery gold of her robes swished, accentuating the roll of her hips. Arthmael marvelled at their luck in finding her. He told this strange porcelain-skinned beauty their story and she seemed to understand. She appeared different now. More empathetic, less brash. He'd quite enjoyed her brashness and her angry, flashing eyes. Their parried taunts had been challenging, entertaining. Unpredictable. But gentle could be appealing, too, he guessed. Now when he obliged her to talk she shyly covered her mouth. That was coy—quite Alteedan—perhaps a little too sweet for his taste. He decided he liked her, all the same.

'May I call you Noriglade?' he eventually asked.

She nodded.

'You hate Riz . . . in fact, all your brothers.'

'Not Drake,' she conceded thoughtfully.

'All right, but you abhor your dear father.'

She bristled. 'That vile demon viper! He be dear to no-one, least of all me!'

Arthmael grinned. 'I believe, instead, I'll call you Prickle.'

'As you wish,' she spat.

They now climbed through the castle gate. 'That be my home,' she said. He followed her gaze past the gardens to a cemetery and crypt. Beyond them lay a summer house with spiralled green turrets.

'It's quaint. Enchanting,' he offered, trying to be pleasant. 'But why so far from the castle? Don't you miss palace life?'

She eyed him strangely. 'It be others who prefer it this way.'

CHAPTER FORTY-FOUR

Inside the castle, day seemed to have begun early. Servants carried breakfasts down marble corridors. Outside, night clung obstinately on.

Noriglade ushered them into a richly furnished hall. Men and women lounged in clusters of sofas or stood quietly talking by marble columns. Incense hung heavily in the air, mingled with the same rotting odour Arthmael recognised from earlier that night. Faces turned to examine him curiously. As the stretcher was laid on a table many grimaced; one group hurriedly got up and left. Three bloodless men and one woman, however, came over to investigate. Their progress was awkward. They shuffled as if battling reluctant limbs. Arthmael's own body stiffened at their odour.

Noriglade whispered into his ear. 'Stay calm, they have supped already tonight.'

The Undead crowded around the stretcher. 'Who might this be?' one asked the soldiers.

'We know not, sir. It be here on the Princess's orders.'

'It be Baron Hoodeneth, perhaps,' offered the woman. 'Some say he has attacked another Undead.' She peered down, macabrely intrigued, and pinged Jatta's jutting fangs.

'Does he not fear the King after all that be done to him?' asked one of the men.

'I think not,' said the woman. 'King Brackensith caged

300

him with his entire household. A strategic error, if my opinion be asked. The pathetic man has naught to lose.'

'Except his life.'

'And what value be that, to one of his kind?'

'Lift his lids,' urged one. 'Brackensith removed Hoodeneth's eye.'

Noriglade hissed dangerously.

They blinked at her, startled. 'Pardon our intrusion, Princess,' bowed the woman. They shuffled with effort back to their sofas.

Brackensith swept in. Everyone rose, hushed. Their eyes followed him as he strode among the groups, acknowledging some. He glanced at Arthmael without apparent interest, though this court had probably seen no foreigner in sixteen years. He stopped by Jatta's stretcher. Taking her snout in his hand he dragged it left, then right, to study her profile. 'I recognise not this face. Immature, it be. A peculiarly powerful soul. Possibly male, but always hard to tell.' He glanced up at Noriglade for the first time. 'Well, wretched daughter. Tell me, who be it?'

Noriglade's grace had deserted her. She jerked into a nervous curtsey, her hand still covering her mouth. 'Jatta, daughter of Elisind, Father.'

Brackensith's piercing pale eyes registered neither surprise nor satisfaction. He clicked his tongue and his audience filed from the room, leaving the four of them alone. He took Arthmael's chin, turning it as he had Jatta's. 'And be I expected to recognise this one?'

'Shall I prompt you, Brackensith?' said Arthmael tersely. 'Eleven years and two months ago you murdered my mother.'

'Hmm . . . Alteedan noble by your vulgar accent. You must

be wretched Arthmael. You look not like your father. Not that your cursed sister seems to, either.'

'I look like my murdered mother.' Arthmael's voice was strained with anger.

'Indeed? After eleven years you can hardly expect me to remember her face.'

Arthmael clenched his fists. He held onto his temper with difficulty, telling himself that Alteeda's future rested on this meeting, wishing he'd insisted Noriglade wait for daylight. For Jatta and her gentle way.

'So, wretched daughter. Where found you these two?' The King settled on a nearby sofa. From there he continued to watch Arthmael with bland disinterest.

'Father, they came of their own free will. They have escaped Riz's clutches.'

'Impossible.' He now eyed Arthmael suspiciously.

'Impossible they came?' asked Noriglade. 'Or impossible they escaped Riz?'

'Impossible that Riz kept her. I visit him daily through the portal.'

'Riz had his own plans for Jatta, Father.'

'Shut your stinking mouth and let the boy talk.'

Arthmael bowed stiffly. 'Majesty, Riz did have plans for my sister. But when you dragged him away from the canyon, he gave fresh orders to kill her.'

'Have you proof?'

'What proof do you require?'

'Don't pose riddles for me, boy. Proof that they met, at least.'

Arthmael crossed the floor to where Brackensith lounged, handing him Riz's betrothal ring.

'Where got you this?' said the King.

'Riz gave it to my sister.'

'Why?'

Arthmael laughed once without humour. 'Why does a man ever offer a woman a ring?'

'I've warned you about your riddles, boy.' Brackensith shrewdly raised one eyebrow. 'You assert these two be betrothed?'

'Be? *Were*, yes. In Alteeda, feeding the bride to dragons is reasonable grounds for annulment.'

The King rose, blandly examining Arthmael. Without warning he struck a blow to the Prince's cheek. Arthmael reeled back with the force.

'That be for sarcasm, blaggard boy. You will answer me straight. Have you other proof?'

Arthmael nodded, massaging his jaw, cursing both himself and Brackensith. 'You yourself witnessed them together. The girl under his coronation cape, the one he ordered dispatched, was my sister.'

'How know you of her?' Brackensith's eyes tightened in suspicion again, but then he held up a hand to block Arthmael's answer. A sly smirk grew to twist the corners of his mouth. 'Maybe . . . It would be like my boy to sacrifice his own bride. But no, he would not risk it. I would hunt him down and destroy him.'

'Unless he destroyed your portal first.'

'The portal.' Brackensith grunted, then chuckled at some private joke. His smirk spread till it flooded his face and he threw his head back to laugh. 'My poor, tragic, imbecile son! How obsessed he be with my portal. How many times be he told: only the King may command it. No mortal may destroy it.'

'You laugh, Father,' protested Noriglade. 'Yet he would betray you.'

'Do not pretend, wretched daughter, that your interest in this be Drake's marital bliss. Nor my happiness. This Alteedan has promised you something. What be it? Safe haven in Alteeda if you plead his case?'

'No, nothing. I help him for the justness of his cause.'

'Rank dragonrot. Perhaps revenge spurs you. If it be revenge you shall have satisfaction. Your brother will suffer indeed, if all this be true. I shall recall Riz today.'

Arthmael could hardly believe Brackensith's promise. Alteeda was free! A hot surge of happiness swept through his body. He shot Noriglade a look of triumph and she beamed back at him from behind her hand.

The King eyed them shrewdly, one eyebrow cocked.

'You flirt, daughter. You make eyes at the pretty Alteedan.'

'Father, please!'

'Do not hide like a courtesan behind your foul hand. No, show the boy. Show him your true, abhorrent nature.'

'Father, he knows.'

'Still you disguise?'

'Father, grant me this last shred of dignity, though you have stripped me of all else.'

'Listen to her, boy. This martyrdom she wears like a crown.' The King strode across the floor, eyes icy cruel. He stopped above her and she flinched, seeming to shrink. Her hand dropped away.

The King grabbed her head, twisting it till she faced Arthmael.

'Smile for the pretty boy.'

Her eyes glistened with humiliation as her mouth twisted, trembling.

'Wider, curse you.'

She opened wide, exposing black glass teeth. Her eyes pleaded with Arthmael's, blinking as if with tears.

Arthmael stared, not knowing how to comfort her. Horrified at her father's cruelty.

'See, boy, how she feeds, that you may be repulsed. As others are.'

Her eyes flashed with hatred. She spun on her father. Teetered and almost fell.

'Repulsed! It be *you* who repulses me!' she spat. 'It was *you* who forced elixir past my lips! It was *you* who made me so!' Her jaws opened, teeth gleaming. A deathly snake-hiss rose from her throat.

Startled, Brackensith stepped back. Next moment his hand was raised to strike.

Arthmael stepped between them. 'King! My sister is stirring.'

Brackensith shoved him aside. He leaned over Noriglade, his eyes holding hers with disdain. The hiss died in her throat and her mouth went slack. Her rage had dissolved as suddenly as it had exploded and she looked fragile and small once more. Only then did the King glance toward the stretcher, and at the windows. The long night was ending.

'Go now, wretched daughter, if you intend keeping your face.'

'Noriglade, I'll visit you,' whispered Arthmael. 'The cemetery? No, the crypt?'

She would not look at him. With one hand trembling over her mouth, the other shielding tears that could never come, she stumbled from the room.

CHAPTER FORTY-FIVE

Jatta had in fact not stirred in her sleep. It would be midday before the paste wore off. Arthmael had lied for the Undead princess.

As he watched over his sister in her new chambers, waiting for her to wake, he was disturbed by unfamiliar feelings. Till this morning he hadn't understood what it felt like to really hate. He knew now, though, that he hated Brackensith. Not only for murdering his mother. Nor for making his sister's life miserable. He had always accepted the Dark King's wickedness, much as he'd always understood that wars killed and disease caused suffering.

Last night, however, he'd watched Brackensith twist his knife in Noriglade's humiliation. He'd witnessed calculated cruelty. Hating Brackensith was one more thing he and Noriglade shared.

He thought about Noriglade, how her teeth had failed to frighten him. Surprised him, yes. Disturbed him a little, even. He chuckled to himself, embarrassed at his foolishness. He'd almost convinced himself she was alive. Warm, with a pulse. It was all so difficult to wrap his mind around. She would never see daylight, never grow old, always be beautiful. But nothing like other Undead. Just a scared, vulnerable girl, trying to cope with unimaginable horror. Like Jatta.

His sister opened her eyes.

'Afternoon, sleepyhead,' he smiled.

She looked around, trying to focus.

'We're inside Brackensith's castle. No turning back now.'

She nodded. 'Did I . . .'

'Eat anyone? No, Jay.'

She grinned weakly; her brother's humour could be indelicate. Then her face screwed up as her stomach heaved.

'Jay? What's wrong?'

She jerked up to hang over the bed, though nothing more than bitter bile surged into her mouth. With an apologetic wince she flopped back into the pillows.

'You all right?'

'Sorry, that happens sometimes,' she said. 'How was Brackensith?'

'Listen, he believes us. Mostly. He's going to pay his son a visit and he wants you with him.'

There was polite knocking on Jatta's door, and slave girls with broad faces and long black hair entered. The bowls of fruit they brought were smothered with thick milk and honey.

'Can you eat?' Arthmael sat her back up.

'I'm ravenous.'

The milk tasted sour. Jatta gulped it down anyway, but Arthmael screwed up his face in disgust. She ate his, then most of the spiced meats, trout, pickled vegetables and sweet breads the slaves returned with.

They had not yet finished lunch when the door opened and Brackensith swept in. Jatta remembered his cold, pale eyes from Riz's tent, his sudden frigid violence. She stood at once. Arthmael followed. The King ignored him.

'Recognise this, Jatta?' Brackensith held out a jade ring.

'Majesty, it's Riz's.'

The King raised an eyebrow.

'Majesty, I'm certain. He gave it to me, but I have cause to believe that offer revoked.'

A dry smile flickered on Brackensith's lips. 'You be a natural diplomat, girl.' He slipped the ring over her finger and gestured for her to follow.

She glanced nervously at her brother. He nodded, mouthing, *'Good girl'*.

Brackensith led her through corridors heavy with incense and into a hall-sized guardroom. Its circular wall was lined with soldiers.

'Above be the Royal tower which I share with my heir. One day you shall live there, too,' he said. They crossed the empty expanse of floor to a single locked door. It was no exit though, but a broad spiralling stairwell abutting his circular tower. They climbed. 'Know you where we be headed?' he said as she struggled beside him in her skirts.

'To Riz, Majesty? To your portal?'

He neither acknowledged her answer nor even looked at her again till they emerged from the stairs. There was a foyer and a bolted door. From the other side came frenzied barking and snarling. Jatta shrank back against the wall.

'Shut up, you cursed curs,' he growled, deadly low. 'Or I shall slice you for my supper.'

Instantly the frenzy stopped. Jatta heard fearful whimpering.

Brackensith turned the key. 'The dogs shall not bother you now.'

He opened the door and four rottweilers came crawling out on their stomachs. They seemed as tense as Jatta, torn by their instincts. Although terrified of their master, their eyes flicked dangerously to her.

The largest started dangerous growls. It bristled. Jatta backed against the door. Stealthily it crept, rising from the floor. Teeth bared. Snout quivering. Poised to lunge.

In that moment Brackensith stepped between them. The dog dropped instantly to the ground, cringing pitiably. The others whimpered, pressing flatter still.

'Shut up, vermin.'

They lay silent as death.

'That be a powerful odour you have,' he said, stepping over their bodies and into the room. Jatta willed her trembling legs to follow.

They entered an immense, circular, windowless den, dimly lit with torches. The shelves were crowded with poisons books, dried herbs, horn and skins, flasks and jars. Against the wall, under a clutter of manuscripts, sat a heavy table. Perched there, peering down at her, was a life-sized golden statue of a winged child. At least, that was Jatta's first impression in the flickering light. As she approached, she saw that the ribbed wings didn't belong to the golden Dartithan girl at all, but to a dragon that formed her back half. Both faces had been crafted with such skill that Jatta tensed, half-imagining the hatchling's nip as she reached to touch its golden cheek.

Brackensith grabbed her wrist and pulled her through the jumble to the far corner, where his portal stood. He handed her a black lace scarf, then strode between the columns. Jatta hurried to join him. He was waiting impatiently for something, one eyebrow arched, eyeing the lace. She stared blankly at it for a moment, then placed it over her head like a veil.

He creased his forehead in deep concentration, holding one hand before his face. Jatta's eyes widened in surprise as visions flickered over his outstretched wrist: Riz's tent, palace rooms. They dissolved as he began an incantation.

'To errant Riz
I would hasten.
Heed me, I imagine it now.'

The floor shifted beneath them as the portal buzzed. Blue sparks flickered all around. Jatta's hair frizzed out, her skin tingled. The floor dropped away and for a moment Jatta dropped too. A sea of swirling blackness opened all around her. She clutched out wildly, fearing she would fall through the void.

She didn't. Flickering sparks returned, suspending her between the columns. Suspending Brackensith too.

The swirling sea's blackness was retreating, the floor re-forming. In the dimness she recognised its marble pattern. She peered to make out Riz preening before a mirror, posing for a fitting with Elisind's tailors. They fussed about him, adjusting his new coronation cape. He'd found another crown to adorn his foolish head. Jatta's mother's.

Her father's throne room grew light, but still Riz hadn't noticed the portal. Jatta recalled the several seconds the portal had shimmered in his tent, realising Brackensith must have watched his son posing then, too. She stole a sideways glance at Dartith's King. His top lip twisted in contempt.

The portal buzzed and Riz squealed in alarm. He hurriedly brushed the crown from his head and shoved the tailors away.

'Father, it be almost lunchtime!' he cried. 'I had quite given up expecting you.'

Brackensith stepped coldly out of the portal, dragging Jatta in her veil.

'I have brought Drake's betrothed to show you,' he said.

'Father, no, I protest. My mission be almost completed! Yes, this morning the Princess has been caught.'

'Rank dragonrot,' growled the King, dangerously low. 'With Fand now gone, you could not catch the plague in a crypt.'

'Father, you be unfair! Was it *my* fault the dragon took him?'

'Filthy right it was.' Brackensith's eyes fell to Riz's nervously writhing hands. 'And where be your ring?'

'I—I lost it.'

'You *what?*'

'It slipped off my finger.'

Brackensith's lip twisted again.

'—and—and the dragon ate it.'

'Idiot son.' The King's face was set in cold contempt. 'You expect me to believe that utter drivel?'

Riz nodded uncertainly.

Without warning Brackensith struck him an almighty blow. The Prince fell to his knees.

Jatta flinched. For once, though, she felt no pity.

'Princess, show him your ring.'

Jatta held out her hand. Riz rose. He glanced at it dumbly then bent low to peek under her veil's folds. Brackensith dragged it off. Her eyes stared into Riz's with disdain.

The blood drained from his face.

His mouth opened and closed, making strangled little sounds. 'I—I—I gave you this heart,' he managed to squeak, swooning a little, clutching at his chest. 'Why must you mutilate it so? Have you no soul?'

'No soul?' Jatta glowered. 'I'd let it burn in the firewall to save Alteeda from you.'

Brackensith's smile was fleeting. 'Fortunately for Drake, that sacrifice be unnecessary.'

'Come, traitor scum.' Brackensith strode to the portal, dragging his son, who whimpered like one of his dogs. He turned to address the room's Dartithan soldiers. 'Gather your fellows, all that you can. I shall return in one hour, then in two nights. After that, never again.' He turned to Jatta. 'For you, too. One hour.'

Blue sparks flickered and his portal faded.

Never again. Jatta felt a giddy rush of triumph and gratitude. Brackensith was keeping his word! Hadn't he saved Alteeda from Riz? From vicious bloodlust? Unlike his son, he felt no delight in destroying life. Though she feared Brackensith, though he'd imposed such suffering since that bleak night eleven years before, Jatta had found virtue even in the Dark King's heart.

The soldiers were already racing from the room. 'Stop!' she commanded. 'You! Take me to King Elisind.'

The Dartithan hesitated.

'Don't you recognise Drake's betrothed, your future queen?'

He bowed, and turned toward the Great Hall.

CHAPTER FORTY-SIX

Jatta had never seen squalor, nor smelled it. What sickened her most as she paused by the first makeshift cell was not the vomit or faeces, but her painful recognition of so many faces. Ambassador Sartora's daughters, who could not yet know of their father's murder, lay against the bars. They blinked up at her, confused. The servant who lit the Great Hall fireplace sat inside it with his sick parents. Pacing the bars was Surgeon Tate. Forlorn groups squatted against the back wall with its boarded-up windows, murmuring in shadows.

'Release them. Release them on King Brackensith's orders!' commanded Jatta.

For several heartbeats silence hung. Then as bars clanged open the palace faithful surged forward, calling and crying and laughing. The next cells started clamouring.

'Riz is gone!' she shouted. 'You're free. Help us heal Alteeda!'

'Jay!' came Steffed's voice through the din.

'Jay!' cried her father from the last cell, where the stage had been. She ducked through the throng to them. Their bony bodies were pressed against the bars, their hands stretched toward her. 'You're alive! You're safe!' they cried. Their beards were rough, their faces gaunt and their eyes full of longing. She wrapped herself in her father's arms, smelling not sweet spices, but putrid sickness. It was by his voice, no more, that she recognised him.

After everyone else had fled, the three walked back together. Steffed and Jatta saw how their father used the bars for support, and both slipped their arms around his waist. Jatta fitted neatly under his shoulder. He seemed as light, almost, as her.

'Where's Arthmael? Where's my boy?' he asked.

Jatta took a deep breath. 'He's safe and well . . . in Dartith.'

Her father staggered. Jatta gripped his waist tighter.

'Brackensith will bring him back, though?' he pleaded.

Her eyes glistened. 'Father . . . Dartith isn't so awful, not like you imagine. He's treated well. And—and he has family. He has me.'

Her father fell against the bars, searching her face for some evidence that none of this was true. 'No, my precious girl! I won't let you follow him.'

'Father, please. Brackensith doesn't give us any choice. We have an hour together, just one. He's given us that.' Sheriff Lerrick's words returned to her, words that had stung. 'Alteeda will survive without its Princess. Not without its King,' she said now, hearing the authority in her own voice, the resignation.

The King's tears dripped as they'd done once before—on cold marble, when a frightened girl had felt them spatter by her face, wanting them to stop. Tears for Arthmael. Tears for her. This time, how could she begrudge his tears?

'Are you never coming back?' asked Steffed.

'I don't know . . . perhaps,' whispered Jatta. She stood on tiptoe, leaning close, though the hall was empty. 'Perhaps when we understand Brackensith more.'

Servants returned with a stretcher, impatient for orders. They carried the King to Jatta's rose garden. 'Go feed yourselves. Reopen the treasury,' he said, and sent them away.

They sat together on the dragon pond wall. Jatta told them stories of sleeping in the desert under heraldic stars, of the dragon and the firewall, of Riz's betrayal and the dwarf's, of Arthmael's heroism, too, and she felt a surge of happiness when her father smiled.

Servants brought cider, cheese and dried fruit. The King and his heir dribbled and stuffed their cheeks like beggars. Jatta's face betrayed her surprise, and they grew uncomfortable.

'You hardly recognise me, do you, little Jay?' said her father.

'I do! Now I do!' she cried. 'It's in your expressions ... and the way we talk. You seem thinner ... and older, that's all.'

'And filthy, and lice-infested, and putrid,' said Steffed. 'I'd appreciate a bath.'

Her brother was grinning for once. She loved that. She splashed him with pond water. He splashed her back, and his aim was better. He threatened to grab her, though they all knew he hadn't the strength to throw her in as he and Arthmael had done years ago, before he'd grown too important to share a joke.

He was joking now, making an effort. They all were, trying to store up each bittersweet moment in memory. She urged them to drink, then squeezed the orb; Arthmael came to sit beside them. Her father wasted barely an eye blink on wonderment before congratulating the phantom on taking such care of his sister. He offered them both advice. Jatta tried not to smile and failed. There was something comforting in her father's lectures on family.

Arthmael faded. Ministers gathered beyond her garden gate, shifting restlessly, waiting for instructions. Jatta's hour in Alteeda had trickled away.

'Could you really use this toy to come back?' asked Steffed.

'We hope so.' Jatta blushed. 'But . . . our plans keep going stupidly wrong.'

She and Steffed supported their father back to the throne room where Brackensith was waiting. Blue lights sparked and Jatta was gone.

CHAPTER FORTY-SEVEN

The black swirling sea dissolved. The potions den returned. Jatta's heart was full, bubbling over with a peculiar mix of triumph and loss. She wanted to dance and squeal and run to Arthmael with the news. She wanted to cry, too. Would they ever sit on the pond wall again? Best not to think on that now. How proud Arthmael would be. He'd want an orb replay.

She bobbed by Brackensith's side through the potions den, past the prostrate rottweilers and down six flights of steps to the guardroom.

Brackensith glanced down coldly.

'You revel in some private joke, Jatta?'

The grin dissolved from her face. 'Majesty, no. I was smiling for Alteeda.'

His features softened momentarily. Had she read approval in his eyes?

'Forget Alteeda.' The steeliness returned. 'Dartith be your home.'

Brackensith raised one hand and two grim-faced soldiers fell into line behind Jatta. 'I go now. These guards be for wolf-moon days, hear? To protect both you and the castle.'

She curtseyed obediently as he swept away. Jatta, however, had other plans; she led her minders to the armoury, coaxed from them any news of her brother, then slipped away as a miniature suit of armour. She raced clanging halfway across the archery range before she remembered to stop kneading. She burst into the fencing studio.

Inside, two men were duelling while another three lounged about watching. All wore hooded mesh masks, though from their dark beaded plaits she guessed the spectators, and one of the duellers, were Dartithan nobles. The fifth was her brother. The tall, heavily built Alteedan was still a half-head shorter than the others. She recognised his parrying style, powerful and unpredictable. She noticed something else as he leapt out of the way of a thrust, then staggered. He was exhausted.

His opponent saw his advantage and lunged. Recovering, Arthmael ducked and jabbed his corked point to the man's chest.

'Game!' called Arthmael, breathing heavily. With a flourish of his sword he bowed. Before he could straighten, another had taken his opponent's place. The man delivered a fresh volley of passes, forcing him staggering back across the room. Arthmael stumbled over his feet and landed in straw. The man thrust down. Summoning what remained of his lion strength, Arthmael thrashed and grunted. The blade flew from his opponent's grip. By the time the swordsman scooped up his blade Arthmael had rolled over and wobbled to his feet. He was forced back against a barrel of wooden swords. He dodged, kicking the barrel forward, and the man leapt out of the shower of swords—straight into her brother's trap. He thrust and hit a score to the man's neck.

'Game!' called Arthmael, dropping to his knees, gasping for breath. 'Enough, please!'

'Two against one,' called a fresh noble, leaping into position. A second swordsman positioned himself behind. Arthmael staggered up, swaying uncertainly.

Jatta held her breath. Arthmael thrust back aggressively at the first opponent, forcing him to retreat with the raw power of his strokes. Then he spun around wildly to the swordsman at his back. Arthmael whacked the sword from his hand as the first man struck his kidneys.

'Game!' yelled the first, triumphant.

Arthmael saluted and bowed, then collapsed to sit.

'Still Dredden's finest. No-one betters us at the archaic arts,' said his other opponent, removing his mask. Jatta gasped. The pale grey eyes, the smooth-featured, flattish-nosed face: the likeness was unmistakeable. She was looking at Riz's younger brother.

All eyes turned to her.

'Welcome to Dartith, little Princess. These last eleven years I be waiting.' Riz's brother bowed elegantly low, his voice syrupy with sarcasm. 'I be Drake, your betrothed. Your future king.'

She curtseyed back uncertainly. She didn't trust the smirk on his face. Nor his professed age. Drake was supposedly eighteen, like Arthmael, but this man's face was almost lined.

'Do not believe my knavish brother,' said the opponent who had struck Arthmael. He removed his mask to reveal younger, mischievous grey eyes. 'I be Drake, your betrothed. Your Prince, little Princess.'

Jatta wanted to believe him. She liked his face better. She suspected, though, that these two were playing a game at her expense.

She challenged all four. 'Princes? Please, show your sister-in-law your faces.'

Another man took off his mask. 'I, for one, intend *not* to be Drake. It be a dubious privilege to be betrothed to this

319

doll-sized Alteedan—as poor Riz, thrown in the dungeon for his trouble, would agree.'

'And I be Ivish,' said the black-haired fourth, revealing a trace of Sludinian accent. 'I hear you have spirit, little Jatta. Do you, indeed, intend betrothal to each of us in turn? Then I hope I shall be last to take your fancy.'

'Princess, choose your betrothed from among us,' announced the first.

Jatta looked to Arthmael for help. He shrugged. Whether the four brothers had not introduced themselves, or whether they had played a similar game with him, she couldn't tell. She studied the four waiting faces. The first Drake and the brother who intended not to be Drake seemed too old.

Both the younger brothers, however, could be under twenty. The cheeky-eyed Drake leaned with both hands gripping his sword, and the black-haired brother who called himself Ivish relaxed against a punching bag with arms folded. She sighed, perplexed. Whatever clues she might ask of them, she guessed they would lie.

In a flash of inspiration she remembered Riz's ring. His initial had been carved in jade under the Dartith crest. She saw now that both older brothers also wore them.

'Brothers, I have Sorceress powers,' she said mysteriously.

Arthmael and the cheeky-eyed Drake laughed. She walked across the floor to this Drake, massaging her temples and half-closing her eyes, as if receiving premonitions from some other realm. 'I'll know my betrothed by reading his palm.' She lightly stroked his uppermost hand where it gripped his sword.

He winked roguishly around at his brothers before

whisking his ring hand behind his back. He held out his other palm and she inspected it, playfully tracing her fingertip in a swirl.

His hand flinched. 'Little doll, that tickles!' He chuckled. She wailed:

'Oomba-goomba, Fidey-fie-fum, fidelly-foove.
I read your name in your palm's etched groove!'

Everyone laughed. There, though, in his thumb pad she read the imprint from his ring. Underneath the reversed Dartithan crest was a letter. *I.* So! The younger brothers had swapped identities. She released Ivish's palm with a wink of her own.

She turned toward the punching bag, suddenly nervous with the significance of this moment. As she approached, taking slow, deliberate breaths, she examined Drake's face for the first time. Not quite as handsome as his brothers. Not warm. Not exactly kind. That did not surprise her. She hadn't seen a truly gentle face since arriving in Dartith. She had imagined worse. Much worse. He returned her gaze with the same searching intensity and she blushed.

She curtseyed before him. 'My Prince.'

'My Princess.'

The others broke into guffaws.

'They be not laughing at you,' he said. 'My brothers Mordis and Fabish bet you would choose Ivish. Girls do. But Father says you be more sensible than most.'

She blushed deep crimson.

Drake twisted the ring from his little finger and slipped it on her middle finger. She had nothing to offer him. Her blush could go no deeper.

Drake smiled sympathetically. 'My wayward brother refuses to remember where your ring be. We shall persuade him. He will be tortured for compromising your honour.'

'Please don't!' she blurted out. She took a deep breath. 'I mean, the ring's long lost. For all we know, Riz tossed it out of the portal mid-flight. Torture won't restore it, or his sanity . . . or my, um, honour.'

He scrutinised her curiously, as if she'd rebuffed a gift of sweetmeats. 'Dartith can hardly remake your ring.'

'No, but . . . I'd accept one with meaning for you—your mother's. I'd wear it till our wedding.'

'You would accept what my father wore? You cannot wish for connection with him.'

'I don't resent King Brackensith. Resentment's a poison, isn't it? How can I learn my queenly duties if I hate him?'

His eyebrows rose in disbelief. As he studied her honest elfin face a gradual, surprised smile spread over his own. 'My gratitude, then. I never knew my mother, but if you would accept my aunt-stepmother Noridane's ring, I would be deeply honoured.'

He leaned in close to whisper, 'Make it truly yours. I be in no hurry for marriage.'

'Neither am I.'

'Neither be Father. That be settled, then. You shall come hunting with us in two days.'

'I—I don't like hunting.'

'You shall learn, Jatta. Now get back to the castle. Our day be almost over, and you have a night in the marble cage ahead of you.'

Marble cage? That hardly sounded like sleeping potion. But as she hurried out of the fencing studio with Arthmael, she barely gave it a moment's thought. Again she felt that giddy rush of triumph.

'Is it true?' burst out Arthmael. 'They say Riz is disgraced!'

'Yes! I've been dying to tell you. And Father's freed. He says he loves you, he's missed you, he's so, so proud. Steffed, too.'

Arthmael whooped and leapt high in the air. He had evidently recovered his breath.

She gazed up at his beaming smile and suddenly felt wildly grateful he was here, grateful her solo portal plan had failed. She couldn't imagine Dartith without Arthmael. 'Father says you've a talent for making the best of any situation. That even here you might find happiness.'

'And what about you? You and Drake?'

Nothing could diminish this triumph. She shrugged, grinning. 'It could be worse.'

Jatta's minders came racing across the grounds. Under Dartith's grey twilight they herded her back toward the castle.

'Remember, Jay, I'll be thinking of you,' he called. 'Tell Brackensith I'll keep you company next time. We can tour the countryside again.'

Arthmael watched until she disappeared, then turned back through the grounds, following the route she, Noriglade and he had taken early that same morning.

CHAPTER FORTY-EIGHT

Arthmael returned to the crypt Noriglade had pointed out. From the outside it was not much to look at, a forbidding granite block with a wrought-iron door. This, though, was merely its antechamber. The real crypt was a vast cavern beneath, cut out of rock. Jatta had shown him pictures from her book.

He wandered outside among the headstones, flicking nervous glances at the horizon. In a few minutes it would be time to descend. But not yet. He had little desire to wait down there among the corpses. On the other hand, it would be suicide to arrive after the Undead had woken.

Angry shouts broke through his thoughts.

'Thieving brat! Where be my purse? It be no use to you when you be drained and dead.'

'Tell us, or we shall leave you here. They be starving when they emerge.'

'I never, never took it!' wailed a terrified child.

Arthmael strode back to the crypt. Three noblemen stood with their backs to him, laying punches into a fourth figure strung up on the iron door. A boy. A scraggy slave child. Blood thundered in Arthmael's brain.

'What, in Glory's name!' he yelled. 'Release that child!'

The men spun around.

One drew his sword. 'Mind your own cursed business. This be nothing to you,' he spat.

His friends gasped. 'It be the Alteedan prince.'

'Release him, I say! Whatever he's done, it's murder to leave him here.'

'I done nothing!' wailed the child through a split lip.

'Be on your way, meddling Alteedan,' said the man with the sword. 'You be one against three.'

'Leave it, Leeth,' said his friend, peering anxiously at the horizon. 'I be arguing no longer around this Undead place.' He turned and ran. With parting curses the others bolted too.

Arthmael drew his sword.

'Don't! I done nothing!' The boy started frantic squeals.

Arthmael cut the ropes from the door. 'I won't harm you, boy. I'm a friend.'

'You be like them others,' whimpered the swollen-faced child, backing away. 'They—they took my coin and now I got naught for meat for my master.'

Arthmael dug into Naffaedan's purse. 'Here, take these. They're silver,' he said, holding out a handful of pennings.

The boy's eyes narrowed warily as he wiped his bloody nose on his sleeve. Suddenly he snatched the coins and ran.

Arthmael was left shaking his head with a soft snort. 'A *thank you* would have been polite,' he muttered.

The boy turned as if hearing him and ran back to hug Arthmael tight. He smiled up impishly, then made a dash out of the graveyard. Something in that smile alerted Arthmael. His hand went to his pocket.

Naffaedan's purse was gone.

Anger surged, and he had the urge to give chase. The purse,

though, was gone. This place, he'd warned his sister often enough, was not Alteeda; if he was to survive here he would have to adjust.

Day had grown dim as night. He dragged open the iron door.

Inside, the architecture was just as bleak. The floor's one feature was a central hole with a winding staircase. Arthmael started his descent.

With every step the smell of damp and decay grew stronger. He climbed down to a vast cavern cut out of rock. Columns, carved like skeletons, stretched up to vaulted ceilings. The walls seeped into puddles on the floor.

The main floor was an empty space. Mosaic tiles depicted people rising out of sarcophagi to embrace the living with kisses to their necks. Whether this represented some Dartithan resurrection myth, or something more gruesome, Arthmael could not decide.

The walls were indented with alcoves. Inside each alcove were seven slabs as high as tables. Resting on each slab was a human body.

Arthmael stepped up to a slab in the first alcove. The remnants of a netted shroud covered what was left of a man. He had long been reduced to bones, but tatters still clung where once there had been fine clothes. Skeletal hands lay crossed over shreds of linen on his ribcage. A ring still hung on one bony finger. Arthmael shuddered, both intrigued and revolted. He stepped over to the next. One glimpse told him the woman under the ancient shroud had not decayed at all. He tensed and backed away.

The next, and the next, and the next alcoves contained nothing more than skeletons. He dared not enter the alcove that followed. One fresh shroud writhed with beetles. Its stench made him gag.

Arthmael moved from alcove to alcove. Forty shrouds along he found another white-shrouded face. Even relaxed in its sleep of death the man's features were disturbingly cruel. His mouth had fallen open, displaying obsidian teeth. Blood was smeared across his part-rotted cheek. Arthmael backed away, shaking his head in disgust, shaking the stench from his clothes. This place was soaked in evil. He'd had enough of the Undead and their dark perversions.

'Lord, what am I doing here?' he shouted to the arrayed dead. If he expected an answer, none came. He bolted toward the stairs.

Halfway up, he stopped.

Somewhere down there was a girl. Someone he ached to know. And tease. And protect. He slumped down to sit on the step and banged his head on the rail in frustration. He groaned, then laughed, at the absurdity of it all: he, Alteeda's second-most-eligible bachelor, was finally smitten.

With a fish-sucking, foul-mouthed Undead.

He dragged himself back down along the railing and returned to the crypt to resume his gruesome quest. He found her hidden behind six vacant slabs. He pulled back the shroud. The porcelain skin. The full lips. It was hard to believe. It seemed she was simply sleeping.

'Prickle, wake up.' He shook her shoulder.

Her collarbone shocked him as if it were ice. Instinctively he whipped back his hand, then cursed himself. 'Fool, Arthmael. You *know* what she is.'

Her eyes opened. All around the crypt Undead were stirring.

He leaned close, his skin tingling with nerves. 'Prickle, remember me?'

She took a moment to focus. Warm recognition spread over her face. Then it crumpled, and he saw the shame in her eyes.

'Why be you here? Go away!' She covered her face with her hands and turned her back.

'I . . . It's all right that you're Undead. Please don't hide.'

'You see me at my worst, among my own kind.' She would not look at him. 'They . . . We repulse you!'

'No, Prickle, not you.'

'Do not lie. I saw it in your eyes this morning.'

'Perhaps just a little. But only your cold touch. And when you hissed. And . . . Listen, this is all new to me. Give me a chance. If I can adapt to Jay, I can adapt to you.'

Someone was slinking through the alcove's shadows. He saw it from the corner of his eye. 'Prickle, please! Is there somewhere safe we can discuss this?'

'You know nothing of Undead,' she said to the wall.

Someone breathed, cold, on the back of his neck. The hairs there stood up. Arthmael froze. Someone hissed in his ear. Like a snake, about to strike.

Noriglade heard it too. She sprang to her knees. One arm whipped around Arthmael's neck. The other swiped at the Undead's gaping mouth. She hissed viciously.

Clutched to her chest in her cold embrace, Arthmael's heart thudded painfully. He heard the rustle of silk as the Undead backed away. He breathed again, breathing in the stink of her robes.

She released him and slid down from the slab. 'Stay close,' she warned. They headed for the stairs.

As they climbed, relief broke across his face; all tension

drained from it. 'Thank you,' he said, then chuckled. 'See, I told you I could adapt. Did I flinch? Even once, when you held me? Not at all.' He tickled her from behind. 'Let's see who squirms now.'

She turned on him, spitting her deadly snake-hiss. Baring obsidian.

Wide-eyed, he fell back against the rails.

She was standing there above him, laughing. Her pale eyes sparkled. He'd hardly seen her smile before. He started laughing, too.

'Now shut up, Arthmael. I be hungry. Starving. I be tempted to attack anything, *anything* that chatters too much.' She turned her back on him and resumed her climb.

'Have I told you how pretty you look? Especially when you laugh. You have dimples—cute, girly dimples.'

'Idiot boy.'

But he could tell from her luscious voice she was still smiling.

He dozed in the moonlight by the castle lake, weary after two sleepless nights, while she fished. She said he was mostly safe here, that Undead were banned from feeding around the castle. While he slept she emerged from the lake, washed clean of the crypt's foul smells. She slipped a wet, writhing fish down his shirt then giggled as he scrambled up yelling.

'You seem fascinated with Undead, boy,' she said. 'Try sucking on *that*!'

'It's not the Undead that intrigue me,' he replied, tossing the fish back in the lake. 'It's you.'

He lay back in the grass. She sat beside him in one lithe, fluid movement that was a pleasure to watch. Her hands rested cupped in her lap and he feathered them with a blade of grass; she didn't seem ticklish at all. She answered his questions in her warm, sensual voice, without self-pity . . . How she hated Dartith, how she'd felt it draining the humanity from her soul just as it had eventually drained the life from her mother . . . as it had long drained the blood from its people. She told him how her adored mother wasted away over fourteen miserable years, how only she and Drake had mourned her, how afterwards she plotted with friends to escape through the portal . . . how they failed. How she begged Brackensith to behead her for her treason.

'But he made you drink Andro Mogon's elixir instead?'

She nodded.

'Why?'

'It was the worst punishment Father could devise. Certainly, some men have aspired to this half-existence when their own lives were at an end, but I have always despised the Undead and the suffering they cause. As, rightly, does the world beyond Dartith. Father knew I could never attempt escape again. No kingdom would have me.'

'Do you still wish you were dead? Have you thought to stay out past dawn?'

'I tried once, but it be not easy to end one's existence. The craving for one's soul be distressing to resist, like . . . like your need for air. Could you hold your breath for three days?'

'Not for three minutes.'

She laughed dryly. 'I lasted *one*. I had barricaded myself in Father's chambers supposing I was strong. With the coming dawn I grew frantic.'

'What happened?'

'I jumped from his tower window.'

Arthmael grimaced. Her aunt Noriward had done the same thing.

'Did it hurt?'

'Indeed.' She winced at the memory, then smoothed her expression. 'Pain be not the worst of it, do not concern yourself about that. I break, I squash, I slice through. But I cannot die. That be the worst. That pre-dawn I picked up the pieces and dragged myself, defeated, back to my slab. I was fortunate, I admit, to find every piece. By sunset I had healed each torn thread, each broken bone.'

'Your soul mended everything?'

'Silk and skin, bone and pearls, all be dead . . . so how can a trapped soul know which be corpse and which be decoration? A soul does not distinguish, understand? In its first Undead morning a soul imprints on whatever be laid on its slab. Every morning thereafter, it repairs the corpse's rot—'

'Don't. You're no *corpse*.' He touched a finger to her full, cold lips. 'You think I haven't seen Undead who stayed out too long? That's not you. You're unique.' His eyes roved over the perfection of her face. 'You're so . . . beautiful.'

Her uncomfortable smile twitched. 'Perhaps on the outside, but by night's end my limbs grow stiff with rigor mortis. You shall smell decay on my breath, Arthmael. Know me as Dredden does, as nothing more than a rotting, animated cor—'

'I don't want to hear this!' He bolted to sit upright, shifting away.

'That be why I must warn you. Handsome Prince, do you still feel like tickling me?'

Arthmael didn't answer while he battled the distaste in his face. Her gaze dropped; her fingertips trembled, pulling blades from the grass. He cursed his transparency.

'Prickle?'

He felt the resentment in her silence. Glory, what a miserable mess. His rejection had wounded her, for all she'd invited it with her ruthless truth. She couldn't possibly have expected him to embrace it, could she? No, not this Undead who'd hid behind her hand. She was brave, he'd grant her that.

'I still want to know you,' he said, not sure what else he felt. 'There's no girl like you in all Alteeda.'

She glared up, abruptly angry. 'There be many like me here in the crypt. Save your macabre fascination for them.'

'Prickle! That's not what I meant, and you know it.'

He leaned in close and forced a grin, fighting back the vision of beetles that flashed in his mind. 'You're our friend now. Where in Dartith would my sister and I find a more honest and courageous friend?' he whispered.

The gesture worked, mostly. Her fiery eyes relaxed, sad again.

'You would expose her to me?'

'Sure, she'll like you. Here, then? Tomorrow night. Just don't shoot her this time.'

CHAPTER FORTY-NINE

'Prince or not, his traitorous head deserves to be separated from his hide!' shouted Dredden's chancellor.

'Behead Riz, and you risk greater bloodshed!' cried the chief minister, slamming his fist on the table. 'Most Undead stand with him. His allies be power—'

Brackensith raised one hand, silencing the minister mid-blast. He was in the throne room, listening as his counsellors argued Riz's fate, when Jatta was brought from the fencing studio. He glanced out the window, then scowled at Jatta's minders. They blanched under his gaze. 'Next time you lose the Princess, you lose your heads,' he said.

He turned his scowl to her, his head tilted as if contemplating some irksome puzzle, and her heartbeat sped up. *He knows*, she thought. He knows about my armour suit prank and the orb. Stupid girl. Careless.

He rose, beckoning her to follow. Again she remained mute, lengthening her strides to keep up, clenching her fingertips into the orb in her pocket.

Eventually he spoke. 'You be not the first wolf in our family, Jatta.'

Her grip relaxed. He had something to explain; perhaps that was all. 'Majesty, I'd wondered about that.' Her tone was quiet, respectful. 'I don't scare people here in the castle. Not like in Alteeda or on your farms.'

'Exactly so. Wolves, Undead. What lesser men dread, we royals embrace. Embrace within safe limits, understand? Henceforth you shall spend wolf-moon nights in the marble cage.'

'Majesty, in your family . . .' she began cautiously, framing the question she'd first considered a lifetime before, back in Redd's hall. 'In your family . . . have there been wolves younger than me?'

'You shall find no infant wolves, Jatta. Thine emerged at puberty when it should.'

She grunted softly, sadly. There it was, an inanely simple explanation for eleven wolf-free years. How completely, how blindly, they all had deluded themselves about Redd.

Brackensith didn't speak again. They climbed the tower stairwell up eight flights past the guardroom, past Drake's chambers, past Brackensith's poisons den and his private bed-chambers to the very top floor. They stepped from the stairwell to face two more soldiers—and a wall constructed of great marble blocks. Curiously there was no door, only a slit in the thick wall no taller than Jatta, and no wider than her shoulders.

'Answer me, Jatta. Why no door?' Brackensith cocked one eyebrow, testing her.

Jatta thought for a moment.

'Majesty, a woman can enter. A man can too. But a wolf can't leave.'

He gave not the slightest response, except to gesture for her to enter. She stepped through sideways and he followed, first ducking his head under the low frame, then squeezing his torso through.

The circular chamber was bare, its floor a mosaic of

semi-precious stones. Its walls stretched up three storeys to a spectacular, leadlight dome. Though the bottom two storeys were white marble, the strip of wall just below the dome was a mosaic mural, a wolf-hunting scene, set with a million tiny stones in painstakingly perfect but gruesome detail.

Attached to the wall directly across from Jatta was a marble water trough. Beside it a woman crouched, grubby and wary like a cornered feral cat. Her hair had once been elegantly styled, though now its jewelled clips lay buried among greasy tangles. Her once rich robes hung loose on her skinny body.

Jatta tensed. 'Get her out, please.'

'She be chained. She shall not hurt you,' smirked Brackensith.

'But I'll kill her!'

'Yes. A welcoming treat for you.'

Jatta felt physically sick at this isle's brutality. And at her own potential for it. She dropped to one knee. 'Majesty, please. This is all too grotesque, too new. Give me time. I swear I'll adjust.'

He scowled. 'She be a wretched traitor, Jatta. Torn apart by you or cursed by others, she be condemned.'

'Then keep her for me.'

'Sentimental girl.' He snorted in annoyance. 'Bloodlust be in your nature, understand? It be holding back the moon's tide to resist it.'

He called back through the slit. 'Men, keep the traitor one month. And, by blasted heralds, fatten her up!'

The soldiers dragged the prisoner out. The King turned and was gone.

She was left alone in her elegant prison. While Dartith's sun tinged the clouds above the dome a murky brown, Jatta sank to the floor, feeling her nose tingle, forlornly resisting. Flesh stretched and pulled. Bestial urges rose.

A ferocious howl rose from her throat, trailing away in eerily beautiful song. Jatta rose to crouch, prickling with pent-up hatred, her snout twitching for prey. Her eyes flicked to the slit and beyond, where two silhouettes watched. Jatta's ears swivelled, listening to their easy heartbeats, their intrigued whispers. Fury erupted. She sprang, clearing ten lengths. Her claws were through the slit and raking the air. The whisperers stumbled back against the stairwell door.

She gnawed chunks from the slit. She clawed holes as if it were chalk. Her pelt powdered white. Sweat and dust mixed to a paste in the creases of her neck and rubble collected at her feet. She launched through, legs first; that had brought rewards once. She stuck at the chest. In frustration she squeezed herself back and thrust her snout through the slit, snapping violently at the fresh meat. She stuck at the shoulders. The whisperers fled down the stairs.

Desperate, she tore around the floor and bounded up walls. She leapt for the dome, clearing the second storey to slam into the mosaic. Claws scraped through a dying slave on her way down. Again she coiled. Driven by bloodlust, she almost flew. This time she collided with the mosaic wolf that leapt upon its slave meal. She gouged wounds in semi-precious stones, in marble too, all the way down to the trough.

A third time she coiled. Jatta launched like a firework, bursting past the mosaic. Her claws snagged the very ledge that the dome rested on. She hung above empty chambers that had witnessed no such feat in seven hundred years. Then effortlessly she swung her colossal bulk up onto the ledge and stood. In the courtyard below, servants stared up at her silhouette.

A tantalising scent wafted from the slit. She sniffed and her hatred prickled. This new creature was powerful. Haughty. Ruthless. The sweeter the taste, then. Green eyes flicked. The fresh meat picked his way through the rubble and her excitement spiked. She contemplated strategy: edge halfway to the slit, then leap down to crack his skull. She was becoming better at thinking, more controlled, less rabid. The meat was not scared. He would be. He stood exposed, watching her watching him. He growled back to the slit.

'Distract her, man. She needs to be fed.'

The words meant nothing to her; it was the annoyance in his voice she enjoyed. Yes, this flesh would be sweeter than most.

She edged around. The whisperers whined on, and he commanded again.

'Did you not hear me, man? I promised her sensibilities a reprieve of one month. No, a challenge. Something to occupy her talents . . . Bring her Riz's pets. He shall need them no more.'

The crushing of his bones. The tearing of his limbs. She could almost feel it as he nodded up at her. As she crouched.

Too late! He ducked out through the slit.

She danced her frustration. She tore a chunk from the ledge and hurled it after the departed meat. She tore another to smash through the dome. And as glass disappeared below, fresh scents drifted in. She thrust shoulders through to the sky. She filled her lungs with this city's vibrancy, and it excited her. In her limited imagination she was already bathed in gore. Herding screamers. Not stopping to gorge. She'd been made for this. She grasped the dome's edge and leaned out to leap to the feast. What she saw tore a howl of anguish from her chest.

The drop to the courtyard was impossible. Armour-cracking far.

Jatta went berserk. She jerked back, rampaging the dome's circuit. Smashing. Finally, when nothing was left, she howled. The moon and heralds heard her torment, and much of Dredden besides.

Many voices echoed up the stairwell. A new odour, one she did not recognise, shut her up. It wasn't compelling, not like her natural prey, but strong. Tastier than whinnyers. Tasty enough, she decided. Metal scraped as the creature's cage was dragged to her slit. Its door slid aside. She watched intently. One enormously long leather wing threaded through, followed by a red-tinged body. It hopped across rubble to allow a second wing through. Its sword-length beak yawned up at her, exposing obsidian teeth. Her eyes narrowed, assessing this bird-lizard creature which now spread its wings without fear. It flapped to spiral slowly past her to the dome. She plotted as it circled above. There was no meat on the red wings, nor on those bird-legs, but the rest would be juicy enough. Her gaze returned to the slit.

A second lizard-bird struggled through to spread its wings. She crouched. It froze, dribbling fear. It squawked as she launched. It toppled onto its back and wings thumped the floor. She landed perfectly, straddling it. Her paws pinned its wings as her jaws swept for its throat. That was as far as she got.

A screech came from above. She snarled in hatred and twisted up. As the red screecher lunged for her eyes, she leapt to gouge tracks down its beak. But a second attacker launched from the slit. She landed to bash its chest, sending it skating into the wall on its back. All three screeched and rose. She bounded after them, leaping as high as ever before, past the mural. Her teeth snapped on the coward squawker and its leg came away in her mouth. She spat it out, falling to the floor with a thud. She launched again, higher yet, as they circled the dome.

A third time she jumped, but onto the ledge. She reached it easily, and relaunched at the squawker. It squawked again as her body thumped down on its back. In panic it burst through the dome, shattering glass. She took the brunt of that.

Suddenly there was nothing except sky. The moon hung within reach. Her urge was to howl.

But her squawker bucked as it floundered. The rock of her weight dragged it down, and it dropped below the dome. It swerved downward, dragging her from her moon. Jatta's jaws wrapped around its skull and she crushed.

Too late, she remembered to look down.

The squawker's neck went limp. Its wings flapped against her like a cape. The drop brought her stomach into her throat. Together they spiralled down, spinning her dizzy. The moon was a ball twirling and the tower a streak of light. The court-yard rushed up.

The thud, when it came, jolted her armour. Plates ground past each other before settling. For a moment there were flashes of light, then her head rang in aftershock. She lay in lizard-bird flesh and blinked up at the moon.

All the odours of panic took moments to soak into her brain.

She shook her head, sat up and inhaled. Human flesh called to her. It was cramming the doorways to escape inside. A feast. She coiled, bristling. She launched through the night.

Claws plucked her legs in mid-flight.

The screechers had her and she was being dragged above the feast. So near, so far. It was unbearable. She writhed up to tear out their interfering hearts. Two beaks waited. That hardly deterred her. They poked at her eyes. They battled, jerking like a dragonfly as they climbed. Up past the tower. Past the dome. Higher. So much higher. She seized a beak and flung it around, the whole body, too, to break its neck. In that moment, as Jatta dangled by one leg with the red screecher thrashing in her grip, the moon caught her eye.

She looked down.

The pavement, its prey too, swayed a world below.

She let go of the screecher and howled. She howled in a crescendo of frustration. For eight nights her hunger had raged without a taste of human flesh. Without the warm wetness in her mouth, the rip of muscle through her claws. She cried to the moon.

The remaining screecher released her.

She was plummeting. With a wolf's instinct she twisted, hurling herself sideways towards the dome. It loomed close. Closer. Not close enough; she fell past its curve, clawing air. The ledge slipped past, a length from her chest. Her thrashing claws caught a twisted strip of lead. Jatta slid down its lifeline to a stop. It stretched into wire. It snapped as she backflipped onto the ledge.

With a wild screech the red was at her again. Jatta had had enough. As the beak closed on her face, she seized it. She prized it open. Even as it fell back through the dome, she dragged it more open than a beak could go. The head cracked before they hit the floor.

While she was still shaking herself up, the last screecher came in all its fury. She snarled her answer and swung the red's body up. Both were knocked into the wall, where they slid into the trough. In two bounds she was on top, triumphant. She started feasting while the last's wing flapped vainly against the floor, her hatred mixed with elation. This, killing, was what she did best.

Shortly after sunrise Jatta staggered out past the soldiers, bruised and cut, holding her slashed and filthy robes in place. This morning she had remembered more of her wolf night.

There'd been the pain again. There'd been the pterodactyls, the rabid delight of the kill. Remembering wasn't the worst of it, though; it wasn't what frightened her most.

It had happened. Her wolf had stayed on past dawn. She'd woken sweating frustration. Seething with hatred. She'd lain on the mosaic floor among twisted lead and glass, among bloody smears and scraps, with bestial urges flashing unbidden through her mind.

Only her plea to Brackensith had stopped her performing an unforgivable crime. But this morning the fragile Princess lay craving the soldiers' blood. Craving the prisoner's blood. The two Jattas were becoming one. After next month, or the next, she was no longer sure she would have the will to plead.

CHAPTER FIFTY

Jatta was skimming through passages, bathed in dreamy happiness, following the wobbling blue droplet. Her mouth opened; her breath drew it inside, a honeyed reward for her tongue. Another droplet formed ahead, coaxing her to hurry, and with a powerful flick of her wings Jatta surged to sample it. Through a warm labyrinth Jatta chased, soupy-thick air buoying her up, drawing closer to home, to a long slit of light, and her excitement grew. One last droplet wobbled through the slit and, tilting her body, Jatta's great wings brushed through too.

She emerged to hover inside a leadlight dome, not her rose garden, and her insides ached in disappointment. She looked around for blue honey and found instead a woman crouched, chained, beneath her. 'Get her out of here!' she cried, suddenly scared.

But the woman smiled up at her, calling, 'Come sleep beside me, little Jatta.'

Jatta's dreamy calmness floated back ... If she could just lie here awhile, sleep through the night, where would be the harm in that?

Jatta woke to pounding outside the chambers. She blinked groggily in the dark, remembering her dream, not remembering where she was.

In a bed, but not her own. There was a window with heralds and a moon. Night, then.

She remembered now. The strange bed *was* her own. She'd returned to sleep here after her dreadful marble cage night. The carnage of it flashed. Her overfull stomach heaved. With all her will she forced its memory back with her first. Her nausea retreated too.

Taking long, soothing breaths, she focused on her dream. Sleeping potion would save her from herself; surely that was the key, her last hope. She would plead with Brackensith. Only a sadist would not understand.

'Jay!' came the muffled call. 'For Glory's sake, how many weeks are you going to sleep?'

She dragged herself up and stumbled toward the door.

Arthmael followed her in as she returned to collapse back down on the bed. 'Difficult night?' he asked.

She nodded.

'You *have* eaten, though? Since, I mean.'

She nodded.

'Good girl. Care for a moonlight walk?'

There was definitely something bothering him, too. His voice was too anxious for his bright smile. He laid shoes by her bed and she obliged him by slipping her feet inside. She followed him to the door, too worn out to slip anything but a cloak over her night robes.

As they crossed the royal forest Arthmael broke the silence. 'There's someone . . . I'd like you to meet her.'

'A girlfriend.' This was a first. She flicked him an exhausted smile.

'No, not a *girlfriend*. And don't use that term around her or she'll flay me alive. Listen, Jay, she's not quite what you might expect. I'm not even sure . . .' He trailed away. 'Be nice, all right? Promise you'll keep an open mind.'

She was hardly in a position to judge. 'Is she a commoner? A slave? I really don't care.'

Arthmael ignored her, steering them toward the lake.

'All right, so what's her name?'

'Noriglade.'

'Noriglade? But that's Sludinian.'

'Her mother was Sludinian.'

'Noridane? Then she's the Princess. What's wrong with that?'

'She has a handicap, all right?' He pulled her to a stop, peering through the trees. Recognition lit in his eyes and his mouth stretched into a grin.

She followed his gaze to the lake. A tall figure stood still on its moonlit bank. Her black hair clung wet to her head and her golden robes dripped. As they drew close the Dartithan Princess smiled nervously, and dimples showed in her exquisite face. She was obviously Brackensith's daughter with her full, defined lips, smoke-grey eyes and smooth features. Unlike her brothers, though, her skin was white. Sickly, bloodlessly white.

Arthmael kissed her cheek awkwardly. 'Princess Noriglade, it's my pleasure to introduce my sister, Princess Jatta.'

Jatta leaned close to kiss her, too.

Noriglade backed hastily away. 'I—I be sorry,' she stammered, covering her mouth. 'Please give me time.'

Jatta tried to set the older girl at ease. 'Of course, you're still wet. Do you have something dry to change into?' She glanced around the bank. 'You must be cold.'

Noriglade frowned, puzzled. Then realisation spread over her face. She flicked Arthmael an annoyed look. He shrugged in apology.

Jatta struggled to read their unspoken exchange. The swim, or her wetness, had something to do with Noriglade's handicap, she guessed. Obviously neither of them were keen to confide it at this stage, so she tried again to smooth over the awkwardness.

'Noriglade, I haven't thanked you for the other night. Arthmael says you no longer live at the castle.'

Noriglade was looking increasingly uncomfortable. She took a breath to answer, then changed her mind.

'Jay, Noriglade lives over there.' Arthmael pointed past the trees to where Noriglade had first shown him. 'In the—the summer house with the spiralled green turrets.' He faltered, seeing Noriglade's irritation grow. She was holding onto her temper with difficulty. She pulled him down by his shirt to whisper in his ear.

In that moment Jatta saw *them*.

Obsidian teeth. Sharp, against his neck.

She screamed. She tore her brother from the Undead's grasp. Blood thundered through her head as she yelled, 'It's a trap!'

Noriglade stood bewildered. Suddenly her face contorted and she flung herself at Jatta. Hissing viciously. Baring her teeth.

Jatta fell to the ground. Her hands shielded her face as she screamed.

Arthmael stepped between them. 'Enough! Shame, Prickle!' he yelled. 'You're terrifying her.'

Noriglade turned on him. Not hissing, but pounding his chest. 'Shame? What of *my* shame? Such loathing in her eyes! Hadn't you the decency to tell her?'

Jatta stared, dumbfounded.

'I'm sorry, all right!' he yelled. 'I thought if she got to know you first—'

'*Know me?*' She spat out the words. 'Only you be idiot enough to want that! Forget me. I'll have naught to do with you, hear?'

She turned and strode toward the crypt.

Jatta lay gaping, trying to take it all in. Her brother was enchanted. And the Undead clearly cared about him also. Jatta scrambled to her feet, her face flushed and abashed. She ran after the pale, dripping figure.

'Noriglade! Wait.'

Noriglade strode on. Jatta raced to catch up, grabbing the white arm. The touch was deathly cold. It sent an unpleasant chill down her spine.

'Noriglade, please.'

The Undead turned around, the pain in her perfect face unconcealed. Jatta looked into eyes that blinked as if with tears, eyes as vulnerable as her own.

'I, um . . . It seems we got off to an abysmal start,' stammered Jatta. 'Please, I want to be your friend.'

'What use be that? Your brother will never accept me, not with his "*summer house with spiralled green turrets*." He wants no unnatural, perverse monster in his life.'

'Of course he does. He already has one.'

Noriglade scoffed. 'You? Your curse does not compare.'

'Can you control your urge to kill? I can't.'

'So? Do you rot through the night? I do.'

'No, but—could you infect others? Those you love? I might.'

'So?' yelled Noriglade. 'Have you been robbed of children? Of life itself? Will your miserable existence stretch out for eternity? Mine will!'

'Will hatred invade you, till there's nothing of the real you left?'

Noriglade raised one eyebrow in reproach, looking uncannily like her father. 'My crypt companions grow more evil with every generation they survive. Why should *I* be different? You at least, Jatta, shall be old and decrepit before your wolf overtakes you. Be you saying your curse be worse? Would you rather be Undead? Answer me truly.'

Yes! Anything but what I am! screamed the voice in Jatta's head. *Because it's happening now.* Jatta took a breath to say it, but her throat suddenly felt swollen. She swallowed to clear it, but these words were too painful to push past the lump. Their squabble, and everything else, seemed utterly stupid.

'Princess Noriglade, I concede victory to you. You have the right to greater misery.' To hide her moist eyes, she bowed low. When her head lifted, Noriglade was awkwardly smiling in apology.

Arthmael approached the girls. 'Are we friends again? Am I forgiven?'

Noriglade turned her back on him. 'First promise not to yell at me.'

'First promise not to hiss at people,' he retorted.

'*Jatta* never minded. We be friends now.'

'Garbage. She thought she was going to die. She was on the ground screaming, remember?'

'Actually,' interrupted Jatta, her voice rough, 'I have to go.'

'Sorry, Jay,' said Arthmael. 'We'll walk you back.'

'No, please. Being alone is what I need right now.'

*

Arthmael returned with Noriglade to the night markets. 'Attacks! Latest losses!' called a pamphlet vendor to a fast-gathering crowd.

'Updated lists of local Undead feedings,' Noriglade explained as Arthmael tried reading over a pot vendor's shoulder; the woman glowered and buried her pamphlet under pans to drive him away.

'Wolf attacks also,' continued Noriglade. 'Though these Dreddeners do not bother with those columns. Victim survival strategies. Drinking profiles of the thirty-eight of us here in the crypt, our preferences—not accurate, but offering these people some illusion of control over their fates.'

'Drinking profiles?'

She nodded up at a first-floor balcony where two matronly noblewomen were deep in discussion. Arthmael noticed nothing unusual about them till one turned her head to study the pamphlet vendor in his booth. Her whiteness under the heraldic stars betrayed her.

'That be Beetress. The other be Theedress,' said Noriglade. 'Their profile says they feed together, choose a brewery worker, let him live if he fills his veins with beer for their entertainment. But Beetress tells me she be tired of the taste, and of restraint.'

Beetress returned her attention to her companion with a flick of her eyebrows. Her companion nodded a kind of bored assent, and Beetress descended the balcony stairwell. The crowd scattered as she wandered, with more languid ease than Arthmael might have expected from a middle-aged woman, towards the vendor and his aged assistant.

'Come. Do not watch,' urged Noriglade, hooking cold fingers around Arthmael's belt and pulling him away.

'Why doesn't he run?' His voice was tense.

'Running will only aggravate her. She will not tire and will readily destroy his father as well, he knows that.'

Arthmael let himself be dragged along, compelled to watch as the street cleared of all except Beetress at the vendor's neck. She had him propped against his booth, and her companion was inside it, leafing through a pamphlet. Arthmael glimpsed the old man cowering behind.

Something beautiful was happening around Beetress's face—a white glow like the moon's halo had illuminated her features. He watched it float down her throat and spread around her whole body. With sudden foreboding his focus flashed to the man's throat. It glowed too, pulsing as though a connection had opened between man and parasite and some brilliant and precious substance throbbed through.

Arthmael shuddered. He stopped. 'We have to do something.'

'What, precisely? Teach her to suck fish?' Noriglade's voice was gentle despite her cynical words. She lifted icy fingers to coax his chin back from the booth. He flinched. Her hand whipped back.

'Arthmael, welcome to our world. I know this vendor. He be in league with Riz's Undead—his pamphlets deny their attacks around the castle. Here everyone be both predator and victim.'

'Not you. You'd never kill.'

Pain flickered over her face. Her gaze dropped to the pavers.

'Prickle? What ... who?' As soon as the accusation was out, he groaned. But there was no taking it back.

'There, I disillusion you. Go, leave. You imagined me different. Worthy, like you.'

'Prickle, please. I didn't mean killing in self-defence. Whatever happened, it's all right, you don't have to tell me. You'd never murder, I know that.'

Her eyes rose to his, hardening, congealing into a bitter, defiant mask. For the first time she looked truly Undead. 'You think not?'

'Help me here. I—I don't understand.'

'Plainly, then. I murdered three good friends who never harmed me.'

'Why?' he asked, feeling a chill along his spine.

She glared in bitter defiance.

'Did Brackensith make you do it?'

She scoffed. 'Still you plead some excuse.'

'I don't believe you.' He watched her mask tell him otherwise. 'Don't—don't you feel remorse?'

'No.' She backed away. 'Despise me, you artless Alteedan. See me for the Undead I am, not the angel of your fantasy. Yes . . . I see disgust there in your eyes.' She turned and strode back up the hill. The gold of her robes gleamed.

Twin aches of desire and loss coursed through him, and he hated that he should want her. What an abysmal plight! Even as he trod behind, letting her gain distance, letting the rotting, murderous creature escape, his mind was busy making excuses for her killings, excuses she refused to provide. Why couldn't he take her at her word? Hadn't she rejected him too many times? But in some screwed-up Prickle way, she probably figured rejection was the other way around. It had been there in her face, in the moment she'd turned from him: a spasm of pain at his betrayal.

CHAPTER FIFTY-ONE

Jatta groaned and rolled over as slaves entered her chambers. They threw open the drapes and dawn sunlight streamed onto her face. They nudged her shoulder, pulling down the quilts.

'Go away,' she mumbled. 'I want to be alone.' She wrestled back the quilts, dragging them over her head.

'My Princess,' whispered Drake's voice in her ear. 'Have you forgotten our trip?'

She bolted upright, blinking.

'I beg you, keep us waiting no longer.' He smiled with amused tolerance, then swept from the room.

Their trip. The hunt. She felt sick.

Jatta came shuffling up, slaves still lacing her robes. Arthmael was waiting, bleary-eyed, with the brothers beside two open carriages. He looked as forlorn as she felt.

'Where are the hounds?' she asked.

The brothers laughed.

'It be stags we hunt, not townspeople,' answered Drake. 'The hounds wait in the lodge beyond Dredden's walls.'

Drake helped her into the first carriage, then he and Arthmael swung up behind the driver. Mordis, Fabish and Ivish climbed into the second.

'It be a long trip, Jatta,' Drake said. 'Will you care to entertain me with tales of Riz's dragon?'

'This I must hear!' cried Mordis, leaping down from his carriage and up beside Jatta.

'Me too!' Ivish jumped up and onto a horse's back. To his brothers' cheers he walked over all four frightened horses to leap down into Mordis's lap. Fabish ran around his carriage to wedge himself on top of Ivish, and all three toppled onto Drake.

'Get off, you oafs,' laughed Drake. 'There be room for four only.'

'Our Alteedan doll be only little. Mordis and I shall sit beside her,' announced Ivish.

Fabish shoved him from the carriage. 'Mordis and *I* shall sit beside Jatta. You lost us Drake's bet, Ivish. You may drive.'

Ivish dragged the driver from his seat and mounted. He grinned back mischievously at them all, and cracked his whip through Fabish's hair.

'Aye, this'll be some ride!' yelled Mordis.

The whip cracked over the four horses' backs. They surged forward at a gallop.

If Jatta was grateful for one thing, it was that the brothers squeezed either side prevented her being tossed out. As Ivish rattled around corners on two wheels, she found less to be grateful for. The two giants were thrust together, guffawing, and she practically disappeared inside their great mass.

She had not seen this route before, though as broad buildings and brocaded people careered by, she could form little more than an impression. If this *was* an upmarket suburb, then its terraces were crumbling, its pipes rusted and its people also the worse for wear.

Little traffic, though. A second thing to be grateful for.

'Make way!' hollered Ivish, standing on the driver's seat. 'Almighty Heir! Make way!'

In the carriage's path was an old woman wheeling a barrow of fruit. She stood stunned for one moment, then shuffled for cover.

They hit the barrow and fruit flew. The carriage, too. They landed on two wheels with a spine-splintering jolt. Ivish was nowhere in sight.

The horses galloped in wild panic, half hitched. Something cracked and they were free. The carriage kept going at full speed across the street. It crashed through a door, taking half a wall with it. Everyone seemed to be yelling or screaming. On its side now, the carriage slid across the floor. Jatta waited for the dreadful crash, the splintering of bone. They clipped cabinets, spinning. Then they came to a gentle thud against a wall.

'Art!' cried Jatta.

'Jay! You're alive!'

Arthmael and Drake dragged her from the wreckage. Mordis and Fabish crawled out and looked around. They'd destroyed a jeweller's shop. Precious trinkets hung from wheels and seats. More lay scattered over the floor.

'Heralds!' Mordis shook himself in disbelief. 'I said this would be some ride.'

'Where be Ivish?' yelled Drake.

A groan came from behind the carriage. They clambered through the rubble to see. There lay the jeweller, pinned beneath a wheel, blood trickling from his mouth. Jatta felt sick at his agony. She forced herself to edge closer. She knelt beside him, hugging her trembling knees. It was almost impossible to look.

'Help me,' he moaned.

Arthmael was at her side, testing the carriage's weight. 'We can lift this,' he said.

She looked to the brothers, confused. Why were they not also at the carriage?

'Help us free him, please!' she said.

They ignored her. 'Where be Ivish?' asked Mordis.

A crowd was gathering outside the rubble. She called to them. 'Please come help! And get a doctor!'

They stayed where they were. Someone reached through the splintered wall to snatch a handful of pearls. Others leaned in too.

'Drake! Mordis! Be you all safe?' Ivish shoved his way in through the crowd.

The brothers embraced with neck hugs and slapping of backs. Ivish peered around. 'Blazing heralds, what a mess! What shall we do now?'

'Please help—' she began.

'If we can find the horses we can still get to the lodge,' said Drake.

'First let's lift the carriage,' insisted Arthmael.

'Arthmael can ride with me,' offered Fabish. 'Jatta can ride with you, Drake.'

'Please, please—' This was a nightmare and Jatta couldn't wake up. She was staunching the jeweller's blood with her skirt and he was grasping her hands. The brothers were traipsing through his blood on the floor and she couldn't make anyone hear.

She had to make them understand.

'Stop! What's wrong with you all?' she cried. 'This man's injuries are our fault!'

Drake peered down, taking an interest in the jeweller for the first time.

The man looked imploringly into his eyes.

'No use,' said Drake. 'He be dying.'

The man's eyes filled with despairing tears.

'No, Drake! You can't do this!' Her pulse pounded painfully in her head. She was trembling again. 'I won't let you leave him like this! Imagine if you were him.'

Ivish snorted. 'Your betrothed would be all perfect manners and die quickly. He would not make woeful faces to distress you.' He scooped up a handful of rings and tossed them to the crowd. 'Nor bleed all over our hunting trip.' Mordis and Fabish laughed. Drake stifled a grin.

Jatta struggled to her knees and grabbed her betrothed's hand in both hers, slippery with blood. Pleading. 'My Prince, I surrendered to Dartith expecting nothing from my marriage. You gave me hope. You're decent. You're reasonable. You, above all Dartithans, will help this man now.'

His forehead creased, as if trying to solve the puzzle of her. 'As you wish.'

He turned to his brothers. 'Here, lift this for Jatta.' He and Fabish joined Arthmael at the carriage.

Mordis grunted impatiently. 'I be off to find the horses.' He pushed his way through the crowd.

Drake scowled at Ivish, still sitting amid the rubble.

'What?' cried Ivish. 'My ribs be all bruised where I landed.'

Drake nodded at Arthmael and Fabish. 'One! Two! Heave!' The carriage toppled sideways, crashing into a bench. The jeweller was silently crying. 'It be done, Jatta. Now we go.'

'He needs a doctor,' she pleaded.

'Enough!' he said in exasperation. 'This be not Alteeda. This man's fate be not your affair.'

'No, Drake, it's yours!' she shouted back, utterly desperate.

'Show me now! *Show me* you're as good a man as my brother. *Show me* you'd be a wiser ruler than Andro Mogon!'

Drake's face had changed as she shouted, growing furious when she mentioned her brother, actually flinching at the Dark Sorcerer's name.

'Cease your blasphemy!' he yelled.

She'd gone too far. She didn't care; the jeweller still lay dying. Only his laboured breathing disturbed the silence.

Trembling, so fragile, she stood defiant before Dartith's heir. 'Show me,' she whispered. He glared down wordlessly, his body rigid above her.

Suddenly he exhaled. His face softened and an expression almost like kindness flickered over it. 'Come, little Jatta. I shall take you from this place.' He slipped his hands around her shoulders and began to lift her. She cried out in pain.

'My ankle!'

He lay her back on the floor among the rubble. Her ankle was red and horribly swollen. He cursed under his breath. 'Fabish, Ivish. We cannot hunt now. Go fetch Jatta a doctor.'

The brothers groaned.

'No, dear Drake.' She screwed up her face, biting down on both lips till the pain seemed to ease. 'Arthmael will take care of me. Go, enjoy your hunt.' Her hand slipped inside his. 'Come back to see me tomorrow.'

Drake's worried forehead creased further into a scowl at Arthmael's name. 'My Princess, you be my first responsibility.'

She kissed his hand, bloodied from where she had grabbed it. 'Go, have fun. Bring me back a small treat.' She stifled a wince. 'A nougat from the markets.'

He kissed her hand too, reluctant to leave—but Arthmael was also there by her side, unlacing her shoe. She whimpered, pulling her fingers from Drake's embrace to lay them on her brother's arm.

'Sorry, Jay. I'll be more careful.'

Neither saw the Crown Prince's jealous scowl.

'Come!' growled Ivish, dragging Drake up from her side. 'Get your heir's backside on a horse. We be too long in this tip.'

'I shall stay with you, Jatta,' said Drake. 'Tell your brother to go.'

It was Arthmael who glanced up. 'No, Drake, we'll be fine. Honestly. I've seen her through worse.'

The heir's face hardened.

'There be a doctor's precinct six blocks south,' called Fabish, tossing his purse as the brothers pulled Drake from the shop.

Jatta leaned across to the jeweller. 'Did you hear that, sir?' She stroked his forehead, like her father used to do when she was ill. 'We'll bring you a doctor.'

He opened his mouth to talk but instead spluttered blood.

'Is it broken, do you think?' said Arthmael.

'Pardon?'

'Can you walk?'

Puzzled, she wrinkled her forehead. Then realisation dawned.

'Me? My ankle's fine. I used the orb.'

He grunted, smiling. 'Jay, clever Jay. I'll be back soon.' He pushed his way out through the crowd.

No sooner had he left than they spilled in. The wealthy in their threadbare finery, the too-skinny poor. They began picking through the rubble. Someone dragged a ruby bracelet out from under her knee.

'Stop! Vultures! What are you doing?' she cried.

*

Arthmael jogged the short distance to the doctors' district. Signs hung from eaves announcing each surgeon's speciality. He scraped open a half-unhinged door, calling, 'There's been an accident! Where's the doctor?'

Several well-bred faces turned to him. One, pressing fingers to a crescent-shaped wrist wound, whispered Arthmael's name. All recognised the curious-looking foreigner, the Princess's brother.

'Where's the doctor, I said!'

One pointed at a door. He burst through.

A woman was lying on her stomach across a bed, her ample bottom exposed to the room. The doctor looked up from the boil he'd been lancing there. The woman opened and closed her mouth, too outraged to speak.

Arthmael ignored her red-faced indignation. 'Doctor! There's a man badly injured under a carriage. My sister—'

'Your sister?' The doctor grabbed his satchel, stuffing instruments inside.

'My sister's with him. His chest is crushed—'

'Your sister be unharmed?'

Arthmael nodded. 'He's only six streets away. Hurry, I'm worried—'

'Stop!' The woman had found her voice. 'Shut that door! Dare you humiliate me before that crowd?' She pointed a shaking finger toward the door, and the faces peering through.

The doctor crossed the floor to close the door. 'Your Grace, remember your manners. He be brother to—'

'And who be *I*? One man under a carriage can wait till you have dressed my wound.'

Arthmael gaped, confounded. 'The man is dying!'

'Then he shall have no need of a doctor,' she retorted.

'As you see, I be busy,' shrugged the doctor. 'Let someone else attend him.'

Arthmael's eyes flashed. 'You, man, have taken an oath to preserve life.'

'An oath? What be you talking of?'

Arthmael's frustration boiled over. He grabbed the satchel in one hand and the doctor's wrist in the other, and dragged him from the room.

'Unhand me, Highness. I shall come,' said the doctor as he was dragged past his gaping patients. Arthmael released his grip, and the man straightened his clothes. 'You will tell your sister I came willingly?'

Arthmael could only glare.

'Please stop! Stop, vultures!' cried Jatta again, hands pressed to her temples, trying to block it all out. A few faces turned. Most simply redoubled their search, stealing away the jeweller's life-time of work. Beside her, a soldier was picking up rings. She kicked out. The booty flew from his arms, scattering across the floor. Like gulls, others converged. They snatched and squabbled. A fight broke out. She conjured a flame that exploded into an inferno. All fled to gawk from across the street.

It frightened her jeweller, though. She gave up, and the scavengers returned.

He was gurgling again, mouthing a word. She bent her head low.

'*Wife?* Your wife?' She touched the ring on his hand.

His eyes spoke yes.

'A message for your wife. You love her?'

The eyes sparkled. He exhaled, his whole body slumped. His eyes' light died.

She sat beside him in a cocoon of numbed misery while the shop gradually emptied. After a time Arthmael came to sit beside her. She wrapped her arms around his neck and sobbed, and the man standing above them left without a word.

Arthmael gently stroked her hair. After some minutes he whispered, 'I'm not sure we could have saved him.'

'It's not just him,' she sobbed. 'It's this place. I hate it. I hate everyone in it. I hate me.'

Arthmael had only once before seen her so miserable, and it worried him. She wanted to walk, but he insisted on binding her ankle as if it was sprained. He found a carriage, and they rode back to the castle, staring out at the streets in silence. A man was beating a woman in a grimy doorway and no-one intervened. Children chased a cat and her kittens, throwing stones. Thieves and thugs roamed the markets while soldiers turned a blind eye.

'I just want to go home.' His sister's voice sounded small and squashed.

A stage had been erected in the main square. As they passed, the driver jerked his head toward the gathering crowd. 'Weekly event, Highnesses. Public beheading.'

Arthmael watched her face sink into deeper misery.

'We could try your idea of escape,' he whispered. 'An accident. We'd use the portal, we'd learn how. A double accident or something, and we'd take Noriglade and her slab . . . if she wanted to come, that is.'

She shook her head.

'Why not, Jay? What's wrong? He'd never know we used it.'

But her eyes told him Brackensith would.

'All right, Jay. Back the way we came, through the firewall. First you and me. Then I'd return with your suit for Noriglade.'

She stared out the carriage for a long time before answering. 'Then what?'

And in that moment he realised. This time there would be no waiting boat, nothing beyond the fire except burning sand and boiling waves, and leagues of empty ocean.

'No escape, Art. Like you said, some of my ideas work. Some don't.'

CHAPTER FIFTY-TWO

Jatta didn't talk again. She returned to bed, lying with her back to her slaves as they drew the curtains against Dartith's sickly sun. Long after she had sent supper away she lay facing the wall, pleading to Dragongirl for some miracle. Polite knocking again intruded on her prayers.

She lay still, hoping it would go away.

The door opened and Drake peered around the edge. Seeing her silhouette, he grinned. He swept in with a basket overflowing with nuts and nougat.

'How fares my fragile little Jatta?' He turned up the lamps and kissed her hand.

She sat up, managing a brittle smile. 'Better, the swelling's down. I can walk on it if I'm careful.'

'You look ill.' Concern clouded his face as he scrutinised hers. 'Be that all?'

That ruined it. Her eyes brimmed and she looked down to fidget with her bracelets.

He waited. Eventually his hand slid under hers to stroke her fingers with his thumb. The gesture was tender and natural, and it confused her. She could not allow him to be kind.

'This adjustment be not easy,' he said. 'I shall make it easier for you than it was for my mothers.'

'Why me?' she whispered.

'As bride? I know not, yet. Every bride brings something exceptional.'

Her single laugh was almost a sob. 'The only exceptional thing about me is my wolf.'

'It was not . . . *reasonable* of Father to curse you. But let me make it up to you. I will find ways.'

She forsook studying her bracelets to search his face, finding sincerity and a peculiar longing that gave her courage. 'Please,' she said. 'My wolf is maturing early. Please let me have sleeping potion.'

She watched his instant discomfort. His face smoothed over as he composed his excuse. She didn't want to hear it.

'I fear that be impossib—'

'No . . .' She shook her head to make him take it back.

'Jatta, has your wolf not been drugged before? Did you not feel nauseous afterwards? Was not the dose a dozen times stronger than your delicate body could bear?'

'Please, no . . .'

'In such heavy doses, potion or paste be a slow accumulating poison. I almost lost you to the canyon. I will not lose you to this.'

She didn't want this audience. She could compose her empty face no longer, nor still the impotent shaking of her head.

'This be bad news. I be sorry. But trust me—no wolf matures till middle age.'

'Will you let me be alone now?'

He got up, sighed, and sat back down. 'One thing. Perhaps it may cheer you. Little Jatta, I came back early to see you—and Father.'

Her face returned to the wall. She barely felt his hand

take hers or something slide over her finger, clinking against his ring.

'Jatta? Father be agreed to an early wedding, before next wolf-moon. We shall live in Cordorlith, in my northern estates.'

The words took a long time to sink in. Her gaze drifted down to the betrothal ring, then dumbly up at him. 'What—what about waiting? What about Art?'

His eyes narrowed in jealousy and her heart crumpled.

'Who will you choose?' he said. 'Him or me?'

How could she defend her brother, their bond, knowing words would only confirm Drake's jealousy? She stared, aghast.

He stared back without apology.

'I see,' he growled through clenched teeth. 'Your brother stays here with the crypt and its attractions. Forget your damnable brother. Your duty and affections belong to me.'

Jatta didn't sleep. Instead she sat in moonbeams on the floor, hugging her knees in her agony. She had lost too much. Her mother. Sanda. Her father. Everyone decent.

Now Arthmael.

He'd said her wolf was different. It was. Somehow her own nature had done battle with its instincts, and it seemed her love for Arthmael had won. How many wolves had ever fought that battle before? The book told of none. Her circumstances were unique, probably. She'd been thwarted or distracted no less than five times before the precarious balance had tipped, before filaments of human memory had woven around her wolf mind.

Now she was maturing too soon. If he'd have been allowed to stay with her this next wolf-moon, might his calming influence have retarded this disease? Perhaps. She thought back to the two times she'd woken to wolf memories. In the desert heat. After her dreadful marble cage carnage. Both times she'd vented her instincts and woken alone. Perhaps with his soothing voice, even without the potion to numb her, she might have been safe another month, another year.

It was only a matter of time, though. Her personality would decay, her wolf-moons would grow more controlled, and she'd teach herself to curse. Eventually this tumour of hatred would prove lethal, would invade each human hour to murder her love for him. How long? There was no precedent. Drake's disbelief had shown that. Only one thing was certain: she would not gamble with her brother's life to find out. She clutched her knees tighter. Better, less shameful that he didn't witness this change.

Where was her guardian?

Memories of wolves and pterodactyls seeped out; no willpower could squeeze them back this time. This cancer of bloodlust was invading her soul. She felt it lurking silently inside to spread with the next wolf-moon. She was sinking, drowning, in dull, deadening hopelessness. She curled into a tighter ball.

Her guardian had rescued her from the labyrinth, for what?

Eventually she would be alone. Alone with her malignant, murderous wolf.

CHAPTER FIFTY-THREE

Storm clouds gathered around the moon, darkening Dredden's twilight and pressing down on Arthmael's already anxious mind. He waited outside the cemetery gate, trying to look invisible in its shadow. Or at least unappetising.

Undead filed past like mine workers disgorged from underground. Some glanced back hungrily. One retraced his steps, sauntering to the gate. Arthmael steeled himself against the stench but stepped back when the big-bellied, shrewd-eyed nobleman tried to wrap a conspiratorial hand around his shoulder. He seemed good-natured about the rebuff.

'Relax, Prince Arthmael, I will not bite. Princess Noriglade sent me, she waits for you down behind the markets. Know you our old grain stores?'

'No,' said Arthmael warily.

'Then I shall take you.' He reached again for Arthmael's shoulder. When Arthmael ducked and laid a hand on his sword, the Undead glanced down with a slow, twisted smile.

A hiss came from beside the gate. They both turned, startled. As Noriglade swept to join them the noble shrugged at her as if saying, 'Who could blame an Undead for trying?' and returned, grinning, to his path.

She was even more beautiful and elegant, though clearly annoyed, than Arthmael had remembered. His heart hurt, and he felt anger that she was not the paragon he had hoped.

By her face she was possibly feeling something the same. As she drew close, the stench of her hair fresh from the crypt hit him. He didn't quite manage to hide his grimace. She noticed that.

'Be there nothing in your actions not suicidal?' she said curtly.

It seemed a rhetorical question. He ignored it. 'I can't find Jatta,' he said flatly.

'And you think I have supped on her.'

He was about to say, 'Don't be absurd, you ill-tempered Undead.' He was certainly worried enough to take everything out on her. Instead, he inhaled slowly and let out a gust that went some way towards clearing his tension. 'You and I always seem to fight.'

'Then quit harassing me.'

He ignored that, too. 'You're my one friend here. I'm desperate. You're the only one I can turn to.'

That punctured her anger.

'Help me, it's been two days. My demands meet stone walls. I've been dragged shouting from the council chambers, from the tower guardroom. She's gone. She was upset—we crashed into a jeweller's shop. I was worried about her then. I should have done something. I don't know what, maybe just run ...' His eyes pleaded. Noriglade's expression softened in response. Her fingers reached tentatively toward his shoulder. He would have welcomed that comfort, but she withdrew them to her lips.

'This be Drake's doing,' she said.

'Has he hurt her?'

'No—he would as soon surrender his crown.'

'Where is she?'

'Drake be in Council now, but we shall wait outside his chambers to ask.'

To her credit she didn't stop to bathe or feed. He found he could handle the stink, knowing it was for his sake she went without. They hurried straight to Brackensith's tower where she threatened the guards until they unlocked the stairwell.

Arthmael paced Drake's first floor foyer. 'What *is* it with this isle?' he growled. 'They'd rather slice off your hand than lend you one. Oh, unless you're *family*.'

'And not always even then.'

'Yes. Right.' He kicked Drake's door as he prowled past. It slid slowly open.

Their brows shot up. They peered inside. Light from the foyer formed a ribbon through the blackness.

'Drake be not careless . . .' she whispered. 'Come, open the drapes.'

Arthmael heard the wariness in her voice. He walked along the ribbon beside her, sword hand poised. He peered for obstacles in their path, for villains too, surprised at the scale of the room. After twenty paces his fingers brushed brocade. He took hold to drag it open.

Footfalls crept behind him. His jaw clenched as the ribbon of light disappeared. A bolt slid across the door. Beside him, Noriglade gasped.

From somewhere to his right came a suppressed giggle. Its familiarity prickled his skin unpleasantly. His first thought was relief that his sister wasn't here. At least *she* need not endure its repugnant sound.

He heard quiet footfalls, one to his left, one to his right. He drew his sword. Its metallic *shloosh* through its sheath sounded too loud.

'That will not help us,' breathed Noriglade in his ear. 'Cannot you smell their stench?'

He could smell only her.

Shloosh. Metal slid on metal. Close. Loud. High. His tense muscles jerked. But it was only the drape sliding along its tracks.

The clouded night revealed a man's silhouette, which stepped offensively close to examine Arthmael, then snorted in disappointment. Arthmael pulled back, for he smelled the man now, and recognised him from the crypt. That same rotted cheek, the cruel face. Only the bloody smear was missing.

'Do it, do it,' whined the giggler.

Arthmael's gaze shot to his right, past a second bored Undead now lighting lamps, to Drake's bed. The mad Prince lay there on his stomach, feet kicking the air.

'Highness, this be not Drake,' said the Undead.

Riz rolled off and came sweeping over, still wearing the cape from his interrupted fitting. He was filthy from the dungeons. Absurdly, an oversized golden helmet wobbled around his ears and eyebrows.

'I know that be not him!' Riz said indignantly. 'Do you think I do not know my own brother?' To Arthmael he said, 'Who be you, infidel impostor?' His darting eyes showed no recognition. His topaz-encrusted 'crown', Arthmael saw now, was nothing more than a handbasin.

'Brother, this be Arthmael,' said Noriglade in her melodic, soothing voice. 'Drake sent us to say he cannot come. He waits for you downstairs in the guardroom.'

Riz petulantly poked out his lower lip. Then abruptly he scowled. 'You be teasing me, sister.'

She shrugged, indifferent. 'Drake be alone and unarmed. Leave these two, come see for yourself.'

'She be teasing me, Ransid.' It was more a question than a statement.

'Yes, Highness. We should hide ourselves before he arrives. Let me deal with the boyfriend.'

Noriglade's apathy instantly vanished. She bristled at Ransid, hissing violently in his face. His jerked back from the onslaught, then he was hissing, too. The second Undead practically flew to Noriglade, lunging at her throat. She darted away.

Two cold hands wrapped Arthmael's wrists as he tried to follow her.

Riz was giggling at the show. 'Ooh, a love interest for the Undead. There be something unnatural in that.'

Noriglade scoffed, indifferent again.

'Kiss his darling throat for me, sister.' Riz batted his lashes, as playful as a coquette.

'I be not thirsty.'

'Pity for him. I shall let Ransid at him.'

Noriglade shrugged and wandered to sit on the bed. 'If you kill him I want nothing to do with it.'

'My *darling*, oh my infidel *darling*.' Riz extended both arms to Arthmael, making kissing sounds. 'This be so precious. But sister, you must learn to distinguish love from prey. You will obey me as heir . . . or suffer further.'

'That would take more imagination than you have, brother.'

Arthmael watched Riz's unstable mood change again. The Prince's eyes narrowed. 'Do it, then,' he said.

Bad move, Noriglade, thought Arthmael as Undead hands dragged his throat to a black mouth.

'Wait,' she called. 'I shall do it, though I have a condition.'

Riz yanked Ransid's plait. The Undead obliged by straightening his neck. His dead eyes were inscrutable.

'Sister, you be in no position to demand conditions.'

'That be true.' Noriglade flopped back among the pillows, bored.

Riz scowled. 'Very well, then. Tell me.'

She came to join them. Even at this moment Arthmael was struck by her grace, the stillness of her shoulders, her tall litheness. She leaned close to Riz's throat, and for one moment desire flashed in her eyes. Desire, Arthmael imagined, to tear it out. For the sake of his own throat he was glad she resisted.

Riz smirked as she whispered.

'So be it, you have my oath as heir. But for that, I expect a good show.'

Ransid stepped away. Arthmael's muscles surged with the impulse to fight his way out. A futile—no, suicidal—impulse. Then, as she moved close, his pulse thudded in his ears. Having her near was so confusing. He wanted to grab her and protect her, to fight alongside her, to push her away, too.

Her fingers unbuttoned his sleeve. They gently brought his wrist to her lips, avoiding touching his bare flesh. He searched her face, tried to connect with her, not quite certain whether she was saving him, or ... *Here everyone be both predator and victim*, she had said. Which was she tonight?

Her eyes lifted to his and his heart stopped. He saw a mask of indifference. But her fingers trembled.

'No, sister. More intensity.'

She nodded and surrendered Arthmael's arm. Her hands on his chest guided him back against the window. Propped there, he felt her chest press against his. He tensed and his heart pounded. As her full lips brushed his throat, searching for his pulse, he closed his eyes.

'I'm not a good actor,' he breathed.

'What you shall experience no man can act,' she whispered to his neck.

Her words chilled him more than her breath. 'Will I live?'

She nodded. 'But you shall experience what it be to die.'

CHAPTER FIFTY-FOUR

Her teeth were slippery wet. His pulse throbbed against them. They sliced sharply and he flinched. Her lips pressed over the wound and she drank in a slow rhythm, working with his pulse, two beats for every swallow. As her tongue massaged, he felt the blood drawing out of him. Something else was leaving him, too.

His self was leaving. His essence, some part that till this moment he hadn't known he had. Noriglade was devouring it in the same languid rhythm. Memories fled. He'd once imagined that when people died they walked to a light. Images from their lives were supposed to flash by, but he was having trouble remembering who he was. And there was no light, only some silent, stark place. He was there, lying on a black beach under a hard, starless vault of sky. He was a sandman. The tide was coming in, eroding his arms, ears and legs. Eating him. He wanted to hold himself together but his hands and chest were gone. The tide washed away his face in its monotonous rhythm. Sadness was all that remained. It ached, like when they'd told him his sister was dead. He was dissolving.

He wished vaguely, forlornly, that the Undead might have let him stay longer, let him right his wrongs ... so much left to do. His final thought saddened him most. He was not the sandman. It had gone, maybe dissolved to light, maybe been devoured ... No, he was the ribs and flesh hollowed out, the nothing, the black silent beach left behind.

Arthmael slid down the window.

The Undead's rhythm quickened.

With a surge came a memory. It flowed into the hollow where he had been, proof he was not yet gone. Yet maybe he was, for he didn't know this memory, this Dartithan girl and her brother clambering over a lap. It confused him. The girl was exceptionally pretty. He floated in and around her, and somehow he felt what she felt: the haven her mother's lap was, her rivalry with the boy for the handful of sultanas held just out of reach. Arthmael felt her pique and complained with her that she wasn't getting her share. Her Sludinian mother, too tired to mediate, rolled her cheek against the armchair's backrest and screwed up her eyes.

A whining, faceless voice intruded, irritating him. 'Not good enough. You promised me suffering.'

The memory faded and another began. Arthmael didn't like this one. It was cold and he could feel it would end badly, but he couldn't pull out.

She was jumping up spiral stairs two at a time. Nervous. He was too, to the point of nausea. She slipped through a wall slit.

Across a mosaic floor, a boy, a youth and a girl sat among chains. Her friends. Keeth. Yorden. Kinna. His friends also. Relief broke over her face. Their friends glanced up and smiled too. There was such sadness behind their relief. She assumed it was sadness for her.

She ran to kneel beside them with keys. But their chains were already unlocked, a bad omen. Perhaps things had gone very wrong indeed. Still she could not accept.

'Praise the heralds you be alive,' she said, 'Hurry now, my brother's horses be waiting.' She grabbed the youth's hand, stupidly forgetting her touch would be cold. He flinched and didn't get up.

'You be too late, Noriglade,' Kinna said. 'Our sentence was decided last night, also.'

Both Arthmael and Noriglade felt her insides heave, knowing the worst. The King's wolves had been, but not to kill, as they'd thought. She slumped to her elbows. The girl Kinna whispered she was grateful Noriglade came. Thanking her!

'I cannot do this,' she and Arthmael said.

'You will,' said Kinna. 'We have spoken all day, planning how we wish it done, and Keeth asks to go first.'

'I have no knife, nothing.' No, that was self-delusion. She'd grown weapons last night.

Keeth, so young, fumbled to unbutton his collar. Kinna helped. They were starting and Noriglade wasn't ready. Arthmael wasn't ready. They'd never be ready. How could they prepare for such a crime?

Keeth's gaze fixed on hers, too terrified to offer forgiveness. To offer consolation. The boy clutched his ribs so as not to shake, then knelt with his back to his executioner. The others knelt, shoulder pressed to shoulder, on either side.

'Tell everyone at home I love . . .' Keeth's whisper faltered.

'. . . love them more than life. I shall,' said Noriglade quietly, though his family would rightly despise her. Hadn't they entrusted him to her? Hadn't she promised him freedom? She ached, Arthmael ached, to kneel there also, to share his soul's journey. But Arthmael's soul had gone, and hers was eternally glass-bound.

Too much, pleaded Arthmael. Let me leave.

'Be you ready, Keeth?' asked Noriglade.

'Be you ready, Keeth?' echoed Arthmael.

'He does not wish to know when,' said Kinna.

Keeth waited. The longer she stalled, the longer Arthmael stalled, the greater the torture for them all. So Noriglade and Arthmael counted one, two, three, chose one moment like all others, chose one particular bony ridge on Keeth's neck. She pulled back her lips and deadened her eyes. Arthmael felt no more self-loathing, no more guilt. He thought nothing at all as her face lowered. Black glass pressed flesh. Black glass jerked deep. The boy rolled sideways into Kinna.

Noriglade groaned and Arthmael joined her, spitting the taste from their mouth.

Arthmael was ripped from the memory. The Undead was pressing cold fingers on his wound and whispering *'forgive me'* in his ear. His own memories were washing back. His soul, too. It had found no beckoning light, only her cold prison.

That repugnant voice came whining back. 'A delightful performance. Was that not tastier than fish? Come sit by me and wait for Drake.'

Instead the Undead ... Noriglade ... was hauling him up. That made him dizzy. His mind wouldn't co-ordinate his legs, couldn't shake the guilt and dread, couldn't comprehend what he'd just done.

Riz giggled. 'No, sister. Leave him to Ransid.'

That cleared his head.

CHAPTER FIFTY-FIVE

Noriglade spun, suddenly furious, letting Arthmael slide back to the windowsill. He clung to the frame with both hands as the chambers rolled.

'You gave your oath!' she spat.

'Did not, did not. Ha-ha. Sister be not the only teaser.'

Noriglade hissed.

Riz glared back. 'Do not look so sour. Nobody likes a vinegar-face.'

She lunged for his throat. The Undead were suddenly between them, pulling them apart. Riz yelped.

'Drake!' she screamed.

Ransid's fingers clamped on her mouth. She bit them off. He yelled and she broke free. She sprang to the bedside tables, grabbed one, swung it into the window. Glass smashed as it hurtled through. She leaned out. 'Riz! Riz escaped! Ransid! Sath!' she screamed.

Both Undead had her again.

Arthmael wobbled to stand, dragged his sword two-handed above his head and lurched to the bed. With a grunt he swung. Hard. Ransid's part-severed head dropped onto his chest, lolling there. It howled.

'No!' cried Noriglade, staring wide-eyed at Ransid, then at Arthmael. 'Run!'

Ransid was still howling as one hand dragged his face up to

see. Arthmael kicked him into Sath. Arthmael toppled too, almost followed them down as they sprawled on the tiles. Noriglade was beside him. Her arm around his waist pulled him toward the door. But the floor was so vast. Boots behind him were running. He cursed all Dartith, cursed his own dragging feet as a bloody hand closed on his neck, jerking him back. Noriglade wheeled and bit. Someone swore—Ransid. Sath knocked her to the floor as the room shook. The door blew off in flames.

The battle froze. Arthmael's wound dribbled under Ransid's grip. He blinked in hope through the smoke. Two more Undead strode through.

Lord. Overkill.

They barely glanced at Arthmael, though, before shifting ruthless eyes to his attackers. They hissed. Ransid and Sath returned the deadly threat. Ransid's sticky fingers uncurled from Arthmael to hold his own head more securely.

It was Noriglade who broke the stalemate. She launched from the floor to ram Arthmael's chest.

'Oh,' he said, falling.

Even as his back hit tiles she was gouging Sath's throat. All five were upon each other. Shrieks drowned out hisses above him. Pieces dropped around. Teeth slashed everywhere in crocodile-like frenzy, and Arthmael was kicked about.

Other arms—warm—dragged him out, back to the wall. He struggled, hearing Noriglade scream. He glanced around for his sword, finding the wall lined with soldiers, feeling his rescuer's knees pin him to the floor. He looked up to see the Crown Prince's bleak face.

Drake broke eye contact to examine Arthmael's neck. 'Best

leave them to it,' he said flatly. 'It be treason to destroy one, suicide to try.'

Arthmael jerked his head away to watch the fight.

How much longer could it go on? Three throats were torn. A fourth was no more than a stump. Ransid and Sath were mutilated. They propped each other up back-to-back, and Ransid held his head ready at his chest like a cannonball. Their assailants shifted around them.

Noriglade's focus was intense, missing nothing, and she weaved smooth as a snake. There was a chill to Arthmael's admiration. Her natural grace looked deadly here. She feinted; her leap landed a breath short of Sath's lunging bite. It was her two companions who grappled him to the ground. He thrashed and wailed. Ransid dived down among the carnage. Or toppled. His feet severed, he had no way to stand. His head hacked at Sath's attackers.

Noriglade stood above it all with tensed limbs, leaning slightly forward. Her eyes watched in readiness.

Something rolled out from under the bodies, splattering wine-red droplets. Sath's head. Ransid realised what that meant one moment after Noriglade did. In that moment his concentration faltered. His grip slackened. She kicked his head from his grasp. It flew to bounce twice on Drake's bed.

At that cue all five relaxed. Those who still had faces turned them to Drake. Soldiers retrieved the heads and, with curt nods, handed them back to their owners.

'Sath. Ransid. Do you admit treason? An attempt on the heir's life?' said Drake with a reasonableness that surprised Arthmael.

'We do,' chorused the two heads.

'Why, then?'

'The deranged Prince be sympathetic to our Undead ways,' answered Ransid.

'And with Fand gone, you imagined yourself his puppet-master?'

Ransid's mouth twitched, almost a smirk.

'On Undead oath,' said Drake. 'Where be he gone?'

Sath's hands tilted his head to the smashed window, where Riz's cape, knotted around the frame, billowed in the threatening storm. Drake's jaw tightened. Arthmael groaned for his sister's sake, imagining Riz scrambling through the courtyard one storey below still wearing his handbasin crown.

'On oath, he be down the sewers by now,' answered Ransid's head. 'You shall not find him.'

'Will you surrender to King Brackensith's judgement?'

'We will,' they chorused.

'Then he grants you one last night in the crypt.'

And then, as if he'd merely chastised them for leaving a mess, all five knelt to pick up scraps. Drake's Undead worked together. Ransid and Sath searched alone.

The soldiers watched from the wall, unmoved.

Wincing, Arthmael saw Noriglade had lost two fingers and an ear. Very little blood though. Wherever his own had gone, it was not there in her veins. Strange, courageous creature who'd saved his life. Creature wounded by crimes committed against her. Wounded by her own crimes, too. She peeked under her arm at him and he tried to nod his gratitude. She turned away. Stupidly, he needed to be with her. Drake's knees on his chest kept him down.

'Let your vein clot. How you survived a throat wound I know not.'

'I need to thank her for that too, then,' said Arthmael.

'My sister did that?' Distaste flared Drake's nostrils, but he let Arthmael get up. Arthmael came to kneel beside Noriglade. She kept her face low, searching. Her damaged hand and her finds she hid in her robes. Respectfully he looked away.

'Prickle—thank you for my life.'

'Go away, pretty Prince,' she whispered. 'You cannot bear to look at me. I be not beautiful now.'

'You are. In your heart most of all.'

'My heart be dead, like my friends.'

'Don't do this. You didn't murder them. If you must hate someone, hate the wolves that cursed them. Hate Andro Mogon's laws. Hate your father.'

'You think I do not? Still, I have plenty left over for me.'

'Then stop—' *Stop all this hating.* The words had almost come out, but he didn't need her hissing again. And how could he, now, tell her what to do?

'Stop what?' She still pretended to search.

'Stop pushing me away.'

At that she glared at the floor, incredulous. 'You be a true masochist, Alteedan. I give you a taste of the desolation of death, the most heinous experience imaginable, and you come back for more.'

His face tightened at the memory of that. But no, his soul's desertion hadn't been the worst of it, he thought. His had returned. He shot a guilty glance at Noriglade, for only Undead suffered extended separation, indeed through every waking hour of their eternities. Was that why they drank, he wondered, to kidnap souls? To escape desolation for just a few minutes? When next he experienced death, *he* would be the departing soul travelling to its eternal home, and not the shell left behind by this Dartithan curse. Wasn't there comfort in that?

No, the worst of it was the image that flashed even now, of Keeth toppling, limp. Arthmael's stomach twisted.

'What really bothers me, what bothers both of us, Prickle, is this death pact we—you—fulfilled . . .' It was strange how Noriglade's memory had meshed itself so completely with his own. 'I understand something of killing, not that I've exactly done this—'

'You shall do it again and again, reliving it in nightmares.'

'Probably. I don't sleep well as it is.' He took a deep breath, and tried again to expose his weakness. 'You're not alone, you know. I've also . . . Well, once there were three thugs, and I k—' The word stuck in his throat.

'Killed them? You could not murder.'

He smiled weakly at that. Hadn't he protested something similar to her? 'Perhaps not,' he said. 'These thugs had already decided I was dragon bait. I had no choice, like you, but that doesn't stop the nightmares.'

'I had a choice. I had no right to risk their lives. My carelessness led Riz to spy on the portal, and expose us.'

'Your carelessness? Garbage. Riz's own greed led him to spy on the portal. Jatta says he's been trying to learn its secrets for years. Honestly, Prickle, how could you blame yourself for him?' He scrutinised her face, the little he could see of it. Doubt twisted it, but she wouldn't meet his gaze.

'Go away, pretty Prince,' she whispered a second time. 'Do not look at me.'

He sighed heavily, not sure whether to respect her wishes, or . . .

His heart picked up pace, as it had in Drake's darkened

chambers, but something other than danger spurred it now. Arthmael reached to touch her damaged hand. It pulled back. Firmly but gently he coaxed it from the folds of her gown. That was enough to make her look up, and humble gratitude saturated her face. His chest felt physical pain.

Her hand chilled his. He cradled it in his palm. Slender, pretty, with a thumb and two tapered fingers, the others lost in defence of him. He could find nothing grotesque in them.

The wrist's veins were not blue, but as bloodless as her skin. His fingers skimmed circles overtop. Soft flesh, like any girl's. His fingertips traced lightly, slowly, to her palm. He heard her catch her breath, this girl who could not be tickled. He yearned for her, too.

His hand closed over hers and his fingers curled through hers. He let her coldness shock him, weathered the unpleasantness of the sensation, reminded himself it was no colder than his sword on a frosty morning, and only expectation of warmth made it disturbing. When he was ready, when he trusted his expression, he looked across. Her face was closer than he'd expected, so open and vulnerable. The pain in his chest flared agonisingly.

What they were to each other, friends or lovers, he didn't know, but he would never accept her rejection again.

CHAPTER FIFTY-SIX

The soldiers had left to search the sewers; the Undead had left for their crypt. Noriglade seated herself elegantly on a sofa, her hand wrapped in one of Drake's sashes. Another sash covered her ears like a scarf. Arthmael lounged beside her, almost touching. He studied the glass beneath the broken window, and glanced occasionally at Drake on the sofa opposite. Drake and Noriglade watched each other calmly, as if they had nothing more troublesome on their minds than the coming storm. However Arthmael remembered only once, in the jeweller's, seeing Drake anything except calm, polite and in control. And reading others' hidden agendas had never been his strength.

'Sister, it has been a long time,' began Drake. His lips twitched with a wry smile. 'I be pleased that you survived tonight.'

'Does it please you that Arthmael also survived?' she said with an answering smile.

'Indeed, for Jatta's sake.' Drake nodded at Arthmael. 'Her tender soul would not have welcomed other news.'

'Then you understand that these two be close.'

Drake raised one eyebrow in gentle surprise. 'No ... I think not. I merely meant that suffering affects her badly.'

'Then she would wish to know for herself that he be safe. You must let him see her.'

'She will know nothing of his danger, nor need she learn of his rescue. She does not wish to. She requests to be left alone.'

'That's a lie,' growled Arthmael.

Drake smiled benignly.

Noriglade glared a warning and Arthmael immediately regretted his outburst. 'Such accusations do not help your cause, Arthmael. My brother does not lie,' she said, then leaned to whisper across sofas. 'Though he may bend the truth.'

'Not this time,' Drake answered, and by his tightened smile Arthmael guessed he disapproved of her smell.

She sat back. 'Drake, I ask you plainly. When may Arthmael see his sister?'

'At her wedding.'

'Not before?'

'She does not wish it.'

'And after the wedding?'

'I do not wish it.'

Arthmael had had enough. 'You're being absurd. We fought our way into this infested pit together, and I'm staying—'

'You be free to return to Alteeda,' said Drake pleasantly.

'Not without Jatta. I'm her only link to everything she loves.'

Drake studied him for several uncomfortable moments. Even Arthmael could tell resentment seethed under his civilised, smiling surface.

'I will inform you of a Dartithan tradition,' Drake said blandly. 'A wife clings to her husband, and to no other.'

'So I was right. You be afraid!' Noriglade started laughing. 'Jealous of their bond! What, you think she will never love *you* so?' But she sobered instantly as Drake's face hardened, unsmiling.

He rose. The dismissal was absolute. Noriglade and Arthmael were forced to rise too. 'Sister, your brashness alienates even your allies,' he said in his unfalteringly even tone.

'You never used to mind it. It be my Undeath that alienates you,' she said, turning reluctantly towards the door. But then she turned back. Her voice was pleading. 'Brother, we once were close, like these two. For the sake of our past, for the sake of our mothers—and because we saved your life tonight just as surely as you saved Arthmael's—give him back his sister. Dartith has ripped her from a gentler life. Do not rip her from him.'

Abruptly Drake's eyes squeezed shut in a pained expression, and he shook his head. Moments passed while he composed his face. Arthmael looked away. 'Sister, I cannot.' His moist eyes opened. 'She challenged me to be like her brother, but I be no Alteedan. It pains me to watch the admiration in her face and know it shall never be there for me.'

Noriglade spoke gently. 'You be half Sludinian. Give her what you can.'

This time Arthmael watched the heir's smooth mask and waited for his final verdict.

'She has hidden away in her marble cage,' said Drake, and again his gracious smile looked effortless. 'For you, perhaps, she will relent. You have till the wedding, no longer.'

CHAPTER FIFTY-SEVEN

Jatta sat hugging her knees under the damaged dome with her back to the slit. She kept beside her a blanket and pillow, a few nougats and the Dartith book.

She had company. Sanda. Together they watched her vision of the rose garden farewell. She didn't hear Arthmael and Noriglade enter.

'Jay, playing that'll only make you more miserable,' said Arthmael gently behind her.

She flinched. Her family and the fountain faded. Sanda too.

'Come with us,' said Noriglade. 'This cage be no place for you.'

Jatta turned around and shook her head. Her eyes were red and puffy.

'Talk to us, Jay. We've been thinking up ideas to stay together.'

She raised her eyebrows, defying him to explain.

'All right, we were mostly hoping *you'd* dream up some ideas.'

Jatta's tears brimmed. Their faces swam before her eyes.

Arthmael's cheeriness dribbled away. Noriglade knelt where Sanda had sat. 'Poor Jatta, you have lost everyone. I understand a little.'

Of course *Noriglade* had a monopoly on misery, thought Jatta, suddenly angry. *Noriglade was keeping her mind. She was keeping Arthmael.* Tears dripped—jealous, angry tears. Arthmael

387

would find consolation with his Undead. He'd forget about his sister, he'd adjust. A black hole in Jatta's heart was expanding, swallowing her up. She would start to dissolve after next wolf-moon, but she was already almost invisible to them; she felt it. She watched them through blurry tears, their thighs almost touching as they shared a sorrowful glance. Something had grown between them. Was pity drawing them closer? Pity for her? She watched Arthmael lean forward to wipe her tears with his sleeve. She wanted to shove him away. *Go away! I don't need you, I don't want you. Goodbye. I've had time to adjust, so goodbye.*

She let him soak up her tears.

'Why are you hiding?' he whispered.

She pressed her nails in the orb as fresh tears fell. *Why? My wolf's matured early, didn't I warn you? No-one believed me, but here it is.* It shamed her. She couldn't say it.

'Go home, Art,' she said instead. 'I've made Drake promise to let you go.'

'You're being silly,' he chided her softly. 'I'm not leaving without Noriglade. And certainly, absolutely, not without you.'

'It's too late for me.'

'I don't believe this. Jay, listen to yourself, you're sinking again. Forget being miserable, I'm not allowing it. Haven't we spun miracles to get here? We'll spin some more to escape.'

It bothered her that he was still arguing. Her eyes squeezed shut for the one performance that would change his mind. They opened to lock on her brother's.

'Yes, I'm crying. I do that. But do I look like I'm not coping?' Her deliberately chosen words, not a lie, were convincingly irate. She let him search her face. 'No, so give me credit for having thought this through. I have Drake, he's smarter than you. I no longer wish to leave. I no longer need rescuing. I no longer need *you*. Listen to me, Art. One day—maybe sooner, maybe later—my heart will be all wolf, and Drake's my future, and Cordorlith's my wolf's home.'

She watched his face screw up as it had when he'd been newly stitched and in pain. That grimace surprised her. She hardened herself against it. He'd heal soon enough. Her brother healed quickly, she knew that.

'Let me stay with you at least till the wedding,' he whispered, his voice strained and choked.

'Just go, Art. Please. Extended goodbyes only hurt longer, and you're not helping with your tragic face.'

He tried a smile, without much success. It broke through her steel. She turned her back quickly and Sanda reappeared.

Arthmael dragged himself up. 'Goodbye, Jay,' he whispered.

Noriglade mumbled, 'Goodbye,' and rose to wrap her arm around his waist. Jatta listened to their retreating footsteps while her rose garden tableau played, hopeless loneliness rolling over her. She had the sudden impulse to beg them to stay. But she couldn't. They stopped at the wall, their heads close together in uncertain whispers. She waited without breathing, willing them to return. They called a second goodbye and were gone. Her vision-Jatta was laughing as Steffed splashed her. Jatta kneaded on, though any meaning had drained from the scene.

Suddenly someone new was sitting cross-legged beside her, someone she'd not heard enter. Both Jatta and Sanda stared in disbelief at the Dartithan child who leaned on her elbows, absorbed in the vision.

'Lordy! How'd you get here?' said Sanda.

The girl turned brown, inquisitive eyes to them.

'Hello Jatta. Hello Lady Sanda.'

Her heart pounding, Jatta stopped squeezing. Sanda and the vision faded, the Dartith child too. Jatta spun around. The chambers were empty. She looked up, half-expecting to find an intruder clinging to the dome. Nobody. She scrambled to her feet, raced to the wall slit, slipped through and into the stairwell. Empty, as far down as she could see.

But someone had hijacked her illusion. She was sure of it, just as she had known when she'd hijacked the dwarf's.

She raced back into the cage.

'Who are you?' she shouted.

'*Who—are—you?*' The walls echoed back her words.

'Stop using Dragongirl!'

'*Stop—using—Dragongirl!*'

'The orb's mine!'

'*The—orb's—mine!*'

'Please,' she pleaded. 'It's all I have left.'

Sinking back to her blanket, Jatta struggled with this final assault. This vision was not hers. How could the hijacker have known Dragongirl? Had she always been an illusion? Who might have hidden among Jatta's roses, or sat with her father on the pond wall? What prankster had been the puppeteer of her friend's game? Jatta hoped, rather than trusted, she was not going mad. She gave the orb five tentative squeezes.

Dragongirl was sitting cross-legged, flushed pink and self-consciously clutching her toes. 'I be sorry, Jatta. I—I meant not to upset you,' she began before fading.

Drawing deliberate breaths, taking comfort in believing she could stop at any time, Jatta kneaded again.

'Who made you?' Jatta asked.

Dragongirl's forehead creased in confusion.

'Who sent you, Dragongirl?'

'My Poppy. He be amazingly clever. He teaches me magic tricks and flying. He heals people, Jatta.'

'Why? Why are you here?'

'Poppy be worried. It hurts him to see you so sad. Poppy tells me to say he knows what you feel—your deep despair, your wolf that haunts you. You fear you have lost everyone, but you have not. For you, it be not too late.'

She had a new guardian. Jatta's skin tingled. She wanted to laugh. She wanted to cry all over again, too. Dragongirl's Poppy would save her, just as he had in the labyrinth.

'Can your Poppy heal my wolf? Can he help us escape?' she blurted out. 'Arthmael and Noriglade, she's my friend—can he save them, too?'

Dragongirl shook her head, curiously watching the theatre of emotions across Jatta's face. 'Poppy says he must help you no more, it be you three who must help yourselves. Go now, shun your brother and friend no more. Together you shall find a way.'

Dragongirl seemed to have finished her rehearsed speech. She giggled, scampered up and skipped toward the wall.

'Who is your Poppy?' called Jatta. 'Why me?'

Dragongirl slipped through the slit and was gone.

Jatta was tingling, spluttering and crackling with happiness. She jumped up, ran out the cage and down the stairwell. After four flights she paused, dizzy and puffed, hearing voices below. 'Art! Noriglade!' she called.

'Jay!' came the answer.

She raced to propel herself against her brother with arms

clenched round his waist, beaming up into his surprised face. Releasing him, she stretched up to kiss Noriglade's cheek. Arthmael broke into a grin.

'Something's happened!' she blurted, dancing on the spot. 'You won't guess. I was squeezing and suddenly Dragongirl appeared, but solid-coloured, not milky, and her grandfather's my real guardian and he says we'll find a way!'

'A guardian? For you?' Noriglade looked as if Jatta had proclaimed a revelation from Redd.

Arthmael's grin widened.

'Stop it, Art! Why don't you two believe me?'

'I do believe you, Jay. I'm just grateful you're back.'

Two Undead slunk past, glowering at Noriglade. She scowled back. 'We cannot discuss this here,' she whispered in Arthmael's ear.

'Oh.' Jatta grimaced, seeing his throat wound. She didn't miss the uncomfortable look he exchanged with Noriglade, either.

'A love bite, it'll heal,' he answered lightly. 'Your cage, then?' He leaned on Noriglade's shoulder and they headed back up the stairs.

They'd slipped through the slit to sit on the blanket before Arthmael would let Jatta explain about her visitor. Jatta kneaded, and the scene replayed beside them. At the part where Dragongirl said, '*Together you shall find a way,*' the whole chamber flashed white. Thunder hurt their ears.

Noriglade peered up to the dome. 'Spectacular. How do you manage it, Jatta?'

'Sorry to disappoint you, but the lightning's not mine,'

giggled Jatta, before adjusting Dragongirl's volume to compete with the storm. When the message was concluded and their visitor had skipped out through the slit, Jatta turned triumphantly to Arthmael and Noriglade, who both smiled back cautiously. Again their faces were lit as if by daylight. 'Everything's going to be all right, don't you see?' she beamed, settling to lie back with her head on the pillow, dragging Arthmael and Noriglade down too. 'My guardian will cure my wolf. He won't let anything terrible happen again.'

Thunder boomed.

'Jay, that's not exactly what Dragongirl was saying,' began Arthmael tentatively. 'She said it's up to us.'

'Remember, your guardian will not help you again,' Noriglade added in a kindly voice.

Jatta's smile dropped. Her eyes' brightness faded.

'Jay, please, don't. Listen, this is wonderful news. Really. It means there's a way to stay together. We just have to find it. Think of it as, well, a sort of test.'

Hadn't she been tested enough already? Horrific images crowded into Jatta's mind: her mother's death, the bloody aftermath of her first wolf-moon, the kidnapping, the labyrinth, the dragon's carnage, the firewall's imprisoned souls, the jeweller's pointless death . . . her tumour, most of all. No, her guardian would not put her through further ordeals. He was good and kind. Hadn't he felt her sadness? Didn't he, alone, understand how her wolf haunted her, how it was taking over, how it wouldn't let them stay together now? But he'd said it wasn't too late.

'This isn't a test, Art. My guardian is helping as much as he can. He's just not very powerful. He made Dragongirl guide me through the labyrinth and now he's offering us hope. My wolf, too. There *is* a cure for my wolf,' she said resolutely. 'We'll cope. It's up to us.'

Arthmael grinned in agreement; it didn't reach his eyes. He seemed relieved at her optimism, but not convinced of her reasoning. That worried her. He'd always seen her wolf more clearly than she, always been the realist anchoring her wild hopes and misery—till that time in the desert, when he'd promised she was different. Perhaps she'd become the realist now.

'All right Jay, think.' His enthusiasm for escape, at least, was genuine. 'Our scale suits won't get us off the Isle. Could we still fake an accident, then resettle somewhere quiet?'

'Idiot boy.' Noriglade's gentle, melodic laugh dimpled her cheeks. 'You two stand out like peacocks in a pigpen. There be no place would not know you.'

'What about the firewall? Prickle, can your dear father be made to extinguish it?'

She bristled. 'He be not my dear father! And he be no match for the firewall. That stinking millpond scum, that parasite—'

'Sorry, Prickle.' He took her good hand to trace its fingers around his throat wound. 'You do bite, though, every time.'

Noriglade scowled at his tasteless joke.

'But doesn't Brackensith control the firewall?' asked Jatta. 'And the long nights?'

'No, Jatta. No king ever had magical power, though without dark magic this kingdom might well crumble.'

Arthmael shook his head in confusion. 'But your father's portal ... he melted our swords. I felt it, this buzzing hum. My ring went hot. My chest vibrated like a bee.'

'Indeed. That be the portal's magic, not father's. It be a magical tool, left over from Andro Mogon's reign. Jatta's orb, too, left over from some Sorcerer before. As for the wall—'

'It's a magical tool too?' asked Arthmael.

'Not the wall, no. Its magic be, like our long nights, unique and most powerful. I shall explain. Riz, in one of his manic phases, once decided to invade some poor neighbour— Sludinia, or your Alteeda, or somewhere. He asked Father to build him a navy and extinguish the wall. Father just laughed in his face—said he could build the ships, but no-one except Andro Mogon could tear down the wall.'

A cold tingle of dread spread through Jatta. She lay tense and still, staring up at the black, cloud-clogged sky. 'Then the Dark Sorcerer is still alive?' she whispered.

'Alive? Idiot girl.' Noriglade laughed.

'Jay means *Undead*. That he didn't simply fade away. That he still exists somehow.'

Noriglade hesitated before answering. 'This be our secret, understand? Father ... I think Father visits him through the portal.'

Now it was Arthmael's turn to gape.

'Once ...' continued Noriglade in a reverent whisper. 'It was the midnight hour. I had sneaked into his den. I was trying to command the portal, to escape this hell-hole. Father came in and I hid. He commanded the portal thus:

Andro Mogon, grant me a moment
Of your infinite time.
My will I surrender,
My soul be yours.

'I memorised the words.'

Arthmael shuddered. 'Lord! So there's one great Sorcerer left.'

As if in answer, jagged swords of light clashed above their dome.

'What happened next?' whispered Jatta.

'Father returned and by daylight Fand's brother-in-law be fed to the wolves. His family imprisoned. For treason.'

'Treason? But I thought your people were too cowered.'

'Father named it treason. More a pitiable act of defiance. Futile. The poor idiot be catapulting stuff out to sea from a cliff, over the firewall. Maps, books, strategic documents, in dozens of wax-sealed chests. Inviting invasion. Liberation. Rescue. Nothing came of it, except tragedy for his family.'

Jatta reached for her book.

Noriglade took it, carefully turning the charred pages. 'So this survived the firewall . . . mostly.'

Jatta decided not to explain its history right now.

'This book helped bring us to you,' said Arthmael.

'By heralds, how pathetic. You two, an invading army?' She laughed, and the lilting music of it made Arthmael laugh, too.

He eased himself to stand. Silhouetted against the duelling lights, he bowed with exaggerated chivalry. 'Behold, Dartith, your liberators! Shall we slay your wolves? Present company excepted, little sister. Depose your King? Or destroy your immortal Sorcerer?'

Noriglade laughed and play-nipped his leg.

But Jatta knew the Sorcerer was not exactly immortal . . . and if he could be destroyed, so could his firewall. And maybe her wolf.

'Undead can be killed with obsidian,' she said tentatively. 'Andro Mogon probably, too.'

'Glory, Jay, I was joking.'

Jatta had sheepishly withdrawn the orb from her pocket.

Lightning arced through the sky and her orb sparkled in modest reply.

'My Brackensith could get close enough to do it,' she offered as the storm broke and rain pelted their faces. '*He* could try.'

CHAPTER FIFTY-EIGHT

Dartith's three intrepid liberators were whispering secrets along the castle's incense-heavy, sombre corridors. They sneaked Noriglade inside Arthmael's chambers with a great deal of chuckling and giggling.

'Tell me of your family and home,' said Noriglade as they settled among cushions on the floor. 'Was it hard to say goodbye?'

Jatta answered by massaging her orb. Her treasured farewell memory replayed itself for her brother and friend. The floor where they sat became a lawn and their fingers sifted through blades of sand. Perfumed roses climbed around the room. Arthmael's bed became the stone wall of her fountain pond, where golden fish trailed gauzy tails. There sat King Elisind and Steffed, and Jatta between them.

Noriglade glanced from Jatta to her twin in the vision and, puzzled, back again. She pinched Jatta's leg.

'Ouch!' complained Jatta. 'Yes I'm real, you just needed to ask. Now let me concentrate.'

Her Elisind was talking about Arthmael. 'He's an adaptable boy, he'll cope—'

'I'm coping very well indeed, thank you Father!' announced Arthmael from the lawn. 'I've been here five nights and managed to free Alteeda. Already I've found a friend, someone speci—'

Steffed peered out through the roses and scoffed. '*You* free Alteeda? You pretty-faced clot. Without your sister you'd still be back in Redd's hall.'

Arthmael made a grumpy *hmpf!* Noriglade giggled beside him. He shoved Jatta. 'What are you doing, Jay? Play the memory without commentary.'

'Sorry, Art, but you interrupted. It just happened.'

But Jatta saw his homesickness. She abandoned her memory's script. The King stood, his arms open wide.

'Arthmael, boy! What did you say? You've *found* someone?'

Arthmael leaned forward, his eyes suddenly bright. 'Father, not exactly. She's more a friend for now, a princess here.' He stood, dragging Noriglade with him. 'I'm bringing her home. She's wilful and foul-mouthed. Prickly as blackberries, but you'd like her, I know.'

'Then let me see her,' beckoned the King.

Arthmael pulled Noriglade toward the vision. Instinctively her hand rose to cover her mouth. He brushed it away.

'You're a fine-looking girl,' said the King. 'Perhaps a little pale. Does Brackensith approve of the match?'

Noriglade's hand crept back to her mouth, her eyes on the ground. 'Majesty, there be no match. I can never give your son children.'

The King had grown suspicious. 'Show me your teeth. Smile for me, Princess.'

She cringed and backed behind Arthmael.

'Father, Noriglade's Undead.'

The vision-Elisind drew back, scowling in distaste.

'Father, listen. She's good in her heart. There's no-one in Dartith with a heart so warm.'

'But an Undead! To feed on—'

'Father, she doesn't! Judge her and you judge Jay.'

The wariness faded from Elisind's face. 'Then for your sake I won't deny her sanctuary. But Arthmael, do not pursue this girl.'

'Father, I'm not.'

Elisind sighed and leaned back, undeceived by Arthmael's overdone sincerity. He turned to Noriglade, beckoning for her to sit beside him. 'Noriglade, is it? Welcome to Alteeda.'

The King asked Noriglade questions. She answered simply. How she'd nursed her mother since she'd been old enough to carry a broth bowl, how she'd struggled to be the perfect daughter, to make her mother happy, to heal her . . . how she'd promised her dying mother she would escape.

Alone on the lawn, Jatta scripted her father's response. Perhaps she scripted it accurately; perhaps she scripted what she knew Noriglade needed to hear. Perhaps in real life, if they ever did meet, both would feel bitterly betrayed. For now though, for Jatta, it felt right.

Jatta let the rose garden fade. Arthmael bid them goodbye, and the vision-King and Steffed hugged the vision-Jatta in turn.

'Be my daughter, too,' the King whispered in Noriglade's ear as he hugged her.

Only then did it occur to Jatta how the lonely Princess yearned for touch. Noriglade clung to her new father, wrapped her arms around nothing more than loose sand, and her eyes almost glistened.

Outside Arthmael's window rain pelted from a lightening sky. Steffed got up from the bed. Their father left, too.

Noriglade lowered herself among Jatta's cushions with furrowed concentration, as if stiff from a marathon, and Jatta tried not to stare. Hips that an hour before had rolled jerked mechanically. Noriglade returned Jatta's awkward smile. 'This illusion be a comfort to me. Your gift, whatever Alteeda decides,' said Noriglade, so quietly Arthmael didn't hear. 'I imagine you worry, also. Will Cabinet accept back your wolf?'

'Yes . . . I mean, maybe.' Jatta concentrated on fidgeting with Drake's rings before glancing up. 'I mean, I wondered . . . perhaps wolf curses are unique, powerful magic, too. Like the firewall. You think so, right?'

Noriglade studied Jatta's face for longer than was necessary to answer such a straightforward question, and Jatta began to wish she hadn't asked.

'For your sake I hope so, Jatta.'

Jatta beamed. She took that as a yes.

CHAPTER FIFTY-NINE

The Dark Sorcerer would be incredibly difficult to fool. Jatta resolved to discover whatever Brackensith knew of him, but first she must learn every gesture, every inflection and nuance, of Brackensith himself.

Jatta woke at midday. Peering up through her window she found a day dull as twilight and smiled. Soon she would be freed of this racing sun and its bleak, false sky.

Her slaves helped choose a Dartithan gown and a short, slippery silver over-gown to hide her bust and arms. Conservative but elegant; the King would approve.

She waited, fidgeting, outside his dining room with several court officials. After a few minutes she was called in. The King sat alone at a table laden with fruits and breads piled shoulder high, meats in silver tureens, salmon, yoghurt and jams.

He glanced up as she entered. 'Ah, Jatta. To what cunning intrigue do I owe this visit?'

She curtseyed. 'None, Majesty. Please, I need to learn. Let me learn my future responsibilities from you.'

'Think me a fool, Jatta? You have some ulterior purpose.' He spat out a cherry pip, which landed in the quince conserve. 'Do you expect me to believe you have embraced your prison so soon?'

'Not embraced, Majesty. I'm resigned, though. My prison is my wolf's only possible home. I'm here of my own choice.'

'True enough. But Drake tells me you now embrace your wedding, and separation from Arthmael, too. Next you shall be professing love and eternal devotion to him.'

'Majesty, Drake is as decent as any man in Dartith.'

'We both ask what game you be playing. You cannot manipulate the heir as you did his halfwit brother. You shall never see Arthmael after your wedding, understand?'

'I accept my Prince's will. I accept the wisdom of keeping Arthmael away from my wolf.'

He cocked one eyebrow. 'So what do you not accept?'

She curtseyed respectfully. 'Majesty, only my ignorance. Teach me my role. You've taught Drake his.'

'You be a strange one. But so be it.' He raised his hand, flicking one finger, and her body flooded with relief. Slaves bowed and a place was set beside him. 'Speak not. Stay here in my shadow till I tire of you.'

'Piercing a heart be not easy,' Noriglade had said. She'd suggested practice, so they agreed to meet in the vegetable gardens behind the castle kitchens that night.

As Noriglade swayed beside Arthmael on their way from the crypt, she pointed to a lantern moving through the pumpkin patch. Drawing close, they saw it was Brackensith.

Noriglade's smile dimpled. 'Jatta! By heralds, be that you?'

Brackensith looked up and the smile died from Noriglade's face. His eyes were icy, his mouth twisted in disdain. He beckoned and she obeyed, faltering more with each step. She curtseyed.

'Father, please. What have you done with Jatta?'

'The traitor Princess? She be thrown in the dungeons, and her brother be soon to follow.' He leaned over her in menace.

'It be twice now, wretched daughter, you have chosen friends unwisely.'

'Stop it, stop it, Jay! You're upsetting her.'

Brackensith blushed. 'S—sorry,' he stammered. 'I was just testing it out.'

Noriglade gaped. Her eyes suddenly fierce, she pulled her lips back to hiss.

'Stop it, Prickle!'

Glaring, Noriglade turned on Arthmael. 'You knew!'

'I swear I didn't! Not at first. Glory, who—besides Jay— would be naive enough to provoke *you*?'

'You lie! You lie!'

'I'm really, honestly, remorsefully sorry!' cried a tinny little voice at their waists. Brackensith's face was pleading up at them, atop a dwarf's fat body. Arthmael grinned. Noriglade gaped. While they watched, the ridiculous dwarf Brackensith sprouted dragon wings and Jatta's curtain of ash-blond hair. He wrapped his arms around Noriglade, clinging at her skirt. 'Really, truly ruly!' he implored. Brackensith's lower lip started to quiver.

'Enough.' Noriglade grinned. 'Get off me, you be forgiven.'

Jatta morphed back and got up off her knees.

'Art, what was I doing wrong?' she asked sheepishly.

'Nothing. It was, well, scarily accurate, but keep your hand in your pocket. I saw the sparkling ball, that's all. I look out for the squeezing thing all the time, whenever you're—' He glanced over her shoulder at a flicker of movement. 'Glory, what's that on your back? You're doing it now.'

Jatta blushed and slipped the orb back in her pocket. Her wings faded.

'Listen little sister, this is important. No more playing

with your ball. Nothing at all, understand, till we're in the portal and on our way to the Dark Sorcerer. Do you promise?'

'I promise.' She knew he was right.

'If Brackensith catches even a hint—'

'She knows. Be you done now?' interrupted Noriglade. 'Good. Then have you the obsidian?'

Arthmael handed his sister a shard of volcanic glass as thick as her forearm. It felt surprisingly heavy in her gloved hands.

'Wrists, throat and heart. We shall start with the heart,' said Noriglade, setting a pumpkin on its side between two others. They knelt down behind it.

'You cannot pierce an Undead's heart, slicing up from his belly, as with a sword blade. Nor between his ribs. A shard struck from his slab be too thick, has many facets but no single knife point. You must force right *through* his ribs, *through* his heart. Use all your might, just here.' Noriglade pressed her knuckles into her left breast to demonstrate. 'You will break some ribs, understand?'

Jatta shuddered at the thought, then drove it from her mind. She clenched the shard in both gloves and raised it above her head. She closed her eyes, concentrating her strength, imagining it ramming through pumpkin flesh. She thrust down blindly.

It stuck in the dirt by Arthmael's knees.

'Watch out! Eyes open, Jay.'

She dragged it out of the earth and again held it high. Taking a deep breath she thrust into the pumpkin. Her gloves slipped down its shaft. It stuck barely past its edge.

'You merely bruised his ribs,' groaned Noriglade. 'He be already at your throat.'

'She's not strong enough, Prickle.' Arthmael searched

around for a rock. 'Here, Jay. Use this as a hammer.'

Jatta obediently took the rock in her right hand. She held the shard in her left, its tip pressed against the pumpkin. Confidence fast ebbing, she hammered down.

She hit her knuckle. The shard glanced off. The rock fell with a thud on her leg.

'No, it be done this way.' Noriglade stole both tools and hammered down hard, gouging out a chunk of pumpkin. 'Ow!' She threw down the shard to examine her long fingers, wiping off blood spots. 'This be doomed to fail.'

'Hmm. You'd probably need both hands to hammer,' suggested Arthmael.

Noriglade wrapped her hem around her fingers before again positioning the shard. Arthmael raised the rock high in both hands. Every muscle tensed. He rammed down. Noriglade's shard plunged deep. The pumpkin's heart cracked open.

'That's how it's done,' he announced.

Noriglade laughed her soft, musical laugh. 'Idiot boy. No-one but Father visits Andro Mogon. Jatta can't smuggle us under his robes.'

'Um, I could try to make you both invisible . . .'

Jatta's suggestion surprised them. She had no idea how to perform such a trick. Nonetheless, she slipped her hand inside her pocket, squeezed, and screwed her eyes shut. When she opened them Arthmael had disappeared. So had everything behind him. She had somehow created a black hole in the pumpkin patch.

'I can't see myself. Has it worked?' came his voice.

'She has lost you, sure, and half of Dredden as well.'

Jatta concentrated with open eyes, gradually painting Arthmael's body with details from the background.

'You've done it, Jay!' He stood and sneaked behind them, his painted canvas sneaking out of its black hole. They watched him reach out to brush Noriglade's fingers. She pinched the extended pumpkin-patch arm.

'Ouch! You can still see me, right?'

Noriglade started laughing.

'This is complex, Art. Every time you move I have to fill in fresh background.'

Jatta concentrated again, and this time she managed it, as long as his movements were slow.

'Now me, Jatta,' said Noriglade. Jatta juggled both. Like riding, once she'd learned the right muscles to use, it grew easier. All over the patch, pumpkins were split by invisible assailants.

'Now you, Jay.'

Jatta morphed into Brackensith. 'Wretched daughter, be you attached to that vulgar Alteedan?' she said, arching one regal eyebrow. 'It be a fate more piteous than any I have visited on you.' They ignored her. Somewhere ahead another pumpkin cracked open.

She tried changing the subject. 'I've had a full day. I've memorised Brackensith bored, Brackensith jubilant, Brackensith brooding. It's all quite the same. We took the portal north to Cordorlith. I memorised that incantation too. Then we sent more soldiers down the sewers, though Brackensith hopes Riz has long drowned.'

'We're still invisible, aren't we?' came Arthmael's voice.

'Yes. But my head hurts.'

'All right, Jay. Get some sleep. We can practise more tomorrow.'

CHAPTER SIXTY

Brackensith was not alone when Jatta was ushered into break-fast the next morning. Drake sat to his right, intently peeling a mandarin.

Jatta tensed with resentment beneath her gracious smile. 'Majesty . . . My Prince.'

Drake looked up. His smile was equally gracious. Without comment he carefully pulled his mandarin apart. One half he placed on the setting laid beside him. She slipped into the waiting chair and he took a breath to speak, then changed his mind. This uncertainty was unlike Drake. He took another breath and leaned down to her ear.

'I have seen what impossible damage you wrought on our cage, Jatta,' he whispered. 'You told me your wolf has matured, yet I did not listen. Might such a tragedy be true?'

The question surprised her. She'd given up on people believing, yet his voice seemed genuinely concerned.

'Would that change anything?' she whispered back.

'Might I send you back to terrorise Alteeda? No, Jatta. I should accept even that. You must see by now, we in Dartith all have our demons to bear.'

What a pretty speech. What a noble martyr she might have married. Yet she had no intention of marrying him. Nor of going home, not till she'd disposed of the Dark Sorcerer, the firewall, the unending nights—and her wolf.

'You're generous, my Prince,' she answered. 'But you were right. I was wrong; my wolf's not going to mature.'

After breakfast they took the portal to Cordorlith castle. Drake walked her through fresh construction above his own bedchambers, a cage of granite and iron. His chivalry never wavered. Neither did hers. Back in the den's flickering torchlight Drake kissed her hand goodbye. She was left alone with the King.

Brackensith settled at his long table to read. After several minutes he looked up, seeming to remember his guest. He chose a book from his pile and shoved it through manuscripts toward her. Jatta found a second chair in a corner by the four rottweilers, and dragged it to the table. There, under the child-dragon statue's golden gaze, while the dogs crunched on bones, she read Andro Mogon's laws.

The shortened day may have already faded (though in the dim, windowless den Jatta had no way of telling) before Brackensith closed his book. He leaned back, contemplating her as if she were a particularly troubling passage, till she felt her face grow hot.

'You must have questions, Jatta. Ask them now.'

Jatta took a deep breath. 'I want to know about Andro Mogon, about who he was. The Dartith book and his Book of Laws tell me nothing.'

He scowled. 'What be your interest in the Dark Sorcerer's life?'

'Our laws' origins, Majesty.'

He eyed her shrewdly. 'You shall find naught of the Dark Sorcerer's life in books, Jatta,' he finally said. He stood, beckoning her to follow.

Brackensith led her up the spiralled stairwell to his

bedchambers. He unlocked the door and they stepped into a circular room, quite the opposite of his cave-like den. Blue-tinted windows stretched to its high ceiling. Dartith's insipid afternoon sun lay trapped in beams on the floor, as did its heat. For the first time since arriving on the Isle, Jatta felt warmed. Her blue-tinted view of the grounds, Dredden and the hills beyond was breathtaking.

Like the marble cage one floor above, and the den below, these chambers were immense. They were decorated with a strange assortment of things, some as precious as the crown sitting on a glass cabinet by Brackensith's bed. Others were exotic—grotesque stone gods from an age before Sorcerers, arranged in soldierly rows either side of the door, and the dragon-scale mirror above it. Brackensith unlocked his bedside cabinet and carefully withdrew a plate-sized glass disc. To Jatta it appeared neither precious nor unusual. She wondered if the transparent platter, like her purple plum ball, might be something other than it seemed.

'Know you what this be?' he asked.

He was testing her again. Jatta's mind raced. If the platter was magical she could not imagine how. Yet it was precious. He held it almost with reverence, as if it was his personal stone god. Into its surface were cut ancient symbols like those on the portal, so conceivably it might also be three thousand years old. Her excitement rose: he'd said Andro Mogon's life could not be found in books . . .

'Majesty, is it Andro Mogon's life?'

His face betrayed only a momentary twitch of a smile. 'In life, the Sorcerer was a scholar and healer. This be his personal account. Clear a space on the table.'

Jatta eagerly scanned the chambers. By a far window sat a

table laden with books. While the King relocked his cabinet she scampered to the table and, scooping up several books, knelt to lay them by the drape.

She gasped, smelling the unmistakeable stench of faeces. Two feet stuck out from behind the drape. One was grubby, with broken nails, while the other wore a blood-spattered, grimy boot. Her heart stopped. She recognised the boot. Her father's. For one absurd moment she imagined he'd come to rescue her.

The obvious explanation escaped her.

The drape whipped open, and there stood Riz. His manic eyes gleamed, like firecrackers spluttering and sparking.

She screamed, dropping the books. She spun around to run, but his hand was already at her throat. The other hand was at her face, clutching a broken bottle.

'Evil Sorceress!' he spat, one eye twitching. 'I have you now.'

'Idiot son!' bellowed Brackensith. 'Put down that bottle!'

Riz was backing Jatta against the window. She'd never seen him this wild, this unpredictable. She trembled in his hands.

'Father, listen! I be here to warn you—yes, this Sorceress bewitched me! Her love spell tempted me into betrayal. It was she who whispered treason inside my head!'

'Rank dragonrot!' Brackensith's face twisted with fury. 'Naught but your own vanity tempted you to treason.'

'Not true! Not true! This Sorceress set her dragon on Fand, on my faithful Fand. Yes, Father, when I left her in his kind care.'

Jatta's pulse hammered against his fingers. 'I'm no Sorceress! Let me go,' she pleaded.

Those murderous eyes roved over her body and he

whispered, 'You shall torment me no more.' He dragged the broken bottle down her cheek and she winced with the sting. His bottle traced down her jaw and to her chest. His breath came shallow and fast.

Fuming, Brackensith laid down the platter. He strode forward two paces.

Riz's eyes flicked up to his father's thunderous face. He panicked and jabbed at Jatta's chest. Holes ripped in her over-gown. Blood spotted its silver.

'Drop the bottle, idiot, or I shall skewer you!'

'No, Father! Bid me kill her and welcome me back as your son! As your heir!'

Brackensith drew his sword. He bounded across the room.

Riz squealed. He looked around wildly for escape and saw the window. His boot smashed through, sending blue shards scattering. He dragged Jatta through the jagged hole by her throat.

Out onto the ledge.

Wind whipped through her hair, billowing her gown. She fought down her dread and risked a glance below. The distant courtyard swam before her eyes. Blood pounded in her brain. Her feet slid on sheets of glass. She pressed her body against the window, kicking at loose sheets underfoot, sending them hurtling down, terrified she would slip despite Riz's grip on her throat.

She stole a glance at her captor. He was staring down blank-faced. Whimpering.

'Let her go!' yelled Brackensith, leaning out through the hole.

Riz was roused from his terror. 'Father! Prove you love me. Name me your heir. Or—or I shall jump!'

'Jump then, and save me the trouble of deciding your fate.'

'Majesty, please,' called Jatta, trembling. 'You aren't helping my cause.'

'Hear that, idiot son? She bids me be nice. Very well, let Jatta go and I shall spare your life.'

'No! I be your true heir! Drake and Ivish and Fabish and Mordis—they all agree!'

'You be completely mad.'

'Father, hear me! I have convinced them this day.'

'Unhand her!' Brackensith's frustration boiled over. 'Damn, I shall just sever your wrists!'

Brackensith thrust out at his son. Riz squealed and backed further along the ledge. He almost toppled, taking Jatta with him.

'Majesty, please!' she cried, her legs trembling so much she could barely stand.

Brackensith seethed, withdrawing his sword through the hole. Waiting for his moment.

Riz was whimpering again. He stared down at the distant courtyard, then back at his father. Jatta watched the desperate, twitching confusion in his eyes. They locked onto hers and she saw all his deranged thoughts congeal into one.

All was lost.

He was taking her with him.

A sort of peace settled in his eyes. The twitch had gone. He let the bottle slip from his fingers. It fell so far she never heard it smash. He lifted those fingers to her throat, too, and she felt his grip tighten as he bent his knees to jump. Jatta did the only thing she could.

She vanished.

Riz froze, astonished. Only his mouth moved, silently

forming the word *Sorceress*. She'd gone. So what invisible *thing* pulsed between his hands? He strangled it.

Something kicked into his groin and his face screwed up in pain. The thing jerked free as he fell against the window. His feet were sliding over the ledge on glass sheets. His body was following. Frantically he clutched at the window frame; his fingertips caught hold. The wind played with his hair as he dangled over the ledge.

Glass crunched on the floor under the window.

Riz cried, 'Father, help me!' He thrashed against the tower, despairing of dragging himself up, hoping his father's arms would reach out. They didn't. Instead he heard him swear, and footsteps bounding away, to the door.

'Don't leave me, Father!' he whimpered. 'I be all you have left!'

CHAPTER SIXTY-ONE

Jatta didn't wait to see if Riz would disappear over the edge. She crawled back into the chambers, glass crunching under her feet. Brackensith was there. Waiting. Eyes flitting. Betraying no surprise. He heard the crunch and he pounced.

She ducked, and he managed to grab only her sleeve. He swore. Even as it ripped invisibly from her shoulder she was racing for the door.

He heard her jagged breaths. He bounded there too, wasting not even a backward glance as his son cried for help.

He got to the door first and scraped its bolt across. She froze before him, barely daring to breathe. He scanned the bed-chambers with narrowed eyes. 'Come out, Princess,' he said. 'Show yourself now, or it shall be worse for you later.'

The orb felt wet in her clammy, pummelling fingers.

Brackensith leaned to pick up a cat-headed god, weighing it in his hand, his eyes searching till they came to rest at Jatta's invisible feet. A smile's shadow creased his mouth. Too late, Jatta saw the spot of blood on the tile.

The stone god *whooshed* past her thigh and smashed on floor behind.

Brackensith threw another god, and another. Jatta scrambled invisibly back to the wall. Her heart was thundering, her mind racing. He would hit her and find her. Or he'd run out of statues and call for the soldiers. Either way she'd be found.

Unless.

A low rumble like distant thunder began at the back of the chambers. It grew, making the bed jump, drowning Riz's scrabbling and yelling. Rising to a deafening roar.

Brackensith stared, every muscle tense.

A mighty creature came crashing through the wall—a dragon as tall as the ceiling. Broken stone flew. Night gaped through the wall's wound as the dragon lunged at the door. At Brackensith. Its great jaws gaped, weaving on the end of a tree-trunk neck. Sulphur fouled the air. Brackensith drew his sword, chest heaving, stumbling back against the door. He fumbled behind him.

Jatta heard the bolt scrape free. She felt triumph surge: one last fearsome display would do it, would send him scuttling through. Her dragon's throat sucked in air; jaws drew back, ready. Fire plumed to the King.

She regretted it instantly.

Brackensith yelled. He dropped his sword to cover his face.

Orb dust caressed his hands.

In stunned confusion he peeped through his fingers, then swiped both arms through her flame. His face was slowly relaxing, his body too. He leaned against the door, gazing up as if the monster was a spectacle on a stage.

Jatta's anger at her stupidity surged into fury at him. She redoubled her efforts. A second head burst out, more terrible than the first, then a third with rotting flesh and wolf teeth. Flaming eyes fixed on their prey. Great ribbed wings unfolded and the beast lifted up off the ground. Its screeches were painful. Three heads drew back to lunge.

Brackensith pressed hard against the door, fresh confusion and fear in his eyes. Three monstrous mouths snapped over his body. Slobber sprayed like sand, putrid chunks of flesh, too. The stench was overpowering.

But he was not devoured.

After a few moments his face resumed its cold indifference. He bent to pick up his sword, then sheathed it while the monster screeched and seethed. He clapped four times, applauding the show. 'Impressive!' he called up to the heads. 'You frightened me, little Jatta, I admit. You be an accomplished performer.'

She screwed up her eyes and gritted her teeth, forcing everything she had into the dragon. Blue lightning arced from its body through the chambers. Three heads took noisy breaths and they rasped, seething with malevolence.

'Let us pass, mortal king! Or we shall grind up your skull like wheatmeal!'

'Enough, Jatta!' bellowed Brackensith, squinting up through her blinding blue arcs. 'You cannot bully your King with magical toys. Pack away your monster now!'

The wall's wound healed itself. Her dragon dissolved.

Brackensith reached behind to slam the bolt back in place, eyes searching the room. 'Jatta!' He held out his hand. 'You shall not leave these chambers till you have surrendered your toy.'

But she would not, could not, surrender the orb.

Riz's scrabbling had stopped. Whimpering came from the ledge.

Brackensith heard it, too. '*Still* here,' he growled.

'Believe me now, Father,' called a tremulous voice. 'She be an evil Sorceress.' Riz's bloodied hands entered through the hole. His nervous face followed.

Jatta's loathing hardened; everything was *his* fault. His murderous attack had forced her to this.

Brackensith's top lip twisted in contempt. 'Make yourself useful, then. Help me find Jatta.'

'The evil Sorceress!' Riz's face drew back behind the window. 'Her dragon will destroy me.'

'Snivelling idiot, she will not harm you. She be no more Sorceress than you.'

Riz edged down from the window. Though his bare foot was sliced, he began whirling around through the shards, with arms sweeping the air. More than ever he looked like a madman. Jatta understood, though. This ploy was completely, effectively, sane.

They'd find her now.

But Riz knew nothing of magic.

Suddenly there was a second twirling Riz. Riz's twin jolted to a stop, dumbfounded. Riz caught sight of himself, squealed, darted behind the curtain. 'The Sorceress!' he wailed.

Jatta pressed her invisible body harder against the wall. Her sand-Riz pleaded with Brackensith, 'No! Father, *I* be Riz! *Me!*'

'No, Father, *I* be Riz! Test me, test me, Father!' cried Riz.

'Impostor!' yelled sand-Riz, groping for him. Riz squealed. He fought free of the drapes and ran.

Brackensith watched the chase, poised like a beast in ambush.

Jatta saw his intent. It was more than she could have hoped. Hardly breathing, she tiptoed toward the King. She edged invisibly behind him to the door.

Brackensith's eyes were fixed on sand-Riz. She let him run too close. With a vicious cry, Brackensith pounced.

To his astonishment the body flowed through his arms. He roared in frustration. Then he grabbed the squealing Riz, shaking him. 'Enough! Get back to work!'

Behind Brackensith the bolt scraped open. The King flung his son to the floor. He spun around, seizing something unseen. Jerking it back into the room. Dragging it, twisting its arm mercilessly.

Jatta screamed and dropped the orb.

She stood bloodied and tiny in his grip. With his other hand the King scooped up her orb.

'What be this?' he demanded with dark menace.

'It be the Sorceress's precious ball!' cried Riz.

Brackensith ignored him.

'Jatta, how does it work?' he asked, releasing his grip on her arm.

'You squeeze it and it sparkles,' said his son.

The King's jaw clenched. 'Get back on the ledge,' he growled.

He raised one eyebrow to Jatta.

'You squeeze it and it sparkles,' she said.

Brackensith kneaded with both hands. White stars danced inside. Fireworks rose to the ceiling.

'A pretty trick, Jatta. What else does it do?'

'As you've seen me do, Majesty. But you're not squeezing right.' She offered her open palm as her brother once had. 'Let me show you.'

His smile flickered. 'You be a cheeky one, a fair match for my Drake.' He kneaded again. A vision appeared between them, ghostly, grainy and distorted. Nonetheless Jatta recognised it—a macabre headless Riz, running in haphazard circles around a bloodied chopping block.

Riz squealed and fainted. Jatta stared at the vision in disgust. Here stood another with imaginative powers, but darker.

Brackensith laughed with grim pleasure at his mastery. He closed his eyes to refine his vision.

In that moment the orb was plucked from his fingers. Jatta vanished.

Instinctively he struck out. But she was not where he'd expected. He whirled around to feel her slip through the door. Even as he yelled, 'Soldiers!' he heard her sprinting toward the stairwell.

He cursed her retreating footsteps. 'Find the Princess!' he yelled. 'Harm her though, and I shall have your heads!'

Brackensith called his commanders to co-ordinate the search. Within minutes the castle was swarming with soldiers.

The King was fascinated by the orb, but it was not his focus. He had reluctantly grown to respect his little Princess. Indeed, he preferred her to most of his own flesh and blood. She'd been another wise choice of the Dark Sorcerer's and would make a resourceful queen. One point bothered him, though. Was she too resourceful, a little too clever, to sit obediently beside Drake's throne? The proper punishment, he decided, would teach the Princess her place without crushing her soul. He had made mistakes in the past. He would be careful how he punished this royal bride.

Within minutes the soldiers had locked all exits. They spread nets, sprinkled flour along corridors, and brought hounds. They herded everyone, from kitchen hands to the chancellor, into the Great Hall.

Jatta bounded down six flights of stairs. Only then did she slow her thundering heart with deep, deliberate breaths. She also slowed her bounds to a stride, a regal, purposeful stride. Soldiers stepped from her path, bowing, as she approached the castle's grand entry. With a scowl and a flick of her hand she commanded to be let through.

She was practising for the most crucial performance of her life: her audience with Andro Mogon. She was Brackensith again.

CHAPTER SIXTY-TWO

The sun was already setting.

Jatta-Brackensith strode regally through the castle grounds and stopped kneading only when she reached the crypt. Again she broke into a run.

She bounded down the steps, two at a time, to where Arthmael waited by Noriglade's slab.

'Art, we have to act now!' she called. 'Brackensith knows about the orb. He has every soldier searching.'

He stared. 'What happened to you? What's that gash down your face?'

She ignored his questions. 'Isn't she awake yet?'

Noriglade's eyelashes flickered.

'Give her time.'

'We don't have any! I told you, he won't rest till he finds me.' Jatta dragged the shroud off Noriglade. The Undead opened her eyes.

'Prickle, are you all right to go?' Arthmael took her hands where they lay folded across her chest. Their coldness no longer chilled him. 'Lord knows we're not ready. But we have to go through the portal now.'

Undead were stirring around them. Jatta imagined their sharp teeth; the back of her neck tingled unpleasantly. Noriglade sat up and nodded. Others were rising from their

slabs, slinking close with hungry eyes. 'These two be mine!'
she hissed, herding her friends closer, pushing through.

They fled up the stairs and out among the tombstones. As
they hurried into the castle Jatta took the lead, again squeezing
her orb. Soldiers jumped to attention.

'Majesty!' cried an officer, falling into step beside her
Brackensith. 'She be not in the stables, nor the fencing studio.'

'Search the grounds, you imbecile. Take your men.' The
officer turned to leave, his belt jangling. 'Wait! Give me your
keys.'

The man hesitated, confused—the King's own set hung
from his sash.

'What be you snivelling at, scum? You will not need them
out there!'

The officer fumbled for his keys, then left with his men.

'Arthmael, forgive my father's language,' said Noriglade
behind her.

Jatta's confidence faltered. 'Too much cursing? Is it too
aggressive, do you think? Then feed me my lines.'

'No, you have him, right enough,' grinned the Undead.

Soldiers and hounds swarmed up and down the stairs. Jatta's
hazelnut-perfumed Brackensith and his entourage climbed past
them unchallenged, to the sixth floor. Here the stairwell was
locked. Jatta struggled with the keys, listening to Brackensith's
commands below. Apparently Riz was missing too.

They hurried through and the foyer erupted with ferocious
barking.

'Father's dogs. They will bring the soldiers!'

'No, listen to this.' Jatta cleared her throat and growled,
'Shut up you cursed curs, or I shall slice you for my supper.'

The rottweilers' agitation rose to a frenzy. She tried not to panic. Had she forgotten the command?

'Glory, Jay,' said Arthmael. 'Give it some guts. You're not in tapestry now.'

'Shut up. Quiet,' breathed Noriglade. She dragged Jatta and Arthmael back into the stairwell. Then they heard it, one floor below—Brackensith's order to search the den.

'By heralds, we be dead meat now.'

'Not yet,' said Jatta. Her Brackensith prowled back toward the den.

'Shut up, you cursed curs,' she growled, deadly low. 'Or I shall slice you for my supper!'

Instantly the frenzy switched to pitiful whimpering. She fumbled with each key in the den's lock.

Soldiers were pounding up the stairwell. The rottweilers were snarling again. Jatta slumped against the wall and groaned. 'No key . . . What now?'

Noriglade unclipped a broach from her robes and, kneeling beside Jatta-Brackensith, began picking the lock.

'She's done this before,' whispered Arthmael in admiration.

'Quiet, boy. Let me concentrate.'

The lock clicked open. The dogs were barking in frenzy. Soldiers flooded the foyer.

'Shut up, you cursed curs,' growled Jatta-Brackensith. Arthmael shoved the door open. The rottweilers came crawling out on their stomachs.

All three jumped over the trembling dogs and into the den, Jatta calling, 'Attack!' for good measure. She raced to the portal as Arthmael bolted the door. She held out a wrist as she'd seen Brackensith do.

'Noriglade, I'm not really sure what to imagine.'

Noriglade was sweeping poisons off her father's shelves with both arms, eyes furious. Glass smashed over the floor. 'I know not, exactly,' she said, kicking over cabinets. 'Imagine Andro Mogon. Imagine primeval evil.'

'Pardon?'

'Imagine a cemetery, then. I shall tell you the words.' Noriglade threw a torch onto the cluttered desk. It burst into flame.

Boom!

Something heavy rammed the door from outside as spilled poisons caught alight. Arthmael dragged Noriglade into the portal. 'Prickle, for Glory's sake! Leave off the wanton destruction.'

Noriglade shrugged free, scowling. 'Ready, Jatta?
'Andro Mogon, grant me a moment
Of your infinite time . . .'

Jatta-Brackensith glared at her outstretched wrist, desperately trying to concentrate. A kaleidoscope of confused images were flitting over it as she repeated, 'Andro Mogon, grant me a moment of your infinite time.'

'My will I surrender . . .'

'My will—' Jatta hoped these words weren't binding.

'I surrender. Go on, Jatta.'

'My will I surrender.'

'My soul be yours.'

What if this was some dark spell? Jatta lost her concentration. Her Brackensith started to fade.

Arthmael shoved her. 'Jay, for Glory's sake.'

'All right! My soul be yours.'

Nothing happened.

Her wrist was empty. The door was splintering. The den was alight.

'Be you imagining Andro Mogon? Try harder!'

'How? *How?*' yelled Jatta-Brackensith, kneading with white knuckles, turning Arthmael invisible.

'Jatta! Again. *Andro Mogon, grant—*'

CHAPTER SIXTY-THREE

Blue sparks flickered all around. The portal buzzed. Their hair frizzed, their skin tingled. The floor dropped away and they clutched at each other, though they didn't fall. Flickering sparks suspended them in a sea of swirling blackness.

Blackness lifted. Beneath their feet they felt rocky ground. Around their portal lay a strangely luminous night, like a field of fallen moons.

From out of the night a voice whispered. Weary, mocking. Cruel and cracked with age.

'Aah . . . What has my portal brought me tonight? Supper, I believe.'

For one dreadful moment Jatta thought her Brackensith had failed. But no. And the others beside her were invisible, though she could feel Noriglade trembling. She fought down her own fear and stepped forward.

They were in a graveyard, one more ancient than anything they had seen. Statues of long-forgotten Sorcerers crumbled into the ground. Obsidian-lidded sarcophagi lay in rows like stony beds, except these beds cradled their dead within. This field of tombs was lit by thousands of floating balls, each glowing with the moon's own white beauty.

'Yes, my supper.' The mocking whisper resonated. It filled the night air. 'Two foolish young royals with delicious warm blood.'

Jatta's concentration faltered; for a moment Brackensith

faded. Something was deadly wrong. Her King's eyes tightened defensively and flashed to the source of the voice.

On a nearby sarcophagus sat an old man, examining her. His rich indigo robes were decayed. His lips pulled up in a taunting sneer and obsidian glinted between.

'Aah ... and one wretched Undead with blood lying cold in her veins. Come closer, Noriglade. Bring your handsome Prince. Bring Jatta too. I wish to see Jatta.'

Jatta forgot to squeeze.

They stood exposed, three terrified young royals. The Dark Sorcerer beckoned. They dared not disobey.

Now Jatta saw his face clearly. It made her want to hide behind her brother. His aged white flesh rippled as though a mass of live grubs writhed beneath it. His pupils were clouded milky-white. She averted her eyes to her brother.

Noriglade and Arthmael stared in revulsion. The Sorcerer, unperturbed, lifted one churning hand to Arthmael's chin, turning it to examine his throat's veins, and Noriglade's handiwork.

'Shall I drink ... or not?'

Noriglade hissed, baring teeth.

What happened next didn't make sense, although it went just as they'd hoped. But why was it allowed to happen, despite every mistake? Why was it allowed to happen at all?

Noriglade ducked to seize a ball by Arthmael's knee. It must have been heavy enough to shatter obsidian, despite the fact that it floated, for she staggered trying to drag it to her chest. Arthmael jerked back from the Sorcerer's grasp to help. Why didn't the Sorcerer see what was happening?

Between them they rammed the ball into the slab. It cracked loudly. Shards flew.

Shouldn't the Sorcerer smite them somehow? Shoot blue sparks from his temple? Flames from his chest? He seemed to have lost interest. He whispered Jatta's name and she met his gaze, compelled to answer his call. His eyes locked on hers with powerful evil. He could have torn out her heart and she wouldn't have resisted.

Noriglade must have found a shard. The Sorcerer held Jatta's gaze and waited while she thrust it between his ribs. He flinched in pain. Finally he freed Jatta, lifting his face to Arthmael.

Arthmael had raised the ball above his head. His elbows shook, but not from its weight.

No blow fell.

Arthmael had frozen, eyes unseeing, mouth contorted with horror. Jatta remembered that look. A nightmare was flashing through his mind—of another's face screwed up in agony; of the sickening slush of his blade through another's flesh; of blood spurting from another's heart.

Had the Sorcerer known?

'Do it,' pleaded Noriglade.

The Sorcerer laughed—a weary, cruel laugh that mocked them both. He eased himself back on his elbows, his chest exposed in invitation, dragging the shard in his ribs down, and Noriglade's arms too.

'You're a scourge. A plague,' growled Arthmael, sweat beading, willing himself to strike.

'Why hesitate?' said the Sorcerer, his tone taunting. 'Aah, yes . . . it was easier to kill in self-defence.'

'It's not killing!' shouted Arthmael. 'You're not alive. What you are is—is macabre, just an animated corpse.'

Beside him, Noriglade winced.

The Sorcerer turned to her coolly. 'Noriglade, revenge feeds like a parasite inside you. Will *you* do it?'

Drawing jagged breaths, she raised the shard above her head, then plunged down blindly.

Flesh tore. The Sorcerer's face screwed up in silent agony. Her shard had stuck low in his intestines, no more. She felt faint, revolted at what she'd done, sickened at the thought of trying again.

Jatta watched the small burgundy stain seeping over his robes. Her tears welled.

'What a tragic trio of assassins you be,' mocked the Sorcerer through his pain. 'You, Arthmael, who cannot wilfully kill. You, Noriglade, who despises your kind because they do. And you, poor, fragile Jatta, who weeps through it all.'

'He's toying with us,' said Arthmael. 'I don't know why he lets us keep going.'

Noriglade wrapped her bleeding hands around the shard. 'Please, Arthmael. Again.'

The air behind them was buzzing. They dared not glance back. Blue light flickered over the Sorcerer's face. 'Meddling Brackensith,' he whispered. He stretched up a finger to Arthmael's ball. It burst into flame.

They gaped.

He dragged the shard from his stomach with a squelch. It crumbled to glass pebbles in his hand. Grimacing, he struggled to sit up.

The King strode into their midst. He scowled menacingly at Jatta and her brother. For his treacherous daughter he reserved a look of pure hatred. He bowed low. 'Great Andro Mogon, my humble apologies for these fugitives' intrusion.'

'Go now,' whispered the Sorcerer.

Brackensith bowed again and took Jatta's wrist. He reached for Noriglade.

'Go. Now.' The Sorcerer's calm, cruel whisper grew threatening. 'I have use for your fugitives myself.'

The King's grip on Jatta was clammy. 'Drain the male, Great Sorcerer. But I beg you spare these two. They be family.'

'I have not yet decided their fates. Wait in the shadows, if you must.'

Releasing Jatta, Brackensith bowed deeply and retreated behind the portal. The Sorcerer fixed his penetrating stare on his failed assassins.

'Arthmael and Noriglade, have you done with destroying me?'

They stood dumbly, like criminals awaiting their sentence.

'Yes? I would speak to Jatta. Till you devise some torture less repugnant to your delicate sensibilities, go.' He dismissed them with a flick of his infested hand.

Arthmael hesitated.

Jatta forced a trembling smile. 'Go, Art. I—Sorry. We tried.'

He pulled away, back to Noriglade. Jatta listened to the grind of pebbles under his boots and felt the dull, dragging sense of loss, the tearing of separation.

'You would have made a worthy queen,' the Sorcerer said.

'Let me, still.'

'Let you? It be too late for that now.'

She waited alone for the Sorcerer's judgement. Too petrified to look, she examined the fallen moons around her hem. Her feeble plan lay there too, crumbled among the dust and broken statues. Time, hours maybe, staggered on. She dared not move though her ears thudded and her legs spasmed with cramps.

Just once he sighed: a gravelly intake of breath that ended in a weary, mournful moan. The tone of it caught her off-guard, almost as if she'd heard it before. She chanced a glimpse. His grotesque face seemed to be pleading with the heraldic stars.

Finally he spoke, with a gentleness she had not heard from a living Dartithan.

'So, Jatta, why be you here?'

'To kill you, Lord,' she whispered to the ground.

He laughed wearily. 'Yes, there be that. I meant, what hope you to gain from my destruction?'

'To free Dartith from the firewall, to escape.'

'And?'

'Nothing else.'

'*Something* else?' he softly coaxed.

'Well, I imagined . . . maybe to lift my curse.'

'Child, my destruction could not give you that.' He took her hand in his. It was as cold as death, yet the skin seethed on hers. She grimaced.

'Don't be afraid, little Jatta.'

She willed her eyes up. The infested face and its milky eyes revolted her, though his taunting cruelty had gone. She *was* afraid, but somehow not of these words or the half-remembered voice. Was he still playing his perverse game? The thought twisted her stomach.

She allowed herself to hope.

'I once knew a child like you . . .' A look of intense sadness flickered over those churning features. He patted her hand, then let her fingers slip from his.

'So, you wish to be an ordinary princess again?' he asked.

She took a deep, shaky breath and perched on the slab's edge.

'Can you do that, Andro Mogon?'

'You never were ordinary, little Jatta. Lift your curse, though? I be very tired, but . . . yes, maybe.'

'Can you cure Noriglade, too? I own something precious, it's yours for helping us.'

'Something precious? How intriguing. What treasure have you, Jatta?'

'I'll show you, Lord—but only when you've cured me, and Noriglade, too.'

Instantly his face turned dangerously hard. He laughed, a cold laugh of brittle irritation. 'Ha! So you would dare bargain? Heed this: you do not bargain with the Dark Sorcerer.'

Jatta bit her lip, tasting blood.

Brackensith stepped from the portal with a bow. 'Great One, return her to me. Such insolence shall be punished.'

'Silence!' thundered the Dark Sorcerer. The cloudy-white eyes narrowed, though they did not look up. Instead he lifted one hand. In his palm a wound opened, putrid and stinking. A thin, translucent tentacle wove out. Jatta gasped. It whipped past her, smooth tip flicking.

'Forgive me!' cried Brackensith.

For a moment it paused by Arthmael. Tasting his heat.

'Forgive me!' screamed the King.

It whipped to Brackensith, wrapping around his throat. He was gasping.

'For—for—'

The tentacle gave one more perverse jerk. It slackened, uncoiled and snaked back to its owner. Brackensith retreated, spluttering, into the shadows.

Horrified, Jatta turned back to the Dark Sorcerer. His

wound was healing, sealing in the nauseating stench. His sneering sarcasm had returned. 'Tempt me, Jatta. What be so precious that I should lift a finger to help you?'

Her heart was pounding. She groped in her pocket for the orb, wary for the next sign of disapproval. For the narrowing of his eyes. She would morph into something. Anything. She would startle him and seize precious moments. When those tentacles wove out for her, she and the others would race for the portal.

But her orb was gone.

CHAPTER SIXTY-FOUR

Jatta's orb was in the Dark Sorcerer's hands.

She stared at the orb, overwhelmed. There could be no escape, no defence against the power of the omnipotent Dark Sorcerer. She raised her eyes to him, dreading what she'd find.

He was again searching the stars. Ganus. Manus. Aedossus.

Jatta watched his expression gradually change, its dark sneer and millennia of cruelty seeping away. After many minutes he sighed. His fingers pressed into the orb.

A child materialised on the slab between them. Her face was no older than six and for the second time in three thousand years it was not frosted clear, but flesh. She looked adoringly up into his cloudy-white eyes. 'Poppy! Make me more wings,' she pleaded. 'I want to fly.'

Andro Mogon's face melted into kindness. He touched Dragongirl's shoulder with a churning hand and she giggled. His fingers closed around its sand, feeling its almost-substance for the first time. Gently he turned her so she faced Jatta, and ran fingers in two lines down her spine. Where he traced, leathery dragon wings unfolded. Her toy wings faded away.

Jatta stared, not comprehending. Not wanting to believe.

'No. Not you . . .' she breathed in disgust.

Pain flickered across Andro Mogon's face. Dragongirl dissolved.

'No,' she said, backing away. 'My guardian is good. He guided me through the caves. He hurts when I hurt. He's a great heal—' Jatta stopped. Andro Mogon had been a healer, too.

'I have watched over you, little Jatta,' he said softly.

'No, you're evil. You let Brackensith curse me. You let him kill my mother!'

'I be evil too, it be true. You know Dartith. You know my dark side.'

'Stop it! I don't want you watching me. My mother's dead.'

'I cannot undo what be done. I cannot forgive myself for your pain.'

'Why didn't you *stop* him?'

'Little Jatta, please understand I could not. The powerful Dark Sorcerer who let her die, who instructs Dark Kings, who greeted you this night, still claims me. His half of our soul rests in obsidian. It be only when we pause to contemplate the stars and remember, that he lets me contact my own soul . . . that half trapped and burning these three thousand years.'

A memory flickered. Of course his voice sounded familiar. It had pleaded with her in the firewall. *Little Jatta, my soul be prisoner to the Dark Sorcerer too. Will you help set it free?*

'How? Why?' she demanded.

'Why might we divide our soul? Pain, Jatta. Destroying our beloved Vardensen was too terrible a crime. It caused us unbearable pain. Some part of us, the vestige of our humanity, had to disappear. That part was me. The Dark Sorcerer buried me deep in a crevice in his mind and excised my half of our soul.

'But power alone be meaningless. Remember that, child. In his search for meaning he eventually resurrected me.'

'I hate you both.' She stabbed out those four words. They

were a lie. She watched them wound him, but she was too angry and confused to care. 'You try to make me pity you, but you keep flipping. You're rotten through. How can you live with yourself?'

'Child, I cannot. And neither can he. For these last two centuries we have existed uneasily together, both despairing in our separate ways. He be haunted by emptiness. I be burdened with remorse, remembering those we destroyed. Those we loved and lost. We have hidden ourselves away. Hidden from the living. Hidden from our Undead also. And waited.'

His eyes in that grotesque writhing face were infinitely sad. Jatta struggled against an impulse to comfort her guardian. Yet he'd reached out to her in her misery.

'I . . . I hid away, too,' she said. 'When I thought I'd lost everyone. In the marble cage.'

'Yes. We be more alike than you imagine.'

'Except—' Jatta recalled Dragongirl's words. *You fear you have lost everyone, but you have not. For you, it be not too late.*

'—except, Lord, for you it is too late.'

He sighed. 'I be caught between this existence I despise and the dread of ending it. Child, I long to follow those I cherish.'

Her guardian pressed the orb and Dragongirl appeared on the slab, tugging at her grandfather's sleeve. He smiled down and patted her sand knee.

'Yes, then. Go play.'

She flapped her leathery wings, rising off the sarcophagus. 'I be off to show Nanna,' she said. 'We shall fly to the moon!'

'Don't tire her out,' he called as she flitted off through the statues.

'She really could fly,' breathed Jatta.

'What does it feel like when *you* fly?'

Jatta blushed. 'I don't, not exactly. I just imagine.'

'And how does that feel?'

'Well . . . I climb through the sky, incredibly high, till I'm alone with its blue. The wind whips through my fingers and hair. It tumbles me. I flit. And hover. I dance and I'm free.'

'Aah, I can almost feel it as you speak. My Dragongirl described it thus.' He closed his forlorn eyes. To Jatta he no longer seemed ugly.

'Am I like her?' Her soft voice coaxed him back from memories. 'Lord, why did you help me? Because I remind you of her? Or because of my orb?'

'Your orb? There be a thousand men could fetch me Alteeda's orb. Yet I waited and led the dwarf to find it, hoping he would surrender it to you. Yes, child, I waited generations for you. You have my Dragongirl's imagination and gentle heart. Ah, her tender heart . . . She could bear to harm no creature. Could see inside my flawed soul, too, and warned me against my elixir. Great Sorcerer that I was, my Dragongirl proved wiser.' He was again sinking into sadness. With effort he lifted a seething hand to Jatta's cheek. This time she didn't flinch. She was glad she hadn't, for his cold touch brought a tingling with it, and something more. Warm emotions soaked through her skin. Gifts. A pride in her that moistened her eyes, a devotion so fatherly and protective it made her homesick. As his hand pressed against her cheek his feelings intensified till they coursed through her, unnerving and staggering in their beauty. She gasped, but did not pull away. Something inside her responded, a stirring behind her heart. It seemed he felt the connection, too, for he smiled.

'There, it be done,' he said.

'Pardon, Lord?'

'It be time, now. Will you stay with me?'

Brackensith edged out from the shadows, his face no longer menacing, nor commanding, but stricken with fear.

Jatta rose to stand. Waiting. For what, she didn't know, but her pulse was racing. She could not help hoping the miraculous cure was coming.

Instead Andro Mogon pressed the orb, transforming the sarcophagus where he sat into a bed. A girl Jatta's age lay there. Her pallid skin was stretched tight over her skull; her eyes were large inside deep sockets. Though her body was wasted by disease, Jatta recognised her first friend. Her throat suddenly felt swollen. She swallowed twice to clear it, telling herself this tragedy wasn't happening, was merely an old Sorcerer's memory. That she'd never really known Dragongirl, not the original. That every flight on their dragon, every giggled secret, her rescue from despair at her mother's death, and in the labyrinth and marble cage, were the gifts of an old Sorcerer's imagination.

His fingers closed over his granddaughter's and squeezed their sand with the tenderest of pressure, and Jatta realised. It was *his* suffering her eyes moistened for.

A dozen people gathered mournfully around the bed. A woman was sobbing while her young son watched miserably, leaning into her waist. 'Father, help her,' pleaded the woman. 'Make my Tammon take your elixir.'

Dragongirl's eyes smiled up into her mother's. Her voice was a whisper filled with pain. 'Poppy and I . . .' She paused to draw a rattly breath. 'Have discussed this . . . I be ready to go.'

'But Dartith needs you,' said a man, his voice rough with anguish. 'We all need you to live!'

Dragongirl rolled her head to her grandfather. 'Live? No, a half-life, only.'

'Better than death,' said the man.

'No. To never stand in warm sun ... never watch sunrise.' Dragongirl coughed. 'To live off others' blood ...'

Andro Mogon tenderly wiped the corners of her sand mouth. 'To witness everyone you have loved grow old and die.'

Dragongirl groaned, closing her eyes against her pain.

'Poppy Andro,' whispered the young boy. 'I will drink your elixir when my time comes.'

Andro Mogon shook his head. 'No, child. You shall see what I have become and reject my dark magic.'

'No, Poppy. We want to live on with you.'

'Indeed you will not. In time my soul will grow as cold as my body and as black as night's shadow. I will bury this Isle in darkness.'

'Not you, Poppy!'

'Father, you could never do evil.'

'Each night I will fill my veins with my victims' misery. There be worse things than death.'

'What be you telling us, Father? That you no longer fear it?'

The old Sorcerer caressed Dragongirl's skeletal hand. He drew in an unsteady breath and closed his eyes. 'Fear death? No, no more.'

Jatta watched helplessly. With her guardian's farewell her own silly hopes were slipping away.

Suddenly Brackensith burst from the night. 'No! I beg you! Great One, Dartith needs your dark magic!' He shoved through Dragongirl's family. Their unearthly bodies offered only sandy resistance. 'I beg you—' He collided with Jatta, knocking her forward through her dying friend, into her guardian.

'Silence!' The word was thunder.

The orb dropped, rolling on bare obsidian. Fury transformed the Dark Sorcerer's face. His body shook. Both hands shot up and the King screamed in terror. Tentacles, masses of them, whipped out from stinking wounds. They coiled around Brackensith's chest and legs. Bones crunched. They forced themselves down his throat to stifle his screams. More and more flicked around, till he disappeared inside their seething, squeezing, frenzied ball.

They released him and he crumpled. His body dropped forward onto Jatta. She opened her mouth to scream.

The Dark Sorcerer's moment of fury was spent. He slumped, letting his legion squirm back through dust; one weary finger pointed to the portal. The body was dragged across Jatta's, pulled toward the portal in gruesome jerks across the stony ground. Blue sparks danced. Brackensith vanished.

Shocked, nauseated, she heard his screams still. Hoarse, choked croaks of dry air. Gradually she realised they were hers. The empty portal swam before her eyes. The stars, and fallen moons, and Andro Mogon groping weakly for the orb: all swam too. She lay sprawled on the slab, vaguely watching him. He seemed to be pleading.

'. . . do not hate me, Jatta . . . free your tormentor, your guardian . . . help me . . . help Dartith . . .'

His sad voice dragged her back to the sarcophagus. *The orb.* He wanted the orb. Trembling, she dutifully crawled off the slab to grope on the ground for it, then placed it in his hand. His eyes were fixed on hers and they spoke one final apology.

He sighed a long, noisy sigh like bubbles of air in water. His breathing seemed painful.

'Who be she?' Dragongirl's mother had returned. The family peered at Jatta for the first time.

'Dartith's ... future. She shall right ... my wrongs,' he rasped. Under his skin the infestation seemed stilled, its life cycle ebbing at last to an end.

He sank to lie beside Dragongirl, propped on one elbow. His arm quivered and threatened to collapse. Jatta reached to cup her hands under his age-weary head, sharing his sorrow as it seeped through to her fingers. She eased him to his bed, accepting that the Sorcerer who had overcome death had chosen this hour to surrender to it. So he surrendered surrounded by memories, held by the only person he'd cared for in these past hundred generations.

Blackness seeped out of the night. Stars faded. Fallen moons, too. Slate sky gave way to the whitish grey of pre-dawn.

Lemon tinged the sky.

'My Dragongirl,' he rasped, drawing long, bubbling breaths. 'Let us share ... one last sunrise.'

While orange bled out from the horizon the old Sorcerer and his granddaughter lay watching. He kissed her forehead as the sun warmed it, and they took their last breaths. He released the orb.

CHAPTER SIXTY-FIVE

The corpse stank.

Jatta snatched her orb and backed away from the obsidian slab. In the light of dawn her guardian's face had already discoloured and was peeling. Her eyes squeezed shut.

She should have been grateful. Some part of her was, she supposed—for the early dawn, for the extinguished firewall, for Arthmael's and Noriglade's chance to escape. But in these brief hours she'd imagined something more. Her life back whole.

Had her guardian grown too tired? Or just too absorbed in his own misery?

She couldn't help feeling hopeless—and confused. She'd cared for Andro Mogon, she admitted it, though his Dark Sorcerer was responsible for millennia of misery, including her own. Perhaps this was what she and he had in common . . . both were half goodness, half cruel beasts.

Behind her, Arthmael and Noriglade were making no secret of how they felt about his end, hugging and kissing and laughing. It hurt to hear them.

'Jatta, look! I be alive! Feel how warm.' Noriglade ran to grab Jatta's fingers and pressed them against her cheek, her ecstasy seeping through.

With a jolt of wonder Jatta felt it was true. Of course! The unannounced dawn should have decayed her friend! It would certainly be rotting many Undead.

'Still white as death,' teased Arthmael.

Noriglade shoved him, laughing. 'So would you be, idiot boy, if you hadn't seen sun for a year. But Jatta, what about you?'

Jatta shrugged, pretending she wasn't bitterly disillusioned. 'Nothing's changed. There's just an uncomfortable lump in my heart.'

Arthmael grunted. 'Don't fret, Jay. The Sorcerer took a special liking to you. What did he say—"*There, it's done.*" Right, Jay?'

Jatta managed a smile, daring to hope.

'Of course you be healed!' said Noriglade. 'Why not? I expect your father will celebrate. Yes, with fireworks and feasts and a public holiday after next wolf-moon.' Noriglade wrapped her arms around her, squeezing Jatta's cheek against her chest. Noriglade's hair smelled dank, like the crypt, but in her warm arms a wave of comfort flooded into Jatta. She held on tight, feeling her friend's happiness and her heart pumping beneath living flesh. No fireworks would be necessary. A cure. That hope was celebration enough.

They returned to the portal, nervous about what they'd find beyond the burnt-out den. Brackensith's body would have been discovered there long before. One thing they were grateful for: with the firewall down, with the damage to so many Undead, with a kingdom to govern, Drake would have more on his mind than three fugitives.

'Be you ready, Jatta?' said Noriglade.

Jatta kneaded and her Brackensith appeared. She was *not* ready, though. Brackensith faded.

'Noriglade, I need a small favour,' she said, blushing. She

stepped from the portal and returned to the sarcophagus. 'Could you read this?' she asked, pinching her nose.

Noriglade followed. With only an indifferent glance at the body, she deciphered the slab's ancient inscription.

'Tammon
Beloved daughter of Mirrim, cherished sister to Harthan.
Sorceress heir to Andro Mogon, forever in his heart.'

Noriglade returned to the portal. Jatta stood one last time before the slab, massaging her orb. Her guardian's features re-formed, his stink masked by her father's spicy cologne.

'Goodbye, Andro Mogon. Your soul is free,' she whispered, knowing no-one else would ever mourn this complex creature. 'Thank you for letting me share your last moments. Thank you, also, for restoring my friend's life. And thank you ... I mean, I think, if that's what you've done ... for repairing mine.'

CHAPTER SIXTY-SIX

The too-familiar *buzz* interrupted Jatta's goodbye. She leapt up to see Arthmael dragging Noriglade out of the portal. Blue sparks flickered.

She raced to them. A man was forming, crouched in a puddle of blood and clutching the column, his head bowed and plait unravelled. Jatta shuddered. Beside her Noriglade whimpered and Arthmael drew his sword.

Impossible. She'd felt his crushed body on hers. But he'd returned, still wearing the Dartith crown.

The King looked up and Jatta's heart did an awful flip. Drake's, not Brackensith's, agonised eyes found hers. He blinked in shock to find her. He focused on Arthmael, then on his sister, whose white face was tinged with dawn's orange light. He stared for a moment in incomprehension, then struggled to stand, peering past them to the sarcophagus.

'Great Andro Mog—' he called weakly, hopefully. He toppled onto his face in the dirt.

Pity wrenched at Jatta's heart. She ran to kneel by him, wiping the dust from his mouth, feeling his pain as he laboured to speak.

'Great Andro Mogon . . . Where . . .?'

'He's gone, Drake. He was tired. There's nothing much left.'

The hope on his face died. 'Then I be doomed. My Dartith be doomed.'

Noriglade was at Jatta's side. Arthmael knelt too, gently rolling Drake on his back. The smell was like a slaughterhouse, but after witnessing so much suffering, Jatta still wasn't prepared for what she saw. Drake's stomach had been bandaged. His shirt and leggings were soaked in blood. Too much blood. What sickened her most was seeing his bandage peculiarly sunken, as if his insides were missing.

'Lord,' growled Arthmael. 'Who—what animal did this to you?'

'Riz,' groaned Drake.

Riz? Riz's whimpers from the ledge trailed through Jatta's mind. *'Don't leave me, Father. I be all you have left.'* Vicious Riz. Loathing tightened in her chest.

'Drake, your brothers—have they survived?'

'All gone. Ambushed ... Father, too.' Drake's face crumpled. He sobbed, a wretched sound. She'd never imagined he could cry.

Jatta spared Drake the real details of his father's death. Beside her, Noriglade and Arthmael exchanged troubled glances. Jatta realised these personal tragedies meant a greater tragedy loomed.

'You said Dartith was doomed?' she whispered.

He swallowed, gulping back tears. 'Riz be heir when I be gone ... his men slaughter mine ... rampage ...'

Arthmael whispered in her ear, 'The castle will be a bloodbath. What other portal commands do you know? Cordorlith, right? We'll go there.'

She nodded without looking up. 'Drake, can't *anything* be done?'

'Nothing.'

Suddenly, his eyes were ablaze. His hand shot up,

gripping hers with desperate force. 'Yes. Help us. Marry me!'

She recoiled, shaking her head. What had days before seemed inevitable was now beyond repugnant. Whatever her guardian had said, she was *not* Dartith's future. She would not, could not, submit to this Isle.

'I beg you, be Queen.' His grip was crushing Noridane's ring into her finger. His anguish and pain bled into her chest. 'Rule in my place. Andro Mogon chose you for some purpose.'

'No. I'm going home!' Jatta frantically tried to unlock his fingers, finding Arthmael's hand prising her free. Drake's hand slid from hers, dragging the ring. He clutched it, the token of two forced betrothals, all he would ever take from her. 'I've had enough, hear?' she screamed, feeling panic rise. 'I owe Dartith nothing!'

Drake's energy was spent. He slumped half-conscious to the dirt, his breath quick and shallow, blood oozing from his mouth. Again his agony wrenched at her heart. *Shame on her.* She'd screeched like an overwrought child, knowing Drake couldn't drag her inside the portal, let alone back to Dartith's hell.

'Drake,' whispered Noriglade as she leant by his ear, her hair cascading into his. 'Can you hear?'

He fought to focus.

'Brother, what would you sacrifice to win back Dartith? Would you suffer an Undead's existence?'

Understanding flickered in his eyes.

'Once you pitied me, told me my wretched existence be worse than death,' she whispered. 'Choose now. Will you stay on to battle Riz? Choose. The elixir. Or death.'

'. . . lix . . .' he breathed.

'Prickle, are you mad?' growled Arthmael. 'They'll butcher us. We can't take him back to the castle.'

'Will you let Riz destroy Dartith?' she snapped.

'Since when do *you* care?'

'Since Father be gone. Since the Dark Sorcerer be gone. Idiot boy, cannot you see? After three thousand years this be Dartith's one chance.'

'No, I don't see. You heard Jay, we're going to Cordorlith. Then home.'

'Noriglade's right,' said Jatta. 'He's dying, we must take him back. Not even Dartith deserves Riz.'

'Jay, you're all sweetness and compassion, but this is suicide.'

'Please, Art. We'll be safe with the orb. It's not too much to ask.'

Arthmael took a deep breath, then snorted the air back out in frustration. 'Prickle, where's this elixir? In the poisons den?'

Noriglade nodded.

'All right! All right, Jay, but you'd better be ready to squeeze that ball.'

Arthmael heaved Drake to a sitting position, then hoisted him over his shoulder. Drake moaned. Arthmael rose and strode heavily to the portal as the girls raced ahead. By the time he stepped between them, Jatta-Brackensith was reciting the incantation with wrist outstretched.

'Portal, your King commands you;
To Dredden's den return me.'

The portal buzzed. Sparks flickered blue, tingling their skin and making their hair dance. The floor dropped away as swirling blackness enveloped them. The girls clutched Arthmael's sleeves; he gripped his burden tighter.

CHAPTER SIXTY-SEVEN

The swirling sea dissolved. The floor returned. Jatta pocketed
her orb as they emerged coughing into the hazy, burnt-out den,
to a shocked audience of two. Jatta recognised Brackensith's
chancellor. The second man she imagined was his doctor. He
rushed to pull open Drake's eyelids and feel his pulse as
Arthmael laid the King on the table.

From the floor below came the gut-wrenching cries of
battle. Light streamed from the foyer through the doorway,
now barricaded. The golden child-dragon Jatta had once
admired lay there, blackened with soot, propped between
charred bookshelves and chests of sodden snakeskin.

Arthmael bounded to the barricade. 'What's happening?
Why isn't anyone here to defend Drake?'

The chancellor joined him. 'We two alone carried the King
to the portal. Others of us fight Riz below. But his rabble
swells. Riz claims King Drake be dead, that the throne be
already his. They come, even now, for his body.'

'Lord,' growled Arthmael.

'He be dying!' called the doctor, his voice close to panic.
'He swore to return whole! He led us to hope for a miracle.'

Jatta stood tensely by Drake's side, watching Noriglade
pick a path through debris and puddles, searching. When
Noriglade spied the golden child-dragon she scrambled to
the barricade. She dragged it upright and ran her hands

frantically over the dragon. Jatta listened intently as Noriglade cursed under her breath. 'Idiot girl! You be wasting precious moments. The catch, cretin. Find the catch.'

Not a catch. Imagination alone will open this child-dragon. Jatta's sudden intuition thrilled her. It also disturbed her. Where had it come from? Jatta knew the sculpture was magical. More than that, she knew—instinctively—how to open it.

Arthmael was already by Noriglade's side, one hand gripping the dragon wing, the other its snout, as he furiously strained to prise them apart. 'Impossible. Senseless,' he fumed.

Noriglade shook her head helplessly, her sooty fingers over her mouth. 'How? I thought ... I do not understand. No opening. No join.'

Yells, thuds and screams came louder. Swords clanged up the stairs.

Heart pounding, Jatta squeezed down beside Arthmael.

'Let me, Art. I know what to do.'

Arthmael didn't ask how she knew. He gave her a fierce look, as if he'd heeded her one time too many, then rolled over to peer through the barricade.

'There's fighting at the top of the stairs,' he growled. 'We leave when I say.'

Not nearly enough time, Jatta thought frantically. She faced the dragon, placed both thumbs between its ears, and cleared her rising fear. As each thumb traced over an ear, down the scaled neck, across the contours of an outstretched wing, she closed her eyes, concentrating her mind on the dying Drake. He formed between her thumbs now. It was his golden torso her thumbs traced down, his thighs. Crouched beside her, Arthmael, Noriglade and the chancellor gasped. When her thumbs felt his heels she opened her eyes. Already Drake's features were transforming back into the dragon's, but the line she'd traced glowed red. Jatta dragged the two halves, dragon and child, apart. Inside, hundreds of crystal vials lined silver shelves. Most stood empty. Some were newly smashed, but inside the dragon's feet were a few vials still containing blood-red syrup. Even as Jatta snatched one she felt a dread thrill. Somehow she'd known they'd be arranged this way.

Noriglade grimaced, revolted at the source of her torment. Riz's mob battled against the stairwell door. Arthmael swore.

'Hurry, Princess!' cried the chancellor.

Jatta needed no urging. She was already scrambling to Drake, pulling out the stopper, flinging it to the floor. The doctor was on the table, his king's head in his lap. She pressed the vial to Drake's slack lips. Elixir dribbled down his chin.

'Majesty, I beg you, drink,' pleaded the doctor. But to Jatta, Drake looked to be peacefully asleep.

'Hurry!'

The door burst open. Howls of triumph drowned the chancellor's words, then thundering boots. In the next moment the barricade was being torn apart.

'Suicide!' yelled Arthmael furiously. '*Now* shall we leave?'

Noriglade raced for the portal. Arthmael dragged the chancellor through the den. 'Jay! Get your Brackensith inside this portal!' he shouted. 'Do it *now*!' He heaved the doctor, still pleading to Drake, from the table.

Jatta ignored him. *I need five tiny seconds*, she thought desperately. She drew her lips close to Drake's, so close they felt a thread of his breath. 'Drink, my Prince,' she whispered, parting his teeth with the vial.

Arthmael was yelling from the portal. Men were crashing through the barricade.

Drake's eyes flickered. His throat swallowed. Overjoyed, Jatta tipped the vial and more elixir trickled into his mouth. 'Drake, my Prince,' her whisper coaxed. 'Save your kingdom.' The vial was emptying as he gulped again.

Arthmael's hands were on her waist, throwing her across the room to the portal. Noriglade was screaming his name.

Jatta landed painfully on her hip. Frightened and disorientated, she spun back around. Arthmael had disappeared. Where he'd stood, a ball of men hacked at something in their centre. It fought back in frenzy.

Not Art! This wasn't happening!

For two heartbeats she stood. Numbed. Hollowed out.

Reality kicked her skull like iron hooves. She was hurtling across the debris. Scrambling back to the table.

'Cease your damned warring!' bellowed Brackensith.

Every face turned. Men surging through the barricade tumbled in a mass to the floor.

Brackensith towered above them all in the hazy torchlight, feet planted astride his fallen heir, rigid with rage.

'Snivelling scum! Lay down your weapons!'

Swords dropped. Axes, bludgeons and flails thudded among debris. Men dropped to their knees in awe of their resurrected King. One man sneaked into the corridor and fled.

Jatta-Brackensith scanned the mob at her feet, searching for her brother. They knelt in puddles among the tangle of weapons and wounded, withering under her cold grey gaze. She barely dared to breathe. Then Arthmael struggled up from under a body. He was pale and shaking, staunching a wound to his shoulder. Even so, her heart leapt. She allowed a shadow of a smile to twist Brackensith's lips.

'Cretins! My father be dead!' screamed the voice Jatta loathed.

Eye twitching, Riz elbowed a path through his men. 'Dead, hear? You kneel to a girly impostor!' He shuffled on bandaged feet to Jatta's table.

Her lip curled in contempt. 'Riz, you treacherous imbecile,' she snarled. 'Men, seize him!'

Riz leapt wildly onto the table as men lunged. He grabbed Brackensith's arm, his hand sinking through sand, disappearing inside till it found Jatta's elbow. The mob goggled in disbelief.

He wrenched her elbow forward, then slammed it back into the wall. Bone snapped against stone. Everyone heard. Her Brackensith's lips pressed tight in a whimper.

'Drop your toy!' Riz howled.

But she wouldn't.

He rammed again. He ground. Her bones made grisly peppermill sounds. She screamed in agony; the orb dropped to the table beside Drake's thigh. Her Brackensith faded. Her arm hung useless.

Murmurs rumbled through the mob. Some men got up off their knees for a better view, others reached for their weapons.

Riz scooped up her treasure and held it high. 'A magic toy! Cretins, you feared my immortal father? He be a girl's magic toy!' He turned back to Jatta, his face horribly close to hers. 'This be how I play with your toy.' He cradled her orb in one thickly bandaged palm. Then he pulled out a dagger and sliced its jelly in half. White stars dribbled out to twinkle on his bandage before dripping into charred books.

Tears welled as Jatta fought her pain. She backed over Drake's body to press against the wall, all hope dribbling away with the stars. Riz now hacked at her orb, working himself to a frenzy. Flecks flew off his blade. 'You turned my father against me!' he spat. 'You betrayed me! I offered you a kingdom. I offered you love!' His eye twitched madly. He attacked the orb as if it were Jatta herself. 'You give your love to *perfect* Drake!'

Staring at the mutilated mess, she imagined him attacking Drake with this same fury. Tears of pain and sadness dripped from her chin.

He paused. His eyes lifted to hers. She watched his fury dissolve into something equally dangerous: the twisted smirk he imagined was playful charm. 'Be you sorry, Jatta?' he simpered. 'Sorry you rejected all I offered? You did not imagine me King of Dartith. You underestimated me, yes?'

Backed against the wall, she stared in repugnance.

'Perhaps I shall spare your life. Would you like that, Jatta? Kneel before me and beg forgiveness. Yes, perhaps I shall take you back to my heart.'

Jatta was sick of pretending.

'Your heart is as shrivelled as your brain,' she said quietly through her tears.

He suddenly giggled. 'That be something Father would say.' He stepped over his brother to her. He raised his blade to absently trace it across her bust, bloodied where he had jabbed it with glass.

'You understand your fate?' he said. Her eyes flicked to the purple mess in his other hand. 'Yes, Princess. I shall have you sliced. You shall plead yet.'

Grinning, he turned to take stock of the room.

Jatta searched the flickering haze too. Noriglade, the chancellor and the doctor watched helplessly from the portal. Arthmael stood unsteadily below her table with swords at his chest. He smiled sadly, bravely, up at her. He mouthed 'Goodbye'.

It was all her fault. She'd sacrificed them. For nothing. For doomed Dartith. Drake would not awaken till dark. He would not awaken at all, now Riz was here. Finally, Jatta had had enough. She was in agony, fatigued beyond measure. This day she'd been dragged through terror on the ledge, through the Sorcerer's pain, through hope and death, and worse pain lay ahead. She was too tired, too puny, too pitifully weak. There was no orb to save them, no guardian either.

Riz was giggling again. He'd discovered a fresh entertainment, prodding Drake's head with his foot, watching it loll to the side.

'I told you, dead!' he called to the mob. 'Dead as a rat on a stick!'

He bent to take his brother's crown, but something there caught his eye. His glee drained away. Riz dropped to his knees to pick up the elixir vial.

Jatta watched through a mist, feeling nothing except sorrow for herself, for Arthmael and Noriglade. Riz was blotting Drake's chin with his bandaged thumb. Numbly she watched him examine the red syrup, his feeble mind eventually coming to some conclusion.

Smirking again, Riz dragged the crown from Drake's head and stood.

'Faithful soldiers! Noblemen!' he called, holding the crown high. 'What be my name?'

'Riz!' they shouted.

'Who be Dartith's rightful king?'

'Riz!'

'Who be my father's *beloved* heir? Who protected you and favoured you and showered you with gifts?'

'Riz!'

'And who poisoned my father's heart against his golden son? Who schemed and blackmailed and spread vicious lies, lies that I be unfit?'

'Drake!' cried a smattering of voices.

'Drake!' echoed others, uncertainly.

'Yes, and who must we punish? Who must we chop up in tiny pieces to feed to our hounds before this sun sets?'

The men stared up blankly. Some exchanged puzzled looks with their neighbours. They were finding it increasingly difficult to guess their unstable Prince's desire.

'Who else?' screamed Riz in frustration. 'Who else but Drake! Chop up Drake!'

'Drake!' they shouted. 'Chop up Drake!'

'So what say you to *this*?' Beaming again, he lowered the crown till it brushed his hair.

'King Riz shall reign!' cried the mob.

He placed the crown on his head. He thrust his arms to them, drunk on victory. A gloating, unbalanced child.

'King Riz shall reign! King Riz shall reign!' they cried.

Jatta gazed sadly down at her brother. He nodded. She understood that look; he'd chosen to die fighting, not tortured by Riz. She mouthed her own '*Goodbye*'.

'King Riz shall reign!' yelled the mob, waving their weapons high.

Arthmael jumped to seize two swords. He slashed at exposed chests with a madman's fury. White as the Undead, he yelled. Bodies dropped. More closed in.

'Kill him!' screamed Riz.

Riz spun on Jatta, whole face contorted. He raised his dagger to strike.

Jatta's good arm was whacking the dagger from his bandaged fingers. Strange. She didn't remember deciding to do that. Time was slowing down; his blade was somersaulting through the haze while flames danced mournfully on the wall behind. His words—*'Kill them both! Tiny pieces!'*—were drifting like a dirge past her ears. His hands had closed on her throat, crushing it . . . It didn't hurt. She was being dragged to the table edge. She was stumbling over her betrothed, toppling to her knees.

Such a pity . . . I'm sorry, Art . . . Real fear was bubbling up through this surreal dream. Someone below was seizing her hips, then she was falling forward on the floor. That hurt . . . but not like her arm. Bubbles of terror burst through. *Let it not hurt too much. Let us both die quickly*, her mind was pleading Men were converging above. Her heart stopped, waiting for the first blade's stab. Her gown was tearing down the back and agony was slicing her spine.

She was almost relieved; dying, it seemed, could be borne. She was lying quite still in the sodden debris and ash, vaguely watching the men back away. Waiting for life to ebb.

CHAPTER SIXTY-EIGHT

Something had burst out of Jatta's back.

Suddenly she felt shockingly alive.

She lifted her head to see, and her eyes glistened with wonder. Two ribbed wings stretched to the ceiling, each easily as long as herself, exquisitely translucent green in the flickering torchlight. She trembled. Her wings quivered too.

She willed them to beat. Their great downward thrust lifted her chest from the debris; their great upward sweep swirled ash through her hair. They repeated their wide arc, dragging her to her knees, and their wind fanned the men's unravelled plaits. Slowly, powerfully, their magnificent strokes lifted her to the ceiling with one arm still hanging.

The mob had backed away. Some knelt again. Others gaped, flicking nervous eyes to Riz for their cue. Arthmael teetered, mesmerised. Noriglade pushed through the mob to his side.

Jatta skimmed below the rafters, her body dipping with each magnificent sweep just as she'd imagined it would. With humble awe she turned her mind inward, sensing newborn abilities shifting inside her like fledglings in a nest. Her mind touched one and it quivered. *Empathy*, she thought, remembering how Noriglade's and Drake's bare touch had leaked their emotions—their pain, too—through her skin. Perhaps empathy's tender embryo had always lain there. She prodded among her abilities for her wolf.

Gone.

Others may need the proof of next wolf-moon, but she felt it was gone, as absolutely as she felt her wings. Her guardian had not forgotten. Jatta's soul soared. She flipped in mid-air, then swooped over the men. Her wolf could no longer hurt others, nor her.

'A trick! A girly trick!'

Riz was shrieking, eye twitching madly. 'Drag her down—'

As she swooped low he jumped, seizing the sleeve stretched over her useless, hanging, swelling arm. Jatta screamed in horrible torment. She streaked to the ceiling, and he clung on, hanging like an anchor. Her muscles ripped. She'd never imagined such torture, slashing red-hot up her shoulder to her brain. Bright stars exploded. Her good hand shot toward her tormentor, palm out. A wound opened. Out lashed a flaming tentacle and he squealed. It whipped around his chest; he called to his father as it tightened. It flung him down. He was on the floor writhing and burning with no breath left. His bandaged hands were alight where they tugged at the tentacle. His face turned purple. Contorted. Eyes flickered, half-closed.

His agony surged through her body, torturing her—even through his doublet and bandages, even along her tentacle. She felt it ten times stronger now that her abilities had erupted. His half-witted terror surged too. Still Jatta willed her fiery vengeance to squeeze out his breath, punishing him for every loss she'd suffered, every horror. Hurting him for her agony, her wolf, her mother—

'Jay!'

Arthmael's cry was a whisper in the firestorm of her fury.

She tore her eyes from its heat. Her brother was white. He was gaping, horrified. At her.

What had she done? Her tentacle uncoiled from Riz's smouldering chest to whip back along its path. Her palm's wound closed.

Riz was drawing jagged breaths as his chest heaved. He stared up, wide-eyed with fright. The sight of him chilled her burning heart. *Was she no better than the Dark Sorcerer? Please, no.* She needed this nightmare to end, needed to curl safely under her quilts in a world without wolves or Undead or Sorcerers.

It was too late for that.

Gradually Jatta realised the mob was staring up at her, at her hanging arm, at her tear-stained, sooty face and its parade of pain and fury and shock. She crammed that heart-convulsing pain, as much as she could, deep inside her mind. Tears leaked obstinately.

She took a deep, shaky breath.

'Who among you remains loyal to Prince Riz—who'll take care of him now?' Her voice sounded clear, though not strong. 'Who'll follow him into exile?'

Some men shook their heads, snorting disdain. Some inched to hide behind others. None dared take their eyes from the vengeful Princess.

'No-one? Then you.' She pointed at the man who'd dragged her from the table. He uttered an odd yelp. 'You at least can carry him to the portal.'

The man knelt to fumble with Riz, who struggled weakly.

'No! King ... me ...' Riz pleaded in gasps.

The man managed to hook under his arms.

'Chop ...'

The man staggered backwards to the portal, dragging Riz

through rubble. He heaved Riz inside. Then, grimacing up at Jatta as if she might strike him down too, he edged back into the crowd. All waited.

'Beloved . . . son.' Riz struggled to his knees.

Battling the pain that leaked out with her tears, Jatta raised her good hand. In it formed Andro Mogon's cemetery. The incantation flashed into her mind just as the mystery of the golden statue had done.

Portal, heed my command;
Banish Riz from mankind.

The arch buzzed and men clutched their chests. Blue sparks radiated from Riz. Then the portal was gone.

Jatta descended to Arthmael and Noriglade while the mob pressed back out of reach. Her pain seared as she lightly touched ground. Her wings folded like a butterfly returning to its cocoon, growing gossamer-delicate as they shuffled inside her back. Only two faint ridges remained. She felt them, one either side of her spine.

She searched Arthmael's sombre face, scared of what she might find, but there was no blame there for her murderous attack. He lifted one hand with effort. His finger wiped a tear from her cheek and his pain surged through her skin. His concern for her, too, something beautiful. She gasped at the tenfold intensity of it, more intimate than whispered secrets, more honest than a confession, more precious than an embrace. She didn't deserve such a gift.

His eyes closed and he settled heavily against Noriglade. His wounds were worse than Jatta had thought.

Noriglade broke the silence.

'How do you withstand such pain?' she asked. 'Does your Sorceress not feel it?'

Her Sorceress. There was a word for what she was, and it scared her. '*You never were ordinary,*' Andro Mogon had said. '*You be more like me than you imagine.*' More like who? His gentle healer? Or his Dark Sorcerer?

'No, I—I'm not a Sorceress, not really, not evil.' It wasn't Noriglade she was trying to convince.

Noriglade's forehead creased in confusion. 'Of course not evil, idiot girl. Your Sorceress's fury saved us.'

'But I wanted to murder. I wanted—'

'Yet you pulled back. Your Sorceress be terrifying, yes. But she be yours to command.'

Hers to command? Jatta clung to Noriglade's words. Like her wolf, this power had come unbidden. Unlike her wolf, she'd controlled it. Andro Mogon had made choices; she would make choices too, wiser choices than his.

Barely moving her lips, she beckoned the portal. It materialised, empty.

'Be you ready?' said Noriglade, wrapping her arm around Arthmael's waist.

They shuffled through the mob.

'Great One, we have no king!' called one man.

'Sorceress! Stay!' clamoured others, pushing forward.

Jatta shuddered at the thought of their skins' touch.

'Men!' she called as they pressed closer. 'Take Brackensith's true heir to the crypt. Tonight you'll have your king.' She'd left them Drake. He would be a better king than most, no worse a king than Dartith deserved.

They shuffled inside the portal. Jatta held out her wrist. Arthmael was trying to speak. Jatta peered up anxiously.

'Jay . . .' He formed the word slowly, grimacing. 'You got . . . the wings . . . you wanted.'

Her miraculous wings. Her murderous tentacles. Her strange, intimate trespass into others' feelings. It was all so overwhelming. What was she? No longer a drab, scared little mouse. No longer a wolf. Mortal. Not exactly human, though.

'Art—I'm still me, aren't I?'

He managed a fleeting smile. 'Sure, little sister ... Full of ... surprises.'

She smiled then, too, as images flashed over her out-stretched wrist. The Great Hall ... the throne room ... her rose garden ...

Her father's study. She'd found him, reading in his armchair under stained-glass windows, bathed in coloured morning light.

Jatta, heir to the last and greatest Sorcerer, formed the words in her mind.

To those I love,

To decency,

Return my heart.

The portal buzzed. Blue sparks flickered and the den floor dropped away.

ABOUT THE AUTHOR

Jenny Hale has enjoyed reading her share of dragon-slaying, sword-wielding fantasies, but she could never quite identify with their heroes. Could she, herself, actually kill someone? Might real heroes sometimes foul things up? Their plans go disastrously wrong? Might they ever feel overwhelmed, and just want to pack up their magic and swords and go home? Jenny's first novel places young people in truly disturbing situations, and lets them discover their limits for themselves.

Jenny is an established illustrator and author of children's picture books. She started out as an advertising illustrator, designer and copywriter, and now she has twenty titles and hundreds of thousands of copies in print. She lives with her husband and writes from a long marble table overlooking Australia's bushland.